The Wrong Stuff
K'Barthan Series: Part 2

Here are some things readers have said about M T McGuire's books.

The Wrong Stuff, K'Barthan Series: Part 2

"This one is even better than book one and if there is any justice it will be a best seller.... " -
Susan (Gingerlily) Watson.

Few Are Chosen, K'Barthan Series: Part 1

*"I found I was turning pages as fast as I could... there wasn't a single character that didn't engage
me in some way"* – http://gracekrispy.blogspot.com

*"Once I got used to the tone and style of the dialogue, I really began to appreciate The Pan's
self-depreciating humour and sharp wit, and how his cowardly nature allows him to look at events
with a more detached view, enabling him to make rational, intelligent observations.*

*"Filled with a host of brilliant characters from various wonderfully weird races, none of the
different personalities introduced fail to fascinate."* – http://www.thebookbag.co.uk

The Wrong Stuff

K'Barthan Series: Part 2

M T McGuire

HAMGEE UNIVERSITY PRESS

First published in 2012 by
Hamgee University Press,
www.Hamgee.co.uk
This version, February, 2021

© M T McGuire 2012

ISBN 978-1-907809-17-0

This book is written in British English, with a bit of light swearing
UK film rating of this book: PG (parental guidance)

Written by M T McGuire
Designed and set by M T McGuire
Published by Hamgee University Press
Edited by Kate Jackson and Mike Rose-Steel
Cover design by A Trouble Halved
This copy printed by Lightning Source UK Ltd, Milton Keynes

For
Mark Jackon and Linda Baxter.

M T McGuire is over 50 years old but still checks inside
unfamiliar wardrobes for a gateway to Narnia.
Boringly, she's not found any.

Thank you for buying this book.
If you enjoyed it you can keep up with
news of the author online by
visiting www.hamgee.co.uk

You can also sign up for the
M T McGuire mailing list by
visiting www.hamgee.co.uk/freebook
or bling your life with K'Barthan merchandise at
http://bit.ly/UHSUshop

Thank you to:-
The Editors – Kate Jackson and Mike Rose-Steel
for help, advice and support over and above the call of duty.
Press Officer and Ninja Sister In-Law – Emily Bell; ditto.
The Beta Readers – Helen Bell – especially Helen, Marc Florent, Hayley
Humphrey, Susan (Gingerlily) Watson, Dr R J Westwell and Young Mr Upstart.
Gerard, at ATH for understanding exactly what I wanted for the cover... as usual.

And thanks to my husband and family, for their support and understanding.

Chapter 1

With a massive bang the window of the Festival Hall exploded in a shower of glittering glass crystals. A small sports car flashed through the flying shards and landed with a squeal of tyres on the polished wooden floor. Yeek, thought Ruth, the people running the Festival Hall weren't going to like that.

She was ahead of everyone because she'd been running to get to the sponsor's reception first, and she froze. If this was a bomb attack she was dead. The seconds lengthened. No explosion. She hadn't realised she'd stopped breathing until she breathed out.

The hole in the window was quite high up, suggesting that whatever had come through it was flying, but the thing in the foyer was definitely a car. Ruth's dream car, to be precise, a type of 1960s Lotus, a small and shiny convertible in two-tone light and dark metallic grey.

That was a conundrum in itself, since it had just smashed the front of the Festival Hall. Was that right? Shouldn't the Festival Hall have smashed the front of the Lotus? After all, this was fibreglass versus tempered safety glass. Ruth would have put her money on the glass, every time.

When she turned round, she realised that the people near her were lying down. She was a lone figure standing in a sea of sensibly prone others, except for two men heading along the top of the stairs and picking their way through the prostrate forms around her. The men were big, unusually pale, wearing grey uniforms, jackboots, sunglasses and swords and, yep, that was definitely a gun one of them was holding. It had to be, didn't it? Now, at the worst possible time, they had to turn up; the strange pair of men who'd been following her—or was that stalking her?—for three months.

"Why me?" she whispered. "What the hell do they want?"

Trying to quell her rising panic she swung round towards the Lotus. Yes, it was still there, blocking her only escape route but, bonus, at least it hadn't blown up. If this was some kind of bomb attack, it appeared to be a dud. Looking back towards her two giant pale stalkers, there was no mistaking the direction in which they were headed; towards her. Great, and she was pretty sure they had tried to kidnap her last time she'd seen them. They'd cornered her on the last tube home and only backed off when one of her neighbours had turned up. He wasn't here tonight though. And since they were, it was probably time for a sharp exit.

Where to run, though? The car was barring her escape.

The driver stood up in his seat and waved. Was he anything to do with them?

"Ruth!" he shouted, followed by something incomprehensible. He was wearing a cloak and a hat, but he looked more like a student playing a prank than a bomber. Very strange. He shouted some more gibberish, which also contained the word 'Ruth' at regular intervals.

Please God, let there be somebody else here called Ruth, she thought, though some sixth sense knew, with cringing inevitability, that he was talking to her.

He finally managed some English: "Ruth! I'm a little teapot!" This was less than inspiring and in spite of her fear, she wanted to giggle. He had a lilting accent that she couldn't place.

She looked around for her boss, with whom she'd been sitting and Lucy, her flatmate, who was there somewhere because Ruth had given her a free ticket. However, the mass of bodies on the floor was beginning to stir. No chance of recognising anyone there. She could see the two scary sci-fi guys though, and as they saw her looking at them they broke into a jog. She could see the Festival Hall's security people talking on their radios, and good, there were the blue lights on Blackfriars Bridge. The police would arrive soon, but not soon enough; the scary big men with the uniforms were going to get to her first.

Not that. Not them.

The driver of the car leapt out and ran up the stairs towards her.

"Ruth," he said.

Who on earth was he? She'd never seen him before in her life. He smiled and despite her unease she noticed it was the kind of smile she liked.

"I'm a little teapot," he said.

He stood on the step below her and patted his pockets as if looking for something – a gun? No. Not the type. A gun wouldn't go with that smile. What then? He made writing motions with one hand. Ah yes, a pen. Ruth always carried a pen, but needless to say, in this one moment of crucial need she'd left it on the signing-in table in the sponsor's reception area. Damn. She didn't have a spare, and presumably he was also without one, because he gave up and started waving his hands in the universal sign language gesture for 'no-no'. Although, he was clearly foreign, so Ruth realised it could have meant 'yes-yes' for all she knew. He pointed at the sci-fi blokes and that was the moment she looked properly into his face and noticed his expression of pure panic. Hmm. The hand-waving was probably 'no-no' then.

"I'm a little teapot," he said and grabbed her wrist.

No. Absolutely not. A step too far. She gave him what she hoped was a look of supreme disdain and yanked her arm forcefully from his grasp. She didn't know what made her turn round again but the sci-fi men were much closer now and as she watched, one of them raised his gun. The world began to move at half speed, as slowly, deliberately he aimed it at her and fired. Not bullets, bolts of red light. A laser, for heaven's sake! Where were these people from? The round hit the steps by her feet and the stone bubbled. Yikes. Ruth decided she wasn't going to be there for the second shot. She turned her attention to the man with the hat. Could she knock him down? No.

In front of her, the slightly – but only slightly – more appealing of two unattractive choices held out his hand, smiled and raised one eyebrow as if to say, 'Shall we?' God in heaven. Oh well, on the up side – a big plus point – he didn't seem to have a gun. Anyway, he'd arrived in a Lotus and he'd broken a plate glass window with it. It would go yards, if he was lucky, before it fell to bits; she'd be able to escape at the next red light. She took his outstretched hand and ran down the stairs with him. Together they jumped into the car, neither of them stopping to open the door.

"I don't know who you are but you look safer than them. Of course, that's not saying much."

"I'm a little teapot," said the stranger, but with all the emphasis on the wrong syllable, as if he were saying something else.

"There's me thinking you were a man. You'd better have an excellent explanation for this later," she warned him.

He smiled at her.

"I'm a little teapot," he said again.

She got that one; something along the lines of 'don't worry I have' she reckoned, but rather more expansively put.

He gunned the engine and, tyres giving off a plume of smoke, the Lotus squealed round in a doughnut. He pressed some kind of button on the dash and as it catapulted itself forward, it rose up, too, as if it was taking off. Oh brilliant. It was. She peered over the side, watching in alarm as wings morphed out of its sills and it flew straight back out of the hole it had made in the window coming in. So much for running away at the first red light. Now what?

Ruth wondered if the big guys with the guns mightn't have been a safer bet after all. She glanced over at her chauffeur and he smiled.

He gestured to her seat belt. "I'm a little teapot," he said. Yes, that seemed like a good idea. He turned left and headed along the river. Ruth was silent for a while. She needed time to think. She was wearing evening dress and shoes that were decorative rather than functional. All she had in her handbag was a mobile, a credit card and a little cash – oh yes, and a small package which the old man who lived down her street, Sir Robin Get, had given to Lucy to take to the concert and give to her. Apparently she would know what it was for but so far, Ruth didn't. Then again, she hadn't actually opened it and she daren't now she was a couple of hundred feet up in an open-top car, in case it blew away. Sir Robin, the neighbour who had saved her from the scary big dudes with the guns, the only person she had told about them other than Lucy. Sir Robin, with his I-have-people-who-can-fix-this tone, and his invitation to tea to sort it all out. He had told her not to be afraid, that everything was going to be alright and she'd believed him. Now look. She was sitting in a flying car, being pretty much kidnapped by some bloke in a hat who she'd never met but who, from the way he was behaving, seemed to think they were old friends.

She leaned over the side of the car and below the shiny wing she could see the lights of London. In the dusk, they were beautiful. The warm wind ruffled her hair and she began to feel less scared. She risked another glance at the driver. Ruth would have called him attractive rather than handsome, but he definitely had something that piqued her interest. He was taller than her but not quite tall enough, she'd have put him at about five foot nine, reasonably fit by the looks of it – well-proportioned, she supposed – broad-shouldered but not out-and-out sporty. He had a massive black eye. Someone had clearly thumped him on the nose, too. She was wary but she didn't feel afraid of him the way she knew she should. Strange, if anything he seemed more afraid of her. Perhaps he was just afraid, full stop. He was looking around him for pursuers.

"There might be a police helicopter if it's not busy somewhere else," she said. "Otherwise, I expect we're set, we don't have too many flying cars here in Britain."

"It's not a little teapot," he began. "Ruth," he said excitedly, "I'm … not a little it's teapot … wearing off … I'm a …"

"Are you all there?"

"Little … nearly … teapot …"

"Hmm."

"It's not a little … car … teapot," he said, "I'm a … it's a little … snurd … teapot." His eyes rolled in exasperation.

"Are you on drugs?"

He turned in his seat, put one finger on his nose and pointed at her with the other hand, charades-style.

"Yes!" he said, turning his attention back to the business of driving with a great deal of relief.

"And you want me to know that?"

"I'm a little … not … teapot … self-administered."

"Somebody else drugged you?"

"Mmm hmm." A nod.

They were flying over the City now and below them, Ruth could see a large office block with a helipad on top. She pointed downwards.

"OK. I think it's time you landed this thing so we can have a chat. You have a great deal of explaining to do."

He managed to say, 'mmm' without any mention of teapots and landed the Lotus smoothly on the helipad. For a moment there was no sound except the ticking of the engine as it cooled and the muffled roar of the traffic rising up from the street below. Then he got out of the car and leapt over the bonnet, except she felt the car dip, and if it hadn't been an inanimate object, she would have sworn that he'd failed to leap high enough and had only cleared the bonnet in one piece because the car had ducked. He opened her door with a flourish and she undid her seatbelt and climbed out.

He put out his hand and without thinking properly about what she was doing, she took it and let him lead her over to the edge of the helipad. It was raised a few feet above the roof of the building and below it a couple of yards of concrete ran to the edge of the roof proper, where there was a safety fence. It was there to stop the unwary from falling off, Ruth supposed, but it wouldn't be enough to stop somebody who really wanted to from throwing her off – this man, for example. That said, she was pretty sure his intentions were friendly and that she wasn't in any danger. He seemed too pleased to see her for that, he could hardly stop smiling. He sat down with his legs dangling over the edge of the helipad and she followed suit making sure she kept a few feet of distance between them. He appeared utterly at ease with her, which made her relax a little, despite stern warnings from the sensible part of her brain about the dangers of running off in space cars with strange men.

He raised an eyebrow and waved a hand at the view in front of them.

"I'm a … nice city you … little tea … have here … pot."

"Thank you," she said, "nice Zorro hat. Your wheels aren't bad either."

He chuckled and took a breath as if to speak but inclined his head in a sort of bow instead. Well, there are only so many ways you can tell somebody you are a little teapot, after all, and he'd probably run out of them. He took his hat off and ruffled his hair with one hand. It stood up. Naturally spiky. No sign of gel. Cool. No, not cool at all, get a grip Ruth. The two of them sat in silence for a moment while she tried to work out what to say and what was going to happen next. She felt disconnected from reality, as if her life was a film and she was sitting in the audience watching, a dangerous sensation because it was stopping her from taking it seriously. He cracked first.

"I'm a little … Arnold when is this … teapot … stuff going to … I'm a little … wear off … teapot?" He stopped. "I'm a … I should … little teapot … explain why I'm a … here little teapot." He grimaced and shook his head.

"It would help," said Ruth, "but I can see it's going to be difficult."

He was exasperated and angry with himself too, by the looks of it.

"OK, I have lots of questions, so why don't I ask the ones which only require 'yes' and 'no' answers?"

A relieved sigh, "I'm a little … alright."

"Good, and when I've asked my questions, you will be driving me home, won't you?"

"I'm a … I will take you … little teapot … wherever you want to go." Another smile. She looked into his eyes. They were dark blue, so dark they looked almost black, the way normally only brown-eyed people's can. He maintained eye contact for just that little bit too long before blushing and looking down at his hands. Hmm. Ruth wasn't super-confident about her looks, but in this case the signs were obvious. He fancied her. Oh well, it could be worse. He wasn't a giant, and he hadn't shot at her, and she had to hand it to him, as smiles went, his was pretty engaging. He had a kind face, too. Those blue, blue eyes had the type of crow's feet round them which suggested he smiled a lot. Perhaps it was time to try and discover what he wanted?

"You know, my life has become very weird of late," she said. "Those guys, the no-no ones," she waved her hands backwards and forwards the way he had done and he nodded, "they've been following me for months now."

"I know," he said.

"I don't think you do, not unless you've been following me as well. Have you?" she asked him sternly.

He cleared his throat and couldn't meet her eyes any more. Result! She'd got him bang to rights.

"You have, haven't you? You're another scary stalker! You're just better at it than them!"

"No. I was … I'm a little … Arnold's Y-fronts!" Deep breath. "Sorry. I have to explain and this stupid … teapot … Truth Serum is making it difficult."

"I'm sorry. When you say, 'Truth Serum' that makes me think 'Secret Police'."

"Then you're a little … right … teapot."

"So. I'm guessing that means you're in trouble where you're from, does it?"

He nodded. She eyed him quizzically.

"With the police or someone else?"

"The … teapot … police."

"And I suppose they're not very nice because nice policemen don't tend to use things called Truth Serum."

Another nod.

"And I'd guess they gave you that black eye."

"Mmm hmm."

"Are you a revolutionary?"

"No, that would make me an idiot."

Oh, a whole sentence in one! Sarky, too. She was impressed. "OK then, are you some kind of criminal where you're from?"

He shrugged and spread his hands when he nodded this time.

"Well, you're obviously a really crap one. I'm not scared of you at all."

"I'm a … little … teapot … getaway man," he looked affronted. "I'm … not … a little … meant to be … teapot … scary. I'm meant to be … a little teapot … scared. Otherwise I'm a little … I won't be any … teapot … good at running away … I'm a little … will I?"

Ruth giggled, the teapot thing clearly got worse when she wound him up. She shouldn't be sitting here talking to him like this but amazingly, trapped as she was on the top of a London skyscraper, with no way off and no hope of help, she felt utterly unafraid.

"Is that how getaway men dress?" His outfit was intriguing; elastic-sided boots, dark blue canvas jeans, loose paisley silk shirt, tucked in at the waist and unbuttoned at the top. He was wearing a greeny-blue velvet jacket and over the top, a thick, dark cloak and the hat. How to sum that up? Mostly back-of-Revolver, a dash of front-of-Help, a modicum of pirate and a sprinkling of Zorro. An odd look, but one that was all his own and one Ruth liked.

"No, I'm a little … that's how I dress."

"I see. It's not a bad look and you're correct, it's not scary. So, are you telling me that, right now, you're meant to be frightened?"

"Mmm hmm."

"And are you?"

A nod and a disarming smile.

"I'm the one with no clue what's going on, I thought that was supposed to make me the frightened one."

He shrugged.

"Are you scared of me?"

He laughed, put one hand out and wiggled it in a way that was clearly sign language for maybe.

"I don't think you are."

More smiling, he raised one eyebrow.

"Quite obviously, no." Another shrug. "But you are a getaway man?"

"Mmm hmm."

"That's a criminal."

"Mmm hmm."

"Then why do I trust you?"

He laughed.

"You are evidently a little—" a deep breath, "a rubbish judge of character … teapot."

"Not usually." She gave him her best don't-mess-with-me stare. There was that smile again. A small part of Ruth wanted to go out of its way to make him smile as much as possible. That was not good. Time for a reality check. He had swept her off her feet, literally—if not figuratively—and driven her through the best bits of London in the soft dusk light, in a flying car, with the top down. There was more than a bit of glamour appeal to this experience and Ruth suspected the fact that the Lotus was the car of her dreams might be clouding her judgement about the man inside it.

"Right then. I know you are probably here illegally, that you have a way cool set of wheels which flies and that you have a very amusing speech impediment." He chuckled and she was unaccountably pleased to have made him laugh. "Anything else you'd care to tell me?"

He took another deep breath. "I'm …"

Ruth watched with interest as he waited for the urge to declare himself teapot-shaped to subside.

"Not from around here," he finally said.

"Yes. I guessed that. OK, let's start somewhere simple. What's your name?"

"I'm The Pan of Hamgee," he inclined his head to imply a bow, "and I am at your service."

"I see." Ruth frowned. The 'I am at your service' bit was quite charming, in an old-fashioned way, "What's your first name?"

"I don't have one."

"You mean that's it?"

He nodded.

"That's not a name, it's a title. What do people call you? 'The'?"

"No. Usually it's 'Oi you! Stop! Teapot! Thief!'" Another long pause, "'Pan of Hamgee' translates slightly differently, so I suppose in your language, you'd call me 'The Hamgeean'."

He was looking shifty again. She knew it! He was lying.

"That sounds like a wrestling hold and it still doesn't give you a first name. I'm not an 'oi you' kind of girl. I can't say 'Hi, Hamgeean, how are you?' It doesn't go. I'm Ruth Cochrane—don't you dare laugh at my surname or make one reference to Eddie—so when you want to get my attention calling me 'Cochrane' is plain weird. I'm fine with 'Ruth' and it follows that, barring cultural differences, there must be something I'd use to talk to you; which you are not fine with, presumably." She waited but he wasn't biting. She sighed. "OK, Mister Pan of Hamgee, we'll have it your way, for now, and keep it formal but don't think you've got away with not telling me. I know you're lying and that means you do have a normal name. Let's try something else. Why are you here?"

"I'm a … the big guys with the … little … Arnold in the skies! … teapot … guns are not your friends. I came here to find you before they did."

"Well done, and thank you. I don't think the people who run the Festival Hall will be very keen on you, though. In fact, I expect you'll be had up by the police as soon as they see your car. I should imagine somebody took your number plate."

He smiled, raised an eyebrow, put one finger up in a wait-a-moment gesture and stood up. She watched as he walked coolly over to the Lotus, leaned in and pressed a button on the dash. There was a gentle electronic whining sound in stereo from the front and back of the car and the number plates revolved. He strolled back and sat down again, closer to her this time, with the air of a man who knows he has done something fairly impressive.

"You just revolved your number plate."

How annoying was that! She was trying to play it cool, trying very hard not to appear overawed, and to her irritation, it wasn't working.

"Are you sure you're not a spy? You have a spy's car."

He laughed, and again, she was glad; such a bad sign.

"Very and it's a snurd. I admit it's the deluxe model but where I come from most of this stuff is standard."

No 'teapots' there, he must be relaxing a little. Bad in some ways but for the sake of coherent conversation, good.

"Stuff like?"

"The aviator and submariner options—everyone has those—and all snurds are made of polymorphic metal."

"Polly what?"

"Polymorphic, it changes shape when you change modes." He must have noticed her look of incomprehension, "You know, from wings to," he shrugged, "no wings. It has to, or it'd be full of hinges and rivets and stuff and it'd be too heavy. The metal is preset for each mode so it knows what to do and of course, if you dent it, it remembers where it should be and goes back."

"OK, I don't know if that has been invented yet on Earth, where the hell are you from?"

"K'Barth."

"That leaves me none the wiser. Are you a space man?"

"Of course not. I'm from Earth, too, the same as you; it's a different version of reality, parallel but the same planet."

"Wow!" said Ruth, as she cast another quick glance at the Lotus. "So, does money work there? Could you take me to your country so I can buy one of those?"

"I don't know about the money but I think you'd be very unwise to come to my country." He gave her a rueful smile. "It's no place for a woman like you."

Sexist prat, those lovely eyes and all that smiling undone in an instant.

"Meaning, Mister Pan?" she asked acidly.

A long pause.

"Meaning that it's full of the wrong sort of people and quite a lot of them are after you."

"Thank you for your reassurance. I assume you mean the scary sci-fi dudes do you?" He looked quizzical. "The no-no blokes, with the uniforms and the laser guns."

"Amongst others."

Amongst others? Oh marvellous, who else then? No, beyond one, the 'who' wasn't relevant, the big question was,

"Why? Why are all these people after me?"

"Arnold in heaven. Where do I start?"

"Well, you could try the beginning."

"What if I freak you out?"

"What if? Are you scared I'll run away? In case you hadn't noticed, I'm stuck on the top of a skyscraper with you, it's not like I can go anywhere."

"You might jump off."

"I might but I'd die. Why would I want that? I'm not going to kill myself, Mister Pan; this is life, not opera."

He smiled and there was a hint of something else in his expression ... admiration, perhaps?

"You're not going to like this." He stopped as if he'd just remembered something and looked at his watch, "Arnold!"

Who was this Arnold he kept mentioning?

"Ruth, there's no time. Later, I promise, but now I have to go." He scrambled to his feet and so did she. "Stay here, you'll be quite safe. I'll be back in," another look at the watch, "five minutes."

"Oh no you don't! You're not leaving me marooned on the top of a building."

"I have to. I won't be a moment, I promise."

"Well, why don't I come too?"

"No, it's too dangerous."

"And now we come to it, 'too dangerous'. What if it's so dangerous that you don't come back?"

"I will."

"How do I know?"

"Because I've promised you."

She stared at him, and he didn't look away.

"You know, amazingly, Mister Pan, I believe you when you say you'll come back, but I find, in life, that there is often a big gap between people's intentions and delivery. What if you can't come back, what if you get yourself killed?"

He ran his hands through his hair and put his hat on.

"I'm rather hoping not to. Nothing will happen. You are safe here and I'll be five minutes, tops."

"You're serious, aren't you? You're actually going to leave me here, like a sitting duck."

"Yes, I'm afraid I am." He stood there, regarding her thoughtfully. "Ruth," he took her gently by the shoulders and looked into her eyes. "It's a big ask, I know, but please trust me." He was searching for some form of reassurance. Yes, there was no doubt he meant what he was saying. He believed he was going to come back for her; it was just that Ruth didn't. Never mind, if it was only supposed to be five minutes, best to get it over with. Ten minutes and she'd call the police and they could come and get her.

"I don't have much option, do I?"

He took her face in his hands and kissed her lightly on the cheek. Blimey! She hadn't been prepared for that.

"Thank you!" he said, "I think you might possibly be an angel." And he turned and ran. He leapt straight onto the boot lid of his snurd, gathering the cloak as he went, threw himself into the driving seat and started the engine. She watched as he took off, circled the building once and then he and his ritzy car disappeared in a flash of light. Ah. He hadn't told her he was going to do that. Without thinking what she was doing, she put her hand up to her cheek.

"Five minutes, Mister No-Name Hamgeean, that's all." And she didn't care how safe he thought it was, she was going to spend those five minutes looking for somewhere to hide.

Chapter 2

In a different version of the same universe, Lord Vernon, the Lord Protector of K'Barth, was glaring at the hole The Pan of Hamgee's snurd had blown in his office wall, where the window used to be. This was a setback and he was angry. Nobody ever escaped Lord Vernon and now this upstart was making a regular habit of it. He turned his attention to the two guards who were standing to attention in front of him. What he was about to do was at odds with his usual management philosophy but he was too angry not to take it out on something.

"You there."

"Yessir," croaked one of the guards. They were frightened. Good.

"Remind me, what is the penalty for striking a superior officer?"

"Death, sir," said the other one smartly. Lord Vernon clicked his knuckles.

"Death. Excellent. Gentlemen, hold on to that thought."

Just as he was pulling his arm back to punch the one nearest him, he was interrupted by the sound of the door opening. Lord Vernon saw the relief in the eyes of the guard and it irritated him. He lowered his arm and rounded angrily upon the person who had dared walk into his rooms without knocking.

"Your Most Gracious Exaltedness, I must apologise for this intrusion." General Moteurs; a Grongle of impeccable honour and the only one to enjoy the same security clearance as his master. Even so, his reason for barging in had better be good.

"What do you want, General?"

"I bring news about the bronze portal, sir. As you suggested, it is a piece of simple, if elegant, quantum mechanics."

"Naturally, General. And …?"

"The labs have reverse engineered it, with partial success. We have five prototypes pretested and ready for use."

"Where are they?"

"Four of them are fitted to military vehicles for further evaluation, sir. I took the liberty of having the fifth fitted to the Interceptor."

"Did you, General?"

"Sir. It is effective, but where the K'Barthan portals are driven by the imagination of the user, ours function solely on input map coordinates."

"That may give us an advantage. Find a way to combine the two and we can move freely, without limitation."

"Yes, sir," the General hesitated. "On another matter, my surveillance team have detected your portal in use here. Our systems are still in their infancy so I came here to verify."

"Your systems are functioning perfectly, General, the Hamgeean has escaped and taken the platinum portal with him. That is why I ordered that the Chosen One be brought here." Lord Vernon hid the rage which burned inside him from his voice but he knew, from the General's guarded expression that he had not kept it from his eyes. He stopped to collect his thoughts. "The Hamgeean's departure is …" and the habitual pause followed while he sought the right word. "Irritating. But he is easy enough to follow, if difficult to catch. I suggest we wait and see what he does."

"Yes, sir, I will have the bronze portal returned to you forthwith."

"No need," Lord Vernon held up the copper thimble. "This will suffice."

"As you wish, sir." General Moteurs' mobile phone beeped discreetly and he glanced at the display. "May I?"

Lord Vernon nodded.

"Moteurs." A pause.

Lord Vernon was intrigued, 'Moteurs', not, 'General Moteurs', false modesty? No. Not from this one. He waited.

"What?" said the General. "I see." His voice was strained. There was a long, long pause. "No, I will tell him myself," a quick glance in Lord Vernon's direction. "No, Colonel, that will not be necessary. Yes, thank you. Good night." He pressed the red button.

"Well, General, not bad news, I hope."

General Moteurs swallowed. He was pale.

"A temporary setback, Your Most Gracious Exaltedness, the Chosen One has evaded my team."

"General, I ordered that you apprehend her specifically to avoid this situation, so she would not fall into the hands of the Underground. Explain, if you would, why your squad was unable to carry out my simple request." Lord Vernon's rage was all but consuming him, he needed to smash something, or someone, but no-one as useful as General Moteurs. Later Lord Vernon would go down to the cells and break some rebel heads. Yes, that would make him feel better. The silence seemed endless before General Moteurs spoke. The tension was evident in his voice but he remained calm and maintained unwavering eye contact.

"It seems the Hamgeean came to her rescue. He broke through the glass at the front of the building and—"

"Took her from under the noses of your troops." Lord Vernon waited. He wanted to give General Moteurs time to appreciate the ramifications of failure, he may be too useful to kill but there was no need for him to know that. "And what do you suggest we do now?" He did not bother to keep the anger from his voice.

"All is not lost, sir. The Underground will not have her yet and the Hamgeean fled with her in aviator mode."

"And that is relevant because …?"

"Because there are no snurds in the Chosen One's reality. My troops are monitoring the emergency services there. The snurd will be reported soon enough and then we will have their location. It will be a simple matter for my team to pick them up."

"I am sure it will. However, since your team has already failed in the 'simple matter' of capturing the Chosen One, I will take her and the Hamgeean. Your team will play no further part in this."

"As you wish, sir." The General's air of businesslike serenity did not falter. Lord Vernon was impressed, for all his anger. The General's phone beeped again and if it was possible he turned a shade paler.

"Answer it, underling," snarled Lord Vernon. 'Underling': a monstrous insult, reserved specifically for non-Grongles. Lord Vernon had not dismissed the guards and now heard a sharp intake of breath from one of them. Good; doubtless the General also realised the depth of his displeasure. Moteurs looked him in the eye a fraction longer than necessary, as if to check he had heard correctly but all he said was a calm, "Thank you, sir."

After a few moments of listening, General Moteurs ended the call.

"Well?" demanded Lord Vernon.

"Sir. My surveillance team has detected another instance of portal use. I believe we may have them."

"May?"

"The detection equipment is still temperamental and unreliable. I cannot guarantee a result. Indeed, I believe it would be wise to approach any action as little more than an experiment rather than an attempt at capture."

"Is that so, General?" said Lord Vernon slowly. "And yet you are confident enough in your technology to bring this to my attention."

"Perhaps, Your Gracious Exaltedness."

"Give me the coordinates."

"Sir." He took a pen and paper from his pocket and scribbled down some figures. "My troops will continue to monitor the emergency services in case the equipment …" An awkward pause.

Lord Vernon raised his eyebrows quizzically.

"Fails me, General? Fails me like its master and his sorry excuse for a team?"

"Sir," said General Moteurs. Still he maintained his composure. In Lord Vernon's usual experience, Moteurs should be on his knees by this point, begging forgiveness. The General had courage; Lord Vernon would give him that. And he was loyal, truly loyal in a way others were not. It doubled the pleasure of upbraiding and disrespecting him, of course. Especially in front of his own troops. Lord Vernon cast a glance at the guards, two very large Grongles who were trying, and failing spectacularly, to make themselves invisible.

"Your Gracious Exaltedness—" began the General.

"Sir is sufficient, Moteurs," growled Lord Vernon.

"Sir. With your permission, I would be honoured to take care of this matter myself, and I know my troops would relish a chance to redeem themselves."

"Doubtless, they would. I am glad that they, and you, understand what it means to fail me. However, there will be no more blunders this evening. I shall see to this personally." He snatched the piece of paper from the General's hand and strode out of the room. The door slammed and all was silent. General Moteurs was locked in his own thoughts and the guards carried on standing to attention, waiting for orders. Eventually he spoke.

"Back to your duties, lads," he said.

"Permission to speak, sir," said one of the guards.

"Denied," said General Moteurs. His voice was stern and his face still impassive but his eyes held the tiniest hint of a smile. "I advise you to be out on patrol when he comes back. The worst is over. He may be volatile, but with time to reflect he is fair. I will be forgiven and you forgotten by morning." He held the door open. At just over six foot tall, General Moteurs was short, for a Grongle. Both the guards were taller than he was.

"You knew, sir, didn't you?" said the bigger of the two. The General said nothing.

"Thank you, sir," said the other and General Moteurs fixed him with a steely glare.

"What for, exactly?"

"Saving us a beating, sir."

"Did I give either of you permission to speak?"

"No, sir."

"Then I suggest you don't. I mean it, lads. Leave, now, or I shall have to put you on a charge."

They went.

Chapter 3

Gingerly, Ruth climbed down from the helipad onto the roof proper. It was only raised up a few feet but there was an alcove underneath. She walked, bent double, under the jutting edge. A full circuit revealed that there was a doorway – locked, naturally – with some stairs up which sensible people could climb from rooftop to helipad level. How embarrassing, she hadn't thought of looking for those.

"Spanner woman," she said to no-one in particular.

She wondered how The Pan was getting on and her hand went to her cheek again. Yes, OK, he'd kissed her and it was quite nice but she needed to forget about it because she was supposed to be hiding and … Wait a minute? What was that? It sounded like a light aircraft engine. Yes! Hoorah, he was coming back. She had hoped he would but she had braced herself for disappointment.

Yet some instinct stronger than her pride stopped Ruth from running onto the helipad, waving. This was lucky because on closer examination it turned out to be a different flying car which was approaching the building. It looked like a 1950s Mercedes, the Uhlenhaut. It was sleek, black, and menacing with glassed-in headlights and the exhaust pipes stuck out of the air vents at the side. But it also had wings, which made it a snurd and most importantly, it was not The Pan of Hamgee's.

Ruth retreated from the steps, into the shadows under the helipad. Whoever this was, might be friendly but she decided she'd wait and see before introducing herself. She heard, rather than saw, the Mercedes land. Someone got out and she listened to their footsteps walking across the helipad. Were they coming down the stairs? She strained to hear as something unfeasibly loud-engined drove along the street below, and under cover of the noise she backed further into the shadows. Then she saw him; tall and immaculately dressed in a uniform. No sunglasses, but that black hair, those chiselled good looks and the unmistakable, tangible sense of malevolence emanating from him like some dark perfume.

It was *him*. The one who had followed her all those months ago – when her normal life ended and the stalking began – the man who had been looking for his Chosen One. Please let him be searching for somebody else. She wasn't chosen. If she was she would know for heaven's sake! Or it would be more obvious.

He put his hands on the railings and looked out over the city. Ruth's heart was racing and she started shaking. He would find her, for sure. No, he wasn't going to, but she had to stay silent and out of sight. Very slowly, to avoid making the smallest noise, she lay down on her stomach and slid further into the shadows.

He flipped open a mobile phone, dialled and waited for an answer. When he spoke, Ruth shuddered. If evil could be expressed as sound it would be this man's voice and somehow, though she thought she'd remembered, she realised she'd actually forgotten just how frightening he was. Who was he?

"General," he said, "I must congratulate you on the modifications you have made to the Interceptor. However, it seems that you are correct on the matter of your detection systems. There is nobody in evidence and pleasing though it is, I did not come here to admire the view." A pause while he listened to whoever was at the other end of the phone. He turned round and leaned on the railings with his back to the city, a vivid, unreal outline against the familiar backdrop of the London night sky. He looked straight at Ruth. Had he seen her? There was no way of knowing. His expression gave nothing away; she guessed not.

"It is unfortunate but there is no sign of activity," and in that soft menacing voice, he continued, "I hope your standards are not slipping, General." He chuckled, as if to indicate he was joking. But it wasn't funny. This bloke didn't do chummy. "Yes. Your systems are evidently flawed, since, whether or not portal use has occurred in this area, there is clearly no-one here now." Another silence while he listened. He was still looking straight at the spot where Ruth was hiding, only now he smiled. It was a horrible predatory smile. Could it be aimed at her? No. It couldn't be or he'd act rather than stare.

"Perhaps … Do not mention it. It was a pleasure to assist you in your experiment. And now, I regret, I must leave you to your work. I am master of a nation and my time is at a premium. Oh, and General, I will leave it to you to discipline those who failed to capture the Chosen One." Another long pause while he listened and, in spite of her fear, Ruth had time to feel sorry for whoever he was talking to.

"I appreciate that, and since your team has maintained such an impeccable record, until today, I can understand your desire to protect them. However, I hope you will not be so …" Ruth watched him wave one hand casually, as if to pluck the word he sought from the air, "lenient, if it happens again." Another pause. "Excellent, I am glad we understand one another. I will return directly. Good evening to you." He snapped his phone shut and ran up the stairs. Ruth listened as the engine noise of his Mercedes-type car receded into the distance. A huge sob of relief escaped her. He had gone and he hadn't found her.

That she had escaped him again was lucky, but what she had heard of his conversation was alarming. It suggested that he owned the scary sci-fi men who had been following her all this time, that he thought she was chosen and that even if she realised she wasn't, he didn't, or wouldn't, and that was a problem. She took a deep breath and crept out of her hiding place. Moments later, she heard a noise a little like a light aircraft engine again. Another flying car? Yes, coming in to land by the sounds of it. Phew. She was going to give The Pan a piece of her mind now he was back, and some. It wasn't until she reached the top of the steps that she realised her mistake. The vehicle that had landed was shaped like a black Mercedes.

He'd hidden so she'd come out into the open. Classic cat and mouse and Ruth knew the rules of that game – the cat always won. And right now, Ruth was the mouse – the dumbest mouse imaginable.

Chapter 4

As The Pan circled the building he watched the lone figure on the roof below. She seemed so small and vulnerable from above and he was torn. Was he doing the right thing? Not sure. But after going to so much trouble to save her from the Grongles, he couldn't take her with him. Not where he was going – because he was going home to the Parrot and Screwdriver, the pub where he rented a room. His landladies, Gladys Parker and Ada Maddox, along with Gladys' son, Trev, were the closest thing The Pan had to a family. But they were also members of the Underground, the more moderate of K'Barth's two resistance organisations – and Lord Vernon knew.

Gladys, Ada and Trev didn't realise their clandestine activities had been discovered and as the only non-Grongle who did, The Pan had to warn them. However, it was nearly an hour since he had escaped from police custody – plenty of time for the Grongles to reach the pub first. Worse, they must realise that The Pan would try to save his surrogate family. Ruth wasn't the only one wondering if he would return, The Pan himself, didn't give much for his chances. That was why he couldn't take her with him – because the Grongles might be waiting for him and if they were, he risked handing her straight to Lord Vernon. She was frightened, and it wasn't kind or chivalrous to leave her alone, but he had to. Warning the others was the right thing to do. Ruth would be safe enough on the roof and hopefully, if he returned in one piece, he'd have time to explain and she'd understand.

He pressed the portal button and the snurd materialised a few feet above Turnadot Street, travelling at speed. He slowed, landed and parked in front of the pub. It was too quiet. At this time of night it should be closing, regulars spilling out onto the street shouting rowdy beery goodbyes – or just shouting. No sign of any Grongles though, and from outside, no sign of a struggle. He tried the door. Locked.

"Mmm," said The Pan to himself. Then he caught sight of a notice in the window.

'Staff Holidays' it ran. *'The staff of this establishment has never had a holiday. So now we are going to see what it's like. Therefore, this public house will be closed for a short time on account of that we are having one now.'*

The Pan imagined Gladys, Ada and Their Trev on the beach and it made him chuckle. Good.

He would have to be vigilant but he suspected that if the Grongles had come here, they had been and gone. Had Gladys, Ada and Trev expected him home? He went round to the side alley. Yes, it seemed they had, because although it was almost impossible to tell from the ground, they had left the landing window open the smallest crack. He climbed up the drainpipe his usual way, opened the window, and slipped into the hall. All was quiet. Definitely away and not hiding then and no signs of a search by the Grongles either. He went into the kitchen. Yes, the fridge was switched off, the door open to keep it fresh. Something smelled though. He raised his arm and sniffed an armpit. Arnold. It was him.

It's a little-known fact that for the escape man, cleanliness really is next to godliness. After all, there's no point in being a master of evasion and concealment if the people chasing you can smell where you're hidden. He checked his watch. No time for a proper wash but he ran into his bedroom, taking his shirt off as he went, and grabbed a clean one from the chest of drawers. Back to the bathroom, where he splashed some water over himself, a quick dab with a towel, shirt on. Oops, don't forget the deodorant. He undid a couple of buttons so he could get the can in and applied some. Not too much, or at close quarters, they'd still be able to track him down by smell – only it would be more pleasant for them. There, that would be better than nothing. Now what?

His eyes scanned the room, saying goodbye to the familiar, comfortable detritus of his life. Ah yes, that was a point.

He ran downstairs to the cellar, reached behind the barrels, and collected a red freezer bag containing a small stash of loot, gathered from his days as getaway driver for the Mervinettes, K'Barth's most famous gang of bank robbers. He wished he could help himself to one of Ada's cheeses but he had nothing to leave in payment except a piece of loot, which was too precious to waste on such a trifle. He could borrow one, he supposed, but it wasn't his to take and Gladys and Ada weren't there to ask for an IOU. It would be sensible, and they'd probably understand, but unfortunately it would also be wrong. He sighed. This principles thing was exhausting. He checked his watch; he'd promised he'd be five minutes and he'd used four of them. Time to go.

He ran back upstairs to the kitchen, took a pen from the pot by the phone and wrote a note for Gladys and Ada on the pad they used for messages. *Lord*

Vernon thinks you are rebels, STAY ON HOLIDAY' it said. He read it through and added, *'Thank you for everything and good luck'* along with his name at the bottom. Another glance at his watch. Five minutes were up. He was going to be late. He bundled out of the landing window, not forgetting to close it behind him, and half climbed, half fell, in his haste to reach the ground below. Another running jump into the snurd and he was off, leaving Turnadot Street behind, and rising above the houses. He shoved the bag of loot under the seat and imagined the building where he'd left the Chosen One stranded. Mmm, she would be pretty mad with him when he came back he expected – and he'd deserve it – but at least this time, he'd done the right thing, in so far as he could, and it felt, yeh, good. He checked his watch again. Seven minutes, not bad. Composing himself for an earbashing, he pressed the portal button.

Chapter 5

The Pan arrived to find the roof was no longer empty. No sign of Ruth, but parked at one side was the unmistakable shape of a black snurd. A lone figure in a long dark coat was walking across the concrete, towards a flight of stairs at one side and as The Pan watched, Ruth ran up them and stopped abruptly. His stomach lurched as Lord Vernon looked up at him, laughing, and waved.

"This is not going to happen. Not to her." He acted without further thought. Wrenching the SE2 round he brought it in to land. He wanted to block Lord Vernon's path but he was going too fast and overshot.

"Ruth!" he shouted. "Jump in!" The top of the SE2 was down. There was still time. She'd seen him run over the back and leap into his seat when he left but would she follow suit?

No, she held her arms out in panic-stricken confusion. She hesitated, but by some amazing stroke of luck, so did Lord Vernon. Right then, time for plan B.

The Pan threw the SE2 into reverse but, even as he did so he realised it was too small to delay Lord Vernon, who was so tall he could practically step over it. The Chosen One was toast. There was no escape and no way off this building unless … Arnold, she wasn't going to like this, not at all, and if it didn't work, he was going to kill them both. Never mind, he thought, as he sped backwards towards her, better to kill her trying to escape than hang around and wait for Lord Vernon to do it – or worse.

As The Pan reversed, he leaned over, fumbling for the catch to open the passenger door. He caught a brief glimpse of Ruth in the wing mirror before he flung it wide and the image arced away. She was looking behind her at the stairs. She must be thinking of backtracking. Arnold's pants. This would give her an even bigger shock than he'd thought. A few yards away from her, he slammed on the brakes, the snurd skidded and slowed, not much but enough. When the edge of its wing hit her on her shins the impact flipped her forwards without breaking her legs. Good, there was a bonus! That bit had worked. As she sprawled onto the wing she hit the open passenger door and The Pan grabbed one of her arms and hauled her half in. The snurd jinked as he used the steering wheel for purchase, her legs were still hanging out over the wing and her eyes met his, wide with fright, or maybe rage.

The Pan accelerated again and they sped backwards off the platform, narrowly missing the apron of the roof but, unfortunately, not the safety fence. The SE2 clipped it with a bump.

"NO!" he shouted as the revs dropped. He stamped on the clutch but what with trying to drag the Chosen One into the passenger seat at the same time, his foot slid off the pedal and the engine stalled. However, the momentum carried them on and, taking the top rail of the fence with it, the SE2 fell off the side of the building. As it tumbled into the void, the snurd turned a full somersault while The Pan hung onto Ruth with all his strength, and yelled in pain as, in the absence of any other spare appendages with which to do so, he pressed his bruised nose against the starter button. Something came out of the footwell, bounced off him and fell to the street below. A red freezer bag containing everything he owned.

As the SE2 turned the right way up again the engine finally kicked into life. They were dropping fast now as, with one hand holding the Chosen One, The Pan fought to regain control with the other.

Ruth fell back in, sideways across the seats and the passenger door closed with a slam. She had landed with her head in his lap. Not ideal but her arms and legs were pretty much all inside now so it would do. Without delay, he pressed the button to put up the roof and the bulletproof metal moved into position. He looked ahead. Arnold! The ground! And a bus. At least it looked like a bus, presumably they had them here. The Pan's eyes met the startled driver's for a millisecond as he hauled frantically at the wheel. There was a rubbery squeak as the SE2's tyres glanced off the tarmac and then the snurd was speeding sharply upwards again.

Well, that hadn't been too bad and they were alive, although it had been close and he had to admit, he was a bit sweaty. The Chosen One was pretty much upside down and for a moment or two seemed to be stuck. Should he try to help her? No, she was too angry. After a struggle, she walked her feet across the roof, squeezed herself round so she was the right way up and settled into her seat. He gave her a moment to gather a few shreds of dignity and cleared his throat. She spoke first.

"You're late," she said acidly.

"Yes, I'm sorry about that." What else could he say?

"You said you'd be five minutes, that was more like ten."

"Seven," he said calmly. Oops. Calm was good but contradicting her might not be. "I'm glad I got to you," he hurried on, trying, tactfully, to make the point that he had just saved her life and lost everything he owned in the process, barring the clothes he was wearing, the snurd and the few things which were still in it.

"Yeh? Well it's lucky I had the presence of mind to hide or he'd have got me the first time, you stupid bloody man!"

The first time? What did she mean?

"I'm—"

"DON'T even think about apologising. I've had months of this! You and all your friends following me around wherever I go, staring, frightening me, making my life miserable. Why? What do you want?"

"I never meant to frighten you or make your life miserable. I'm here because I want to help."

"Oh shut up! You sound like some crap psychiatrist."

"Well tough, because you need to listen to me, Ruth, there's a lot of stuff I have to explain and, trust me, I will, but now isn't the time."

"Oh, I'm so sorry, when is a good time, Mister Pan?"

"When we are not being chased by the most dangerous snurd in K'Barth," he said. "And I'd do up your seatbelt if I was you, this is going to be dicey." He risked a glance across at her. She was clearly as angry as she was scared, but did as he had asked without demur. Yes, he was going to get a massive earbashing later. That much was obvious. Never mind, he almost certainly deserved it and at least if she sulked now, it would mean she'd shut up and he'd be able to concentrate. He could apologise and make it up to her afterwards—if they survived—and saving her life yet again might pour a little oil on the troubled waters between them. Although he had to concede that, as a conciliatory initiative, life-saving was proving to be spectacularly unsuccessful so far.

The Interceptor was upon them in an instant and The Pan settled into what he did best; escape and evasion. The SE2 had better shielding than he had believed possible, as he discovered when Lord Vernon began firing. The Interceptor would be difficult to shake off and The Pan, who was usually confident and incisive in an escape, was unsure as to the best approach. In K'Barth snurds were commonplace. Here, it was clear they were not. He knew nothing of the police – were they armed? Could they, would they, shoot down a snurd?

Relieved that the Chosen One was sulking, The Pan realised, as he flipped the snurd down a narrow alley between two buildings and the Interceptor came

close to cutting them off by flying round the other side, that he was going to
need her help. Back home his knowledge of his surroundings was so good that
finding the best places to hide, or ditch a pursuer, was almost instinctive. Here,
he was in foreign territory, he didn't know his way around and he needed
someone who did to guide him.

They were flying out across the river with the Interceptor looming in his
rear-view mirrors.

"Where do I go?"

"I don't know. You tell me," she snapped. "You're the one who does this
for a living, right? Although, you're not much cop so far, are you?"

"Wait and see, wait and see." Yep, she was fully lit and would be for some
time. This was up to him.

He skimmed the snurd low over the water and rolled it several times in a
row to avoid a volley of laser fire. A stray round caught a cast-iron lamp post on
the riverside walkway and it collapsed to the pavement with a metallic groan.
They swooped under a bridge and he turned the snurd towards the other side
of the river. A huge Ferris wheel loomed ahead, all white steel and glass pods,
revolving slowly.

"Aaaaargh wires," he shouted as he swung the snurd on its side. He glanced
at the Chosen One. Her hands were over her eyes. The SE2 passed safely
through but the laser fire from Lord Vernon's snurd hit an empty pod, sending
it crashing into the river. Another roll: to evade machine-gun fire this time. The
Pan was waiting for something bigger. He knew the Interceptor was armed with
missiles and wondered why Lord Vernon hadn't yet fired one. They reached a
second bridge and he bumped the snurd up this time and along the road on top.
A third bridge, a red and black one, crossed overhead. It looked as if it should
carry a railway but when he bumped the snurd up again, The Pan discovered it
carried another street instead. He followed it to a roundabout, a huge blue tower
block loomed ahead and ah yes, here was the missile. The Pan flew towards the
building and at the last minute headed up a wide road to its right. A shower of
blue glass flew past them as the missile hit the building and exploded.

They spent a few more minutes flying low above the asphalt in grim silence
with the Interceptor in close pursuit. Lord Vernon was still firing but he had
reverted to using the lasers. They saw bright explosions of light as the rounds
that missed the SE2 hit other things; buildings, trees, traffic lights. They flew up
over the roofs where they almost collided with a spinning metal ball glowing
with lights. The Interceptor hit it with a bang and the ball fell, in a shower of

sparks, to the road below. The Pan flew down again into an open square and doubled back round a tall column as a second missile from the Interceptor exploded against it. The blast dislodged a statue on the top which narrowly missed the SE2 as it fell to earth.

"No!" shouted Ruth. "Stop it! That's enough."

"There's a plastic bag in the glove compartment—" began The Pan as he sped down a side street.

"No, you stupid man. I'm talking about the destruction. That was Nelson's Column! He's breaking London."

"What do you want me to do about it?" More laser fire flew from the Interceptor. "It's London or he brings us down," shouted The Pan as he rolled the SE2 to avoid it. "And he might want you alive but if he brings us down, he'll kill me. So I'm happy to settle for London."

"Well I'm not. This is my capital city. I *refuse* to let him trash it," said the Chosen One through gritted teeth.

"That statement would imply you have a choice. You don't. Anyway, in case you hadn't noticed, he's done a pretty thorough job so far," said The Pan as he jinked the snurd sideways and a speed camera bit the dust.

"Then it's up to you to stop him from breaking any more."

"Look, I'm just trying to get us out of this. It's not my fault."

"Yes it is, you *left* me. 'I'll be back in five minutes, tops,' that's what you said and you weren't and if you had been he wouldn't have even found us."

Arnold's pants, she had a point but not one he was going to admit.

"He would have found us, we'd just have been sitting on the side of that ..." What was it? He took one hand off the wheel to wave expansively, "... landing thing, where we couldn't escape and you'd be on your way to prison, or worse."

"We aren't exactly escaping now, are we, Mister Pan?"

He winced.

"Not yet," he said.

"Any time today, then?" Arnold she was sarky!

"I'll be losing him just as soon as I can, alright?" he said, painfully aware that the only thing he was losing at this precise moment was his temper.

"Then please can you hurry it up?"

"How? I told you. I'm doing all I can."

"Well, why don't you try a little harder and while you're about it, why don't you try doing it in a way that doesn't involve the wholesale destruction of London?"

"Of course, I'll just stop, shall I, and ask him? 'Hello, please can you not shoot at us, only you're breaking the Chosen One's town and she's upset … Oooh I'm sorry, where did my head go?' Again, how, exactly?"

"Take some of the flack. Doesn't this thing have armour?"

"Of course it does but only so much and when it's gone, we're stuffed."

"Well sacrifice some." As if to accentuate the point, there was a loud bang and the snurd juddered as Lord Vernon's lasers scored a direct hit. It was followed by a short beep as the shields in question recharged and reset.

"Are you out of your mind? What if I sacrifice us? I came here to rescue you. If I wanted to hand you over to him, not to mention getting fried, I could have stayed at home."

"Then why don't you stop faffing and actually rescue me, Mister Pan?"

"Stop faffing?" asked The Pan incredulously. "Listen, Chosen One. I'm the best getaway man in K'Barth and I'm the only man alive who has ever outrun him."

"Then perhaps you could try doing that here."

"Trust me, I'll ditch him quicker than anyone else can," he paused to concentrate while he negotiated the portico of a civic building of some description, flying sideways through the space between the columns and the doorway at top speed, Lord Vernon followed but there was a clunk as one of the wheels of the Interceptor clipped the brickwork. "Back home I know where to hide and I could lose him like that." The Pan clicked his fingers. What a massive lie! Never mind, she wasn't going to know. "Here," he paused. How to approach this? Honesty? Yes, honesty. "Here, I'm lost. I don't know this city but you do, so instead of sitting there whining why don't you help me? Think where the geography would give us an advantage and guide me there."

"Oh yeh, sure. What if I can't?"

"Then shut up and stop distracting me."

"OK. What type of geography do you want, Mister Pan?" Her tone was icy.

"The narrowest streets, underpasses, pipes, factories," he shrugged. "Places where he will have to concentrate so hard on not hitting things that he'll forget about catching us!" As they sped back, more or less the way they had come, The Pan took in the felled lamp posts, broken traffic lights and singed buildings. He saw the tower block with the big hole in it. Mmm. It wasn't good. He bore left at the roundabout, down the hill, left again, straight on for a few hundred yards, down a wide street, up over the top of a building and at last he saw a brief glimpse of something they could use to escape.

There was an underground railway in an open station and a train; he had an idea. He flipped the snurd round and with the Interceptor still on their tail, he headed down towards the tunnel, the one at the back with the overhead power lines, to make it more difficult for Lord Vernon. The train began to move. It was going to be a close-run thing. The gap between the edge of the tunnel and the driver's cab was narrowing fast, and seemed impossibly small as they approached, but it was too late now. As they skimmed under the wires he activated aviator slim mode and the SE2 sped through the tiny gap, ahead of the moving train, its wings automatically folding backwards as it went, and flew into the tunnel. Lord Vernon and his Interceptor were left stranded behind the carriages.

Chapter 6

The Pan slowed the SE2 right down.

"I'm guessing you know about as much of the way down here as I do," he said.

"You're guessing correctly," said the Chosen One. Her tone was still caustic. A few minutes and they emerged into a disused station which had an open roof, and The Pan flew the SE2 out over the wall. They had lost Lord Vernon but not for long – they were dangerously exposed and they needed to hide. He regarded the shiny buttons and switches on the dash. Some of them were new to him, one in particular. He wondered … Worth a try. Up ahead was a hotel with one of those porches in front to allow people to get out of their cars in the dry. That would do. He flew under, slowly, flipped the snurd upside down and flicked a switch labelled 'anti-grav'. Immediately the snurd landed on the ceiling and stuck. No sign of Lord Vernon and no chance of being seen here from the air. Precious few staff around at this time of night either, nice and quiet.

"I think that should have done it," said The Pan. He looked over at the Chosen One. She was pale and clearly emotional.

"You broke London."

He sighed. He hadn't expected thanks but he had just saved her life, twice, in as many hours and he felt that some sort of cursory acknowledgement would only be polite.

"Yeh, I broke your precious city, but you're still alive aren't you?"

"No thanks to you."

"No, of course not, without me you'd be in the clover, wouldn't you? Home free."

"If you hadn't smashed the front of the Festival Hall then yes, I probably would be."

Arnold. Another excellent point there, not about the window and the Festival Hall or whatever she'd called it, but about the Grongles. The Pan knew that if he hadn't escaped, they wouldn't have been trying to capture her in the first place. He sighed. She was right, it was all his fault. Should he admit it though? No.

"I'm not in the mood to argue with you, Chosen One," he said.

"My name's Ruth and I am not the Chosen One."

Mmm. Pity she was so much in the mood to argue with him.

"Well, Ruth, I have some bad news for you there. You are the Chosen One."

"No, I'm not. If I was I'd know, or somebody would have told me."

"Somebody is telling you."

"Somebody I trust."

Ouch. That stung.

"Why, thank you—" The Pan began, but bit his lip. If he didn't shut up they were going to have a row or at least, the row they were having was going to get to the point where someone started shouting.

"Don't mention it," said the Chosen One waspishly.

The Pan didn't usually lose his temper, not properly, he was in unfamiliar emotional territory and he didn't like it. He was fed up with being upside down, too, all the blood was running to his head. He turned off the anti-grav and the snurd fell to the road, with a startling crash, on its roof. There was a brief pause.

"Smecking snotty—" The Pan began.

The Chosen One's eyes met his. Was there a hint of a smile in them? Difficult to tell and even if there was, it was probably 'at' not 'with'.

"Perhaps you should try that again, Mister Pan," she said. Was her tone less frosty? Possibly, but only in the way that some parts of the Arctic tundra are marginally less cold than others. She reached out and flicked the switch to 'on' before he could. With an equally startling crash the snurd snapped back up to the ceiling again.

"There," she said sweetly, "when you're ready."

The Pan was aware there was no such thing as a whole body blush but he reckoned he was close to achieving one. He pressed the starter button.

"Fingerprint ident accepted," said the SE2's sexy voice and the engine started. He selected aviator mode.

"You're not going to fly again, are you?" said the Chosen One as the wings unfurled.

"Unless you can think of another way to get us off this thing, yes, but only for a few seconds." Arnold, could she not give him a moment's slack? This had all gone wrong. He was even crazier about the Chosen One now that he'd actually met her. All that mock formality, the way she called him 'Mister Pan' gave him goosebumps; and up on the roof before he'd left her alone, he'd kissed her and she'd looked into his eyes and, Arnold …

"Well? Are we going?"

"Yes, we're going," he said quietly. He took off for a brief moment, turned the snurd over, landed on the tarmac and drove out into the road.

Chapter 7

The dark form of the Interceptor climbed into the night above Farringdon Station, as Lord Vernon cruised the still-smoking sky searching for his prey. Another escape would be intolerable, but he was nothing if not pragmatic. He must devise a backup plan to entrap the Chosen One. Wresting her from the protection of The Pan of Hamgee would be difficult. Not impossible, of course, the Hamgeean would not be able to hold onto her forever, but there must be simpler, less time-consuming ways to lure her into his power. Lord Vernon was impatient to move to the next phase of his plan but without her he could not.

He would go home and rethink his strategy and then he would take the Chosen One. Yes, he smiled to himself, she would be his and the Hamgeean … The Hamgeean would wish he had never been born.

Chapter 8

"Where to, Ruth?" asked the Pan as they drove.

"Home," she said. She realised she was sitting where the driver's seat was in her car.

"And we drive on the left-hand side of the road in this country."

"And you all speak Grongolian, I guess I should have worked that one out for myself."

"Only if you were Einstein and actually, we all speak English," Ruth corrected him.

"Not where I come from you don't," said The Pan and they headed off.

He was angry. She sneaked a quick look at him and unthinkingly, she put her hand to her cheek. She remembered the expression of helpless resignation on his face after he'd got the anti-grav wrong. When she'd rubbed his nose in it, he'd taken it pretty well. She began to feel guilty.

Get a grip, Ruth. It was time to be angry and she was angry with him on so many levels; for leaving her on the roof and swanning off like an idiot, she was angry that he'd deemed a trip with him to warn his friends as 'too dangerous' – that was so condescending. She was even angrier that he had come back and dragged her off, pretty much by the hair like some Neanderthal, she was angry about the pain in her shins, she was angry about the damage the other one had done to London, she was angry that The Pan was angry with her instead of supplicating and sorry the way she felt he should be; and she wanted to stay angry so she could tell him exactly what she thought of his actions with proper conviction. Last, but most of all, she was angry with herself because underneath all that bile she couldn't deny that she was also, secretly, impressed. Impressed enough to believe that The Pan of Hamgee probably was the best getaway man in K'Barth or wherever it was he was from.

Once road-bound, Ruth noticed he seemed to have an irritating mental block with traffic lights which merely served to enrage her further. He swore blind that back home red was at the bottom and meant go, but apart from that they managed to make it to Kilburn, where Ruth rented a flat, without incident. Just short of the end of her street, he parked.

"I think we should drive past first to make sure everything's alright," he said.

"Isn't the car," he glared at her, "snurd," she corrected herself, "going to be a bit conspicuous? Even with a completely different number plate. I have a sensible plan." She took her mobile out of her bag. "Why don't I ring home? My flatmate should be in and if she isn't I can always try her mobile."

He tried, and failed, to hide his amazement.

"You have a mobile phone?" he said.

"Most people have a mobile phone this side of the Dark Ages," said Ruth.

"Not where I'm from," he said. "Non-Grongles aren't allowed them."

"Who or what are Grongles?" she asked, as she dialled.

"The people with the Truth Serum and the over-active fists, your big sci-fi guys," said the Pan, "and Lord Vernon, the one who chased us, though since he was also the one with the Truth Serum, perhaps he only counts once."

Wait a minute! Ruth pressed the cancel button abruptly. She could feel herself going pale.

"OK Mister Pan, why would these Grongles be interested in me? For that matter, why would you be?"

"At the risk of getting into a conversational loop, because Arnold knows it doesn't seem to be going in, you are chosen, you—are—the—Chosen—One."

"No—I—am—not, Mister No-Name. I haven't a clue where you people are from but it's clearly a long way away; inter-galactically far away, I'd say, from the look of your wheels. So, why would any of you be interested? Why would you come schlepping all the way out here to choose me when you have a planet of your own people? It doesn't make sense."

He gave her a look of something approaching contempt.

"It doesn't have to make sense. It's just the way things are. You are the Chosen One."

She took a moment out to give him a withering glare.

"I don't think so," she told him shortly, selected her home number, pressed send and with the phone clamped to her ear, got out of the car.

The house on the corner of the street had a large privet hedge which enabled her to peep down the road. Was that the faint ringing of the phone in her flat she could hear? She let it ring but nobody was picking up. She tried Lucy's mobile but it went to voicemail. Ruth didn't want to worry Lucy. She was probably on the tube or, since she was a lawyer she might even be on the phone to a client; clients with the kinds of problems Lucy dealt with, regularly called out of hours. Even so, she hoped her friend was alright. Ruth couldn't imagine what might have happened at the Festival Hall after her departure with The Pan but she could imagine that, for Lucy, watching her friend disappear through a window in a flying car would have been pretty alarming. As she slipped the mobile back in her pocket Ruth was startled by a faint rustle behind her and before she could react somebody clamped their hand over her mouth, dragging her backwards. Unable to scream she bit the hand, which was removed straight away.

"What did you do that for?"

She rounded on him angrily. "Because a tap on the shoulder would have sufficed. Don't you *ever* do that again."

"Arnold, this is getting worse and worse, I had no idea you'd be so completely stupid—"

"Look who's talking! Keep digging Mister Pan, you're not doing yourself any favours."

"Neither are you," he snapped. He looked on the brink of finally losing his rag. He took a deep breath and let his anger subside, "Look, I'm sorry alright? I was afraid you'd scream. Here, let me show you." He took her arm, with surprising gentleness and she allowed him to lead her back to the corner. "That's far enough. See the guy down there?" He pointed. "And those two there." He gestured to another two men the other side of the road. Even to Ruth's untrained eye they looked like policemen. "It seems you have a reception committee."

"Is that a bad thing?"

"Don't ask me. I don't know do I? Where I'm from, yes it is but you're not on the most-wanted list, are you?"

"And you are?"

"Yes, I am." He sounded bitter.

"Well, much as I dislike having to agree with you, you're right on this point, I'm not a public enemy, so I can go back there on my own and tell them everything's OK, can't I?" she said, knowing, even as she said it, what a stupid idea it was. All the same, she was annoyed when he just laughed sarcastically at her.

"Interesting plan. They're bound to ask you some awkward questions about me though. What will you say? I may have pulled at your arm a couple of times but you got into my snurd of your own free will. They'll think you know me. How will you explain that broken window, not to mention broken London? Then there's our two Grongolian friends, why were they shooting at you? The police will expect you to know. If the Grongles have been following you, it means they know where you live and you know that they're after you now. Do you really want to go back there and risk meeting them again, because if your police are here, I'd bet my life the Grongles are, too."

"Not necessarily,"

"Arnold! Wake up Ruth! Why won't you listen to me? Which bit of this are you not getting? You are chosen, you might not want to be but you are. There's nothing you or I can do about it and I'm the only person who can help you—though The Prophet knows—not much."

"Then how, exactly, do I get un-chosen?"

"We have to find the person who picked you and persuade him to change his mind."

"And where is this person?"

"He's in hiding."

"Where?"

He shrugged, "That's the problem, I don't know."

"So he gets to screw up my life from under a sofa somewhere and I don't even have any say?"

"No. You don't."

"Have you any idea how unfair that is."

"Yes, funnily enough I have."

Ruth swore. She couldn't help it. All she wanted to do was go home, have a shower and flop into a nice warm bed. Instead she was stuck on the corner of her street looking at her home and unable to go near it. She had lots of friends and her parents would probably put her up – though they'd ask some difficult questions, especially with a strange bloke in tow. Trouble was, she'd been followed for the best part of three months and she betted her gun-toting stalkers knew the whereabouts of every single person in her life. They might not know where Sir Robin lived – the old man who'd saved her from them on the tube and invited her to tea to sort it out, but they'd know about everyone else. Tea with Sir Robin. Her only chance and a slim one at that. Most likely she'd read far too much into his invitation anyway. It was ludicrous to think he'd be able to help and it wasn't until tomorrow. Right now it was the middle of the night and he was old and almost certainly in bed. She could hardly knock on his door because she'd give him a heart attack and anyway she couldn't be sure these Grongle people didn't know where he lived, too.

That left a hotel, which would be traceable through her credit card records, or a night awake in a very small car with a man she was lividly angry with and who had probably been stalking her too.

"All right Mr Too-bloody-clever-by-half. You know about this stuff. What next?" He was looking at her coldly. "I'm sorry," she added, she was tired and irritable but, worst of all, afraid she might cry. "I've had a rough day and I'm completely fed up about … *this*!" She flung her arm out at the street to try and encapsulate everything.

"Yeh well, looks like we're both sorry, doesn't it—" he began angrily.

Ruth's patience ran out.

"You can bet I'm sorry. I'm sorry you had to smash in the entire front of the Festival Hall like a moron instead of parking outside, walking in and talking to me like any normal person would! I'm sorry you had to leave me at the mercy of your Lord Vernon on the top of that building, I'm sorry the pair of you had to smash London and I'm sorry, really sorry, to inform you I AM NOT BLOODY CHOSEN." It shouldn't be possible to shout while whispering but Ruth reckoned she came close to achieving it. It would have been cathartic to shout for real, but the police in the street might hear. For a moment he said nothing. When he spoke his voice was cold and distant.

"Really? Well Ms Cochrane, I can tell you, categorically, that you are chosen and while we're about it, pardon me for saving your life," he looked her straight in the eye. "Twice." He won the eye contact and he knew it. "Most people would be quite grateful but clearly, you are not most people."

Oh just lay it on why don't you? As well as anger she felt guilt, exactly the way he intended, no doubt.

"Most people would have a basic modicum of subtlety and wouldn't smash an entire city."

"Most people would have more than a few seconds to get to you first," said The Pan. "Ruth, just stop a moment and think." He grabbed her by the shoulders.

"Don't you dare touch me!" She tried to kick him but he twisted his body sideways and dodged it. "Let go of me NOW," she hissed.

"No." He glared into her eyes. "Listen to me." He shook her on each word of the 'listen to me' to give it emphasis but he was careful not to shake her very much, she noticed. "I realise this is the worst thing that could happen to you; believe me, I understand how this feels. So, here's something for you to think about. At home, I'm a blacklisted person. That means I'm classed as vermin by the state and my very existence is treason. It's illegal to employ me, it's illegal to pay me, it's illegal for me to own anything and I can be shot on sight. I'm twenty-one years old and I've lived like that for five years. I have no education and no prospects and I never will have. All that vanished for ever when I was sixteen. My family are dead and even though my dad was a rebel the odds are it's my fault because I bumped into Lord Vernon in the street. He was chasing someone at the time, someone he really wanted to catch and because he tripped over me they got away. He didn't like that so he killed my parents and my brother and sister and blacklisted me."

"Listen, I'm sorry. I didn't realise—"

"No. You listen, Chosen One. I had a chance to start again here. To be a normal person, of no interest to the police, with no criminal record and no need to be afraid every day of my life. I could have friends and a job and some peace. That was my plan, to come here and live as soon as I found out enough about this place to fit in without being noticed. Fat chance of that now. So not only have I saved your ungrateful arse, although, Arnold knows what for, but I've also blown my only chance of a new start and a life worth living. For you." He let go of her arms, suddenly, as if they were hot and burning him, hesitated a second or two with his hands still up, as if he was going to grab hold of her again but instead, let them drop to his sides. "I've had enough, I've done my best, you can sort this out on your own. Have fun with the Grongles and Lord Vernon. I'm sure you deserve each other." Shaking his head he turned and strode off towards his car and presumably, out of her life.

Great. Decision made. She could walk down the street and back into her flat, if the police came and questioned her she'd just make something up.

Except she couldn't.

"Wait!" She ran after him and put her hand on his arm. "Please don't go like this."

He turned round suddenly, shrugging her off as he did so and looked her up and down. The orange street lights merely exacerbated the look on his face; weary resignation and more than a hint of disgust. She was mortified.

"Why not?" he asked her coldly. Oh dear. Time to eat humble pie. And some.

"Because I've been so stupid. I haven't done this before and I know you mean well but I'm tired and I don't want to be a criminal and I'm worried about Lucy and my boss and everything is just—"

"Just what?" he demanded.

"Complicated. I know it wasn't your fault and I know you were only trying to help, so go away if you have to but for what it's worth, I'm sorry." She felt uncomfortable saying the words, they seemed snivelling and crawly and insincere, even if they were genuinely meant.

"Yeh, well, maybe in future, you should try using your brain, always assuming that you have one, before you say the first thing that pops into your head."

He was still angry with her, she could tell but perhaps he'd reached the point where he didn't want to be because he flashed the briefest of smiles.

"Like I should have done just then." He took his hat off and raked his hands through his hair. "You will be the death of me, Ruth Cochrane," he said, with a seriousness that suggested he might actually believe it. "Look, it's late. My father used to say that if you're going to live by your wits you should rest them." A terse smile, at least he was making the effort though. "We should probably try to sleep. Do you know somewhere quiet we could park up where we won't be noticed?"

Tricky. In the end she decided on South Mimms. It was less likely she and The Pan would be conspicuous, sleeping in his car and yet, if she couldn't trust him, there'd be lots of people around to help her if she needed them.

"Please don't take this the wrong way but I don't know you from Adam. I'm not sure I want to go somewhere quiet." Instead of anger at her distrust he appeared to be surprised but good surprised, in the way a teacher might be with a pupil who had worked out the right answer to a difficult question. "There's a motorway services not far away though, it's busy but anonymous too. If we stop there for a snooze we'll just look like knackered motorists and we won't attract any attention; but at the same time, if you try to molest me, there are lots of people who will come running if I scream the place down."

A definite thaw now. He laughed, which seemed to surprise him almost as much as it did her. Thank goodness, he'd found his sense of humour.

"I will certainly not be molesting you," he said, as the two of them got into the car, "unless I am asked, of course, in which case I think it would be ungentlemanly to refuse." A slightly hopeful tone there, she noted – perhaps the disgust had been temporary. He raised one eyebrow quizzically and as usual, she tried not to be impressed. "Obviously, it would be entirely for your sake," he added, "and would bring me no pleasure."

She giggled. "Yes, I'm sure it'd be a terrible chore. Luckily for you I have no intention of asking you to molest me!" He turned in his seat to face her and it took her by surprise. Aargh! Why was she so flustered? She hoped the sodium light coming in from outside was concealing the damage. Oh dear. It seemed not. When she looked into his eyes, they were smiling but there was something else there, too; a certain confidence, the air of a man who realises that the girl might be interested.

"Alright, Ms Ruth Cochrane, where do I go?"

"Well," she laughed, "left at the end of the street, Mister No-Name Hamgeean." And they drove off into the darkness.

Chapter 9

In another, different version of the universe, Lord Vernon sat in a comfortable chair on the balcony of his palatial apartments in K'Barth, looking out over the city. He did not subscribe to the official Grongolian view of Ning Dang Po as a reeking cesspit of a place with no redeeming features. It was uncivilised and certainly did not have the beauty of Grongolia – perhaps that was due to the fact the Grongles had bombed large areas of it to bits when they invaded and in many places the city hadn't grown back.

However, Lord Vernon liked the scars and, in so far as he could like anything that wasn't Grongolian, he liked the city. It had a rough and ready charm, possibly even beauty in the right light and of course it was his, to do with as he pleased. It was a place of history, of significance, the spent powerhouse of a once great and proud nation – he leaned back in his chair and stretched – and now, if he chose to crush it, it was his to destroy.

He took a sip of fruit smoothie. It tasted good.

To business. He must dispense with the last shreds of the old order and it was proving complicated. He turned his attention to the dossier of information General Moteurs had collected.

"You can run but I will have you, Chosen One," he murmured.

It was a long time since Lord Vernon had been required to work at anything. He was used to getting what he wanted first time, and this minor setback, though galling, did not unduly concern him. He saw it as little more than an interesting novelty. He would get what he wanted. He always did. His reputation was bulletproof.

He was feared, not just for his propensity to argue with the blade of a knife, but also for his political skills. He had attributes that were essential to good government, in an abundance that even his bitterest, pro-democratic enemies had envied – before he killed them all. And he could destroy them as comprehensively on the debating floor. Anyone who was uneasy about his 'management style' could readily convince themselves K'Barth was in 'a safe pair of hands' – the High Leader of Grongolia for example. The High Leader feared Lord Vernon and when the most powerful being on the planet is afraid of you, you know you're going places.

He pictured the High Leader sitting opposite him and raised his glass.

"Enjoy your last days in power. You will not be there long."

Which reminded him. There was time enough to plan the end game. Later; Grongolia. First; K'Barth. He picked up his mobile phone and called General Moteurs. A short time later there was a light knock on the glass balcony door.

"Good evening."

"Your Gracious Exaltedness." As always, the General began by addressing Lord Vernon formally.

"Sir is sufficient. Sit." Lord Vernon gestured to the chair opposite him.

"Thank you, sir." The General sat. As usual, his face was an inscrutable mask but underneath his calm facade Lord Vernon sensed wariness. The General feared him and he liked that. It made the game of testing his courage so much more interesting.

"Thank you for your excellent information." He held up the dossier and dropped it on the table. "A return to form, it would seem. You have left no stone unturned."

"Sir."

"However, the Chosen One is still at large. Despite our combined efforts," he stressed the *combined*. "Perhaps I was hasty in upbraiding you since I, too, have failed to capture her."

"Sir." Doubtless the General realised how rare this was. An admission of failure was a massive concession from Lord Vernon.

"It would be hypocritical of me to hold you, alone, to account." General Moteurs inclined his head in a half bow. He was shocked and unsettled but still hid it. "It seems our simple task is not so simple. We must act decisively. I am impatient to reveal my hand and proceed with my installation as Architrave but for that I must have the Chosen One."

"Sir." The General hesitated. "We might use her escape to our advantage."

"How?"

"The Underground do not know where she is but my contact assures me that she will be with them the next time I see him."

"Then we must strike fast and take her before she reaches them."

"Indeed, sir. Or we can wait."

"Why would we do that, General?"

"They have a secret headquarters in London. They believe the Candidate and the Chosen One must meet and they intend to introduce them to one another ..."

"Go on."

"If we wait you can have them all; the Chosen One, the last three living members of the Council of the Choosing, the Hamgeean, the Candidate and a number of other sundry vermin."

"All of our quarry in one place at once. Would they be so foolish?"

"I believe they would, sir."

"How very convenient of them. An excellent plan but for one small detail. If their headquarters is secret, how are you expecting to find them?"

"With ease, sir. My contact is to take me there, tonight."

"They trust you?"

"Oh yes, sir. As you know, I have told them I am working against you. They have swallowed my story completely."

"Really," said Lord Vernon.

He watched the General carefully.

"Yes, sir, if you will allow me to guide you, you can have them all within forty-eight hours."

"I would like to be present …" Lord Vernon paused to pin down the right phrase, "at the kill."

"You can be, sir."

Oh yes. What an enticing thought—but was it too good to be true? Lord Vernon fixed the General with another laser stare but Moteurs' face remained blank and expressionless. Perhaps it was time to puncture his air of imperturbability.

"General, we have been working together for some time and until last night you have never failed me. However, tempted though I am to put myself, 'in your hands', I cannot help but be a little wary."

"Sir," said the General. A brief hesitation before he went on. "I apologise if my error has shaken your faith in me. You can rely on me to do my duty."

"Oh I trust you, Moteurs." Lord Vernon chuckled. "I know exactly whose side you are on." There was a long silence. The General sat calm and still. "I merely express a small doubt. You see, what concerns me in this situation is who is playing whom. Sir Robin Get is a highly intelligent man and a supremely manipulative one. Be assured if he and his agents were using you, you would not necessarily realise."

"Sir. I am cautiously optimistic that we have the upper hand at present."

"Are you?"

"Yes, sir." Lord Vernon looked into the General's eyes. There was no deceit but the General put a hand to his face briefly. A gesture of insecurity. "Your Most Gracious Exaltedness …" The full title, eating humble pie Lord Vernon noted. Excellent. "I assure you this matter with the Chosen One is nothing more than an unfortunate blunder."

"Very unfortunate, General, especially for you."

"Sir. If you wish to relieve me of my duties I will understand completely."

Brinkmanship. Perhaps he should call the General's bluff. Lord Vernon sat back in his chair and regarded him coolly. General Moteurs' gaze was steady. Interesting. It seemed he was genuine.

"That will not be necessary, General."

"Sir."

"However, you appreciate, I am sure, that our situation is about trust and perception." Lord Vernon watched Moteurs tense as he spoke. Good.

"Sir."

"You play a dangerous game and I am allowing you to do so because I have absolute confidence in your loyalty to me. Why should I not? You brought me the portals and until yesterday, you have never failed me. I trust you implicitly, General, so I merely advise you that in the light of recent events you would be unwise to betray that trust."

General Moteurs was silent for a moment. Again he put his hand to his face.

"Sir?"

"I am interested in your motives, General. You are honourable. I cannot imagine your role as a spy comes naturally to you. Perhaps this is about your daughter?"

"My daughter is dead to me—" began the General.

"Since her execution for treason, she is dead to all of us," Lord Vernon cut in. Harsh words. A flicker of emotion crossed General Moteurs' face but only a flicker. Impressive.

"I tried to stop her, sir."

"Perhaps you should have tried a little harder."

"Maybe, sir. But if you doubt my moral strength, I would remind you who administered her punishment."

"Yes," said Lord Vernon slowly. "If a father executes his own daughter he must truly love the state." Lord Vernon knew the power of blood ties, he used them often for the purposes of information retrieval. Such an act of honour and loyalty would have cost General Moteurs.

"Sir," said the General. "She was young and foolish. It was the Underground who brainwashed her, perverted her into shaming our family name."

"And you wish for revenge?"

"Atonement, sir."

"Call it what you like, General, but it sounds like revenge to me."

"Sir."

"No matter, to business, General Moteurs. With the help of this useful information," he put one hand briefly on the dossier he had been reading, "I have laid my own plan to capture the Chosen One. Once she is mine, they will have no choice but to try and save her. However, the Hamgeean guards her jealously. I fear it may take more than my endeavours. If the Underground await my next move I would not wish to disappoint them. So, General, if I am in your hands, what would you have me do?"

General Moteurs took a deep breath.

"Stake your claim, sir. Announce your intention to be installed as Architrave."

"That is what Sir Robin wants?"

"Yes, sir."

"Interesting. If I grant Sir Robin his wish, what's in it for him?"

"In truth, I cannot say, sir. They are in no position to oppose you. They cannot act until the Candidate has understood his calling and it seems he has not."

"He?"

"Yes, sir. I have not met him but Sir Robin tells me he is male, not much more than a boy. He lacks the confidence and self-belief to realise who he is and K'Barthan tradition dictates that he must do so unaided."

"So, until he does they can do nothing?"

"Sir. If he fails to realise within the week then Sir Robin believes it will be too late. The portents will favour us and there will be no more Architraves and no more Candidates after this one."

"I doubt this will be so simple."

"Sir. He believes that the most appropriate date for your installation is next Saturday."

"I suppose, by the law of averages, Sir Robin and I must agree on something. My reading of the Prophet's writings also suggests that next Saturday is the most auspicious date—in the eyes of these K'Barthan savages at any rate."

"Sir."

"Perhaps he wishes to force my hand."

"Sir."

"Or the Candidate's." Lord Vernon paused for thought. "I am tempted to grant Sir Robin his wish. But for the people to believe my claim I must engineer it so that, for appearances, at least, the Chosen One picks me. Your plan puts the onus on us to capture her."

"Yes, sir. But it is unlikely you will fail on that score; and if you do it will not stop us. We will take her with the rest of them." General Moteurs' phone beeped quietly.

"Go ahead," said Lord Vernon.

"I have a message on the secured text system from my source within the Resistance."

"Yes?"

"They are establishing a false Candidate."

"I am not surprised. Keep me informed." Lord Vernon stood up and General Moteurs followed suit. "Excellent work, General. I think this concludes our business for now. This evening you will tell your contact that I am about to announce my candidature; you will hint that my installation as Architrave will take place this Saturday, and you will report to me directly upon your return, no matter what time that is."

"Sir."

"For my own part, if we do not harry the Underground I believe they may become suspicious."

"Agreed, sir."

"So, while you set the trap, I will continue my sport and visit Mr Chatterton-Dix."

Chapter 10

Deirdre Arbuthnot sat sullenly outside the throne room of King Denarghi XVII, leader of the Blurpon nation and, more significantly, the K'Barthan Resistance. King Denarghi had been in a foul mood since The Pan of Hamgee and Big Merv had escaped. Deirdre could sympathise with him. The reward money for those two would have paid for enough weaponry to equip a small army, which was the point of the exercise, of course. On the up side, at least the escape was nothing to do with her. She had delivered them to Denarghi by that time and gone to check that the sentries were discharging their duties correctly, before retiring to the officers' mess for a plate of salad.

Since it was Denarghi himself who had let them escape, he had immediately instigated what he called 'a re-evaluation of this entire organisation to determine how such a blunder occurred'. It seemed sensible to Deirdre but her more cynical colleagues were calling it a blamestorming session. Since then, word had leaked out that Denarghi also intended to formalise the hierarchy of the Resistance with a new system of rank. No-one really knew why. Thus far, the Resistance had been led by Denarghi and a band of senior operatives who were known as lieutenants; below them, ten groups, each one commanded by a Group Leader. The groups were made up of ten cells of five people, each led by a corporal. They were broadly similar but different groups had different areas of expertise; the skills of the cells within them were even more precise. It was a useful system which left the lieutenants free to pick and choose the most appropriate cell or group for any missions they undertook. Sure, there was a pecking order – some lieutenants were more important than others – but it was simple, straightforward and it worked.

Deirdre, like everyone, had been lying low until such time as Denarghi's black mood lifted. Unfortunately, because of the reorganisation, she had been summoned to see him to learn her new rank and receive new orders.

She was escorted to the Throne Room – rather a grand title for a space that was little more than an office with a big chair in it. She wondered what Denarghi wanted and hoped the pointy finger of suspicion was not involved. Letting the prisoners escape was a rare gaffe and there were rumours someone else was going to take the rap. Again, Deirdre didn't believe it. Denarghi was honourable, decisive, incisive: a fine leader. If he did make someone a scapegoat, it would be the firing squad for them. A creature of such impeccable principles would never stoop so low.

"Arbuthnot," he said. Denarghi was a Blurpon, that is, about three feet tall, red, furry, uni-pedal and quick to anger. Like the rest of his species, his facial features and ears were catlike, but he had furry arms and hands as opposed to front legs and paws. Even for a Blurpon, Denarghi's fuse was short and as Deirdre approached him her spirits sank. He was still in a filthy temper – that much was obvious.

"Your Majesty …" She bowed and when she straightened up she tried not to look her full height. Deirdre was nearly six foot, and Denarghi was not only small (even for a Blurpon) but chippy about it.

"Lieutenant Arbuthnot," he said sharply. "This organisation must move with the times. Our chain of command is outmoded, old-fashioned and unsuitable for its burgeoning size. I have established a new rank of colonel. From now on, only colonels will report to me, and as a lieutenant, you will not."

"But—" she began. He cut her off.

"I have conducted a thorough investigation into the escape of the Hamgeean and the Swamp Thing, and since you were responsible you will forfeit your promotion."

"But I—"

"Consider yourself lucky. If you were not the Candidate, you would have been court-martialled for dereliction of duty and shot."

Deirdre regarded herself as an uncomplicated military woman, but even she could see what was happening here.

"Permission to speak, Your Majesty," she blurted.

"Denied."

"This is so unjust—"

"Or should I demote you to Group Leader?" He spoke smoothly over her protestations.

Deirdre stopped talking and glared at him.

"Next, your orders: to reinforce your position of Candidate, the people require a fairy story. You must take a lowly job from which, when the time comes, you may be raised up to greatness. You will be pleased to know I have found you just such a position."

That didn't sound good.

"Thank you, sir."

"You will report to the Security HQ in Ning Dang Po, the old Palace, at the earliest opportunity. There is a new staff intake this afternoon and a vacancy has been created for you in the laundry. This is an important mission and your job, apart from laundering the Grongles' shirts, is to keep your head down and stay unnoticed." 'Deirdre' and 'unnoticed' were not two words that usually went together, especially if she was surrounded by the male members of any sufficiently compatible species.

"Your Majesty—" she began.

"I would expect even a simple operative to be capable of a covert operation."

Deirdre got the message and with a petulant sigh she shut up.

"You are there to reinforce your humble origins, as required by the proper procedure for candidature."

Deirdre wondered if she could wriggle out of this to some alternative humble origin. She was a woman of action, a military leader, and did not hold the laundering arts in the same high regard as Denarghi did. He was wrong about the humble origins, too. Deirdre's, and those of many of the Candidates, were far from humble, but she forbore to point this out.

Denarghi continued. "You may not carry arms on this mission. Do I make myself clear?"

"Yes, Your Majesty." Deirdre had carried arms for at least five years and wasn't inclined to stop. OK, so she'd leave the big stuff behind but what was a throwing knife or two among friends? It was insubordination but in this case it was also self-preservation. It would be hard to blend in when she'd never washed a shirt in her life.

"Do you have any questions?" The answer Denarghi would be expecting here was 'no'.

"Your Majesty, if I am working in the Palace I will be there on a three-month tenure. What if something goes wrong, how will I get out?"

"Lieutenant, if you make sure nothing does go wrong I fail to see how it could be an issue."

"But if it does, I will be trapped there, sir."

"You question the wisdom of my orders?"

Deirdre said nothing.

"Good. You are lucky to be part of this organisation after allowing such important prisoners to escape."

"I was in the mess eating a salad—"

"Exactly, Lieutenant Arbuthnot, whereas a vigilant operative would have been ensuring their charges were handed over safely."

"They were handed over safely. You signed for them and dismissed me."

"That is not so."

"You did."

"Do you accuse me of lying? Are you losing your dedication to the Cause?

This is not an organisation for those of lukewarm intent."

"Your Majesty, you know I have never faltered in the defence of freedom but you are punishing me for your own shortcomings …" Arse. She'd used the word short, not good. She started again. "I mean that I have done nothing wrong and surely, a good military leader—even a proud one—"

"—knows when to keep quiet and obey the will of her commander," said Denarghi. "You have your orders, Lieutenant, and I expect you to follow them."

Deirdre didn't want to go to the laundry. She tried another tack.

"Then … I will need some training. The laundering arts are …" She stopped.

He cocked his head on one side and looked up at her.

"Beneath you?" he asked quietly. His red fur bristled with rage. Uh-oh.

"No," she said hastily. "It's just that I haven't …" again, she hesitated.

"You have never washed a shirt?"

Deirdre shook her head, "No, Your Majesty." Her family had little people to wash their shirts, little red furry ones as far as she recalled, although she felt it prudent not to say so. Since joining the Resistance she had always bullied, cajoled or, later, ordered others to wash her clothes for her.

"Of course not," said Denarghi acidly. "Your fat, rich parents wouldn't sully themselves with a job of honest labour. Then I am pleased your time there will not be wasted. You will learn a new and useful skill. Your brothers and sisters in the Cause will teach you. We have thoroughly infiltrated the laundry."

Deirdre was disappointed. She hadn't spent all that time training and clawing her way up through the ranks to be consigned to washing other people's smelly shirts.

He handed her an envelope. "Here are your papers. You are not Deirdre Arbuthnot, you are Rosa Trampleasure, simple Tithian maiden, seeking work and your fortune in the city."

"Why do I have to be Tithian?" asked Deirdre, who felt too modern and metropolitan to have come from a backwater like Tith.

"Because you cannot sign up to a three-month work tenure in the Palace under your own name. It is known to the authorities."

"I realise that, but—"

"Your colleagues will make themselves known to you."

Never mind, it could have been worse, at least he didn't want her to be Hamgeean. For all their lack of sophistication, at least no-one in Tith ate squid.

He held out another envelope. "This is the password. Read it, commit it to memory and eat it."

Deirdre felt the second envelope between her fingers. In the name of The Prophet could he not use rice paper? Clearly the digestive system of the average Blurpon was stronger than hers.

"Yes, Your Majesty."

"You will not stand on rank. You will be working under cover as part of a cell." This was getting worse and worse. "You are to discover what the Grongles are planning and anything they know about the Underground. If the rumours I have heard are true you will not be a laundress for long. Lord Vernon plans to be installed as Architrave, soon. Your secondary mission at the laundry is to keep your eyes and ears open and discover the details."

"Yes, Your Majesty."

"And Lieutenant Arbuthnot, if you want people to trust you, sharpen up your appearance, cut your hair and wear some proper feminine clothes." Deirdre opened her mouth to protest. "That is all, you may go."

How dare he? She did not move. Deirdre took pride in her appearance, not to mention her ability to appear extremely female when required – but in a mostly male environment she tended to play it down. Unless she wanted something, or someone, she kept her hair tied back in a simple pony tail and wore military fatigues like her male colleagues. Denarghi was a Blurpon and he simply didn't understand the laws of attraction among the baldy tall races – as the Blurpons and the Spiffles, their similarly-shaped brethren, called, well … pretty much everyone else. Deirdre felt put upon. King Denarghi had always praised her, held her up as an example and when her colleagues had shown any trace of cynicism about his motives she had leapt to his defence. Surely a good leader does not blame one of his most loyal disciples for his mistakes.

"You have your orders," said Denarghi ominously.

Deirdre had one last try.

"Your Majesty," she said. "My loyalty and dedication to our cause and to you have never faltered. Why are you punishing me for something I have not done?"

"I am the leader of this organisation and I will decide what has been done and what has not. I do not make mistakes and on this occasion you have. Is that clear?"

"Yes, sir," said Deirdre and she trudged off to pack.

Chapter 11

Nigel was pleased to be home.

He had enjoyed his business trip. Sabrina, his assistant, had been very accommodating. He smirked to himself as he remembered. The two of them had taken an early flight out of Prague and, on top of that, he'd spent a long day in the office. So much catching up to do.

Now he was tired, it was late and he looked forward to relaxing alone. It was good to have some time to himself. He threw his case into the corner of the hall, walked into the bathroom and turned on the taps. He strolled back into the hall, removing his coat as he went and hanging it on one of the hooks by the door. Loosening his tie and flipping it over his head, he went into the drawing room without turning the light on and poured himself a brandy.

Ah, Sabrina. She was beautiful, and the fact her uncle owned the advertising agency Nigel worked for merely added to her many attractions. He swirled the brandy round the glass and smirked again as he recalled the highlights. Booking adjoining suites had been a master stroke, and when he'd given her first choice she'd seemed touched by his old-world courtesy. She'd chosen the best room, of course, but by that time Nigel was aware that reserving a second was merely a formality.

Sabrina had made it clear from the moment they got on the plane that she would be interested in far more than his technique with a laser pointer, if he pursued her with suitable flamboyance and attention. So he had, and the results had been incredible …

He sighed and drank a sip of brandy. "Goodbye, Lucy, and good riddance." He raised the glass and took another mouthful. Yes, a man like him needed a special kind of woman. Sabrina would stand beside him, look up to him, flatter him and want him, whatever he did.

Nigel had already phoned Lucy and informed her, via her voicemail, that she was dumped. It wasn't his fault if she couldn't be bothered to switch her phone on when she knew he might call. Which reminded him … he swapped screens and checked his emails.

Nothing much, just a text from Sabrina. He closed his eyes and allowed himself a moment's fantasy. He would see her again. Soon. Whistling happily, he strolled back towards the bathroom to turn off the water.

"Good evening, Nigel."

He hesitated. Had he imagined that? Yes. He took another step towards the open door and the light of the hall.

"In my culture, Mr Chatterton-Dix, it is considered impolite to ignore a greeting." Something about that softly spoken voice. Quiet, yet carrying and malevolent. For a moment Nigel was very scared but then he rallied. OK, so this guy was good but he didn't know who he was trifling with because Nigel knew he was better. He had money and power, not enough yet—or at least not enough for his taste—but plenty to deal with some two-bit burglar.

"In my culture," said Nigel, "it is considered impolite to enter a person's house without permission." He held up his mobile phone with three nines entered on the screen ready to dial. "You have thirty seconds to replace anything you have stolen and leave or I will call the police."

There was a flurry of activity and white hot pain as something struck his arm and then wrenched it behind his back. As he watched the glowing screen of the phone, his lifeline, spin away under the sofa, somebody lifted him bodily into the air and slammed him face down on the glass coffee table. Ouch. This was going to be worth a monster lawsuit. Especially if the wretch had broken his nose.

The intruder grabbed a handful of his hair and pushed his head into the polished surface. It hurt, but with a detachment that surprised him, Nigel calmly pictured in his mind's eye what he must look like were he seen from below as he mentally prepared his response.

"I warn you, whoever you are, I am a very powerful man and I have even more powerful lawyers," said Nigel, calmly. Except that the fact his face was being ground into a coffee table, with some force, meant that one side of it was unable to move quite as freely as the other and somewhat spoiled the effect. Still, it wasn't bad; dignity was scarce in a situation like this.

The stranger laughed and Nigel suddenly knew he would go to almost any lengths to avoid hearing that laugh again. It was … Could he use that word? Yes, he could. Evil.

"And I warn you, Nigel, that you are in no position to argue with me." Whoever it was, pressed his face into the glass that little bit harder, just to make the point. "And if you are unwise enough to do so I have the means to show you the true meaning of power in a way you may find … uncomfortable."

There was something distinctly ominous about the way the intruder said, 'uncomfortable'. Nigel made one last effort to assume control of the situation.

"I have lawyers," he said. He meant to sound authoritative but it came out nearer to pleading.

"I am beyond the authority of this nation, your lawyers are of little import to me," said the voice quietly. "As far as you are concerned, Nigel, I am the law and you will obey me or suffer the consequences. I assure you, it will be far more pleasant for both of us if you cooperate. Otherwise, I will be forced to kill you and assume your identity."

Not a threat, more a statement of fact. Nigel examined his situation. He was sure of one thing, the intruder was bigger than him, would clearly regard murdering him as nothing more than a minor inconvenience and had him pinned to a coffee table. Hell. That was three things and they were all bad.

"What do you want?" he asked.

"I have a business proposition for you …" Oh yeh, of course! Nigel wondered what he really wanted. "If I release you and you try to escape," the voice went on, "I regret that I will be forced to snap your spine and that would be a shame." The tone suggested a spine-snapping would occur at the slightest provocation. "So …?"

"I will not try to escape," said Nigel. That came out wobblier than he had intended.

"Good, I am pleased you have seen reason."

The vice-like grip was removed and Nigel stood up, rubbing the back of his neck. His shoulder ached, too. Bad move, intruder. Nigel was rubbish in a fight, but when it came to negotiating, he was a ruthless operator. Ha! His confidence returned. Pity about the bath, it was bound to overflow, but he wasn't going to sit in the dark. He walked over to the uplighter in the corner and kicked the sliding switch with his foot. That was better, now to get a good look at this person so he could describe him, in detail, to the police.

Ah.

His intruder was certainly a commanding presence; tall, armed to the teeth—complete with sword—and wearing some kind of uniform. He looked about six foot six, possibly more, and gave off an aura of intense hostility. Nigel swallowed. The levels on his confidence-o-meter sank substantially. If he negotiated at all, he was going to have to do so carefully. This was not the kind of person he wanted to mess with. He watched as the stranger strolled nonchalantly over to the sofa. Not the stainless steel and leather ones he reserved for visitors but the comfortable antique sofa which had belonged to his grandparents, *his* sofa for heaven's sake, and sat down. The intruder walked like a panther, every movement smooth and controlled, no energy wasted, and as he had already demonstrated, he had similarly lightning big-cat reactions. Who the hell was he? An assassin? A gang lord? Bad news, that was certain.

"What can I do for you, Mr …?" croaked Nigel.

"Lord Vernon." An emphasis on the word 'lord', Nigel noticed.

"Lord Vernon." He gave the 'lord' similar emphasis. No point getting his spine snapped over trifles and absolutely zero doubts about this Lord Vernon fellow's capacity to do so.

"A small favour."

"A small favour," said Nigel flatly. He might be on the back foot but he was going to have to stop repeating everything his visitor said. Even so, it was hardly going to be a favour if being murdered was the alternative. And small? No. He looked at the giant sprawled on his sofa, sprawled and yet so clearly coiled, ready to react with extreme violence in milliseconds. Nothing asked by a person like this was going to be small.

"Yes. You appear to have a certain …" a wave of the hand, while Lord Vernon sought the exact word. "Technique with women." Uh-oh. Where was this going? "A successful one."

"Hell yeh!" Phew! Nigel began to relax. His way with women was the envy of the entire male staff at his workplace. "I have them running after me as if they're on heat. I'm a dead cert. There isn't a woman on this earth I can't bed eventually."

"Then this will be easy for you. I require you to become close to a woman, somebody with whom I believe you are already acquainted."

"I'm acquainted with many women."

"Naturally, and that is why you are so useful to me. This girl's name is Ruth." Nigel felt a sinking feeling in the pit of his stomach. Scratch the dead cert, here was the exception which proved the rule.

"Not Ruth Cochrane."

"Yes," said Lord Vernon slowly. "You will lure her here and deliver her to me." Nigel tried to disguise the shiver which ran down his spine. He loathed Ruth but even she didn't deserve delivery to this … was he actually a man? He seemed unusually tall and his skin was pale, almost greenish.

"That might be a problem."

"You are here to provide me with a solution, Mr Chatterton-Dix." The ominous tone again.

"No, *the* problem, just one, is that she doesn't fancy me."

"And yet, you assure me you are irresistible to women."

"I am—but not to that woman."

"Then you will talk her round." Nigel tried to meet the dark grey eyes. Lord Vernon was good-looking, film-star good-looking, more so even than Nigel. Why couldn't he do his own dirty work?

"Pardon me for asking, Lord Vernon, but why do you need me? You're a handsome fellow, why can't you talk her round?"

"I have better things to do with my time." More likely, Nigel surmised, Ruth had already met Lord Vernon and decided that once was enough.

"If you don't mind one further question, what do you want with her?"

"That is my business."

Nigel knew he was pushing it asking anything more but he had to know.

"Are you …? Will she survive meeting you, Lord Vernon?"

"She will come to no harm. I want her alive." That statement should have comforted Nigel but somehow, the way Lord Vernon delivered it made 'alive' sound more ominous than dead.

"I will try my best, but she's irrational—you know how women are—and the problem is, she hates my guts."

Lord Vernon drew a large knife and began to twirl it casually from hand to hand. "I am not certain you appreciate the seriousness of your situation, Nigel," he said calmly. "Let me help you to focus. If you wish your guts to remain where they are you will do more than try. You will succeed and change her mind. Soon."

Help.

"Even I can't do that straight away …" Hmm, how long would it take to tie up, pack up and disappear? "It might take as long as a month or two."

"I am feeling magnanimous this evening so I will allow you forty-eight hours."

Nigel gulped and with great difficulty, swallowed what felt like a large apple.

"I'll think of something." He wanted to sound in control but it was all he could do to talk. His throat had gone dry, unlike his bathroom which, from the sloshing sounds he could hear, was clearly awash with overflowing bathwater.

"Yes, you will."

Desperation aside, Nigel was also angry. This Lord Vernon had him on the rack but clearly he couldn't get to Ruth on his own. He needed Nigel and that meant that if he could revive his self-belief, then, despite the threats, Nigel was in a position to bargain. If he'd learned anything in business it was the value of bluff. Deep down, he was not comfortable with the idea of delivering Ruth to Lord Vernon but Nigel liked being alive. If that meant Ruth had to suffer, so be it, but he was going to make sure it cost Lord Vernon dearly. He looked his malevolent visitor up and down, trying to appear confident.

"You are clearly a wealthy m …" No no, this guy might not be a man. He started again. "You are clearly wealthy, someone of means. I'm sure I would think faster and bring Ruth to you sooner if I knew there was something in this for me."

"Oh, but there is. Your continued existence."

Lord Vernon stood up, suddenly reminding Nigel of his sheer presence, not to mention height. Nigel pretended to think for a moment and then he did the hardest thing he had ever done in his life. He argued.

"I'm sure that's very kind of you, Lord Vernon, but let's cut to the chase. You're a smart guy and so am I. We both know what this is about. You need my help. If you didn't you wouldn't be here. You want me to get something that you can't: Ruth. Am I right or am I right?"

Lord Vernon made a low noise, somewhere between a growl and a hiss, which Nigel took to be a 'yes', and his visitor waved one hand dismissively. He was wearing black suede gloves, Nigel noticed, with jewelled rings over them. They were the kind of monster rocks the Borgias might keep poison behind and Nigel wondered, fleetingly, if Lord Vernon did.

"Then you've made the right choice, Lord Vernon, because I can do that. I can give you Ruth. But on my terms or, if you can't wait that long, you pay me. Because I'm good, Lord Vernon. And that makes me expensive." He made an all-encompassing gesture to his surroundings. "Quality like this doesn't come cheap. I want gold. Two kilograms. One now, one afterwards."

Lord Vernon gave a derisive snort and fixed Nigel with a laser stare. The depth of his hostility was frightening. His eyes burned with a dark fire so evil it made Nigel feel faint, but he paused to collect himself. He had a thick skin, he worked in advertising, he was a hardened negotiator, a smart cookie; Lord Vernon's anger might be frightening but it was good news, it meant Nigel was getting to him, suggesting a weakness that could be exploited. Nigel wasn't going to faint. No-one normally stared him into submission, although in this instance they did. He avoided passing out by looking away for a brief moment and steeling himself, before meeting those scary eyes again.

"What do you say, Lord Vernon? Do we have a deal?"

"You believe I will click my fingers, like so," Lord Vernon's voice was mocking and the light flashed from his rings as he did just that, "and conjure up gold for you?"

No. Nigel didn't, although he was pretty sure that if anyone could, it was Lord Vernon.

"I think not. You will work on my terms and I will give you what you deserve when and only when, you have done what I require." Another dismissive wave of the hand, and Nigel's gaze was drawn to the rings again. One in particular shone with mesmerising clarity: a ruby, blood red, it seemed to glow with a life of its own and as Lord Vernon noticed where he was looking his expression changed. Not much but enough to show the tiniest hint of unease. It was hardly noticeable but it gave Nigel an idea.

"I can see you are honourable and I trust you, Lord Vernon, but I'm afraid I can't settle for that. I want something up front." Nigel was in the zone now, he was the best of the best with his eye on the prize. Oh yeh, he couldn't fight Lord Vernon but he could negotiate and he was going to get some payback for his wrecked carpets. "What about a couple of those rocks you're wearing? That ruby. Yes. I tell you what, Lord Vernon. You give me that ruby ring and I'll give you Ruth. Tomorrow."

"This ring is not subject to negotiation. I tell you what, Nigel," Lord Vernon imitated the way Nigel spoke. "What if I were to kill you now?" Lord Vernon's rage was almost a physical presence.

Half of Nigel was petrified that his sinister visitor would lose control and let his anger speak, the other half was exultant that he was controlling this monster, calling the shots. He had turned this round and he was winning. Everyone in his office knew he was the best at cutting a deal but even he hadn't realised he was this good. Lord Vernon didn't want to give up the ring but Nigel was going to get it, or one of the others. It was time to press home his advantage. Time to close the deal. Fast.

"Ah, but you wouldn't kill me Lord Vernon, do that and you'll never get Ruth. OK, so I see there's a problem. Let's talk about solutions because I think I've found a way out of this that will make us both happy. You want Ruth and I want to give her to you but I need something, a sign, from you. Call it a demonstration of trust. But I can also see that I'm asking a lot in that ring. So how about this? You lend me your ruby ring for a short while, as security, and I'll know you're going to come back with my gold. And when you do, the day after tomorrow—because I understand it might take you a little time to get that much gold together—I'll give you it back. With Ruth."

There was a long, long silence.

"I admire your spirit, Nigel, but my rings are not for sale and I do not carry gold about my person," Lord Vernon paused and Nigel hardly dared breathe as his visitor put one hand to his belt. It hovered over the holster and for a terrifying moment, Nigel thought Lord Vernon was going to draw his gun. Instead, he opened one of the pouches and removed a black velvet drawstring bag. "I find diamonds pique the interest of my contacts far more effectively than gold. I am surprised you did not ask for them."

Damn. Nigel knew he'd missed a trick. Lord Vernon tipped the shiny rocks into his palm and selected the largest. Then he put the rest back in the bag and secreted it securely away in the pouch on his belt. "Perhaps this will help you with your motivation?" He held the diamond up to the light. It sparkled and shone. "I will let you keep this for your trouble—over and above the gold—but in return for my … largesse, I want Ruth faster and I do not expect you to fail. You will give her to me, tomorrow." He held up the diamond and walked slowly across the room until he was standing very close to Nigel, closer than was pleasant or comfortable. Nigel took a deep breath to stop his hand from shaking and held it out.

"Thank you," he said, with no hint of politeness as, with sneering disdain, Lord Vernon dropped the diamond into his palm.

"I will return here *tomorrow* and if you disappoint me, human scum, you will pay a high price."

Nigel tried not to notice the depths of malevolence in Lord Vernon's voice.

"That won't be a problem," Nigel gestured to the expensive furnishings around him. "I can afford some pretty high prices. You are gracious in defeat, Lord Vernon and I assure you, I'll get you what you want."

"Good," said Lord Vernon, except the word sounded more like a snarl. "And now, I must leave." He pushed Nigel out of the way and walked out into the hall. Nigel followed. At the door, Lord Vernon stopped to hand him a card with someone else's name and number on it. "If you need to communicate with me, General Moteurs will deal with you. I will return here at six thirty pm …" A pause. "Tomorrow. I hope, for your sake, that you will have what I want."

He glanced down and pressed one foot a little further into the carpet. Water squelched up around the side of his immaculate, black suede boot. He looked back up, or at least, less far down, at Nigel with a sadistic smile.

"I hope I have not inconvenienced you," he said softly, menacingly, daring

Nigel to state the truth that yes, he bloody well had. Not to mention destroying a very expensive carpet and precipitating another round of complaints from the collection of hopeless, whinging drones who passed for neighbours in this block.

"Not at all." Nigel would have liked to have loaded the return statement with sarcasm, but negotiating with this monster had cost him, and in the face of prolonged exposure to those merciless grey eyes his voice, not to mention his courage, seemed to have deserted him.

"Good."

"I'm sure the gold will cover it," managed Nigel, just to remind Lord Vernon who had come out on top in the preceding negotiations.

"Yes, Mr Chatterton-Dix. It will," said Lord Vernon. He put on a pair of sunglasses and waited expectantly. Presumably Lord Vernon had little people to do things like opening doors and—little people in absentia—he was clearly assuming Nigel would step into the breach.

Trying not to get any closer to his unwelcome visitor than was absolutely necessary, Nigel did.

"Good evening, Nigel," said Lord Vernon as he stepped out into the hall. Nigel wondered if Mrs Balls, from downstairs, would be up to complain. He hoped so. She never missed a chance to have a go. Miserable old trout. He wanted to see her face if she came up now and met this gentleman. Sure enough, he caught a glimpse of her in the hall as he closed the door. He bolted it quickly, leaving the two of them to get on with it.

With any luck, a run-in with that monster would send her scurrying back downstairs for a lie-down. Nigel went and checked his face in the hall mirror. Phew. Nothing broken, though there would be bruising. He examined one side and then the other. Yes, he'd have to make up a suitable story about what had happened. One that made him out to be brave and intrepid and put the other guy in hospital, or police custody, or maybe both. Even so. That was one hell of a deal he'd clinched. Nigel pointed his first two fingers at his reflection and pretended to fire.

"Kapow!" He blew across the tops of them as if they were a smoking gun. "Oooo yeh see the magic. Nigel the Chatterton-Dixter is red hot."

What was that noise? Oh yes. He swore volubly as he remembered the bath and ran down the hall to turn off the taps. This was going to take a lot of clearing up. Never mind, the water was warm. He glanced at the towel hanging over the radiator.

Why not?

He took all the other towels he possessed, spreading them over the floors to soak up the rest of the flood and padded into the sitting room. His original glass of brandy lay on the floor, half spilled. He picked it up, downed the dregs and refilled it, helped himself to a large cigar, lit it and puffed the smoke gratefully into the air. Someone was banging on his door. Mrs Balls, no doubt. Or she'd enlisted the help of one of the others. Nigel wasn't popular with the other flat owners, too many 'comings and goings' they said. In other words, too many women—or at least—too many different women.

"And none for them," said Nigel, to himself. They were just jealous.

Ha! Screw them and Mrs B. The water was off now and it would stop leaking through the ceiling soon enough. Meanwhile, miraculously, he was alive and he had twenty-four hours to entrap Ruth.

No problem. He'd think of something, he always did. In the meantime it was important he cleared his mind and relaxed. Dealing with the flood could wait until morning, after a good night's sleep. In the meantime a long soak would be just the thing. He wandered down the hall, brandy and cigar in hand and undressed. Carefully, to protect the cigar, he climbed into the bath.

Chapter 12

Following Ruth's instructions, The Pan drove his snurd, in a very pedestrian manner, on the road, to South Mimms – a huge complex of cheap hotels, service station, car park and other 'amusements' for the tired motorist at the intersection between two major roads. Ruth informed him these were called the A1 and the M25; all very Grongolian-sounding. The Pan, who was used to roads with proper names, was intrigued. They chose a spot in an empty corner of the car park and tried to get some rest. As he lay on his side, feet entangled uncomfortably among the pedals, he shut his eyes. He was tired but he was also hungry and sleep wouldn't come. He supposed it was meeting the Chosen One at last. In real life, with sound, she was even better than she'd been in the thimble. She was funny, smart and brave. A lot braver than he was but then, he supposed that wasn't very difficult. And she was prettier, much prettier then he'd expected and lying next to her, here, while she slept, was distracting. More than distracting. When he closed his eyes he was back on the roof with her, before he messed things up and instead of a hurried peck on the cheek he was taking the time to kiss her properly. He sighed. This getting to sleep business wasn't going too well. Perhaps it was better not to close his eyes. He listened to the sound of her breathing.

Hang on a moment.

That wasn't right.

It was irregular, as if she was pretending to be asleep; a sharp breath in, a long pause, half a breath out, another pause, a further breath out and a hiccup.

Was she crying?

He was lying with his back to her, and he opened his other eyes abruptly, the ones in the back of his head. Another sharp breath inwards from Ruth – more of a gasp – and she looked straight into them. Had she seen? No. Surely not. Why would she? Nobody else ever had. He watched as she bit her lip and closed her eyes but in spite of her efforts, a tear escaped. She screwed up her face and her mouth silently framed the word 'no'. She was crying. And she didn't want to. What on earth was he supposed to do now? He pretended to wake up and she pretended to turn over in her sleep and face the other way. He got out and shut the door quietly. He patted his pockets which contained a lint-covered boiled sweet, his snurd keys, a blood-spattered handkerchief, his own thimble and a couple of scraps of paper. Mmm, the handkerchief was too filthy for anyone else to use and it had blue blood on it, which might cause an issue. He didn't know if it was normal in K'Barth, let alone this place.

He sauntered into the main building and headed for the gents, berating himself as he went. He'd been such a fool, there was bound to have been another way if he'd only stopped to think. He'd damaged her city. That wasn't a good start. He had always managed not to break any of the important bits of Ning Dang Po; but it's easier to avoid smashing the important landmarks in a place when you know what they are. Broken London aside, what was the point of saving her life if he went and ruined it at the same time? How was that going to make things any better? He'd also broken the concert hall. She was right. Why hadn't he parked outside and just talked to her, like a normal person? Well, no, that was because he wouldn't have reached her before the Grongles otherwise; but he wished he'd checked her surroundings more carefully. Materialising inside the building would have been less conspicuous than flying through the window. Then he'd compounded his error by leaving her on the roof. Why had he let her out of his sight? How could he, the best getaway man in K'Barth make such a glaring, elementary mistake?

"Schoolboy error," he muttered bad-temperedly. He was her protector and no matter how risky it had felt taking her to K'Barth he should have kept her with him. Arnold, he was an idiot sometimes. Then, subsequently, when she'd pointed out what were, after all, only a few obvious truths, he'd been so angry, so disgusted with her that he had frightened himself. And she realised. He could see it from her point of view, on the run from the police and unknown others, with some man who, she would assume, from that one unguarded moment, found her morally repulsive. No wonder she was crying. He helped himself to a mound of lavatory paper along with some paper towels.

Back at the snurd he peered in. She was really crying now, curled up in a small ball, her face turned downwards in the seat and to see her like that tugged at his heart. He had planned to live here as a normal person, find a way to arrive without scaring her and get to know her. Maybe his feelings would abate and they'd have been friends or maybe she'd have fallen for him in time. Now he would never know. He, the outlaw, the blacklisted pariah, had come to her world to save her and merely made her an outcast, too. Not the cleverest move for a man who wanted to start a romance. Opening the passenger door as quietly as possible, he knelt down on the tarmac and put the tissues on the sill. She was still crying but now that she had noticed his presence, she was also pretending to be asleep. He was unsure how to proceed. All he knew was that he had to try and help her; couldn't leave her the way she was. She'd probably smack him in the face if he touched her. Perhaps he wouldn't mind. He almost certainly deserved it.

"Ruth," he said gently. He brushed her hair off her face, which was red and blotchy and covered in tears. "I'm so sorry." She looked into his eyes and it was so easy to look right back. He wondered whether to try and wipe away her tears with the loo roll but on second thoughts decided against it. He wanted to be gentle and on his current form he was more likely to stick his hand in her eye. "I've been such a fool. What can I do to make things right?" She sat up and shook her head sadly.

"Nothing," she told him in a very small voice.

He took her hand and pressed a few more feet of the lavatory paper into her palm, it smelled antiseptic and now he was handing it to her, he realised that though soft, it was a softness which veered dangerously towards the scritchy end of the tissue spectrum. She smiled wanly at him and to his immense surprise, flung her arms round him, buried her head in his chest and sobbed in earnest. He didn't know what else to do or say, so he held her tight and let her cry. He stroked her hair and every now and again kissed the top of her head and told her everything would be fine, even though they both knew it wouldn't. Her hair smelled of almonds with a hint of something else, was it her perfume? His mind began to wander in absolutely the wrong direction. He wished he wasn't quite so crazy about her. Eventually, when she had thoroughly soaked the front of his shirt, she let go of him and sat up.

"I'm—hic—sorry," she said, hiccupping again, for good measure. "I—hic—leak when I'm—hic—stressed." She gave him a rueful smile.

He handed her yet more of the loo roll and tried a joke.

"Who's the one with the interesting speech impediment now, Ms Cochrane?" She laughed, thank The Prophet, and blew her nose, still hiccupping. He smiled. "Listen, in a few hours when we've had a bit of sleep and you're feeling better, I'll take you to the police. Not here but somewhere else where there's less chance they'll know us. You can make a statement. Whatever you like, it's up to you what you say, but be sure to tell them it's my fault. I have the snurd, I can sell it, we'll pay off the damage and everything will be fine."

"And you'll go?"

Ouch.

"If that's what you want."

"Actually, it's not."

Yes! Result! Thank you Arnold! She glanced at her watch.

"And no way are you selling your space car on my account. There has to be another way, so listen Mister Pan. It's nearly six o'clock, I'm not going to be getting any more sleep now. What I really want is some breakfast and I know just the place; but first …" she opened her minute handbag and took out a mobile phone. "Damn, the battery's dead. I hate this thing."

"Can't you recharge it?"

"Not without a charger."

"Ah, then you don't …?" The Pan realised he was miming rubbing an imaginary phone in his hair and felt stupid. She laughed.

"No Mister Pan, we haven't yet harnessed the power of static electricity at this end of the galaxy. We still have to make it with things that will destroy our planet and store it, inefficiently, in crappy batteries that last about six minutes."

He laughed.

"Seriously, it's useless. You're better off without a mobile than one like this—though they're all pretty rubbish."

"Not when they run on static, then you can charge them up anywhere and … um … I'm not from another planet you know, I'm from this one."

"That's difficult to believe with your lasers and snurds and all."

"It's the same place just a different version; a parallel reality."

"Yes, of course it is. OK that's enough for now, I'm not even going to try to get my head round any of that until I've had some bacon and eggs, preferably with several gallons of coffee. You and I need to have a proper chat Mister Pan, soon. But right now I have to go in there, find a payphone and ring Lucy." He'd no idea who Lucy was. "My flatmate," she explained. "I want to make sure she's alright and tell her that I'm OK and that you are," she smiled wryly, "not bad either. And I should probably ring work, too. I need to take some time off to sort this out—if I still have a job." She took a deep breath. "*And then*, when I've done that and I know exactly how the ground lies, we can go get breakfast and you can tell me the whole story, who you are, why you're here and what, exactly, is going on."

"I'll do my best."

"Good, because I have lots of questions so when you've finished and I am able to make a proper informed decision, *that's* when I'll decide what I'm going to do. So, if you could stick around, at least until then, it would be great because I get the impression you're a repeat offender and since I've never been on the run before, I'll need a seasoned pro to turn to for advice."

As Ruth returned The Pan's smile something tied his stomach in knots. There was no mistaking the depths of his affection. Not now that he'd actually met her. This was love. But could she love him back? That was the big question. She seemed to like him but was it the right kind of 'like'? He had no clue. It was too early to tell.

He wished he could talk to Sir Robin, but until he had won Ruth's trust, he could hardly drag her back to K'Barth on such a flimsy pretext, especially not when it would undoubtedly put her in danger. If only he was in a position to be objective. He'd be more likely to understand the truth about Ruth if he could seek a second opinion from somebody level-headed who wasn't utterly besotted with her.

Chapter 13

In the dormitory set aside for female laundry workers, Deirdre Arbuthnot had spent the night awake. She had never had doubts before. She had always followed orders, sure that she was on the side of good, but being punished for Denarghi's mistake had shaken her faith. Around her, the ladies of the laundry snored and occasionally farted in their rows of beds.

"You aren't helping me," she told their unconscious forms. Not that they would hear her. Deirdre wondered how it was that she could sleep through a mortar attack in a freezing foxhole but, so far, had never been able to cut out snoring. She'd have to go to the staff shop and get some earplugs tomorrow. "Shut up!" she shouted. A couple of the others sat up and looked blearily about them, before flopping back into their slumbers. Just in case, Deirdre pretended that she, too, was asleep. The loudest of the snorers made a gargling noise, turned over and started breathing normally. Great! Blissful silence.

Or not.

Three beds away, another of Deirdre's colleagues started making a kind of whistling bubbling noise with every breath. Arnold's Y-fronts, that was about the most annoying sound she had ever heard.

"Three smecking months of this is going to be a tough mission," she muttered. Perhaps she shouldn't have brought the throwing knives; any minute now she'd find herself using them on her colleagues. She plumped her pillows irritably and lay in the darkness reflecting on her situation.

The security implications of having a K'Barthan workforce enter and leave the Palace every day were immense, so all non-Grongolian life forms working there—NGLFs as they were called—had to sign up for three-month residential stints. They were paid more to make up for the time spent away from their families and friends, but they were not allowed out of the Palace until their period of work was up. Indeed there were stories of people dying at work and still not being released until the day stated in their contract.

Some of the day's events had reassured her but Deirdre didn't feel settled or comfortable in the Palace. Part of this was because 'Rosa' was so very different from Deirdre, and it was difficult pretending to be someone else the whole time, especially when playing the part convincingly meant allowing herself to be walked over by every halfwit in the vicinity. She might get used to it in time but the fact that she was trapped would not change. And she hated the fact that as well as being some useless bumpkin from Tith, she had the most stupid, stupid surname imaginable. That was unnecessary spite on Denarghi's part. She lay in the dark, fuming, yet bored. Why couldn't she just go to sleep? She sighed and turned over, but the day's events kept replaying in her head.

Having passed through extensive security to get in, her first afternoon at the laundry had not gone well. Her Resistance colleagues were Blurpons to a man, and were helpful enough, but they seemed to think she needed to learn about laundering shirts. Why, Deirdre couldn't understand. It was typical of Denarghi. She pictured him laughing as he imagined her cleaning up after the Grongles. Little git. She had believed in him, looked up to him and this was how he repaid her loyalty. Well, tough. She wasn't interested in servitude. She would gather information and familiarise herself with the layout of the Palace.

The dress was annoying. Even thinking about it now made her roll her eyes. The Blurpons and the Spiffles in the laundry, being furry, never wore clothes. Both were similar in appearance, the only real difference being that Spiffles had orange fur and two legs, whereas Blurpons had red fur and one leg. The Spiffles were a great deal more relaxed though. Deirdre had almost forgotten how spiky Blurpons were until she saw the two species working side by side. Both the Blurpons and the Spiffles wore belts with pouches to carry the items they needed. Lucky them. Like all the ladies, Deirdre had to wear a uniform—an old-fashioned corset, long frilly skirts and a white shirt—low cut and off the shoulder, of course, because for all their aloofness, the Grongles liked a bit of feminine allure. As long as it was vaguely humanoid they weren't that fussy about the exact species. The uniform was flattering, but to Deirdre's dismay, not in a way that would further her aim of remaining incognito. It was also uncomfortable and restrictive. She thought with longing of her military fatigues. She felt so much more at home in them.

The laundry was insanely busy, hot and dusty—or muggy depending whereabouts she was—and the staff were constantly interrupted by the Grongle who oversaw the running of the household, an ugly great brute called Captain Snow. His shifty, bloodshot gaze always slid to wherever Deirdre was working and remained on her. It wasn't a look Deirdre liked. Simple Tithian maiden or not, she was going to beat him to a pulp if he tried anything. She betted he would, too. The laundry, indeed the whole Palace, was significantly lacking in female employees under middle or old age. Deirdre guessed that Captain Snow, and others like him, were the reason.

Considering what a mundane boring job it was, laundering things was surprisingly difficult. Deirdre's lack of skill became annoyingly apparent early on, when she put a red sock in with a whole load of white shirts. The Head Launderer, an affable Spiffle called Sid, gave the baby pink results to the Head Bleacher for correction and reassigned her to ironing sheets. Even for a laundry task this looked as if it would be incredibly boring but Deirdre never found out for sure. She worked the ironing tables for approximately thirty seconds before setting one of the linen presses on fire. A glaring error from the point of view of blending in but a good result in the sense that it was unlikely she would be given ironing duties again. Once the flames were doused, the Head Launderer, completely at a loss, assigned her to collection of soileds, as the dirty laundry was called, until such time as he could find a job she was able to do safely. She was to be sent out with a trolley and a map because no-one could think what else to do with her. It would have been a pretty ignominious start for a genuine Tithian maiden like Rosa Trampleasure, but for Deirdre Arbuthnot, trained Resistance assassin, it was a fine result. At last, she would get to do some reconnaissance.

Due to their tendency to extreme violence, the Blurpons were discouraged from leaving the laundry, except along certain routes that were considered best served by the non-humanoid species. However, in this instance one of Deirdre's Resistance colleagues, a Blurpon called Snoofle, was assigned to accompany her on her human-only route. He rode shotgun on the trolley as she pushed it along the corridors.

Snoofle wasn't like the other Blurpons, not at all.

"Here you are." He handed her a photocopied map with notes all over it.

She looked closely: *'Ugly beardy chap with sword—Commander Thistwith-Mee?—by Gloombin of Tith.'* Deirdre knew very little about Gloombin of Tith, other than that he was an artist and sculptor but Commander Thistwith-Mee was one of the greatest military strategists in K'Barthan history. The Inter-Species Wars had gone on for years until, after a run of decisive victories, Commander Thistwith-Mee had given the warring parties a choice of living in harmony or being annihilated by his forces. Funnily enough, after that they had all suddenly hit on ways to overlook each other's differences. She examined some of the other notes; all of them detailed the positions of works of art.

"What is this supposed to be?" she waved the paper at Snoofle.

"A map."

"I meant these," she demanded, turning it round and pointing to one of Snoofle's notes. "Do you know who I am?"

"Yes," said Snoofle.

"Good. Then you'll know we're not on a sightseeing tour. I'm here on serious military business."

"I should have explained," he said equably. "This place is about two thousand years old. Labyrinthine doesn't begin to describe it. Away from the state rooms, many of the corridors are similar, but the art works are all different. I navigate by them. Let me show you. This is our route, left out of the laundry, right at the Mong vase, up the stairs, left at the Bunn Jones window and so on, d'you see?"

"That's … lateral." And absolutely not what Deirdre would expect from a Blurpon. Blurpons were into combat and clean clothes. She was impressed and a little depressed, because she wasn't sure Snoofle's navigational system would do her much good—what she knew about art could have been written on the head of a pin.

"Don't worry, I'll show you each artefact and when we're done, you can try it out for yourself by navigating us back. Then, if you think it works for you, I can show you the other routes."

Getting lost was only one of the trials Deirdre had to contend with. The Arbuthnot effect on males clearly extended to Grongles. By the time she and Snoofle had made three collections Deirdre had been pinched and groped, and one particularly foolish Grongle officer had tried to steal a kiss. Deirdre had accidentally tripped, elbowed and lightly gouged each of her tormentors in turn. Since she was prepared to pretend their injuries were inflicted accidentally, they were happy to play along. Anything rather than acknowledge that a human woman had got the better of them. She was relieved at how easily she could use their pride against them and to her delight, they were clearly cautious about any further interaction with her. That was progress. She began to feel more confident.

However, Snoofle declared that they had done enough for one day and though Deirdre was all set to explore the Palace further, he persuaded her it would be wise to return to the laundry. That didn't stop him pausing frequently to point out important architectural features, over and above the navigational requirements: art works, frescoes and even a mosaic floor. They strayed from the route so he could show her the Upper Quadrangle with its ancient statues, historic central garden and cloisters.

Deirdre was grateful for the chance to see more and to try to improve her knowledge of the building. It was ludicrously complicated, but then, as Snoofle had said, it was two thousand years old and forty generations of Architraves had built on, enhanced, redecorated and generally messed about with it.

At the end of the Quadrangle, Deirdre and Snoofle stopped and she listened with uncharacteristic patience as he expounded the artistic merits of yet another statue. He knew all of the bizarre trivia that made history alive and interesting—right down to which museum, in Blurpostan, the Grongles had looted it from. He glanced cautiously up and down the corridor to check there was no-one about.

"OK Lieutenant, ma'am," it was the first time he'd addressed her by anything other than her cover name. "Time to go back. D'you want to take it from here?"

"Yes." She looked carefully at the statue and examined her map. "Snoofle, are you sure you're *all* Blurpon?" she asked him as she set off in the direction, she hoped, of the laundry.

"One hundred per cent."

"But—"

"But what? Not every Blurpon has a flair for the laundering arts and I can do the combat. I'm a black belt at hoo-flung-yoo. You want a sparring session sometime?"

Deirdre liked the idea. She was a black belt, too. Her expertise lay in a different martial art: ka-pa-tee but the two weren't so different.

"There's a gym?"

"Not as such, but we can improvise. There are plenty of empty rooms in a place like this."

"Do you like it here?"

"Arnold yes! The laundering arts leave me cold. It's the visual arts that ring my bells. I'll never get a better opportunity to study them than here. There's going to be a lot of clutter collecting in a building this age, fabulous clutter. I'll tell you something for nothing, the Architraves knew about works of art; all the best artists, designers and craftsmen from every era. I got into the attic once. That was a revelation. Then there are all the wonderful things the Grongles have looted from everywhere else."

"Yeh, but when we get into power that's going straight back," said Deirdre as she stopped at a junction between two empty corridors and examined a huge painting of a rather flabby middle-aged female nude. Though completely starkers in all other respects, the lady was wearing a long white scarf which floated in the breeze, helpfully obscuring her rude bits.

"It should, but …" he hesitated. "You've a lot to learn about Denarghi."

"Denarghi is a fine upstanding—" she began leaping to her commander's defence by force of habit. She stopped. "Then again …"

"Or maybe you haven't." Snoofle smiled. He stopped and looked thoughtful. "Rosa. Come here a minute. There's something I want to show you." Deirdre spent a couple of seconds looking for 'Rosa' before she remembered he was talking to her. Arnold, she was totally pants at this undercover stuff. That's why she was in strike operations, of course, but it was still really embarrassing.

"Sorry. I wasn't concentrating."

Assuming he was going to show her some more art she followed him down a side corridor at the end of which was a door. It led outside onto a tiny gap of roof between two of the Palace's many turrets. It wasn't even halfway up the building but it was high enough to command a picturesque, if limited, view across the city.

"There are a few places in the Palace where it's safe to talk. This is one of them. It's quiet, secluded and private. There are others and I'll show them to you but I've kept this one to myself, so if you could keep it secret, I'd be very grateful. I come here when I need a bit of space."

"And you're sure we can talk freely here?"

"Oh yes. No-one can see or hear us." He hesitated. "Lieutenant, I appreciate you are a superior officer and if I'm out of line you don't have to answer but I need to ask you something."

"Proceed," said Deirdre, letting the 'Rosa' thing drop for a moment.

"What are you really doing here? I know you're the Candidate but that makes it more dangerous. Nobody who looks like you should have been sent to a place like this."

"I'm more than a pretty face, thank you."

"Yes you are. I didn't mean—"

"If you must know, some of our prisoners escaped. It's Denarghi's fault but he's blaming me, even though I was in the officers' mess eating a salad at the time." She couldn't keep the anger out of her voice.

"Ah," he nodded. "Yes. I can see the problem. If he'd blamed anyone else he'd have had to execute them, but you're the Candidate so …"

In Deirdre's eyes, the problem was that Denarghi felt compelled to blame anyone, even so, the idea that there might be some logic behind his actions cheered her up.

"I suppose it had to be me. I haven't been very understanding," she said.

"From what you're saying, neither has he. So he sent you here for three months until the heat dies down?"

"No. I'm here to prove my proper credentials, by being a humble laundress, so that when the time comes I can be …" Who was she kidding? She shrugged. "I guess so. Yes."

"That's harsh." He looked thoughtful.

"I can see it from his point of view but I still don't understand. He made an error. It happens. He should be big enough to admit it."

Snoofle's whiskers bristled a little.

"Not big," she corrected herself, "but you know what I mean. No-one'll think any less of him if he admits a mistake. I'm not in the way of making errors—it isn't in my nature—but the one time I did, I accepted responsibility. I know my troops appreciated that. That's why this is so unfair. I'm being punished for someone else's blunder or at the very least an accident. That isn't our code. And he said I lacked commitment! No-one is more zealous in the Cause than me, no-one."

"I believe that," said Snoofle. He glanced at his watch. "Thank you for your honesty Lieutenant, ma'am, we can speak again later, but we'd better go now." He held the door open.

They walked the length of the corridor in friendly silence. Deirdre turned left at the painting and before long they reached the lift. She stopped to check her map and noted a set of duelling swords hanging on the wall. As far as she could tell she was in the right place.

The lift arrived and they trundled in. After a few moments it reached the basement and Deirdre pushed the trolley into the corridor. There, at the end, was the laundry.

"You may not know much about art but you can certainly read a map," said Snoofle as he jumped off the trolley and held open the laundry door.

"Considering who I am, I should hope I can," she said frostily.

"Point taken," said Snoofle. "I don't think you should go out too often though, you're pretty conspicuous."

"Meaning?"

"Meaning that I'm a Blurpon and you're a big baldy but even I can see you've got something. Just don't let Captain Snow see you, that's all."

"Too late."

Snoofle was concerned.

"Oh dear. That is not good." He thought for a moment. "If you will excuse me, I must talk to Head Launderer Sid for a minute and see if he's decided what to do with you." He grimaced. "If it helps, I know how it feels not to excel in here, I'm not much better at laundering than you. With any luck it'll be the drying room. They're good folks in there and it's out of the way of Captain Snow. You'll be fine."

So Deirdre had waited while Snoofle spent several minutes in earnest discussion with Head Launderer Sid.

Snoofle was right. Deirdre was assigned to the drying room where Mrs Doreen (pronounced D'reen) Pargeter and her team of 'girls' (who were all well into their eighties) hung up washing, because it was light work and nobody minded if it didn't happen very quickly. The first thing Deirdre noticed was a large rat.

"Oh, it's been terrorising us for months. It's disgusting, running along the washing lines doing its business all over the clean sheets," said Mrs Pargeter.

"Not any more," said Deirdre, who didn't much care for rats either, and with one lightning movement, she despatched it with her throwing knife.

"Gosh! What do they get up to in Tith these days?" asked Mrs Pargeter.

Bum. Deirdre had no clue.

"Er … my dad was a knife-thrower in the circus." Circus? Knife-thrower? What was she doing? "I don't have any brothers so he taught me all he knew."

"Gracious," said Mrs Pargeter. "He must have been quite a man."

"He was." Oh no, this was getting worse and worse, Deirdre's father was the mayor of Prang, a suburb just outside Ning Dang Po. She mustn't make up stuff like this. She'd forget it. She needed a change of subject, and fortunately Mrs Pargeter obliged.

It turned out that, in killing the rat, Deirdre made a friend for life of D'reen Pargeter, who had sent Glynis, one of the other girls, to find one of the few non-Resistance Blurpons in the laundry and extracted a promise that he would teach Deirdre how to launder a shirt if it killed him. In return Deirdre would teach D'reen and any of the other girls who wanted to know, how to throw a knife through a rat from twenty yards—hopefully without killing anything else.

The drying room was great, mainly because D'reen and the girls, though old, seemed refreshingly youthful in outlook. Even so, Deirdre eagerly anticipated getting out again soon, so she could carry on with her mission. Snoofle might have reservations about her looks but she felt more confident now she had met some of the Grongles. Sure, she must be careful—she was supposed to be Rosa Trampleasure, humble country girl, after all—but she was also on a fact-finding mission. And she wanted to find some facts. Information that would leave her colleagues in awe and show Denarghi what a big mistake he had made in his choice of scapegoat. Tomorrow, she must persuade them to let her back out again, collecting soileds.

Chapter 14

After a brief and restless night, Nigel sat in the remnants of his destroyed flat contemplating the tiresome job of clearing up after the flood: hiring industrial dryers, having his hallway measured for a replacement carpet and worst of all, eating humble pie with Mrs Balls. Even so, he congratulated himself at how rude he could make an apology sound—all the right words, so she couldn't argue—delivered with the utter loathing he felt. Nothing from Lucy, yet. He was surprised that she hadn't tried to contact him.

He checked his emails, answering machine, and voicemail messages to be sure.

Nothing. Not even a call to tell him what a heartless git he was, which, he appreciated, he had been.

It was surprising. He knew Lucy was fond of him. That was half the fun of seeing her. The guilty pleasure of manipulating her out of pure devilment. The ease with which he'd compelled her to abandon, or at least adjust, her smaller principles had delivered an intense thrill. Simple things like where and what to eat, what clothes to wear, where to go out of an evening … and oh, the pleasure of watching her wrestle with her conscience and go against it, fully aware that she was being forced to by him.

He regretted his haste in throwing her over for Sabrina. If he was no longer dating Lucy it would make it more difficult to get to Ruth.

It was annoying. He usually considered himself to be lucky. Sure, he believed that to an extent a person makes their own luck but he was aware that he didn't have to try as hard as some people. He won premium bonds and raffles galore, he was the kind of person who won board games because he could always throw a six. He was confident in chancy situations, but this situation needed more than luck. He must be careful with Lord Vernon. He'd been threatened before, of course. He had trodden on enough people's hands as he climbed the ladder of life for some of them to be angry. A few had even said they'd kill him, but he'd never taken it seriously. The types of people he'd walked over would only ever lie down and stay down. He was confident of that. This time, it was more difficult. If he didn't find a way to lure Ruth into his clutches Lord Vernon would kill him; with relish and enjoyment. He had to think carefully and make sure he got this right. Sure he was scared, but that just added to the frisson because he was good, really good—better than Lord Vernon. The diamond in his safe was testament to that.

He picked up his phone and began idly spooling through the numbers stored in his address book. At R and Ruth's name, he stopped. A get-out plan struck him so forcefully he felt weak at the knees. It was a master stroke; clever, devious, downright sneaky and best of all, Ruth would never be able to refuse it.

"God, I'm more than good," he said shakily as he sank into his sofa. He laughed. His luck was still holding. Lucy hadn't called. The difficult part would be persuading Ruth to listen to what he had to say. Once he'd achieved that, he was home free. He must hold his nerve until the moment was right. He looked at his watch. Now was as good a time as any.

He clicked on her number and pressed the button to dial. After a couple of rings she answered.

"Hello …"

"Hello—" Nigel began before Ruth's voice continued.

"I'm sorry I'm not available to take your call right now but if you leave your name and number after the beep …"

He hung up. Well, that figured. They were hardly friends and it was early. This was going to take courage and brinkmanship but Ruth was soft-hearted and cared about Lucy. His plan would succeed. He just had to make sure he got hold of her in time.

Chapter 15

Lucy was woken by the phone. She rolled over in bed. A quarter to six. Her mobile was switched off so it must be the landline. Who, in God's name, would ring the flat phone at a quarter to six on a work morning? Not that it mattered, she supposed. It was only a quarter of an hour before she normally got up, anyway, but those fifteen minutes were important, especially today. Wondering why, exactly, she was in such a tizzy over such a trivial number of minutes, she rolled over. Then it hit her. She groaned. The phone was reverberating strangely and yes, she had the mother of all headaches. Seriously though, who in the name of …? Gradually the previous evening's events came back to her. She'd gone to Ruth's concert, said 'hello', passed on a package Sir Robin had asked her to give to Ruth and then she'd been dragged off to an emergency client meeting before it even started.

The law never sleeps—or goes out or has time off. Yeh, and when you choose to specialise in human rights, the people involved tend to have an even looser grip on that side of life. She hadn't given the emergency lot her home number had she? Could she have been that stupid? Difficult to tell, and now her head was so muzzy that she didn't remember. Who else could it be? Nigel in trouble? Maybe. No. He wouldn't ring her. Realistically, there was only one option; the death—or dire illness—of a relative. It had to be answered and Ruth hadn't answered it. That meant Lucy was going to have to.

She leapt up. Sheeesh, why did she do that? The room spun and she clung onto the bedside table. She had to get to the phone. What if it was one of her relatives? Please let it be something uncomplicated like work. She'd tell them that she was on her deathbed and pass them on to a colleague. She ran into the hall, grabbed the receiver and pressed the green answer button.

"Hello?" Ouch. Slowly, she slid down the wall until she was sitting on the cold tiled floor. Not ideal but a lot better than standing up. She was shivering and wished she'd had the presence of mind to put on her dressing gown. Then again, no, because if she had she would never have got to the phone.

"Luce?"

"Ruth?" she glanced at the door of Ruth's bedroom. She'd come home late and assumed Ruth was already asleep. "Hang on … why aren't you here? Are you OK?" Slurred. How had that happened?

"I'm fine. No time for questions Luce," Ruth stopped. "You OK? You sound terrible." Lucy looked sideways down the hall, eyeballs only, keeping her head still. The eyes moved but reality followed oh so slowly.

"I'm feeling a bit rough." Her voice sounded croaky. "Flu I think. Where are you?"

"Can't say, they're listening. Did you stay over at Nigel's last night?"

"No. Nigel's in Prague, remember? After you'd gone off to your pre-concert sponsor's thing I got called into an emergency meeting. I didn't hear a note of the concert and then I had a pig of a journey home, security alerts all over the place. I finally found a taxi but by the time I got in it was so late I thought you must already be here, asleep." Ooo. Lucy shut her eyes. No more long complicated bits of speaking. Now her brain hurt as well as her head.

"Would you be able to meet me later?" asked Ruth.

Could she leave the house, Lucy wondered. Hmm, possibly, if she ate an entire bottle of aspirin in one go.

"Sure." Yeh, it'd be OK. She'd take a taxi. "Make it late, later."

A pause at the other end.

"Sir Robin invited me round this evening. Why don't you meet me round his?" Oh bless her, somewhere close. Hang on.

"He's old. What if he hasn't had a flu jab?" A brief hiatus while the world did some interesting spinning. "Trust me Ruth, this'll kill him."

"Just meet me by the door Luce, we can wing it from there, right?"

"OK."

"Six?"

"Six."

"Gotta go, they'll be listening."

"Who? Ruth, what's going on? Are you OK?"

"You haven't seen the news yet, have you?"

"It's quarter to six, I haven't got dressed yet," she said. And she wasn't going to. Her next call would be to her secretary's voicemail with instructions to cancel everything.

"I should have thought! Sorry I have to go. Later, OK?"

"OK."

"Don't talk to anyone, not the police or anyone until I've sorted this out, OK?"

The police? What had Ruth been doing?

"OK."

"And don't watch the news either, not until you've heard my side of it." Click and the dialling tone.

Lucy rolled onto all fours and crawled to the bathroom. Not a great start to the day. And where the hell was Nigel when she needed him? Never there. Despite promising to come to Ruth's concert with her he had flown to Prague on business two days before, with his very attractive assistant who everyone, including Lucy—whether or not she was prepared to admit it to herself—thought he was having an affair with. She felt tired and low and she needed him. Whenever that happened, Nigel had a trying proclivity either through chance or device, she couldn't be sure, of being elsewhere.

No. She could be sure. She might be besotted but she wasn't stupid.

She was far keener on him than he was on her and she really ought to stop seeing him. Ruth was right, he was using her, but she loved him and when he was on good form and being charming he was wonderful to be with.

Git.

Rummaging through the bathroom cabinet in search of medication she found a thermometer which she stuck in her mouth while she continued her quest for aspirin. Success at last! She found a new box of the expensive effervescent ones she favoured and read the back.

"No more than twelve Asprofizz should be taken over a twenty-four-hour period," she read aloud. Only, because she had a thermometer in her mouth, it came out more like, "Go gore gan gelve gasgogiz gould ge gagn ogre a gentygore gar geriod." She consulted her watch. Good. The thermometer was ready to read.

ONE HUNDRED AND THREE! She squinted at it carefully, that had to be wrong. Nope. It was really what it said.

Ooof!

No wonder she felt so bad.

Stuff twelve aspirin in twenty-four hours. This bug called for the atom bomb of pain relief. She dropped four into a glass of water and watched them dissolve. Blimey! Did they have to be quite so noisy?

The doorbell rang, the sound lanced through her ears and made her fevered head buzz. Ugh! She wasn't answering it, she thought as she drank back the aspirin in one go, claggy half-dissolved bits and all. No way.

Ah ha! Hanging on the back of the bathroom door was a hot-water bottle. Hoorah! She'd never noticed it before but she was very happy to see it now! She unhooked it and still crawling because standing up made everything go a bit weird, she made her way through to the kitchen.

It was time for a hot toddy and then bed, forever. Ruth had bought a bottle of whisky when she was trying to make some pudding or other a few weeks ago. It must be around, there were oranges in the fruit bowl and there was a jar of honey, or at least the dregs of one, in the cupboard. Lucy was pretty sure that Ruth wouldn't mind her drinking some of the whisky, especially not if it was for medicinal reasons. A hot toddy would knock her out, especially on the back of all those aspirin. The doorbell rang again. Studiedly, she ignored it and put the kettle on. It rang a third time and kept on ringing. Her head rang with it. If it didn't stop she was going to die. Only one thing to do.

She turned and crawled down the hall to answer it, formulating a few choice phrases to say to whoever it was as she went, most of which had the word 'off' in them.

Lucy opened the door.

Chapter 16

Two smartly dressed people stood on the doorstep, a man and a woman. Please God, not the Jehovah's Witnesses, she really couldn't deal with that right now.

"Lucy Hargraves?" asked the male one.

"Yes," said Lucy. Only it was more of a croak, she hadn't noticed her sore throat until now. Never mind. She would have her revenge. It was flu, after all. They'd almost certainly catch it from her. Take that you irritating, irritating people.

"DI Philip Softone," he said, holding up a wallet with one of those special plastic windows containing an identity card. "This is May Gurney," May Gurney—of unspecified rank—did the same.

Lucy took a sharp breath but had the presence of mind to buy a bit of time by pretending to read May Gurney's card too. DC, she was. 'Don't talk to anyone, not the police or anyone until I've sorted this out.' That's what Ruth had said but they were here and Lucy would have to tell them something.

Oh God (sorry God) not now, she thought. DI Philip Softone raised his eyebrows. Oh no. "I didn't say that out loud did I?" A smirk from the May Gurney woman. "I did, didn't I?"

"Yes madam, I'm afraid you did," said DC Gurney, but her tone was sympathetic, despite the smirk.

Bum.

"I'm very sorry, I'm not feeling all that bright."

They looked her up and down.

"That's understandable, madam, we appreciate it is early for most people."

"No. It's not early for me, I'm usually at work by seven thirty but I have flu and a temperature of one hundred and three so I'm not at my best."

A hesitation. Good, maybe they were getting the hint. Short of telling them, baldly, that she would rather they went away she wasn't sure how much more unsubtle she could be.

"We would very much appreciate it if you were able to spare us some time," said DI Softone.

For heaven's sake! Which bit of 'go away now' were they not getting?

"I'd be happy to—but are you sure you want to speak to me right this minute?" 'Don't watch the news' Ruth had said. What on earth had happened?

"Yes. This won't take a moment," said DI Softone, smoothly.

Complete gits. The pair of them.

"OK then. Come on in," said Lucy. Very carefully, so as not to move her head too much, she turned and led them down the hall. Perhaps coffee would help. "Do you want some coffee?" she asked them as they followed her into the kitchen.

"Tea please, milk one sugar."

"Just milk in mine."

They wanted flipping tea. Typical. Because coffee was good to go, she had set up the filter machine the night before, but tea would take faff and—worse—bending down. She flicked the switch on the filter machine and left it to brew while she filled the kettle. Her head thrummed. She couldn't believe how noisy a kettle and a coffee maker could be. They were even louder than the aspirin. Then the fridge came on. Good grief! How did people live with all this racket going on around them? Never mind, at least when the kettle had boiled, she could put the rest of the water in the hot-water bottle.

The police officers sat at the table and waited expectantly while she crept around until, finally, it was done, the tea was made. She placed the cups in front of them and was careful to sit at the end of the table, at right angles from them rather than at the other side, facing them, like some kind of—well, yes—it was an interview.

"How can I help?" she asked them. "And please make this quick or the way I feel this morning, I may die, here, in front of you." Nothing like laying it on thick but it wasn't as if they had taken any of the other hints she'd dropped. They looked at one another. God help her, if they so much as mentioned biscuits, then, police or not, she was going to lamp one of them.

"We are conducting an investigation into last night's events at the Festival Hall," said DI Softone.

"There was a concert as far as I know, I was called away before it even began and I—wait a minute. Has something happened?"

"I'm afraid so. It seems somebody drove through the window in a car, picked up your flatmate and then drove away again."

"In a flying car," added DC Gurney.

"What? Actually in the sky?" asked Lucy.

"Actually in the sky," said DI Softone.

"This … this can't be true. Are you serious?"

"We don't tell lies or make jokes at the Met, Ms Hargraves," said DI Softone.

Lucy swallowed, her head was spinning even more now and it wasn't a hundred per cent down to the flu. She closed her eyes for a moment and tried to collect her thoughts.

"Excuse me for asking, but I have quite a high fever and I'm just wondering if you could confirm something for me."

"Go on …?"

"Are you real?"

DI Softone smiled.

"I'm afraid so."

"Do you know anyone who might fit this description?" asked DC Gurney. She pushed a photograph along the table. It was a still from the Festival Hall's CCTV. Lucy picked it up. Yes, there was Ruth, about to take the hand of a man Lucy had never seen, who was wearing a hat and cloak.

"Not that I know of. Inspector, Detective Constable, I've got flu and a temperature of one hundred and three. I'm not very sure what's going on or if you are even here. Why don't you come back in a few days when I may be more equipped to give you some coherent answers?"

"Because we don't have time to wait that long. Not if this is a kidnapping."

A pause. DI Softone was irritated, that much was clear, but probably not as irritated as Lucy was at his insistence on interviewing her when all she wanted to do was sleep.

"We need to know if Ms Cochrane has contacted you?" he said. Oh so formal.

"No." Of course it wasn't a lie she was simply disagreeing with them. They didn't need to know whether Ruth had contacted her: not at all. "Is she in trouble?"

"That depends. First of all we have to understand the circumstances of her disappearance—whether she has been kidnapped or went of her own free will."

"Whether what?"

"If she was kidnapped," the inspector continued smoothly, "then, clearly, we have to find her. If she went of her own free will she may be charged with criminal damage, wasting police time and possibly terrorism offences." That didn't sound right. They were playing hardball, they had to be.

"Terrorism?"

"The flying car she took off in reappeared later with another one and the pair of them did a lot of damage." Lucy's heart sank, she wished she was able to think straight but her brain was definitely subpar.

"What sort of damage?"

"Major destruction; a pod off the London Eye, a couple of the cast-iron lamps along the Embankment knocked down, the ball knocked off the Coliseum, numerous sets of traffic lights damaged, Nelson's Column …"

"Don't forget the Daily Mail building, sir," said DC Gurney with the tiniest, tiniest hint of a smirk.

"Yes, not forgetting shooting the Daily Mail building with some sort of high-explosive missile," said DI Softone. "Luckily no-one was hurt."

"Several terrorist groups have claimed responsibility," added DC Gurney.

"No. That's not Ruth. She is absolutely solid. She'd never do anything like that."

"Then she sat in the passenger seat while her friend did it."

"No. She'd never—do you have a shred of evidence that she was in the car? You said it disappeared for a while. Where did it go? How do you know he didn't drop her off somewhere?"

Whoa there Lucy, too close to giving something away. DI Softone looked at her and narrowed his eyes.

"Are you sure she hasn't contacted you?" asked DC Gurney.

Lucy was used to telling the truth and as a solicitor, technically it was her job. She took a deep breath.

"OK people. Right now, I have a very high temperature and I'm not sure of my own name …" Would they buy it?

"I see," said DI Softone but he didn't take his eyes off her. No. Then again, if they thought Ruth was involved in terrorism Lucy had to put them right, but tactfully.

"Ruth would never commit a terrorist offence and she would never voluntarily be involved in one either. If she really was in a flying car blowing up bits of London it would have been against her will and this would be a kidnapping." Not bad but still dodgy.

"I see. And you think it is?"

"No, I don't. What if Ruth's on the run?" Yes, that was probably alright.

Both police officers were instantly attentive.

"Why would she be running?" asked DI Softone.

"Because some bunch of nutters have been following her about for months." Too much information? Possibly, but it was nothing they didn't already know.

"What bunch of nutters?" asked DC Gurney.

"Giants in strange, futuristic suits. They would make me run away, too. She was followed by the first one three months ago and they've been cropping up wherever she goes ever since. If you look in your files, you'll see she reported it. Some gopping great bloke who scared the hell out of her and called her 'chosen'. Not that any of you did anything."

No! Dammit. Stop already. She'd promised Ruth she'd say nothing. She had to say something to counter their ridiculous theories about terrorism but Lucy realised she was too tired, ill and angry to think through what she was telling them. It was time to get rid of these two police officers—and fast—before she shot her mouth off and said something she, or worse, Ruth, would regret.

"What about Ms Cochrane's mental state?" asked DC Gurney. "Does she have a history of mental instability?"

"Are you kidding? Of course not! I told you. She's about as reliable as it gets."

"We're trying to understand her part in last night's events."

"Then why don't you find her and ask her?"

"Have you seen the news this morning, madam?"

"Do I look in the state to watch telly? I have a temperature of one hundred and three," she reminded them. Lucy wondered how many times she was going to have to mention that she was ill before they reined it in? She stopped talking and rested her head on the table. Ah that was better. She made a mental note that later once the aspirin had kicked in and the visual disturbance subsided she must find out what was going on. In the meantime, she was missing something big and obvious. A giant get-out-of-gaol-free card. It'd come to her if she could only get her head out of feeling maudlin about flu and into work mode. For now, enough was enough, she would beg them to go away. With a great effort she straightened up again and looked DC Gurney in the eye, woman to woman.

"If you don't mind, I'm going to have to end this conversation and ask you to leave because I have some serious recuperation to do. You can put a man outside if you like, or a woman, I won't be going anywhere, I will be here in bed, sleeping, probably for the next two weeks."

"One more question," said DI Softone.

Lucy's memory finally came up trumps.

"Are you going to arrest me and take me into custody to answer it?" There it was. Go brain. She might be ill but her thinking equipment was still on form, even if it had taken a little time to warm up.

"Not at the moment, no."

Of course not. Ha! Pass go and collect two hundred pounds. Lucy was a human rights lawyer, after all, and she had a growing reputation. They weren't going to be giving her any crap. Legalities aside though, she knew the real reason for this was nothing to do with her fledgling reputation. It was because if they took her to the station everyone down there would get flu and Inspector Softone's name would be mud, that was why.

"Then I won't be answering it. Let me show you out."

They made nothing more than mild protestations as she walked them carefully and slowly to the door. Once she'd closed it, she leant against the wood for a moment. Ugh, her head was really hurting now, she could hardly see.

Police despatched, she returned to the kitchen, filled the hot-water bottle and went back to bed. Almost immediately, the doorbell rang again.

For heaven's sake. It was like Piccadilly Circus. Couldn't a woman be ill in peace for five minutes? Quietly, so as to give herself the option of not being in, and on all fours because God knew she couldn't stand, Lucy crept down the hall and squinted through the peephole in the middle of the heavy Victorian door. She could see two blokes, one greasy-looking in an ill-fitting suit, the other fat and balding with a camera.

Press.

Now what? Go back to bed. That's what. As she started down the hall she heard the letterbox opening and ducked into the kitchen just in time as one of them peered in.

"Come on luv! We're looking for Ruth!" he shouted. "Open the door. There's cash in it for you. You can sell us your story."

"Get stuffed!" thought Lucy but she said nothing. They hadn't seen her and by rights she should be at work or on her way there so it was unlikely they were expecting to find anyone in. Trapped in the kitchen, she made herself a hot toddy and drank it in her pretended absence while she waited for them to go. They spent a good ten minutes hedging their bets and trying to persuade anyone who might be there to open the door before they finally gave up and left.

Good. Now, finally she could get some sleep.

Except that first she needed to find out what had happened, but the breakfast TV shows were all busy talking about an MP who'd had an affair, so she switched to a rolling news channel and even though her head thumped and the letters swam in front of her eyes she managed to get the basics. The police were telling the truth. That was a slight comfort, but the facts were grim.

Somebody actually had driven a car through the window of the Festival Hall and spirited Ruth away. It had disappeared and then returned with another one, just as the police had said. The two flying cars had then chased through

London, randomly destroying buildings, street furniture and several major landmarks as they went. Lucy switched the TV off. Was this honestly real or was it just a dream that was getting clever?

It was so difficult to tell.

She thought about sparking up her laptop but she knew her limitations. She would check her emails, see the hundreds piling up in the inbox waiting for her attention and then panic or, worse, try and answer some. No, she must be sensible and disciplined about this. She was not in a fit state to help Ruth, or anyone else, until the aspirin started to work and she'd had a lie-down. She went back to bed and switched on Radio 4. They had a panel of experts discussing whether or not the London Outrage, as they were calling it, was a deliberate attempt by terrorists to destroy the city and cause chaos, or whether it was something else. One panellist pointed out that it might not be an act of terror on the grounds that nobody had been hurt and terrorists usually aim to kill as many innocent bystanders as possible. Then, amidst expressions of derision from the other panellists, the anchorwoman of the show read out an email from a Harrier pilot substantiating this view. He explained that the action in the TV footage showed all the hallmarks of a dogfight as opposed to a rampage. Lucy shuddered. She almost hoped it was deliberate damage. If it was a chase, the car Ruth had got into at the Festival Hall was the one being pursued. To be in it at the time must have been horrible. Lucy hoped her best friend was OK. Wide awake, she listened as the voices burbled away. Her head still thrummed. She needed to rest but there was no chance. Not until she'd worked out what was going on. She wished she wasn't ill. It made it so difficult to concentrate.

Stuffed inbox or no, she would have to check the computer. She looked at her watch. And in a little while, she'd phone her boss, too, and discuss Ruth's case. Because it was a case, and she didn't have a solicitor and since Lucy was one … She steeled herself to get out of bed again but instead promptly fell into a fitful, feverish sleep. While sleeping, Lucy had the kind of vivid uber-realistic dream she always had with flu. She dreamed she heard a strange sound, like bathwater going down the plughole, a loud pop and breaking glass. Then there was a brief murmured conversation: male voices, two of them talking quietly as if they didn't want to wake her. Except that they did wake her. She looked around the room. Even though she knew she'd been dreaming she felt a strange sensation, as though somebody actually had been there. Relieved, she turned over and was just going back to sleep when she heard the noise again, but without the breaking glass this time.

What in the hell was that? The press people? She looked at the window. Still intact. The breaking glass bit must have been imaginary—or outside.

So what had the other noise been? Something leaking? She sat up and listened, waiting to see if it happened again but it didn't. She got out of bed and crept round the entire flat checking for leaks, anomalies, broken windows or other signs of false entry, and anything else that might have caused the sound. All the while her head buzzed and crackled and her eyes felt as if they were melting out of their sockets.

As she searched the kitchen she was startled by a rustle from inside the bin, it was pretty full. She'd had to push the surface of the rubbish down to put some kitchen roll in the previous evening. It was probably just settling, except it shouldn't be rustling now. Please god don't let it be a mouse or something.

She moved closer … amazed at her own jumpiness, and put her foot on the pedal. The lid flipped up and hit the wall with a metallic ding that made her head ring with it. She peered in. The fragments of a jam jar had appeared which she didn't remember breaking; it was one of those tiny ones they give you at breakfast in some hotels. After thoroughly checking the rest of the flat again she found nothing else. Finally, after ten minutes, she concluded that it had been a fevered dream and went back to bed. More aspirin, another lie-down and blissful oblivion for a minute or two.

Again she awoke. This time, on her bedside table, a large mug steamed gently. In front of it was a piece of paper, folded so it stood upright, which bore the legend 'Drink me'.

"Very Alice in Wonderland," she said to nobody in particular, and through force of habit—because heaven knew she couldn't smell anything—she sniffed it.

"Ugh." She could smell that, and it was rank! Since she couldn't smell anything else it was clearly strong, to boot.

"That is redolent of the sewer," she said, mentally noting that she had to be very feverish not to remember getting up, going out and buying herself such a vile concoction. Then again, here she was, talking out loud to herself, and she'd broken a jam jar, swept it up and put it in the bin without remembering. She swirled the mixture round the mug and sniffed it again. Yes, it stank, it would probably taste horrible and would therefore be likely to follow the standard cough medicine rule of vileness; the more revolting it tasted and smelled, the more likely it would be to get rid of the symptoms.

OK. Here went nothing. She necked it and immediately the doorbell rang.

"Go away!" she said, got up and put on her dressing gown.

Chapter 17

The Pan of Hamgee stood next to Ruth as she fed coins into a phone at South Mimms motorway services. He knew how coin phones worked, they had them at home; they had to because non-Grongles weren't allowed mobile phones. In K'Barth, though, someone was always listening in on a payphone; in fact a well-scripted conversation over the payphone system was one of the most reliable ways there was of misinforming the Grongles. Contrary to the K'Barthan tradition though, payphones here were the safest ones to use and it was the mobile phone system which was easily monitored. Interesting.

He stood at a tactful distance and watched as Ruth phoned her flatmate—she wouldn't want him to listen but that didn't stop him having a go. However, he couldn't pick up much and she kept turned to the wall so lip-reading wasn't an option. When she'd finished she told him she'd arranged for them to meet her flatmate later that day.

Ruth seemed nervous about using the phone. As he understood her, she thought the authorities could listen to calls fairly easily and possibly also use them to trace her whereabouts. She believed the payphone was a safer option but couldn't guarantee that either. She thought the authorities would almost certainly know the number of Lucy's mobile and be able to listen to and monitor her calls, and they were probably tapping the flat landline, too, so as far as The Pan could tell, there was probably a third party listening to any exchange over the telephone.

It was all very complicated and not helped by the fact that Ruth's only knowledge of these things came from films which, she'd explained, meant it was, most likely, wrong.

The Pan could offer little assistance, coming, as he did, from K'Barth where it was so different.

Next they moved to a different phone from which Ruth rang her work to try and explain herself. She'd told him she started work at nine but, amazingly, there was someone at the other end that early, someone sympathetic by the sound of it. Good. The Pan watched the people moving past him and felt a familiar sense of loneliness. They belonged. Even here he knew he was an outcast.

A little old dear with a bag full of knitting came out of the ladies and stopped, looking him up and down. She peered round the side of the phone at Ruth, shook her head and wandered off muttering. Ruth's eyes were still red and her face blotchy, while The Pan looked exactly the way he would expect to look after being beaten up by Lord Vernon: rough. He was unshaven, too. If the old dear thought he and Ruth were together, what must she be thinking?

Drawn to the bright lights of the retail outlet, he caught sight of a pile of newspapers. He wandered over and picked one up. It was all in Grongolian but he could read it reasonably well, not that he needed to when he saw the picture on the front.

'Terrorists rampage through London,' read the caption in big, shouty letters—The Pan was intrigued to notice that four terrorist groups had already owned up to his and Lord Vernon's exploits. Worryingly, the article made no mention that the SE2 and its occupants were innocent of any contribution to the 'orgy of damage,' as the paper colourfully called it, meted out to London. Not great news that. No mention that the SE2 was being pursued, either. He sighed. At home he was regarded as vermin, here it seemed they thought he was a terrorist. He suspected both labels resulted in a similarly high Most Wanted ranking. He read on. Below, in a smaller font, it said, 'Drama captured on CCTV'. Living in a police state, he knew what that was. It seemed they had more here than at home though. Strange. The picture showed a series of stills. First, a set of the SE2 with Lord Vernon in hot pursuit. Mmm. They looked pretty good if a trifle blurry. Next, a series showing the foyer of the Festival Hall, his snurd just visible through the front window, the explosion of glass as he arrived, and him standing on the stairs, holding his hand out to Ruth. Mmm, not a bad shot. He held it up. Yeh, he always felt that little bit more confident, more himself, when he wore his hat and cloak. He liked the look and here in these pictures it worked. He had a kind of glamour, even with the black eye and the bruising across his nose. Yep, he'd have to keep it. He folded it up and put it under his arm.

"Are you going to buy that, sir?" said a female voice. The tone was polite, sweet even, but he could hear the steel beneath it.

"Yes I am," he glanced over at Ruth who was beckoning to him frantically. Ah yes, money for the phone, "In a minute …" He dumped the paper into the shop assistant's hands, rushed back to the phones and held out the handful of coins Ruth had given him. She selected a big, seven-sided silver one and shoved it into the slot. The machine spat it out. Another attempt, with the same result, and yet another.

The Pan retrieved the coin from the floor, turned it round and with a deft twist, flicked it into the slot. It stuck and the LCD figures on the machine changed from three seconds of talk time to three minutes. He raised his eyebrows at her and she gave him a warning look—as in—don't go back over there, presumably. He held up one finger, ran back to the scary lady and took the paper.

"Here," he held out his handful of coins. "Please take one." Her hand hovered over one of the gold-ish ones and then she stopped.

"No. You pay at the till." She pointed to a long queue of disgruntled people snaking through the shop and out into the distance.

Arnold's hair.

He put the paper back on the pile and returned to Ruth just as she put the phone down.

"You have the attention span of a gnat on acid, you know that, don't you?" she said. "It's like hanging out with a two-year-old."

"I'm assuming the implication here is 'short'."

"Well done, Mister Pan."

"Well, Ms Cochrane, you might want to see this." He grabbed her arm and dragged her over to the pile of newspapers. She picked one up and her hand went to her mouth.

"Oh no," she whispered in alarm. There was a fourth picture which showed the pair of them running hand in hand down the stairs towards the snurd. She was clearly recognisable, a fact she would undoubtedly regard as bad news. Ah. Probably best to try and jolly her along.

"Not a bad shot," said The Pan with a smile, "you look quite—well—" embarrassed cough. "I would."

She wanted to be angry, he could tell, to cry, perhaps, or shout at him and she was definitely trying to glare crossly, only a laugh bubbled up and she started giggling before she could stop herself.

"Not you again," said the shop assistant, less sweet and more steel in the tone this time. She snatched the paper from Ruth. "As I told your friend, you have to buy it if you want to read it, over ..." Her voice petered out. Oh dear. Another bad sign. She looked at the paper in her hands and then at The Pan and Ruth. What was she seeing, he wondered. Ruth, who had obviously been crying and him, so like those grainy photos. A suspected terrorist with a woman in distress. What would she be thinking? Like the little old dear earlier with the knitting, absolutely the wrong things.

"It's OK. You keep it," said The Pan. "Come along darling." Ruth's head snapped up in surprise as he grabbed her by the arm and dragged her towards the door. "Time for a sharp exit."

"What are you doing?" She slowed and angrily wrenched her arm free.

"Nooo!" he pleaded. "Don't do that in here."

"Then stop dragging me around by the hair." Through gritted teeth. "It's the second time."

"It's not your hair, it's your arm."

"I'm referring to your caveman antics."

"D'you mean the calling you 'darling'?"

"No." She blushed. Ah. Apparently, she liked cheeky. "It was the dragging me off without explanation, the treating me like an idiot."

"I'm sorry, I would never knowingly treat you like an idiot but I don't have time for the niceties." He pulled her towards him and spoke quietly into her ear. "She's recognised us. Ruth, we need to leave."

The woman was talking to someone else and a wave of understanding seemed to pass across the crowd like a contagion. You could almost hear the metaphorical pennies dropping as people stopped, turned and began to point. Ruth stared over at them.

"Listen to me," said The Pan. "We must go, I mean it. Really, right now, this minute. Are you going to start running or do I have to pick you up and carry you?"

"You won't get far, I'm heavier than you think."

He laughed as she grabbed his hand and they began to run.

"Stop right there!" An overweight man in a uniform stepped into their path. They let go of each other's hands, Ruth dodging to his left and The Pan to his right. Yeh, a retired policeman by the looks of it, unfit and burger-fuelled; he had no chance. They ran into the car park and above the roar of the traffic on the nearby road he heard a new sound. Sirens. The Pan reckoned they meant the same thing in any version of reality.

"Police?" he asked her, as they ran.

"Yeh."

Arnold.

They headed towards the place where the snurd was parked and were both brought up short by what they saw. It was surrounded by a large crowd.

"Now what?" asked Ruth.

She was out of breath but not as much as he expected. More power to her and how—in The Prophet's name—could she run in those shoes?

"We can hardly march over there and get in," she said.

"No. I'm afraid we'll have to draw attention to ourselves again," he said. "I don't see how else we can get out of this." He took the keyring out of his pocket and pressed the button.

"What d'you mean?"

He nudged her arm and pointed at the lardy security guard who had recruited some leaner, meaner colleagues along with a large posse of the general public and they were heading purposefully in their direction.

"We can't go over there and get in but it can come over here and get us."

She gave him a totally nonplussed look. Oh dear. Further explanation required, he glanced over at the crowd heading towards them, it would have to be succinct. "I mean we are going to have to start running and stay ahead of them until it finds us."

A slightly panicky expression appeared on the Chosen One's face as they sprinted off again.

"What if I can't?"

"You can. You're fitter than you think."

She'd have to be. He took her hand again, pulling her along as they fled.

From where the SE2 was parked he heard shouts and the sound of the engine revving. The shouting got louder and more desperate and the revving got, well, it was more of a growl than a rev.

Tyres squealed.

The lean mean security guards were gaining.

The sound of the SE2's engine altered, it was moving, he could hear it changing gear. Good. He and Ruth ran out into the roadway between the shiny strings of parked cars. The snurd flashed past them at high speed and screeched to a halt at the end of the row.

"Nice handbrake turn!" shouted Ruth. "Who's driving?"

What was she talking about?

"No-one," he said as they started running towards it.

"What d'you mean no-one?"

"Exactly that. Stop talking, you need your breath."

"It's you with a remote, right?"

"No." He held up both hands, the keys dangling on the ring from one finger so she could see he wasn't pressing any buttons.

Uh-oh! A luridly checked car full of—yes there was a certain set to policemen which didn't change whatever version of the universe you happened to be in—pulled up alongside the SE2. The flashing lights and wailing siren were a bit of a giveaway, too. The snurd started to move again, towards Ruth and The Pan, picking up speed. They stopped. It was transforming itself into aviator mode and putting its roof down. It would do, wouldn't it? Oh well, not that it could do much else. He looked at the Chosen One. This was going to be a big ask.

"Ruth, do you trust me?" he shouted above the din of squealing tyres and revving engine.

"No!" She was laughing.

"Well, you're going to have to. Hold my hand, run and jump as high as you can when I do," he shouted as the snurd approached. It was flying low, but still flying, fast. He turned and they started to run, together, towards their pursuers. The snurd was gaining but not as quickly as The Pan would have liked. Would it reach them before they ran headlong into the gaggle coming the other way? He ran faster. Ruth was having trouble keeping up, not too fast then or she would never make the jump.

"Ready?"

"Yes."

The crowd loomed a few yards ahead of them, bearing down with intent to arrest, probably, knowing crowds and The Pan's luck, in an exciting, adventurous way that involved rescuing the poor sweet girl from certain death and giving her abductor a good kicking.

"Three, two, one … now!" They leapt into the air, there was a slight bump, as if the snurd had needed to move down in order not to hit them and they landed inside, Ruth, smartly in the passenger seat, The Pan with one leg either side of the transmission tunnel.

Arnold! Show the girl you're a klutz or what?

His eyes watered and he just had the presence of mind to flip the autopilot switch to off and put it into a climb. It would have been tactless to plough through the crowd of people barring their path.

"Arse!" he said.

She was laughing again, "I dunno, it looks more like your—"

"Yes. Ha ha. Very amusing. Can you steer for a moment?" He plonked her hand on the wheel. The passenger footwell wasn't made to accommodate three legs and what with Ruth's two being in there already, an extra one of The Pan's made it a snug fit. He finally extricated himself and managed to wriggle into the driving seat. By the Prophet's earwax that smarted! A quick sideways glance. Yep, she was trying not to laugh. The impress-the-girl side of this adventure wasn't going smoothly, indeed, it wasn't going at all. He wrenched his thoughts back to the important matter of escaping. A quick check behind revealed that there was a—what was that?—a big long thing with a fan on top. Whatever it was, it appeared to be following them. He pressed the button which put the roof back on. "Buckle up," he told her as it slid into place. "We might need to do a little aerobatics. I don't know what that thing is but I expect it's after us."

She did as she was told and then checked her mirror.

"Hang on, I can't see properly, I'll have to look." She slipped her arm out of the seat belt and craned round to peer out of the tiny rear window. As she leaned towards him he happened to be reaching towards the dash to press the button which locked the roof. Her hair brushed his neck. For a second the world stopped as his brain headed off at a tangent. Arnold in heaven not now! This woman would be his undoing! He could feel her leaning against his shoulder. Did she need to look for that long? He decided to tell her to hurry it up and they turned to face each other at the same time. They were so close they almost touched noses. Flustered, she took a sharp breath.

"It's a police helicopter and yes, I think it probably is after us." Studied matter-of-fact delivery, trying to cover her confusion.

"How fast can it go?" he asked her.

"How should I know?"

Oh well, even in K'Barth, he doubted there were many law-abiding people who shared his encyclopaedic knowledge of the speeds of police vehicles.

"Well, we can go about …" It was a sure bet that if they spoke Grongolian they measured in it. What was the snurd's top speed in Grongolian millimiles? Come to think of it, now it had been rebuilt by Gerry, what *was* its top speed? "Actually, I don't know how fast we can go but I'd guess it's about three hundred of your, what do you call them?"

"Miles."

Ha! No milli but otherwise, bang on.

"Yes. Three hundred miles an hour, or thereabouts, maybe more. So if I knew how fast the whirly thing goes, I'd know whether or not we can outrun it."

"It's a helicopter, and no, we shouldn't even be thinking about trying to outrun it. We should land and talk to the nice policemen politely."

"No Ruth, landing is the last thing we should do, we must get somewhere safe, well-hidden and out of arm's reach. You said yourself we need to talk about this and you're right, we do. That's when we can decide what we are going to say and send the nice policemen a message." A very apologetic one. This was not going well at all. He was supposed to be helping the Chosen One, protecting her, not dragging her deeper and deeper into the doo-doo. Oh. And there was a thought. "Unless it has guns on. Does it have guns on?"

"Not that I know of."

Every cloud has a silver lining.

"If only we were at home. I'd find a busy patch of sky and lose it amongst the traffic."

"What?" She grabbed his arm excitedly and the sudden weight pulled his elbow down, causing the snurd to wobble alarmingly in mid-air.

"Easy tiger, it's not a good call to touch me when I'm doing my thing."

Out of the corner of his eye he saw hers roll. She was debating whether or not to say something caustic, he could tell and made a mental note that the phrase 'easy tiger' might have been a bridge too far. That sort of thing was all very well with gangsters like Big Merv but this was a real woman. Eventually the bit of her that was in a hurry seemed to win out over the rest of her and she said,

"What did you say just then?"

Arnold, she wanted him to repeat it?

"Um, easy tiger."

Could a silence be sarcastic? Yes.

"No dear, before that."

"I'd find a busy patch of sky."

"Brilliant! There you go. I've got it!" She opened the window and leaned out. "See the big road down there?" she shouted above the roar of the air coming in. "Follow it. And go lower! I need to read the signs."

She clearly had a plan and since he was in unfamiliar territory and fresh out of ideas, he did as he was told.

They skimmed into a cutting and he was so busy trying to find the signs she was talking about that he nearly collided with two bridges over the road. He dropped the snurd down just in time to fly between them. The Chosen One turned a little pale.

"I'll take care of reading the signs shall I, Mister Pan? You stick to flying."

"What was that?" he shouted as the bridges receded into the distance. She wound the window up.

"The M1. We're going the right way."

He realised the M1 must be another road.

Unlike the Grongolian police these ones were not to be tempted into a chase. They merely stayed high and followed the snurd from a distance. He wondered if he should try and outrun them but he had to fly slow and low enough for Ruth to read the signs. His thumb hovered over the portal button but he didn't know what to imagine other than Ruth's street or the motorway service station, both of which were probably being watched. Even if he'd been able to imagine somewhere safe he didn't feel comfortable using the thimble. Not after Lord Vernon had turned up last time. It could have been a coincidence but the fact he'd arrived just after The Pan had used his portal was ominous; and the fact he'd known the exact spot to arrive at, even more so. Yes, keep the thimble as backup for now. They were in enough trouble as it was, without Lord Vernon arriving to liven up the mix.

"We're not doing very well at losing the whirly thing," he said.

"Don't worry, we will." She checked out of the window again. "Go left a bit and up. I think we need to be about two thousand feet high and circling over that big reservoir over there." She pointed. Yes, she clearly had a plan, he was glad he had subdued the urge to run.

He pulled the wheel towards him and the SE2 began to climb into the clouds. The vapour ahead of them parted for a moment, long enough for The Pan to realise they were on a collision course with the largest snurd he had ever seen. It was the size of a ship, in aviator mode still, but coming into land by the look of it.

They both screamed as he yanked the wheel and the SE2 bucked and dipped in the turbulence as it passed.

"What in the name of The Prophet was that?" he shouted over the din of its receding engines. She was looking at her watch, seemingly counting seconds.

"We have our own flying things called aeroplanes but they only fly. They don't do anything else," she told him. She was speaking quickly. "It's kind of like buses—do you have those?"

Yep, K'Barth had buses run by a company called 'Vite K'Barthan', except it was 'Vite K'Barthan wholly owned subsidiary of Go Grongolian' at the moment.

"Yes," he said.

She was still looking at her watch as she talked. "Right, well, imagine something like buses, only ones that go in the sky instead of on the roads. That was one of them. They have to land in special places called airports and they all land on the same path at this particular airport, every ninety seconds. That means it's tricky for the helicopter to follow us immediately—UP NOW!"

A wall of noise hit them and the snurd climbed steeply as The Pan avoided another of the huge aeroplanes.

"They'll clear a path, they'll stick all the aeroplanes in a holding pattern going round and round and round so they can come after us but it'll take a few minutes; and even if they do they can't leave the aeroplanes there for more than five minutes. So I thought we may be able to get away while they're waiting or once air traffic control kick them off and let the planes start landing again."

"Have you ever thought of a career in crime?" he asked admiringly.

"No. Mister Pan. I'll leave that to you."

Yes, they could probably get away. Where would they escape to though? Not sure. Another flying leviathan was approaching the runway and, as he prepared to avoid it, The Pan had a bright idea. Or was it a dumb one? They'd soon find out.

He let the snurd lose some height and as the plane screamed over their heads, accelerated upwards until they were flying a few feet underneath its huge belly. It had what appeared to be engines on each wing, but they were of a type he'd never seen before so he was careful to stay away from them, in the middle. Should he use the anti-gravity button? No, it was hardly taxing flying, just a case of holding the right line. Wheels came out of trapdoors either side of them. A quick glance at the Chosen One. She was very pale, sitting bolt upright and clutching the edges of the seat with both hands. He'd seen that look on Big Merv and—another quick check—yes, her knuckles were white.

It was much darker under the aeroplane and incredibly noisy.

"What are you doing?" she asked, at least he thought that was what she said. She was doing her best to make herself heard but he was lip-reading, all he could hear was the screaming of the aeroplane's engines. A message scrolled across the head-up display.

"Activate noise cancellation?"

"Yes please," said The Pan and the snurd was suddenly silent.

"Ruth," he shouted and stopped. He started again, speaking normally. "I mean, sorry, Ruth, I think I know how we can disappear."

She looked nervously around her.

"Disappearing temporarily is OK by me but if you mean a more permanent form of disappearance—like dying—I'd rather not if it's all the same to you." By the looks of things, switching off the noise had merely worried her more.

"We'll be fine, I promise," he said. As the plane dipped lower he stayed with it until they reached the edge of the airfield, then, as it disappeared over the security fence he peeled off and landed on the public perimeter road. No sign of the whirly thing. Good. Had it seen them? Who could tell? The Pan quickly pressed the button to morph the snurd back into road mode and headed towards the side of the airport which looked busier, full of houses, offices and—thank The Prophet—cars. That would help them to blend in, at least. They were heading back in the direction they had come from, a mistake possibly, if the whirly thing was still searching for them there, but it might be far away, travelling in the direction it had last seen them moving.

He drove, on the ground, through a village called Sipson, heading back towards the main road. They passed a hotel and went straight on at a mini-roundabout, down a small lane, which seemed to be going nowhere, with a grey bus parked on the verge a little way down.

Good, that should do. He drove past the bus and parked behind it, under some overhanging trees. Plenty of places for the snurd to secrete itself nearby, under cover. It could stay where it was if it liked. The bus had flat tyres and had been turned into a—what would it be? As he turned off the engine, the smell of greasy breakfasts frying assailed his nostrils. Ah yes, a café of sorts. He realised he was very hungry and as Gladys, his inimitable landlady, often said, ''S not much beats a good fry-up first thing'. He said something to the Chosen One to that effect, being careful to do the accent.

She laughed but there was an edge of hysteria to it that he didn't like.

"You alright?" he asked.

"Yes," she said, but he didn't believe her. From the way she looked down, blinking, he could tell she was in danger of bursting into tears. She wouldn't want to cry. She was proud, the Chosen One. He needed a distraction to change the mood and caught sight of something in the footwell. The tiny handbag had fallen open and spilled some of its contents over the carpet: a credit card by the looks of things, the dead mobile phone and a package addressed to her.

"Aren't you going to open that?"

A puzzled frown followed by grateful comprehension. Yep, she was smart, too, she knew exactly what he was doing and grabbed at the straw.

"I might have been about to post it." A game attempt at a smile.

He shrugged and said, "You might. I suppose it would save you carrying it home."

"How so?"

"It's addressed to you, Ruth Cochrane, that *is* your name isn't it? So I'm assuming the address is where you live."

"Yes." She laughed, properly this time, and it broke the tension. The danger moment was over. No tears now, or at least, not for a while. He checked his watch.

"I think we have time for a spot of breakfast. Shall we open it in there?" asked The Pan, pointing to the bus. "Or do you want to go with your original plan and eat at your greasy spoon of choice?"

"My choice is ace but it's on the outskirts of the City of London and it's rush hour so we might not make it until lunchtime."

"It would only take two ticks if we—"

"No," she interrupted him. "We can't fly, because nobody else can, and after all the trouble we've taken to ditch the police it would be foolish to do something conspicuous and attract their attention."

"Fair point. Shall we have a look, then?" He nodded his head in the general direction of the bus.

"It would be good, but how can we? What about the newspapers?"

Ah yes. He rummaged about under his seat. Like the revolving number plate, a range of emergency disguises, to The Pan, was the equivalent of a jack, a spare tyre or a box of handkerchiefs on the back shelf. He was relieved they hadn't fallen out with everything else, but at the same time, a little vexed that it was his hard-won loot which was gone and the disguises which had stayed put. He found a fake grey moustache with a can of hair paint, a pair of big sunglasses and a long blonde wig. She eyed him doubtfully.

"I appreciate there are not many people who carry a wig and a fake moustache in their vehicle, but not everybody is committing high treason by existing," he explained. "Mmm," he held the moustache towards her as if sizing it up, and put on a silly voice, "I'm sorry, I think this is wrong for your colouring dahling! Change your hair instead." He handed her the wig and the sunglasses. Would it fit? "Can I be of assistance putting it on?"

She started to giggle again.

"You are such a clown! Why am I laughing? The police think I'm a terrorist, I'm consorting with a wanted felon and I probably owe the Festival Hall about £100,000."

Ah if only he had that one million Grongolian, thought The Pan. He'd buy something that would be of value anywhere, gold, or diamonds maybe. Then he'd pay off the debt and all would be fine. As it was, Arnold's smelly sandals! All he could do was jolly her along until he could think of a plan or, more likely, until she did.

He peeled the backing off the moustache and smoothed it across his upper lip.

"How do I look?" he asked as she replaced her spectacles with the huge sunglasses.

She started to laugh again.

"Like an ageing porn star who's been punched on the nose." He started to spray his hair and the paint made her sneeze. "Ugh, careful what you do with that stuff!"

"Sorry," he smiled at her and checked his face in the mirror again. "All done."

"Good. My go now."

She screwed her hair up into a bun but it was too curly to be controlled without kirby grips and it kept popping out when she tried to put the wig on.

"Would you like me to help you with that?"

"Yes please, people who wear wigs must have a special secret arm which pops out at rug-on time!"

"Well, people who wear wigs are quite often bald …" She gave him a sideways look. "And doubtless, bald people don't have quite so much hair to tuck in."

She coloured a little.

"Easy, Mister Pan—or—should that be 'tiger'?!" She guffawed. "I can't believe you used the phrase 'easy tiger' and then said you were doing your thing!" She was clearly comfortable with him, even if that last remark had stung a little.

"I was a trifle stressed."

"Take it from me, talking street is not for you and talking seventies street is an absolute no-no!"

"Now then, Ms Cochrane, that's no way to go on if you want one of my arms. I'll leave you struggling with that wig, go in there without a second thought and stuff my face with bacon butties all on my own!"

"You won't! You will only be able to sit there watching people eat bacon butties until you are delirious with hunger because I'm the one who has most of the money. Then you'll have to come back here, drooling and incoherent, and beg me to come and buy you some breakfast. Although, without me to tell you when your moustache has fallen into your tea, I'll only have to wait until it does, you're recognised and the police come and take you away. Then I'll get to keep this amazing space car."

She was thawing nicely now. He took mock offence.

"It's a snurd. Not a car and I would never trust you here with it and the keys." He held them up and jangled them for extra effect. "Not without me. So, while you win with your cruel barbs this time—because you are correct about the moustache—I will have my revenge later."

"I don't think so," she said.

"Mmm. We shall see." He smiled at her again. It was difficult to stop.

She held her hair up and he put the wig on for her with no further trouble.

"Thank you."

"Don't mention it. Shall we?" He got out, jumped over the bonnet and opened the passenger door for her.

"Milady," he said, bowing and gesturing to the road with one hand. It made her laugh.

"Shut up!" she said and climbed out.

Hand in hand, they walked across the rutted tarmac.

Chapter 18

Lucy shuffled down the hall in her slippers, aware that her nose was bright red, her hair greasy and that her breath if it wasn't vile already, would certainly be now because it would smell of the potion she'd just drunk. The doorbell rang again. She looked through the peephole.

Oh. Hang on.

It was black, as if somebody had put their finger over it.

"Ahem."

What the ...? Yes, she had heard a polite cough. Behind her. Inside the flat. She froze. There was somebody there, pretty much next to her. She could feel their body heat.

"Don't be afraid, I ain't gonna hurt yer," said a male voice.

"Says who?" asked Lucy.

"Says the fact you're still upright, girl."

Should she test out her self-defence training? That was sort of asking for a dig in the ribs with a nice sharp elbow, or a stiletto down the shin. Except she was wearing fluffy sheepskin moccasins and a dressing gown. It was tempting but he was probably a fevered vision, anyway. She'd look a complete spigot fighting with herself while what was probably just another couple of press spivs listened and chortled outside.

"Don't let him in," her new visitor, the one inside, or very possibly inside her head, told her.

"Why?" asked Lucy, beginning to turn in the direction of the voice.

"Don't turn round." Whoever it was took her by the shoulders firmly—but gently—and swivelled her back. "He's bad news, girl. I ain't joking."

"What about you?" said Lucy. "Are you bad news?"

"Not for you, treacle." Treacle? "You have to trust me though, when I tell you that that geezer out there is."

Well. He'd put his finger over the spyhole. He was obviously bad news.

"It's probably just the press again," she said. She wasn't going to admit she was scared.

"Take my word for it. He's no journo."

"OK, for now I will." She put the chain on and opened the door. Outside was a tall gentleman wearing an immaculate long black trench coat with understated military insignia; epaulettes, something round the arms. The coat was open, and underneath he sported a military jacket and a white shirt with, yes, that was a cravat. His trousers were black with a red stripe down the side and he was wearing knee-high suede boots, black, spotless and with spurs. Across his chest and round his waist he wore a black belt with a silver buckle and slung onto it were a couple of pouches, one of which, Lucy noticed, contained a gun. He had pale skin, almost greenish in the shade of the porch, black hair, chiselled features and he was wearing sunglasses which he removed to reveal a pair of dark grey eyes. He would have been very good-looking had his whole demeanour not been so totally devoid of warmth.

He rested one hand on the door frame and as the other curled round the door itself, she realised he was wearing suede gloves with a selection of rings on the outside. The trench coat fell open further as he moved and she caught a glimpse of a large star, a knight-of-the-garter kind of star, pinned to the chest of his jacket. He was tense. Tense in a lithe, big-cat-about-to-attack kind of way and she had a strong impression that if he wanted to, he could easily break the chain and force the door, which was disturbing. Her fevered mind clutched at a straw.

"Oh right. It's a hallucination," she said, with more hope than conviction.

He made eye contact.

"No. It is not."

His voice was horrible; soft, menacing and—could she use the word 'unspeakable' here? Yes. She could. Unspeakably evil. The hairs on the back of her neck stood up. And the way he looked at her. It felt as if he was looking into her very being in a most dark and malign way. As if he was taking something from her, her soul, her very essence, her spark of life. She was almost mesmerised. She wanted to look away but he held her gaze and she stood there, petrified, little-bunny-in-the-headlights style, feeling herself weaken as the energy drained out of her. He knew what he was doing and he was enjoying it. As her head began to swim she watched the corners of his mouth turn upwards in a malicious smile. This was the man who had followed Ruth, who had called her 'chosen'. It had to be. Without meaning to, she shuddered.

"You are afraid?" he asked.

Wow. The visitor standing behind her wasn't wrong, this guy was seriously bad news.

"No," she lied. "I have a temperature and flu." She coughed, ensuring she only made a half-hearted attempt to put her hand over her mouth. Whoever this was, she had no compunction about launching germs at him after the way he'd scared Ruth. Yes, and it wasn't just Ruth who was afraid of him, she thought as she looked up at him, probably everyone was.

"I am looking for Ruth," he said. "I am a friend."

Lucy suspected he was using the word 'friend' loosely; in the sense that he had heard Ruth's name and nothing more. Her flatmate would never, ever be friends with somebody like this, she was far too good a judge of character.

"I don't think you are," said Lucy's mind. "Oh, I see," said her mouth. Phew! Her brain was still at the controls.

"I am …" he took the hand off the door and waved it while he sought the right word, "concerned for her well-being."

"Like hell you are," said Lucy's brain. "That's very kind," said her mouth.

"It is imperative that I find her. You will tell me where she is," he said quietly.

"I think it's imperative you don't find her so I shan't," said Lucy's brain. "Oh I wish I could! I'm so worried about her," she told him. Oops, careful, don't lay it on too thick. "After she was kidnapped last night." She shrugged helplessly. "I couldn't say." Not a lie if he interpreted it the way she hoped.

He did.

"That is a pity."

"I'm sorry too." She put her hand to her mouth but made sure she left a big gap to funnel the germs through and coughed at him again. Take that, Mr Evil!

"No matter," he said casually. "I will find her."

Impressive how much malevolent intent a single human—was he human? probably—could load into a seemingly innocent statement.

"Let me know when you do." said Lucy.

"Yes," he said slowly. "I shall." He paused. "Should you hear from her you will telephone this number." He handed her a business card with a mobile phone number on it.

Lucy looked at the card and up at him.

"Of course, it goes without saying." That she would not be phoning him.

"Excellent. Good morning, Lucy."

Wait a minute. How did he know her name?

He turned on his heel and walked down the path and into the street. She watched him out of sight.

"That was a close shave." She shut the door and rested her head against it.

"Too right girl. You done good though," said the voice behind her, cheerily. "'S not many people could talk to 'im an' not crack."

"Have you just saved my life?" she said as she double-locked the door. Not that it would stop Mr Darcy's evil alter ego for more than a moment or two if he came back, of course.

"Might've done."

"Then thank you."

"'S OK."

She turned to face her—well yes, he probably was her saviour.

Behind her, or at least, in front of her, now, was a tall man-shaped thing. He, she guessed it was a he, was about six foot two and dressed in a pinstripe suit, like a 1940s gangster, except it was a perfect fit and the body inside it was definitely gangsta rather than gangster. He worked out. A lot. In fact, judging by the size of him, he probably didn't have time to do much else. She'd bet he boxed, too, judging by the look of his nose. Heavyweight, Lucy imagined. Yep. He was definitely uber buff this … was he a man? Lucy wasn't sure.

He smiled. It lit up his face and he had great teeth, she noticed. It was the rest that was scary. His eyes were a very unnatural shade of green, not unattractive but definitely not natural. She looked at him a bit more closely and began to feel rather strange. Yes, it wasn't a trick of the light, he actually did have orange skin, slightly clammy to the touch by the look of things and oh no—time to sit down possibly—antennae, one either side of his head. She knew it was rude to stare and that her mouth had fallen open but she didn't seem to be able to stop herself. She watched, wide-eyed, as the antennae tied themselves in a reef knot and then undid, slowly.

Everything seemed to wind down, he was speaking to her, his voice concerned but unclear, fuzzy, as if he was in another room and blackness started to creep in from the periphery of her vision.

"I think I'm going to faint," she whispered, and passed out.

Chapter 19

For what felt like the umpteenth time that day, Lucy woke up. The first thing that struck her was how much better she felt. More than better, well. The second thing was the smell of fish fingers, chips and peas which turned out to be real and which were beside her bed – not forgetting a bottle of ketchup – on a tray. The third thing was that, despite the fact the curtains were pulled and the room was very dark, she could tell it had been cleaned up, all the dirty paper hankies and half-used packs of aspirin had been tidied away and her work suit had been moved from the back of her desk chair where she'd flung it, put on a hanger and hung on the peg on the back of the door. Who had done that? Ah well, she'd find out soon enough. She turned to the most pressing matter on the list. Food.

Mmm mmm! Comfort food. She had forgotten how much she missed comfort food. Nigel was into fine dining and so was Lucy. Where they differed was his opinion of the humbler dishes in the culinary spectrum. She thought fish fingers were delicious and was a founder member of the SAS (Scotch egg Appreciation Society – they'd dropped the E because SAS sounded cooler). Nigel called fish fingers unsophisticated peasant food and scotch eggs *Las Bolas de Satan*. And Lucy was pretty sure the *Bolas* he was intending to refer to were actually called something else. Along with many other dishes, he regarded both as beneath him. Then again, Nigel was a snob and while Lucy was in love with him, there were a lot of aspects to his personality that she didn't actually like. He could be terribly pompous sometimes – most of the time really, she thought wryly. Hmm. She should forget about her absent boyfriend for a moment and concentrate on the important matter of eating. She sat up, plumped up the pillows, leaned back and put the tray on her lap.

Yep. Six fish fingers, chips, peas, ketchup and yes, result! A glass of blackcurrant.

She began to eat. Boy! That felt better. What a strange morning. She glanced at her watch, OK, day. She tucked into her fish fingers and took stock. She wasn't sure where reality stopped and fantasy began.

"Right," she said aloud. "The facts." No. Facts was the wrong word. "The course of events my brain is presenting me with? That'll do. What do I know for sure?

"One, I've been ill. Two, some kind soul has cleared up in here and made me one of my favourite comfort dishes. Three, I've been asleep. Those are the constants, the irrefutable truths.

"Now we get to the other things. One, unless it was a dream, the police came to see me this morning. They told me that Ruth disappeared last night in a flying car. If I hadn't had flu today I'd know whether or not that actually happened but frankly I think I might have dreamt it because nobody but Ruth would make me a lunch like this unless Nigel ..." No, definitely not Nigel.

"OK, two, Ruth rang me, I think, and told me the phone is bugged." That didn't sound very likely either. A brief sigh. Onwards and upwards. "Three, the press are looking for her along with very possibly the most frightening man I have ever met and they all came here to ask me. Four, I forgot to add the police to the list of people in number three. Five, I went out and bought some vile concoction to cure my flu without remembering. Six, amazingly, I drank it. Seven, even more amazingly it worked. Eight ..." Did she really want to say this out loud? Ah what the heck? "I think it's just possible that a six-foot slug in a zoot suit saved my life."

That was when she noticed a shape in the corner, a large, formidable shape and it moved.

"Seeing as you're foreign and you ain't never seen one, I'll let that go, but usually, you'd only say something like that to a Swamp Thing if you was hoping he'd give you a smack in the mouth."

"Oh, it's still going on. This is a trip, isn't it?" she said flatly. "I took too many aspirin and I'm delirious. Or am I in hospital, in a coma?"

"Nah, you're alright. You're in your bedroom with a Swamp Thing."

"A Swamp Thing. You."

"Yeh."

"Like in the film?"

"Yeh, like in the film." It growled resignedly. "'Cept I ain't green. I drew the curtains because I wanna talk to you before you see me again and get scared. I'm here to take care of you."

"I wasn't scared, I was shocked. There's a difference."

"You reckon?"

"Yes, I do reckon."

"Suit yerself."

"So. You're protection?" The dark shape in the corner shrugged.

"If you like. You ain't nuts, girl."

That was a relief even if having a very tall, very big orange thing in your bedroom was a little scary. Whatever was going on, this was a delicate situation so it paid to be polite.

"Thanks," said Lucy.

"'S no bother. There's this geezer who owes me a lotta money but he can't get hold of it unless I give him a hand. So if I want my cash, I gotta protect you, 'cause that's the hand I've gotta give him. 'S only for a day or two till the heat dies down. I brought you the flu stuff. There's a box on the tray an' all. You gotta eat one of them every four hours or the flu's gonna come back. 'S worst bit."

"Thanks for the warning." Lucy read the wording on the box. 'Mrs Poldark's Gnissoids, for efficacious relief of colds and flu.'

"They ain't exactly tasty."

"Never mind, neither is flu. So, they come from your home. Where is that?"

"A long way away, sweetheart."

"I see," she proffered the tray towards him. "Leftover chip?"

A laugh.

"Don't mind if I do."

Ah stuff it. She turned on the bedside light. He stood up, carried her desk chair over and sat on it the wrong way round, leaning on the back. Yes he was orange – really, really orange – with antennae. She tried not to stare. Uh-huh, concentrate on looking into his eyes then she wouldn't see anything weird. OK, she would, that was not a normal green. Good colour though, and they really did light up when he smiled.

"Who are you?"

"Big Merv." Yeh, she looked him up and down, she could see where he got that name from.

"What do I call you," she tried a joke, "apart from Sir?"

He smiled again. Displaying the perfect teeth.

"Merv's OK. What'll I call you?"

"Lucy is good."

"OK Lucy, how do you do?" He held out a large hand. It was going to be clammy and she didn't want to touch it but she didn't want to be rude either so she shook it. It was surprisingly warm and didn't feel the way she expected. She tried not to show her relief because that would have been rude too, and he was

built like the Incredible Hulk and as yet she wasn't one hundred per cent certain
he was on her side.

"How do you do, Big Merv," she said. "Thank you for being so kind to
me."

"'S no bother."

"It's still appreciated," she smiled, "I'm not sure what's been going on in the
last twenty-four hours but I think I need some help to work it out. If all this is
real then something's happened, something major and I'm even more worried
that my flatmate is the person it's happened to."

"My getaway bloke. That's what happened to your flatmate."

"And that's a good thing?"

Another shrug.

"Depends on your point of view, girl. He rabbits on like some bird with a
cop-on but he's a red-hot escape man. If she can stand all that backchat without
getting a headache she couldn't be in a better place. He's a top boy and no-one'll
catch up with them."

"What if she would actually quite like to be caught up with?"

"He'll wait, won't he? Hang on a mo'," another laugh. "You ain't thinking
the little squirt's kidnapped her are you?"

"Um, well, the police do. To be honest, I'm not sure yet. That's why I was
wondering if you knew." Except that if Lucy was being entirely honest she
meant 'yes' because she feared the police were right. Sure, Ruth hadn't sounded
kidnapped on the phone, frightened and nervous, maybe, there against her will,
possibly, but not on account of any particular person or at least, not in the
traditional he's-standing-next-to-me-pointing-a-gun-at-my-head manner – and
as a human rights lawyer, Lucy did have some limited experience of how that
sounded. Even so, the whole thing was too odd.

The Swamp Thing laughed.

"He wouldn't kidnap no-one. Not in a million years, girl, and when you
meet the fella you'll get the joke. He's yellower than a bowl of custard and he
couldn't hurt a fly."

"Is that a good thing?"

"Course it is. It's why he's the best."

"Can Ruth trust him though?"

"One hundred per cent! You've got no worries on that score, lady. He may
be yellow but he's salt of the earth. Saved my bacon a ton of times. I'd trust him
with my cobblers on a chopping block. Don't tell him I told you that though or

he'll never shut up about it. Blimey! To think the boys and I was gonna chuck him in the river." Lucy concentrated on keeping her face impassive and failed. She could feel her eyebrows disappearing upwards.

"You were going to chuck him in the river? I thought you said he was salt of the earth."

The orange turned a little darker, the result of a blush, presumably.

"Yeh." A shrug. "Didn't know that when I first met him though, did I?"

"Er, right. So you're not just any old Swamp Thing, are you? What do you do for a living?" she said cautiously. OK, so this Big Merv had saved her life but she was beginning to feel nervous again.

"I'm a businessman."

Yes. He would say that. The difficulty, now, was that Lucy was pretty sure everyone else would describe him differently.

"A businessman."

"Yeh, was, I'm retired, temporarily."

"I see—but occasionally your 'business' involves dropping people with lead boots on into rivers or incorporating them into concrete motorway stanchions?"

"Nah. Not often. If I make them think I'm gonna, that's usually all it takes. 'S a criminal waste to go on and kill 'em unless they're the sorts of blokes the world can do without."

"You *have* done it though, haven't you?"

The green eyes looked calmly into hers.

"Yeh. Once or twice." No hint of apology or regret; a simple fact.

Gulp.

"You asked," he added.

"Yeh. I asked. That doesn't make your answer any less sinister." She wasn't nearly as scared as she'd have expected but then, she didn't really believe him. He was bound to be laying it on, playing the hard man.

"I ain't proud of it but it had to be done." Oh yeh? She eyed him warily. "'S not like this place, where I'm from, girl. Anything sticks on me there and I'm dead meat, public execution, nonce on a spike." He tapped his forehead with one finger. "I got the Resistance and the Grongles on my back, and then there's all the blokes, who wanna be the boss, wanna fill my shoes," he counted them off on three fingers. "When it gets so it's me or them, it's gotta be them."

This didn't feel real. Lucy wondered, could she be in a coma? Best not to rule it out. Be wary but carry on as if everything was normal. Well, not normal but … oh never mind, carry on.

"If you're telling the truth, I'm very relieved to hear that you're on my side, Mister Merv," she told him cautiously. "In the meantime, would you mind waiting in the sitting room while I have a shower and get dressed?"

He went maroon.

"Sure girl. Sorry," he said and hurried out of the room.

Lucy needed time to clear her head. Yeh, she was going to have a shower and then she was going to find out what the hell was going on. First things first, though. She switched on her phone. A text arrived to inform her she had a message. She didn't want to get dragged into other matters straight away and she decided it could wait a minute. Instead, she rang her secretary with instructions to pass the crisis client to a colleague, along with her profuse apologies. Good. Now for some insurance. She couldn't tell her colleagues about Big Merv, she couldn't tell anyone the truth but she could tell Nigel enough to ensure that the police would be alerted if she disappeared. As usual, his phone went to voicemail so she left a message to say that if she disappeared he was to call the police and tell them to look for her body in the Thames. She also told him that someone called Big Merv would be the culprit. A bit melodramatic, perhaps but then again, Nigel was her boyfriend and as such he should be able to make allowances. Feeling slightly more reassured, she headed off to the bathroom.

Chapter 20

Ruth and the Pan chose a table in the beaten-up bus. It was full of mostly large and rotund men and women – although the odd one was small and stick thin. Very fast or very slow metabolism, she supposed. The fluorescent yellow high visibility jackets they were wearing, or which they had hung over the backs of their chairs, reflected the light and gave the room a strange artificial glow. It was like an advert for healthy breakfast cereal. They were clearly jolly types, laughing, joshing one another and generally having a good time. She wondered what they all did.

She sat with her back to the wall and watched them. At the counter, The Pan of Hamgee—she must find out his real name—queued to order breakfast with one of the meagre stashes of notes from her purse. They were going to run out of money soon. She would have to think about that. Where was the safest place to use a cashpoint? It would have to be sooner, rather than later, or the police might trace it or worse, her bank might stop her card. Perhaps there'd be a hole in the wall at the airport. Yes, there must be. After breakfast then.

Through the window in front of her Ruth could see a large building and when she read the sign on the side, the size and attire of the clientele began to make sense. It was a coach depot. These were people who sat at the wheel of a coach all day and when they weren't sitting at the wheel of a coach, judging by the shape of them and the amount of laughter she could hear, they were sitting at a table in this derelict bus eating bacon sandwiches and taking the mickey out of one another.

Ho hum. She watched the Pan's car—uh-uh! snurd (one day she would remember its proper name)—as it drove itself through the gate and parked behind the hedge among the bus drivers' cars, under a tree.

Smart move.

No! Get a grip, woman! Not smart, just programmed by somebody smart. This was a vehicle, an inanimate machine, it wasn't objective or clever and it certainly didn't have a personality. Except that the way it had revved at South Mimms, when the crowd gathered round it; that had sounded aggressive. And she had difficulty accepting it was a simple collection of nuts and bolts (albeit complicated ones) when it took the initiative and did things on its own. No it hadn't taken the initiative and done anything on its own, it was probably set to stealth park or something.

What was she going to do? This wasn't a drill. She was going to have to get her head round the events of the last twenty-four hours and fast. More importantly, she was going to have to do something about them. It was unpleasant to discover that a part of her life which she had more or less written off as nervous fantasy was real. Except the Pan of Hamgee. She kind of liked the Pan of Hamgee—not that it would be a sensible move to tell him—and she was going to have to educate him a little, especially around traffic lights. She watched as he walked over to their table and sat down.

"I've ordered a Bang On K'Barthan Greasy Fry-Up—they tell me you would call that a full English."

A Bang On K'Barthan Greasy Fry-Up? Please no.

"You didn't actually ask them for that, did you?"

"Do I look like a fool?"

"No, you just act like one." She smiled to make sure he realised it was a joke and he seemed pleased.

"I do believe you are taking the rip, Ms Cochrane. I told them I wanted what they were having," he pointed to a couple of the larger high-vis crowd who were tucking into a pair of loaded plates. "Twice. I didn't know if you wanted a whole one but I haven't eaten a square meal in twenty-four hours so I thought I could always help you if you were overcome by the quantity."

No chance. Not after Ruth had missed supper.

"Thank you, but I think I'll manage."

"Good. I like a woman who eats properly."

"Oh yeh? I don't reckon you're that fussy. I think you'd just like a woman, full stop."

He smiled and inclined his head.

"Usually, there's an element of truth in that but there's only one woman on my radar at the moment."

"I see," said Ruth, she locked eyes with him, intending to give a stern, I'm-not-remotely-interested stare but was surprised, not to mention alarmed, to discover she couldn't see it through. He smiled, undaunted but hopefully not unduly encouraged, and she looked hurriedly down at the table. Damn.

He waited, perhaps hoping she would ask for clarification. She decided it would be best to ignore what he'd said and pretended to concentrate on her knife and fork. He relaxed and turned his attention to the café's other patrons.

She seized the opportunity to examine his face more closely without being noticed. The bruising on his nose showed markedly in profile. It was coming out nicely; black and blue. Very blue. Like her shins. Yes, she was grateful to have been rescued but she was going to have to have a calm, non-angry word with him about the execution when the time was right. Although his bruises seemed almost too blue to be normal. Was he wholly human? Hmm. How could she put that thought in a way which would alarm her less? Was he different? Yes, 'different' was the word, coming from a parallel version of the universe and all of that. If he wasn't human, what was he? How long did he live? Was he, as near as dammit, immortal, with two hearts and an ability to regenerate like a Time Lord? Unlikely. He didn't behave like a man with lives to spare.

Ruth wondered where to start. The Pan of Hamgee was the only person who could help her. She'd never felt so at ease with anybody, outside her family, as she did with this strange and anonymous man. It felt good but it also made her nervous.

A corpulent, cheery chef brought over two plates piled high with full English, except that there was square sausage and potato scones; more of a full Scottish then. It was followed up with a pot of fresh filter coffee, on a tray, with milk and two mugs.

The Pan appeared to know what coffee was. He sniffed the pot appreciatively and poured it. There was a brief hiatus while they helped themselves to milk. Ruth took a sip. It was good.

"How are your shins?"

"Very bruised and they smart, *a lot*." No harm rubbing it in. He was embarrassed, close to the point of actually physically squirming. He couldn't look at her either. Good.

He shrugged helplessly.

"I'm sorry."

"So you should be. Although I'd guess you're not the biggest idiot round here because, heaven defend me, I'm going to ask for your help." He tried to conceal his reaction but this news clearly made him feel like a small child who has been given a big toy. He was pleased to be trusted and he couldn't hide it. Not at all. He'd be rubbish at poker.

"Your wish is my command," he said, with a little more relish than she was comfortable with.

"Good. I need to ask you some things," she said.

"Yes, I can imagine." He smiled wryly. He was trying to strike the right balance: to jolly her along but not at the expense of taking her seriously. It was kind and she was grateful.

"I need to tell you some things, too—about being inconspicuous."

"I see," said The Pan, the smile widened. "Where would you like to begin, the asking or the telling?"

Where indeed? There was a lot of ground to cover, although Ruth suspected he was clever enough to figure out most of the do's and don't's of existence in her version of the universe unaided. She glanced beyond him, across the road and into the car park where the paintwork of the Lotusy thing, the snurd, glinted through the hedge. With the benefit of hindsight, Ruth realised her memory was already dumping the reality of both escapes; presenting them to her as adrenaline-fuelled fun rather than the fearful flights they had actually been. He sat there, smiling at her.

"What's so funny?" she said and he stopped smiling abruptly, making an obvious effort to compose his features. Unfortunately he was incapable of keeping the smile out of his eyes which ruined the effect.

"Nothing in particular."

"Nothing in particular? Is there a bogey hanging out of my nose or something?"

He burst out laughing and she felt another flurry of panic because it pleased her to amuse him.

"No, Ms Cochrane, no bogies, I promise. If you want the truth, cheesy though it might sound, I'm just happy."

"Happy," she said guardedly.

"To be honest, I've been looking forward to meeting you for some time and now I have you are …" he looked her up and down. "Well, let's just say that in the flesh, you certainly don't disappoint. I'm delighted to be here that's all—please be assured I am taking you very, very seriously." Mocking her, mocking himself and too obviously the truth for her to be properly scathing. Even so, she gave it her best shot.

"You're happy, are you? With nowhere to go, on the run from the police—not to mention Lord Vernon."

"Ah yes …" He held his hands out and inclined his head in a slight bow. "I can see your point." He unleashed a dazzling smile. "However, you forget, I live like this every day, except it's better here. I'm far more afraid of the police where I come from. As for being relaxed, trust me, our current situation has nothing on the trouble I'm in at home."

Yeh, well, she could believe that one.

"Strange as it may seem, I don't need any convincing of that, Mister Pan. It's not just the disguises, it's that little hint you dropped about committing treason by existing. OK then, let's start with your car," she held her hand up in a no-don't-correct-me gesture, "I mean, your snurd."

"What about it?" Proud. The tone of a man who knows his wheels have impressed the girl.

"Well …" Flustered, because they had and she didn't want him to realise. "It's the only one of its kind on this planet." OK, so it was possible the CIA might have something similar but if she started to explain about them, things were going to get complicated. Ruth was too tired for complicated right now. "That means it makes us stick out like a sore thumb unless we can pretend it's a car. If we're going to do that, it can only do the things cars can do. So, while I think we have managed to get away with it, here, letting it park itself is probably a no-no."

"You mean I have to park it?" He looked shocked.

"Yes, Mister Pan. You have to park it, yourself, like everyone else." Her sternest possible tone. She wanted him to take this in.

"Why on earth would I do that?"

"Because, here, it's dumb not to. The only things in London which drive themselves are some of the trains; and most of those still have a bloke on them to sit there pretending. We're not good at machines which take the initiative on this planet. That means your snurd is going to be very conspicuous if it keeps going off on its own."

"But," he shrugged and spread his arms out. "How can I stop it?"

"What do you mean how can you stop it? It's a machine, isn't it? It's not supposed to have a mind of its own."

"Not officially, no, but I find myself wondering."

"OK, I can accept that. Can't you tell it to keep a low profile or something?"

He held out his hands, palms upwards in a theatrically Gallic gesture.

"I can try," he said.

Ah. She was thrown. She'd meant that last quip as a joke.

"I'll have a little chat with her, shall I?"

How sexist was that?

"Her? Listen buster, everyone knows all sports cars are blokes!"

"Not this one—and it's not a car, Ruth." No apology and the way he'd tacked that 'Ruth' on the end was a little more condescending than was called for.

"Don't get cocky with me, Mister Hamgeean," she told him coolly.

"Then don't get hot under the collar about nothing. If we're going to sort your life out, we have to get along." He paused. "I think we do get along. Perhaps a little too well, maybe that's the trouble." He wasn't wrong there but Ruth said nothing. "I'm sorry," he continued. "My nerves are probably as frayed as yours. I know I can be a bit prickly sometimes, I don't mean to be."

"You're not prickly, just very upfront. Do you talk to everyone like this?"

"Actually, no."

"Then why me?"

"Because we don't have time to stand on ceremony …" He stopped. "Alright, and also because it's easy, it's as if we've met before, as if I already know you."

"Ah yes, but as you sheepishly admitted earlier, Mister Pan, you've been stalking me, so it's only natural that you should dream up some imagined personality for me."

"It doesn't feel like it. As I believe I may have mentioned, you are …" A roguish smile. "Everything I hoped you'd be."

"Behave yourself, Mister Pan."

They ate in silence for a moment or two.

"When you were having a hissy—when we were having a bit of a tiff yesterday, you said something about having been followed for months," he said.

"Yes I did. Three to be precise."

"Was that by Grongles?" he asked cautiously. She nodded.

"I didn't know what they were then, I thought they were just big blokes." She thought about their colouring. "OK, big blokes who don't get enough daylight. The first one was Lord Vernon, after that it was just—"

"Lord Vernon? Himself?" asked The Pan in alarm.

"Yeh, he came looking for me and I hid."

"And he went away without you?" Incredulous.

"Yes." She was irritated. "Is that such a big surprise?"

"Don't take this the wrong way, Ruth, but yes. Are you sure it was him?"

"No. I thought it was the Queen of Sheba."

"Who?"

"Forget it, I was being sarcastic, the implication being, Mister Pan, that of course I'm flipping sure because Lord Vernon is difficult to forget." She pictured him in her mind's eye, standing on the roof, looking straight at her as he talked on the phone. He had radiated malevolence so strongly it was almost physical; swirling round his ankles like a cloud of poisonous, black, dry ice.

The Pan eyed her with concern. Her fear must be showing.

"Could it have been anyone else?" he asked, a definite tone of hope in his voice.

"Well, let's see. Is Lord Vernon the big scary guy who helped you to break London?"

"Yes."

"There we are then, it was him."

"Arnold." A short silence. "What happened?"

"I went to a comedy gig with some mates and missed the night bus, so I decided to walk home. I heard footsteps behind me and I realised somebody was following me; so I pretended I hadn't noticed and then, when I rounded a corner, I ran. He ran after me but I hid and, get this … While he was trying to find me, he sniffed the air. It was as if he could smell my fear."

"This might sound strange but he may have been trying to do that. Fear makes you sweaty and well … you know … sweat gets a bit smelly."

"That's completely vile."

"I know, but unfortunately it's true." He raised one arm a little and sniffed an armpit. "I'm not exactly minty-fresh, myself."

She laughed.

"You are unbelievably gross."

"I aim to please."

"And you're right, you honk but then I expect I do, too. If you've got a wig in your ca—snurd, how come there's no deodorant?"

"There usually is but the one in my room ran out so I took the can from the snurd and forgot to replace it." He stopped. "Sorry, I shouldn't have interrupted you, please, go on."

She told The Pan how frightened she had been. How she had shut her eyes and held her glasses behind her back as Lord Vernon shone a torch into the hedge where she was hiding. How it had startled a cat, which had bolted from a spot near her, making him think it was that he had heard, not her and how, finally, he had gone away. The Pan listened attentively throughout her story and after she had finished he was silent for some time.

"Mmm. Well Ms Cochrane, welcome to a small and exclusive club. Not many people escape from Lord Vernon once, let alone twice."

"That's what's worrying me. I keep wondering how long can I keep running and when I do that, I start thinking that the truthful answer is probably not for very long."

"I've managed five years so far."

"Yes, but even after this short time I can see you're different. Being chased by Lord Vernon would make most people insane after one week …" she stopped. "Actually, are you still sane?"

He laughed. "Relatively, and if I'm not I'm hardly going to tell you, am I? Did you see Lord Vernon again, I mean, between then and yesterday?"

"No. It was only the others. They might have been meant to get me on the tube, the night before last, but one of my neighbours turned up and scared them away."

"A neighbour?" The Pan looked thoughtful.

"Yeh, an old guy who lives at the end of my road, I carried his shopping home for him once and after that we—me and Lucy—we kind of adopted him."

"Mmm," said The Pan. He cast his eyes down and pushed a bit of sausage around his plate for a moment. He seemed thoughtful, as if filing away her words for later but kept to his current line of enquiry.

"Alright, so after three months of being followed by Grongles, you were on an underground train, on your own in the middle of the night."

"Well … yes."

"You're one brave woman, Ruth Cochrane."

"Not really. Until you showed up, I'd half convinced myself I was just being paranoid. People don't get followed and kidnapped in Britain. Not without an obvious reason, or at least, not often. So I wanted to get over it. Get back to my normal life and stop being such a massive wimp."

"I'm not buying this wimp business. You're far too bright for that."

"Yeh right. What's brain got to do with it?"

"You have the intelligence and imagination to realise exactly what's happening but you carry on regardless. That's true bravery. Courage is easy if you're too stupid to realise what you're about to do. I'm afraid the heroes I've met have been very disappointing; boneheaded rather than lionhearted, to a man."

She laughed.

"Not bitter and twisted about that, are we, Mister Pan?"

He pulled a face.

"Very possibly. I, too, have an imagination but unlike you, I'm yellow to the core. So I expect my cynicism is merely a convenient way of deflecting my attention from my own cowardice." No shame. He seemed totally comfortable with the idea. "And of course, they do tend to get all the girls, these brave thickies and that *is* galling." Ah, now there was the nub of the issue. She laughed.

"I expect you're chasing the wrong types of girls."

"I doubt there is a right type of girl for someone like me."

"Don't be daft, of course there is, somewhere, you idiot!"

He chuckled, "Possibly, Ms Cochrane but at the moment, it's too early to tell."

"What's that supposed to mean?"

"You'll have to wait and see, won't you?"

Chapter 21

Lucy returned from the bathroom, got dressed in her weekend clothes – there was no point in going to work now – and checked her phone. There was a text from her secretary to say he had sorted out the emergency client. Hoorah! There was a second text from her voicemail message service too. She dialled the number and listened as the plastic lady told her she had a missed call from Nigel's phone number. She was relieved. The message played automatically.

"Lucy," said Nigel's voice. Phew. She sat down on the bed and listened to the rest of the message but her relief at hearing from him turned quickly to dismay. It was short, pithy and eloquent enough to leave her in no doubt that she was absolutely, comprehensively dumped.

For a few moments Lucy didn't know what to think. Part of her was almost grateful to Nigel for doing what she knew she should have done herself, but had lacked the courage to do. Part of her was cringingly embarrassed at having rung him for help, without picking up his earlier message binning their relationship but, unfortunately the biggest part of her was broken-hearted. And there were ways of doing these things and Nigel's method was about as cruel as it got. Was it so difficult to come and see her and tell her to her face? Well, clearly, yes. Then again, on the upside being dumped by voicemail was marginally better than being dumped by text. No, actually it wasn't. Not at all.

The tears bubbled up and she threw herself onto the bed and sobbed. A short time later, she was disturbed by a gentle knock on the door. She ignored it and after a few minutes she heard the sound of quiet footsteps retreating back down the hall to the sitting room.

Chapter 22

Back in K'Barth, Deirdre was giving Mrs Pargeter her first knife-throwing class.

"No, D'reen, you're holding it wrong," she turned the blade round and adjusted the elderly lady's arm and hand. "There. Try now."

Mrs Pargeter threw, and there was a metallic ping as it glanced off a washing machine several feet to one side of the wooden barrel she was aiming at. Deirdre dodged as it flew back past her ear.

"Oh dear."

"It's an improvement. At least you got some force into that one. But that's enough for today."

Deirdre pulled the knife out of the wooden washing prop behind her, glad of her excellent reflexes, and tucked it back in the holster strapped to her thigh. The dress had its uses after all – for the purposes of concealing weaponry it could have been sent by The Prophet himself.

"Oh I did enjoy that!" said Mrs Pargeter, beaming.

"Good. We'll try again tomorrow with something less sharp." Mrs Pargeter was almost as clueless at throwing a knife as Deirdre was around laundry. Even so, Deirdre couldn't help liking her.

Things were going slightly better this morning. Deirdre and Mrs Pargeter were on late lunch, which meant they had half an hour to themselves manning – or at least womanning – the laundry, while everyone else went to the servants' hall and ate. It was the perfect opportunity for some private weapons training, even if the knife throwing was far from perfect.

"All that excitement has got me in a dither," said Mrs Pargeter. "Would you be alright on your own if I just popped to the lavvy?"

Deirdre could hardly refuse, even though she knew her colleague would be ages. Mrs Pargeter moved slowly and the ladies was a long way away in the next quad. Never mind. Deirdre held the door open for her and then spent a few minutes hacking the end off a piece of wood used to stir vats of bleach. She was starting to whittle it into a replica of her knife when the phone rang. She picked it up.

"Laundry," she barked and remembered just in time that she was supposed to be humble. And polite. "At your service," she added hastily.

"This is Corporal Puneschment. Laundry collection required from Room A."

There was a protocol for this, she remembered. She scrabbled about and found the collections book. All collections were ordered by phone and scheduled in advance. Room A? Where was that? Was it one of the Blurpon-only routes? She wasn't sure. Never mind that now, she could ask Snoofle or Mrs Pargeter when they got back. Best take the booking, they could sort out any errors later.

"We have a space at half-four."

"No, you come now."

"I can't, my colleague's gone for a—is otherwise engaged and I'm the only one here."

"You are new here, underling?"

"Yes."

"You would be. Then, let me make this easy for you. What we've got here is Lord Vernon's laundry. So, either you come and collect it now or he comes down there and rips your head off: choose."

"Alright," snapped Deirdre. "I'll be up in a minute." Undercover or not, she didn't appreciate being upbraided by someone of inferior rank. Better do this properly, though. She asked him directions and wrote them down. Deirdre knew she would get into trouble for leaving the laundry, especially if Room A was a Blurpon-only pickup, but she'd get into even more trouble for disrupting its good relations with the Lord Protector. Anyway, no-one would find out. Mrs Pargeter would be back soon enough and so would she.

She ripped the page of instructions out of the notebook, grabbed a map of the Palace and a trolley, and set off.

Chapter 23

Lord Vernon was still no closer to finding the Chosen One or the wretched Hamgeean but now that he had spent the morning venting his frustration, all in the laudable purpose of questioning political prisoners, he felt a great deal more relaxed about the situation. Washed and dressed in a clean uniform, it was time to turn his attention to the daily round of papers to sign before lunch. But first he must send the soiled uniform to the laundry. He had approached the interrogations with enthusiasm and while it had made him feel better, his clothes had suffered. Perhaps he should put aside one set of uniform for interrogation only. Yes, that might be the answer. He would also return the latest batch of suede gloves which had not been cleaned to his exacting standards. He picked up the internal phone and dialled to have his laundry collected.

He sat in his chair and while he waited for one of the launderers to arrive, his thoughts revisited the morning's bloodletting.

Usually, he preferred clean precision to gore and mess but today he had surrendered to his anger and frustration with no attempt at self-control. The results had been cathartic, not to mention spectacular. He closed his eyes and saw again the blood—so much blood—and the fear of his victims, so strong he could smell it. These worthless K'Barthan non-beings would be cleansed from the planet soon enough but for now he was their god, their vengeful god. They were his, to use as he pleased; and there were millions of them.

He opened his eyes abruptly. No more fantasising, he had indulged himself enough. A little excess was all very well but his baser instincts must be channelled, honed, restrained and—he smiled—used creatively.

Within minutes there was a knock at the door. Lord Vernon turned in his swivel chair.

"Yes?"

"Laundry," said one of the guards outside as he opened the door.

A tall, leggy blonde stood in the doorway and at once he was intrigued. He had not seen her before, she must be new. He stood up and walked over to where she was standing.

"You work in the laundry?"

"Yes, Your Gracious Exaltedness."

He raised his eyebrows.

"Sir is sufficient. Our launderers are usually Blurpons."

"Yes, Your Gracious Exaltedness but the Master of the Laundry prefers that they remain downstairs." Her tone was a little sarcastic for Lord Vernon's taste. Perhaps he should teach her some manners.

"Really. And why should that be?" He moved closer to her, invading her personal space.

She stood her ground.

"Poor people skills, Your Gracious Exaltedness." That defiance and her continued use of his full title, after he had ordered her to call him 'sir', would normally have annoyed him. However, nothing vented his frustrations like an hour or two taking care of state business, especially at the levels of indulgence he'd allowed himself this particular morning. Right now, Lord Vernon felt almost tolerant. He was supremely relaxed.

"I believe I told you that 'sir' is sufficient," he said.

"Yes, sir. Thank you, sir," Lord Vernon was especially feared by the non-Grongolian female staff. Naturally, to females of his own race he was suave, debonair and a picture of decorum. Casual liaisons were frowned upon in Grongolian society, so, like most red-blooded Grongle males, Lord Vernon got many of his sexual kicks from the females of other species; in his case, the less willing the better. It was useful that there were so many in his employ. As non-beings they were fair game and he used them at will. This one was human; a pleasing sight, good-looking for a piece of worthless K'Barthan trash; so much so that he wondered about putting aside his papers and inviting her to sit down. It wasn't as if she could refuse, he owned her. His gaze travelled slowly down to her cleavage and up again. Her ice blue eyes met his, her expression cold and haughty. She was different. Confident to the point of defiance but that didn't change the balance of power. He could do what he liked with her. He would, too. And even better, she would fight. It would be exquisite. What a pity he was so busy. No matter, she wouldn't be going anywhere for three months. He added her to his mental 'to do' list.

"Get these cleaned, please." The strong, metallic smell of blood rose from the laundry bag that Lord Vernon thrust at her. Her eyes met his, knowing and still unafraid. There was something about her that Lord Vernon recognised in his own face. He was looking into the eyes of a killer. Very interesting. This was no laundress.

For the easy dissemination of misinformation, and to make them feel they were achieving something, Lord Vernon had inferred to General Moteurs that the Resistance should be allowed to infiltrate the Palace in some small way. With all those angry Blurpons in their ranks, and the entire race's lauded laundering skills, he supposed the laundry was the obvious place. However, clearly the Resistance Blurpons were rusty when it came to their traditional skills. It explained why they had cleaned yesterday's batch of suede gloves so badly, of course. Which reminded him: he leaned past her and grabbed the offending items, still half-wrapped in their brown paper, from a shelf by the door.

"I would be grateful if you could inform your Blurpon colleagues that I require my gloves pristine. These," he dropped the paper package, disdainfully, into the bag she was holding, "are not."

"Sorry, sir," she said.

Her voice, her demeanour and her tone all unrepentant. That was annoying and yet also, interesting. Should he teach her some humility right now? No. He had already gorged himself and he preferred to ration his treats. And this would be a rare treat, he thought, as he gave her another slow look up and down. The temptation was almost irresistible as he imagined how he would bend her, break her, use her up. As she read his intentions he saw fear in her eyes for the first time and he savoured it, holding her gaze well beyond the point when she wanted to look away. Wide-eyed, half mesmerised, unable to defend herself, she let him see into her soul. She was not so tough. He ran one finger down the side of her face. Oh he could do it now if he wanted but he would wait. Such a tasty morsel should not be rushed and he must ensure he set aside a suitable amount of time to appreciate the experience. For now he would let his anticipation build, fantasise, plan until he could contain his desire no longer. Then he would have her brought to his rooms and she would learn some deference. He closed his eyes and took a jagged breath in. Oh yes, and how he would teach her.

"Get out." He pushed her into the corridor and slammed the door in her face.

Chapter 24

Nothing had prepared Deirdre for meeting Lord Vernon in the flesh. The minute he opened the door she saw the danger she was in. What had made her think she could brazen it out? Her confusion, she supposed. When he handed over his laundry personally it had thrown her.

However, for all the aura of latent menace emanating from him, Lord Vernon had been polite and clearly did not realise she was anything more than her alias: Rosa Trampleasure, a simple country girl from Tith who had come to work in the city. It would have stayed like that if Deirdre hadn't allowed her relief to make her complacent. Arnold. Was it so hard to act the part? She was so unsuited to this kind of mission it was laughable. Then Lord Vernon had handed her the bag of soggy uniform and the wheels had really fallen off because even in front of Lord Vernon, himself, when her life depended on it, Deirdre couldn't be 'Rosa'. And he'd looked into her eyes and she could hide nothing from him. When he had finished, she realised he knew exactly who she was. And, just in case she didn't understand what that meant … She shuddered as she remembered the sensation when he touched her face. He had made his intentions very, very plain.

Somehow, Deirdre got to the service lift and waited until the doors had closed, before she fell to her knees in the corner and retched.

What had she been thinking of? Everyone knew what the worst Grongles did to women. Everyone. And Lord Vernon was the worst of the worst. And he got anything he wanted and Deirdre realised with sickening dread that, right now, he wanted her. She wondered if she would survive the experience. No, judging by the way he had looked at her.

She would have to find Snoofle and she'd be in trouble for going out of the laundry without an escort. She'd be in even more trouble for wrecking her mission. So much for being incognito, she had just made herself conspicuous with a capital C. She wasn't dead yet; one objective achieved out of three then, but it was time to leave or hide, now, before one became zero.

Chapter 25

Lucy lay on her bed clutching a sodden handkerchief in one hand and her phone in the other. She had been there too long. She had to go and look in the sitting room to see if there was anyone there – if the orange Thing in the suit was real or imaginary. Best to stop crying before she checked, just in case. The problem, of course, lay in the fact that Lucy was beginning to wonder if she ever would stop crying. She lay, face down on the covers, mentally berating herself for being such a soppy fool while the sobbing continued. She didn't notice the door open, or even register when somebody sat down on the bed, but then Big Merv scooped her upright, pulled her against him and put his arms round her.

The shock stopped the tears for a brief moment. She pulled back from him a little and then realised that he felt soft and warm, and that the sensation of his arms around her was comforting and kindly meant.

"There, there, girl. You cry it out," he said. She buried her head in his chest and sobbed some more while he patted her back gently. He seemed to realise what the problem was because he added, "There's plenty more fish in the sea."

"Bloody Nigel," she mumbled into his lapel. For a moment Lucy was distracted by Big Merv's cologne. She liked it. She could hear his heart beating. The lapel of his jacket was soggy against her cheek but she could still feel the quality of the fabric. It was a fantastic suit, bespoke-tailored with consummate skill, with a pure silk lining by the looks of things. Lucy felt guilty crying all over it and said so. Big Merv laughed.

"'S only a suit. I got plenty more. You wanna talk about it? C'mon, tell Uncle Merv."

Uncle Merv. That was the way her grandad talked to other people's pets. The thought almost made her giggle and she felt a bit better. She sat back and smiled weakly. It wasn't great, as smiles went, and she was snotty-nosed, puffy-eyed and her face would be all red and blotchy but never mind, it would have to do. He kept one arm round her shoulders and without saying anything, handed her a clean handkerchief.

"Thanks."

"'S OK honey. Who's Nigel?" She blew her nose with an embarrassingly loud parp.

"Nigel is my boyfriend—or, at least, he was. It seems that, as of this charming message, he is my ex-boyfriend." She dialled her voicemail.

"You gotta mobile," he said. "Sweet. We ain't allowed these back home."

"Most people have a mobile here," said Lucy, navigating the menu to replay Nigel's message and handing the phone to Big Merv. "Here. Have a listen. That's my boyfriend, dumping me." She noted, with relief that she was already getting onto the angry stage. Good. When Big Merv had finished, he handed back her phone. "Why am I in love with a sap like that?"

Big Merv smiled.

"I was gonna ask you the same thing."

"It galls me to the core. I'm an intelligent, aspirational, career woman. You'd have thought I'd know better."

There was a pause.

"Nah. Don't beat yourself up sweetheart. There ain't no accounting for the heart. He sounds like a right tool-bit. I'd say you're well shot of him. Ah, you ain't gonna see it that way now but I reckon you will."

"Oh, he was completely vile quite often. I was going to end it myself but I was waiting until, well …" she sighed. "Until I was a bit less in love with him. I know I'll get over him but what a git, swanning off to Prague with his assistant and then dumping me over the phone. Not even over the phone, by voicemail."

"Yeh. Still, it won't be so hard to get over the little scrote now, will it?" Big Merv smiled and squeezed her shoulders. "Not now he's shown you who he is. Course, if you want, I could always pay him a visit. Teach him a few manners."

"Big Merv, you are clearly very bad and seeing how tempted I am to say yes, so must I be. I can just see his face if you turned up. He'd be petrified. He'd probably pee his pants." She burst out laughing but in a slightly manic way that scared her. "It would be wrong, though. I'm a lawyer, that's not how we're supposed to behave."

"It don't stop 'em at home."

"Maybe but I live here and British lawyers aren't that morally dubious."

He nodded. "Yeh, I get that. Suit yourself." Gently, he disentangled himself from her and stood up. "I reckon it's time we was going," he said. He went and picked up a wide-brimmed trilby from her dressing table and she watched the tips of his antennae turning themselves inwards and disappearing underneath it as he put it on.

"Where to?" asked Lucy warily.

"Place called the Royal Automobile Club. You know it?"

"Yes, I do."

"Good. You gotta pack an overnight bag and one for Ruth an' all if you're able."

"Whoa, whoa, whoa! We're not going away."

"Yeh, we're going away. I gotta keep you safe."

"Can't you do that here?"

"No can do, lady. Remember that guy who paid you a visit? Good-looking bloke, sunglasses, uniform …"

"He's difficult to forget."

"Yeh. Well, sooner or later, he's gonna come back and when he does, we wanna be somewhere else."

"Can't you just … protect me?"

"Nah. I ain't no match for the likes of him."

"You look like a match for most people."

Big Merv shook his head emphatically.

"Not him. He's one evil mother."

"And you …?"

He chuckled.

"I'm just a bad one. 'S not for long, girl. A couple of nights until the end of the week, tops, while we fix things up for you and—wait a mo." He put his hand in his jacket pocket and pulled out a letter. "I forgot. The old geezer what brought me here, the one I'm doin' a favour for, he ain't got the time to stay to explain himself, so he asked me to give you this. It's all in here. You gotta go stay with Sir Robin Get." He handed her the envelope.

"Oh, that's not so bad then, he only lives down the road."

"Nah. At the RAC. He got the flat here to look out for you two. But since it ain't no safer than this one he's inviting you to his real pad."

"At his club?"

"Yeh. It's swanky, girl, you'll like it."

Lucy looked up at him doubtfully.

"I tell you what, take a butcher's at the letter, have a think and let me know if you're gonna hang around here or come with me."

If it meant Mr Evil would come back, there was no way Lucy would stay where she was. A broken heart was bad enough, she decided, without risking a broken neck to go with it. Even so, she took the time to read the letter. Looking at the handwriting, she was as sure as she could be that it came from Sir Robin. He had invited her to stay for a night or two and he'd written that he 'encouraged her most strongly' to trust Big Merv. She glanced over the top of the letter at her visitor. This was quite an adventure. She sent a brief text to her secretary asking him to call her at the club at eight o'clock the following morning. If she wasn't there, he was to ring the police and get them to look for Sir Robin. It wasn't much but it made her feel a bit more sensible about what she was about to do which was, basically, to be utterly foolish. Finally, she packed an overnight bag for Ruth and herself and carried it into the hall.

"I'll take that," said Big Merv.

"Thank you. You may be a bad mother but you're also a gent."

He smiled.

"A few manners never hurt no-one. You ready?" he asked when she had checked for the umpteenth time that she had her wallet, her mobile phone, the charger and her keys.

"Yes."

"Good," he stopped. "This is gonna surprise you but we ain't going out the front. 'S a load of blokes out there, watching and we don't wanna be seen. You get me?"

"Er … yes … I'm not going out the back though. Garden hopping is not for me."

"Nah. You won't have to do none of that." He slung the overnight bag over his shoulder before taking a small jam jar out of his pocket and unscrewing the lid. "Here." He held out his hand.

"You want me to hold hands with you?"

"Yeh."

Lucy sighed resignedly and did as he asked.

"Give us a sec, sweets. I gotta remember this right." He screwed up his eyes and thought for a moment. "Should do," he muttered, and curled his thumb over the edge of the jar. There was a sucking sound, like bathwater going out, only louder. Lucy tried to withdraw her hand but Big Merv was holding it tightly and there was no escape. Her surroundings blurred, seemed to whizz past for a split second and then she was standing in a small side street. Big Merv threw the jar swiftly onto the pavement and stamped on it, grinding it to dust beneath his heel. Lucy was impressed. Swamp Things must be pretty strong and she was glad this one was on her side.

"Wh-what did you just do?" she asked.

"It's an illegal portal, one use only then you smash it fast so they can't get no trace. They'll know someone used one and they'll know it was in London but with any luck no more 'an that."

Blimey. Interesting but not the information Lucy was after.

"No, I meant the thing before that, with the noises and the um ... teletransportation."

"I dunno how it works but it's safer than walking outta your front door past all them blokes watching to see what you do and where you go."

"Who would be watching my flat?"

"People who wanna find your mate. There's a lot of 'em about. Now we've gotta go. It ain't safe to stay here. I can tell you more when we get indoors." He held up an A to Z. "I reckon we go up there, left and it's on our right ..."

"Who the hell are you? What have I got myself involved with here?"

"Lady, we ain't got time for this. We gotta get out of here, fast. Sir Robin Get told you to trust me. Are you gonna do that?"

"Yes, but what now? You're orange, and you have antennae and you can't just stroll around London. People will ... talk," she said weakly although privately she was more concerned that they'd faint the way she had.

"Nah. If you're happy to carry the bag, no-one'll even notice but we gotta go, treacle, pronto."

Treacle? Again? No. "OK, we'll go but Big Merv ..."

"Yeh?"

"My name is Lucy and I'd really like you to use it," she smiled, hoping he wouldn't be upset. He just laughed and held out the overnight bag.

"Sorry Luce."

Luce ... well, usually only Ruth called her that but it would do.

"You can call me 'Merv' an' all. No 'Big'."

"OK Merv." She took the bag from him and hefted it over one shoulder.

"You ready?"

"Yes."

"Then c'mon." Once again she was amazed at the way a little thing like a smile could light up such a stern face. Yeh, and he really did have great teeth.

Chapter 26

Lord Vernon's guards interrupted him again, this time to announce the arrival of General Moteurs. Lord Vernon made a point of reading and signing the papers in front of him before standing up, suddenly.

"General, how convenient. A word, if you please."

"Certainly, Your Gracious—"

"Sir is enough."

"Thank you, sir."

Lord Vernon strolled over to one of the easy chairs and sat down. As usual, General Moteurs remained standing, waiting to be invited before he sat. Always at pains to please his master, he seemed uneasy. Still aware of his failure to capture the Chosen One, perhaps? Even if, having met with a similar lack of success, Lord Vernon was now a little readier to show some understanding on that score.

"Please join me." Lord Vernon gestured to the other, less comfy chair. "You have news for me?"

"Yes, sir. It is possible that an opportunity has arisen to locate the Chosen One—if you are not too busy."

"No General, I am not too busy."

"Thank you, sir. We have intercepted the police communications in her reality, it seems she is still with the Hamgeean and they have taken to the air again. The humans lost them near something called …" he flipped open his phone and tapped the screen a couple of times. "London Heathrow, it's an airport, sir, where—"

"I know what an airport is, General."

"They disappeared over one of the runways. According to the transmissions we've intercepted, all routes out of the area are being watched. Thus far, there is no sign of our quarry. They may have stayed nearby, lying low, waiting for their pursuers to leave. That narrows the search area, although there is still a great deal of ground to cover."

Lord Vernon took his smartphone and the Interceptor's keys from an occasional table between the chairs.

"Send me the coordinates, General."

"Yes, sir." General Moteurs tapped away swiftly and adeptly at his own smartphone with his thumb – a humble army-issue smartphone, Lord Vernon noticed. That was an impressive lack of pretension. The General was authorised to use a top-of-the-range version like his master's. "It is done, sir."

"Thank you." Lord Vernon watched the screen of his phone, waiting for the General's text message to come through. "A quick query while we are waiting, General. It seems the Resistance have infiltrated the laundry."

"Yes, sir."

"I appreciate they can do less to upset the household there than in many other places. However, should they wish to stay there, could you find a handful of their more peaceful brethren to teach them at least the rudiments of the laundering arts? I do not appreciate looking like a vagrant."

"Consider it done, sir."

"Good." Lord Vernon's phone beeped as the coordinates arrived from the General's. Again he turned his attention to the screen.

"Thank you," he said distractedly. "That is all. You may go." General Moteurs rose to his feet but hesitated. Unwillingly, Lord Vernon dragged his attention away from his phone. "There is something else?" he asked.

"Yes, sir."

"Well?"

"As I have explained, the search area is sizeable. If you require some of my team to assist you—"

"No, General," Lord Vernon cut in. "I may trust you but I am afraid I do not trust your team—nor my powers of restraint if they fail me again. I shall see to this, without interference from others. In this manner, only I am to blame if I fail."

"Sir."

"Is there anything else, General?"

"No, sir."

"Then that will be all."

Chapter 27

Back in the bus café Ruth and The Pan were enjoying their breakfast. "You said your neighbour saved you from the Grongles. That's interesting, he must be some bloke," said The Pan.

"I think maybe he is. Can I ask you something?"

"Go ahead."

"How did you end up being a getaway driver? Only, you don't strike me as the criminal type."

She listened as The Pan told her how he had fetched up working for Big Merv, a gangland boss. She tried not to show her shock as he explained how he had agreed to drive, in exchange for his life, after accidentally setting fire to a block of flats belonging to Big Merv. He told the tale with wit and humour, like a joke or a tall story and when he finished she guffawed before she could stop herself.

"You complete spanner!" she said and he laughed with her.

"Yeh, he was a trifle upset."

"I bet," said Ruth, still laughing. "So, being a bank robber—"

"A getaway man."

Was the difference so important? "Whatever, is that why your existence is treason?"

"No," a shrug, "I was already on the blacklist. That was the reason why I ended up working for Big Merv, though. When you're a GBI, you can only work for people who pay cash and aren't afraid of offending the government. When you're blacklisted, even the Resistance tend to prefer the reward money. Not that I'd want to get involved with them. They're a bunch of nutters."

"Don't tell me. Extremists," said Ruth.

"Yeh. They say they're fighting a holy war to liberate the people in the name of Nimmism—that's our religion—but really, they just want to control everyone. If they got into power they'd be no different to the Grongles; no freedom of speech, everything run by the military. Except it's more of a betrayal from them. I'm sure they'd say it was for our own good and all done in the name of The Prophet, but nothing would change for the people living under them. Well, except the names of the bunch at the top."

"Swapping the people holding the whip."

"That's a very good way of putting it. Do you know they want to exterminate the entire Grongolian race? I find that hard to reconcile with a religious viewpoint when the central command of Nimmism is that we should be decent to one another. Most of us are smart enough to see that genocide and brotherly love don't sit well together but they think we're so stupid we'll miss it. They pretend to be something they're not and treat the rest of us like children. At least the Grongles make no pretence about what they are."

Hmm. She got that.

"Have you really been on this blacklist five years? Only, it sounds like a long time."

"Yeh, longer than most. It was my sixteenth birthday present from Lord Vernon. I'm good at running away."

"It can't have been very nice." Nice? Aaargh no, no, no. So anodyne, so gauche. What was she thinking? He gave her a searching look as if he wasn't sure whether or not she was genuine.

"No, it wasn't. It was only a few days after I bumped into him. We'd had a massive family row about how I couldn't keep my mouth shut and I stormed off to the beach to sulk. When I came home the house was empty. The Grongles had ransacked the place and nailed a note to the door informing me of my status."

Ruth thought about what she had been doing when she was sixteen; exams mostly, falling in love for the first time, holidays – one with family, and her first trip away with friends. Definitely the odd row, too. What would it have been like to come home one day and find everyone gone for ever?

"So, what did you do?"

"I packed some clothes, the few portable things of value the Grongles hadn't taken and took off. I didn't expect to last long on the blacklist. Nobody does. They'd only have put me on it to save resources, couldn't be arsed to hang around and kill me I expect. It's ironic that I'm still here, isn't it? Especially when it's my fault that my family aren't."

"Oh come on! It can't have been."

"No, trust me. It was." His voice was bitter. "When Lord Vernon tripped over me I didn't just insult him. I told him my name and address. He'd have put two and two together and come up with the perfect excuse to get Dad. He was probably looking for one, I didn't know it at the time but my father was a bit of a rebel, a leader in the Underground."

"I thought you said—"

"No, not the Resistance. Different organisation. The Underground. They're moderate, the people who ran the old state, I suppose. Lord Vernon would have found a way to get Dad in the end, I just wish … I would do anything to be able to put the clock back and not be the one who handed it to him." He stopped. She didn't know what to say so she waited, listening. He rallied a little. "I'm sorry, there's no point getting maudlin. It's too late now. The people I love are dead. All of them. And there's nothing I can do."

He raked his hands through his hair and a load of the grey dye came off. She passed him a napkin.

"Then maybe you should try to let it go," she said gently. "If your Dad was a rebel he must have known what he was doing. I read somewhere that when stuff like this happens the person who escapes often gets something called survivor's guilt. It's a known psychological phenomenon."

A mirthless laugh.

"Oh really, is that so?" Dry, almost acid. Not a happy man.

"Yes."

She ignored his tone, if he was angry with anyone it was with himself, not her.

"Nice try, unfortunately I was an out-and-out arse. I gave Lord Vernon the perfect excuse. Of course, he was only Sergeant Vernon then, and he ran a tinpot rural police station. Now he's Lord Protector of all K'Barth and I am a dead man walking. As you can see I pick my enemies with panache and style. Pity I keep my intellect so far out of it."

She smiled but couldn't laugh.

"There you go. So if your father was a rebel, and already known to the police, that's proof positive that it was only a matter of time before they arrested him. From what you've told me about K'Barth it sounds inevitable—the only difference is that you weren't included. Think what that must have meant to your parents, to know that the Grongles hadn't got the whole family; that you were still out there, alive. It would have given them hope."

Yeek! Slow down, Ruth. She could hardly say she knew how it felt, could she? These things were beyond the limits of her experience. Who was she to offer opinions about any of this? She waited, expecting, at the least, a withering retort. Instead he gave her a long measured look. His emotional response was unmistakable: respect. She was half surprised and half worried by how good that made her feel.

"I've never thought of it like that," he said.

"Beating yourself up over it isn't going to make it any better or bring them back."

"I know. You're right. You sound exactly like them, you realise that, don't you?" A hint that this wasn't necessarily a good thing. "They were a lot wiser than me." A shy smile. "I think they would have liked you."

"I'm not that wise, you know."

"Mmm. You can say that Ms Cochrane, but I think you might be."

"No. Not yet and certainly not when I was sixteen." Her cheeks were burning. For heaven's sake, it was only a simple compliment. Why did her face keep doing this to her? "For what it's worth, I think you should give yourself a little leeway, Mister Pan." Hiding behind mock formality again, anything to deflect his attention from her embarrassment. "I bet I'm not the only one who thinks that, either. What do your other friends say?"

"I'm on the blacklist, consorting with me is treason. I have no other friends."

"You mean you've never told anyone this?"

"No."

"What?" A sharp intake of breath before she could stop herself. Carrying all of that on his own took serious strength of character. Didn't he realise? "Blimey. I think I am honoured Mister Pan."

He drained his coffee and perked up a little.

"Perhaps you are," he said and moved the conversation swiftly on.

Chapter 28

"Any more questions?" The Pan asked as he poured himself a second cup of coffee.

"Rather a lot, actually."

"Go on then. Hit me."

"OK. The chosen thing. Who would choose me and why? You've a whole world of your own to pick people from, why do you all have to come here and pester me?"

"Well, Ms Cochrane, it's complicated," said The Pan.

"I'm sure it is but that's no excuse. Explain please."

"You've been chosen by the Candidate. Normally, that isn't a problem. He's the ruler elect. He sweeps you off your feet and when he's installed as Architrave, you get to be First Lady living in happy, pampered splendour for the rest of your days."

"I might not like that."

"No, no, trust me, you will." He paused to gather his thoughts. "Alright, look, it's a religion thing. K'Barth is a theocracy. The reason we're all Nimmists is because our country was founded by The Prophet, Arnold of Nim. He was a holy man but he was also a wise one which is why he kept the central command of Nimmism so simple. Of course, he wrote eight books of handy hints on how to be decent and another seven prophetic works to help us plan for the future; the prophecies are so convoluted you need to be close to genius to sort them out and most of us can have a crack at decent without eight volumes of guidance." He was trying to make this as easy and entertaining as he could. "Arnold united the different countries on one continent into a single state, K'Barth, and he was its first, temporal and spiritual ruler; the first Architrave. When he grew old, he searched for a successor and found another person who was similar to him, not the same soul but astrally related. You're looking sceptical."

"Not exactly, we have something similar here." She was thinking about the lamas of Tibet but she wasn't sure she could begin to explain about them nor was she inclined to interrupt. "Go on."

"So, they found the first Candidate and when The Prophet died, she became Architrave. The Prophet left criteria as to how the future Candidates should be chosen and that process is called the Looking. It's how we've selected our leaders, ever since. Except that, right now, it's illegal. So after the last Architrave was beheaded, nobody searched for a new one. Until recently, no-one knew if there was a Candidate or where to find him. Then you came along. You're the Chosen One, absolutely no doubt about it, which means there has to be a Candidate because otherwise, nobody would be there to pick you."

"So this guy is in hiding somewhere?"

"Yes."

"Here?"

"Possibly, although he might be back home, I'm not sure."

"He must be here, surely. After all if he was in K'Barth how would he find me?"

"Ah, now that I *can* tell you." He rummaged around in his pockets for a moment. "At least, I think I can." He put a thimble on the table and pushed it across to her. It was gold, intricately decorated and looked as if it belonged in a museum. "I'd guess he used one of these. It's a portal."

Ruth picked it up, balanced her borrowed sunglasses on her head and examined it close up. The tiny people delicately carved into its sides were taking part in a story. What was actually happening was anybody's guess. All she could really tell was that every molecule of it shouted quality.

"Is this yours?"

"Sort of. The Mervinettes, the gang I drove for, they nicked it—but only incidentally. It was in a bag with some other things which looked like a load of junk. None of us knew what any of it was, so they gave it to me because they didn't think it was worth anything."

"Are you kidding? You can tell it's as old as the hills."

"Forty generations, I believe," he said drily. "It was in a case with a ruby ring and I suspect my colleagues didn't look at it very carefully."

Blimey.

"It's beautiful," said Ruth.

"It is, isn't it? Those are scenes from the life of Arnold, The Prophet."

"I've just thought. When you say 'Arnold's this and that' all the time, does that mean you're swearing?" she asked.

"I'm afraid so, yes." Apologetic.

She giggled.

"It's not funny, I'll probably be damned for all eternity," he said, with irony.

"I can't help you there. The only Arnold in my life was a great-uncle."

He laughed.

"So ... forty generations is a couple of thousand years. You know that, don't you?" said Ruth.

"It has been pointed out to me, yes." Defensive as if it was a bad thing. "I believe it should belong to the Architrave, usually, although right now, it belongs to me." Very firm, it wasn't going to be surrendered lightly, that much was clear. "It's how I found you and it's the way I moved from K'Barth to here."

"OK, so how does it work?"

"Telepathy."

Yeh right.

"Seriously. Think about somewhere you like and look inside it."

Ruth did. In the bottom was a circle of white, like daylight. She eyed him with a quizzical expression.

"No way ..."

"Yes. Have a look."

She did. Instead of white light she could see a slightly fish eye view of the beach near her home.

"That's incredible." She was about to put her finger into it.

"No, don't do that," said The Pan hastily. "It's how it works, you think of something, put it on your finger and it moves you there."

She turned the thimble this way and that.

"So, you're saying that you and your ritzy wheels got here through this?"

"Yes."

She held it up and squinted past it at him.

"Wasn't it a bit of a tight fit? Come to think of it, isn't putting anything through it a tight fit?"

"No. It works on a quantum mechanical principle which I don't begin to understand. However, I have another in the snurd—there's actually an option to plug it into the dash. Then the whole thing gets wired into my thoughts somehow. You could put my snurd through this without using the onboard portal but there's hardly any point."

"How did you find me with it?"

"It was more of a case of stumbling upon you. One day I looked into it without really thinking about anything and I saw you. I thought you were ..." he hesitated, "interesting."

"And so you spied on me."

"Mmm. I'm afraid I did." He held his hands up. "I'm sorry, alright, I didn't intend to. I was looking for a way to join you. There are no Grongles here and that's a good thing for a man like me. I wanted to learn about this place so I could come here and blend in. My only link was you so …" Another shrug. Cracking excuse: credible, watertight and yet patently a load of old tut.

"So?"

"That's all there is to it really."

"Oh really."

"Alright, so I might have been planning to bump into you somehow, once I'd arrived," he said.

"I see and is this how they'll come after us? Lord Vernon just pictures you in his mind's eye and bingo, here he is?"

"No. It can't be or he would be here already. I know he can watch us and hear what we are saying. He was kind enough to show me how he does that. I have to admit the 'bingo' technique is how I do it but I believe that's unique. Most people would need time and special equipment, Lord Vernon included."

"So you're a portal genius, are you?" said Ruth, carefully avoiding the important information because the idea that Lord Vernon might be listening was too horrible to deal with.

"I suspect it's more of a case that I'm ill-informed. I have no idea which things are possible, or impossible. Maybe that makes the difficult stuff easier for me."

"And do you think Lord Vernon found me like you did?"

"No. I suppose the Candidate might have done but Lord Vernon would be looking for an abstract concept, a title, the Chosen One. He would have used advanced equipment—he's studied Nimmism and he's razed enough temples and killed enough priests to have all the right stuff—but the Candidate must have seen you first because Lord Vernon would only have been able to pinpoint you from the moment you were actually selected."

"OK, what if there was a portal detection system only up on that skyscraper, the first time—"

"The first time? Arnold yes, I meant to ask you about that."

"Yeh, and now I'm telling you. He turned up, he made a phone call to some general and talked about detection systems for portals. He knew somebody had used one but he said the system must be flawed because there wasn't anyone there. You know what happened after that."

The Pan was silent for a while.

"Yes," he said eventually, "I'm sorry, I was a fool. What you say sounds plausible and it would explain Lord Vernon turning up like that. I would imagine it causes quite a bit of disturbance in the fabric of reality, using something like this." He picked up the thimble and regarded it thoughtfully.

"Do you think he can trace it when we look through it?" she asked.

"I dunno. If he can, there's not much we can do about it now."

Ruth stared at him, aghast. Why wasn't he gibbering with fear? After all, he'd told her he was a coward and it was all she could do not to.

He continued. "The way I see it is this. We know Lord Vernon has a portal because he can get here and chase us around London. But if he could imagine us and step through it he'd be here now. Last night, while he was chasing us, when I threw him off our tail, he'd have come back, in fact, not even that, he'd have imagined himself in the snurd with us and landed in my lap—or more likely with his hand round my neck. Likewise, if he could detect you looking through it just now and pinpoint where we are, he'd be here already. I may be wrong but my theory is that most people can only use this to go somewhere they've actually been. Clearly there have to be exceptions or I couldn't have got here and neither could Lord Vernon. Unless the Grongles have discovered some other way of using it that means they can go to new places."

"Then, how long before he finds us again?"

"I'm not sure. It would probably take him a while to get a fix and it depends how badly he wants us of course. Presumably, he could have come after me any time since he got hold of his portal but he never did. So, either he chose not to or he couldn't. There's no way of knowing which of those is the right answer but I'm pretty sure he would come for me straight away if he was able. Hence my thinking that it must take him time to get a fix. We would be wise to keep moving but otherwise, if we're reasonably vigilant, I reckon we should be alright." He took another gulp of coffee and stuffed a forkful of sausage into his mouth.

"OK, let me get this straight," said Ruth. "You've just said Lord Vernon is probably watching us. All that news makes me want to do is run and run and never stop but you … you're *eating*."

"Well, yes," he said nonchalantly. "For me, this is situation normal. I'd have died a long time ago if I let that sort of thing put me off my food. Being vulnerable doesn't mean anything's actually going to happen, it just means we need to be on our guard. We're blending in nicely and I'm keeping an eye on things."

"How can you keep an eye on anything when you have your back to the door?"

"Trust me on this alright? I'm the—"

"Best getaway man in K'Barth. Yes, you told me. So here's my next question and it's a big one. Do you know how I get my life back?"

Chapter 29

The Pan of Hamgee looked thoughtful and then a bit sheepish.

"It's a simple question," said Ruth.

"Mmm."

"Go on then."

"To be honest, I don't see how you can."

"Are you saying that unless I can find this Candidate and persuade him to un-choose me, then Lord Vernon and a whole host of other nutters will be chasing me across the universe for ever."

"Yes and all I can do is keep you ahead of them," said The Pan hopelessly. "The trouble is, this isn't really about who you think you are. It's about other people's perceptions …"

"No choice for the chosen, then," said Ruth acidly.

"No. I'm sorry." When the blue eyes met hers they were full of sympathy and although it was well meant, it made her feel worse.

"So, the Candidate wants me and because he does, Lord Vernon wants me too?"

"Yes. No-one can find the real Candidate so in his absence Lord Vernon is one of two people who are hoping to set themselves up as fakes, the other one's a member of the Resistance. There are a number of reasons he wants you but I suspect the main one is so that he can lure the real Candidate out into the open."

"Oh great. I'm guessing he doesn't want to hand over a bunch of flowers."

"No."

"You know, this Candidate gig doesn't sound like a job for life or at least, if it is, it's only a short one."

"Yeh. You can't blame him for lying low."

"I don't." She hated him for it but she definitely didn't blame him. "So, if Lord Vernon captured the Candidate what happens to me? I mean, he won't need me any more, will he?"

A long pause.

"Well, it's not really so much about finding the Candidate. Before long it will be too late for him to turn things around, anyway. What Lord Vernon wants is to be sure. He wants the people to believe he's the real Candidate and since you're the Chosen One, the best way for him to underline his credentials would be to take you as his wife."

Honesty. Good in small doses but that was quite a large spoonful. Ruth wondered, for a moment, what it would be like to marry Lord Vernon and could feel herself going white.

"What if I don't want to be Lord Vernon's wife?" she said, except an automatic reflex which she couldn't control lowered her voice to a whisper.

"I said 'take' didn't I? He doesn't have much of a handle on the concept of choice."

Ruth tried to put on her brave face and accept what was being said but it was impossible. She began to cry, not proper crying but silent fearful tears which spilled out of her eyes and down her cheeks.

"I'm not marrying Lord Vernon," she said. Her voice sounded stronger than she had expected.

He reached out across the table and took her hand in his.

"No, you're not," he said gently. "Not if I can help it," he squeezed her hand. "D'you want a hug?"

"Yes, but please don't or I'll start blubbing in earnest and I don't know if I'll be able to stop." She smiled wanly and pointed to her cheeks. "This isn't proper crying, my eyes are just leaking because I'm stressed."

Ruth was joking but from the expression of pained surprise on his face, he hadn't meant to laugh outright. It broke the tension, though, and she joined in. She took a napkin from the dispenser, wiped her eyes and made a decision.

"I'm not doing this. I am not losing control of my life. I am not chosen."

"Oh, but you are," he sighed. "You are."

"No. Not if I refuse to be. Will you listen to yourself, Yoda?"

"Who?"

Could she really be bothered to explain who Yoda was?

"Look, Mister Pan, my life is mine, my future is mine and I make my own destiny."

He shook his head.

"Nobody makes their own destiny, only other people's. Your future is shaped by others. All *you* can control is the way you react to what happens."

"That's deep."

"That's Arnold."

"He's still wrong."

"I don't think so, he was a very bright bloke and he's usually right."

"Whatever. It still seems amazing to me that Lord Vernon, who I actually heard mentioning that he had a whole nation to run, came all the way to London to look for me."

"Not really. It just shows how important you are."

"Or how insane you all are. None of you has a shred of evidence."

"Lord Vernon does. He has a machine and your reading—"

"Oh, so that's all right then! A machine," she cut in. "Do you not know how crap machines are?" She was on the brink of shouting and stopped.

"Not where I'm from."

She looked past him, out of the window where a glint of sunlight on the dark, metallic, silver-grey paintwork of the snurd caught her eye. OK. Maybe not. This was hopeless.

"How sure are you about this?"

"A lot surer than you'd like me to be."

"What if we found the Candidate and got him to pick someone else?"

"What if? You'd be condemning someone else to the situation you're in now. I don't have you down as the type to dump your misfortunes on others."

Once again, he was right.

"Isn't there someone who'd like to marry Lord Vernon?"

"Only a Grongolian someone and finding them would be extremely risky."

"So the only way I can get out of this whole sorry mess and go back to my normal life is to doom someone else to marrying Lord Vernon or kick his invincible butt?"

"As things stand now, yes."

"Then I'll just have to kick his invincible butt, won't I?"

"Look, it may not be that drastic. I think there's someone who can help us, Sir Robin is—"

"Sir Robin?"

"That's his name."

Suddenly, in the midst of a very dark outlook, Ruth saw a tiny glimmer of light.

"My neighbour, the one who saved me from the Grongles and invited me round to tea to sort it out, his name's Sir Robin, Sir Robin Get, to be precise."

The Pan laughed.

"So's mine."

"You don't think …?"

"I'd bet my life," said The Pan. "In fact, he used to be the High Priest of all K'Barth."

That explained a lot about Sir Robin, not to mention his I-have-people-who-can-fix-this attitude when he'd invited her round for tea.

"So how did you meet him?" she said.

"He's a friend of my landlady's," a beat, "more than a friend by the look of her son. He's smart and he's pretty ruthless. He came and blackmailed me into asking Big Merv if we'd rob the world's most impregnable bank."

"Did you rob the bank?"

"Yes, but Lord Vernon brought us down and the Resistance got us. They killed Frank and Harry 'to focus our attention'. Bastards. Big Merv and I got away, but when we got back Sir Robin had got himself arrested so we went to the Palace and rescued him. Sir Robin and Big Merv got out but I didn't, and that's how I ended up being questioned by Lord Vernon."

"Blimey. You lead an exciting life, Mister Pan." And now it looked as if she was going to be starting one exactly similar. Oh dear.

"On the whole, I try to keep things a little quieter than that. I don't think Lord Vernon was best pleased about what happened. I doubt I'm flavour of the month," he shrugged. "Same old same old, it's not as if I ever have been."

"Public Enemy Number One, I'd say."

"Very possibly."

Ruth hadn't meant that seriously. Was he joshing? Nothing to suggest he was. That was kind of impressive. She tried to hide any traces of admiration which might be crossing her face but she wasn't any good at poker, either. He smiled. Damn.

"Don't go thinking it's cool or anything," he warned her.

"I'm not."

"Good. I'm glad to hear it," he said, except he'd seen through her and was blatantly delighted. "Sir Robin owes me a lot of money for my part in his robbery, if I can get that off him, then, at least we can sort out some of the trouble I've got you into."

"You are very sweet but I can't take your money," she said. It was hooky money for starters, though it wasn't politic to mention it.

"I bet the concert hall will."

"Even if they do, the newspaper was talking about terrorism which doesn't go down well here, especially not on the back of what Lord Vernon did to London. They'll take it as a national affront and no amount of money will clear that up. Anyway, if we do sort it out, I'll still have the Grongles to deal with, won't I? With their laser guns and statically powered torches and a whole load of other gizmos which haven't been invented here. How do I get out of that, Mister Pan?"

"I don't know, myself, but I know a man who does. We have to find Sir Robin."

Chapter 30

In his apartments in K'Barth, Lord Vernon examined the coordinates General Moteurs had given him. The General was right, the search area was extensive but Lord Vernon was not unduly worried. The combination of the K'Barthan imagination-driven portal and the Grongolian coordinates-driven model was indeed powerful. This time, he believed he would succeed in locating his quarry.

Whether or not The Pan of Hamgee knew it, the presence of his thimble would interfere with the signal from Lord Vernon's. And yes. When Lord Vernon pictured the Hamgeean in his mind's eye and looked into the copper thimble, he saw nothing but a grey blur. Switch the image in his head to the Chosen One and Lord Vernon saw the same grey blur. This proved that she was close enough to the wretched Hamgeean for his thimble to be masking her, too. Even if the image had been clear, Lord Vernon could not transport into the presence of a person without time to make the right calculations. Ruth and The Pan would have to stay in one place—or move no faster than walking pace—long enough for him to make those calculations and they weren't. They were moving often. As plans went, it was a non-starter.

However, Lord Vernon believed he had found a way to gather enough information from his K'Barthan portal to enable him to find the Chosen One's coordinates, thus reaching her, using the Grongolian portal.

He put the thimble to his eye examining the edges of the blurred grey views where he knew he would find blobs of colour and light. He concentrated on these tiny pieces of The Pan and Ruth's background surroundings until they began to resolve themselves into shapes and objects. He saw the metal side of a window, with a rubber seal: a ship, a plane? Maybe? A vehicle, definitely. Through the window, he caught glimpses of a building upon which, blurred and foreshortened but fully readable, hung a huge company logo.

"At last."

It should be enough.

Chapter 31

The Pan and Ruth sat together in silence for a moment. It didn't seem to matter that the lull in the conversation should have been awkward. She reached for her coffee cup and knocked something off the table. Ah yes. Sir Robin's parcel. The Pan picked it up.

"You should probably open this," he said as he handed it to her.

"You're too nosey for your own good, you know that, don't you?"

"Mmm. Shall I sing Happy Birthday?"

"You do that in K'Barth?"

"No, but they do it in Grongolia."

Oh they would, wouldn't they? She gave him a withering look, took a knife and sawed open the tape. She could feel him watching her. The envelope was largely empty, with something small and metallic in the bottom with a white business postcard folded round it. She took the card out first. It had a crest on top, the RAC, and it wasn't signed but somebody had written a message.

"You know where to find me," Ruth read aloud. "How strange." She handed it to The Pan who looked at it too.

"The place on there, which I'd better not mention, in case anyone's listening." He pointed at the crest on the paper. "What is it?"

"It's difficult to explain without giving too much away but if we need to find it, I know where it is and I can direct you from here."

"Fair enough. Anything else?"

"A box." She held it up and looked at it. When she tried to get the lid off, it was stuck fast. Or it was a fake lid?

"A box," The Pan repeated. His voice was faint as if he was in shock. She squinted at him. Hmm. He was having to concentrate very hard on breathing normally.

"It's a snuff box, isn't it?" she said.

"Mmm …"

"So, why your spectacular reaction?"

He hesitated. He was trying to say something but he didn't seem to be able to speak. Oh dear. Was this some delayed effect from the Truth Serum? Was he having a turn? What if he was sick?

"Are you alright?" said Ruth. "You look like a beached salmon breathing its last. I'm half expecting you to turn blue."

She thought she could see The Pan's lips moving as he counted to ten in his head but he rallied impressively. When he spoke, his voice was calm and the way he gestured to the box would have been almost suave if his hands hadn't been trembling.

"You know I said we robbed a bank for Sir Robin?" She nodded. "Well, that box is what we stole. I should have expected something like this from him. It's a message. He's sent us a message. This is a sign that he's the same guy here and in K'Barth, that he trusts us and that we can trust him."

Slowly Ruth held the box out to The Pan.

"You nicked it. You'd better have it back."

"Mmm. Actually it wasn't me that nicked it."

"Bit of a technicality that, Mister Pan."

"Mmm." He was in shock.

"Are you OK?"

"I think I'll live."

"Good. What do they do with it?"

"It's used in the Looking. It's the one definitive item that proves whether or not someone is the Candidate."

"How?"

"You have me there." He turned it over and on the second attempt popped the lid open with his thumb.

"It's loopy—I mean, it's old and pretty and beautifully made but it's only a box."

"Yep," he said and opened and closed it a couple more times. "The lid's a bit sticky."

"Age?"

"Or grime. It could do with a clean-up."

He opened the box, peered in with an expression of alarm, closed it and opened it again. He relaxed and took out a small lump of paper. Ruth was surprised because she was sure that on the first occasion he'd opened it, the box had been empty. No. The paper must just have been tucked away at one side. The Pan unfolded it and laid it flat on the table. It was dog-eared and covered in mathematical symbols.

"What's that?" she asked him.

"It's a piece of paper."

Sarcastic git.

"Yes, I realise that. I meant what *is* it? Presumably all that stuff means something."

"I imagine it does, unfortunately my education isn't what it might have been so I have no more idea than you—unless you do have an idea." Hopeful. "Do you?"

She turned it round so she could read it.

"No. Sorry." As she pushed it back across the table to him she noticed something written on the back. "Hang on." As he reached out to take it she snatched it away. *"Stolen by the Mervinettes in return for amnesty for all misdemeanours,"* she read. She raised her eyebrows at him.

"Why do I think this is your handwriting?"

He was embarrassed.

"Alright, yes. I just wrote that to make it look more official. That piece of paper was tucked into the thimble when I found it. I didn't think I should throw it away in case it was important. But I can't keep it there in case it gets lost and it was getting even tattier in my pocket so after the robbery, it seemed right to put it in the box. I suppose I might have hoped the Architrave would find it one day and think some long-dead priest had pardoned us."

"And to let everyone know who nicked it in the first place."

"Ah. Yes."

"Duh."

He chuckled as he put the paper back and opened and closed the lid a few times.

"They strike me as a set, don't you think?" He placed the box on the table between them and put the thimble beside it.

"Yes. So now what?"

"When we've finished breakfast, I think we'd better go and find Sir Robin."

"Should we, though?" asked Ruth. "I mean, if Lord Vernon has a portal mightn't he be watching us? Isn't there a risk of leading him straight to Sir Robin?"

"Yes. That has occurred to me. But we need the money and we need help. Lord Vernon wants Sir Robin but he wants the Candidate more. He blackmailed me. He was going to let me go but only on condition I worked for him—I was supposed to get into Sir Robin's good books, wait until he trusted me with the location of the Candidate and then tell the Grongles. That's why I made such a bog-up of rescuing you … I had no time, they were going to …"

Oh this just got better and better.

"They were using me to get to you, right?"

He nodded sadly.

"Yes."

"So you escaped and came to get me to save your friends from … well … you."

"Yep."

That was a bit of a surprise and sort of touching. More than touching. It was almost heroic. Not the behaviour Ruth would associate with a man who painted himself as a coward.

"That's quite a grand gesture, Mister Pan," she said.

"Thank you." He looked at her thoughtfully. "I never considered it grand, more expedient."

"Grand, I think. All you need is some armour and a white horse." Argh no! She felt a blush rising. Quickly she tried to ham it up, turn it into a joke. "But don't kid yourself, the armour would be rusty and the horse would probably be lame."

He raised an eyebrow.

"I'd be lucky if it had three legs."

Chapter 32

Back in K'Barth, Lord Vernon opened the web browser on his smartphone. General Moteurs' boffins had managed to connect the internet in Lord Vernon's version of reality to that in the Chosen One's.

It seemed the humans there were averse to getting lost. They had photographed every street in every city, every house and much more besides. With the General's helpful information he should be able to narrow this down. He opened Boogle Earth, tapped the company name in the box labelled 'find me' along with the name of the airport and clicked search. So simple. There it was. He clicked on the pin man logo to activate WAM – Walking Around Mode – moved the cursor forwards and the building with the logo came into the frame. He made a note of the coordinates and turned the pin man round in a full circle. With the building behind him now he saw an old bus on the road opposite. He put the thimble to his eye again and as he pictured the bus, two men in fluorescent yellow coats came out of it carrying greasy paper bags and takeaway cups. However, more tellingly, parts of the bus seemed blurred. Lord Vernon knew why and now, as he double-checked the coordinates given by Boogle, he knew exactly where to find the Chosen One.

"Excellent," he said. General Moteurs was right, the Grongolian portal in the Interceptor would serve him well. Phone in hand, he took the stairs up to the roof three at a time. The Interceptor was waiting for him, engine running. He slid into the seat, punched the coordinates into the onboard computer and as he took off, he pressed a button. The Interceptor and Lord Vernon disappeared in a flash of light.

Chapter 33

In the café, Ruth looked idly past The Pan out of the window. A black Mercedes pulled up outside. It resembled a very obscure model from the mid 1950s; like the really cool one with the gull-wing doors except it was sleeker, the headlights were sloping and glassed in and it had two exhaust pipes coming out of the air scoops at the side. If she didn't know better, Ruth would have thought it was—oh no—the Interceptor.

The Pan looked up at her abruptly and their eyes met.

"Get your stuff. It's time to go."

Ruth's stomach turned over as one of the doors of the vehicle outside hissed open and the driver got out. He had his back to her but even out there, he was radiating malevolence like dark fire. She caught a glimpse of the interior as he moved away from the door. It wasn't the leather and chrome of the real article. It was all black suede with blue and red lights. The door closed, hiding it behind smoked glass and Lord Vernon turned round. He held up his key ring and as he blipped the button the indicator lights flashed on and off as the alarm set.

Ruth couldn't move. Her world went into free fall. Oh no, please no, not here, cornered in a bus with no way out, no escape. Opposite her, The Pan was pale but he gave her a reassuring smile. It didn't quite work, it didn't hide his fear, but it was enough.

"Come on Ruth, we have to get moving." He sounded amazingly calm as he stood up, swiping the box and thimble off the table. As she rose unsteadily to her feet, she gathered up her handbag and slipped her feet back into the implements of torture she currently called shoes; no heels over two inches again, ever. How had The Pan known, before she'd said anything, that Lord Vernon was standing in the car park? Did he read it in her face? Was he telepathic? Or could he see behind him? At South Mimms, in the snurd, she'd had a kind of waking dream that he'd had eyes under his hair. Did he? Is that why he was a good escape man?

"I know you're frightened but it's going to be alright, I promise," he said.

Lord Vernon stood there in broad daylight, wearing a white shirt with a cravat, an immaculately tailored black military-style jacket – Regency military-style that is: V-necked to show the cravat with a stand-up collar and it was fastened with brass buttons in the middle. Pinned to his chest, he wore a diamond-encrusted, order-of-the-garter-style star. He wore gloves, suede gloves, with the rings on the outside, black trousers with a red stripe down the side, immaculate suede boots and sunglasses. The dark hair was blacker in the daylight and contrasted with the pale colour of his face, throwing those sneering good looks into stark relief. He had a Sam Brown-style utility belt with a holster on it containing a gun – she had no doubt that it was real – and there was a knife and what were they going to do? Her hands began to shake uncontrollably.

"It's—it's—we—" She couldn't finish the sentence. Paralysed with fear she stared glassily ahead of her. She knew she mustn't panic but it was all she could do not to, every part of her was shaking and she couldn't steady herself enough to speak. The Pan of Hamgee moved swiftly round the table and took her gently by the arm.

"Trust me, Ruth, you're going to be fine." He steered her towards the door. Walking took all her concentration. They stopped. A couple of deep breaths and she felt able to talk. She leaned over and whispered in his ear.

"He's going to kill us."

"No," said the Pan quietly. "Not if we can keep calm and even if he recognised us, he would never kill you."

"What about you?"

"We're in disguise, remember?" Avoiding the question. "That won't be enough on its own but the giveaway is our clothes, not our faces and it's our faces he'll scan first. If we can sneak past him he may not notice what we're wearing, especially if we help ourselves to these." He casually removed a yellow jacket from the back of an empty chair and another from one of the pegs by the door. "Here, put this on," he handed her the smaller of the two. She let go of his arm and did as he said. "Good. We're going to be fine. I'll go in front and hopefully that'll hide your outfit. One more thing, if we show our fear, he will notice. We need to walk tall. Ready?" She nodded. "Good," he smiled. "Here." She took his outstretched hand and he slipped his other arm round her waist, under her coat, holding her up. She stayed close to The Pan as he opened the door to reveal the figure of Lord Vernon, arm raised to grab the handle. Up close, she noticed the rings over the suede gloves were old and antique.

"Sorry mate," said the Pan in a passable London accent.

He stood to one side and waited for Lord Vernon to come in. Ruth shrank behind The Pan, trying to keep all but the blonde wig and the sunglasses hidden.

"Thank you," said Lord Vernon with utter contempt, despite his veneer of politeness. No flicker of recognition though. He strode past them, into the bus and they ducked out into the fresh air.

"Can you walk?" asked the Pan.

"Yeh, I think so."

"Good. We need to be out of sight before he comes out again."

He walked quickly across the road, with Ruth leaning heavily against him and hobbling, jelly-legged, alongside. They ducked behind the hedge where they removed their jackets and hung them over the gate. That was good. Ruth felt guilty about stealing the coats, at least the owners would find them now and avoid getting into trouble for losing their company-issue clothing.

Something nuzzled the back of Ruth's legs. She managed not to scream but couldn't stifle a small squeak. It was the snurd.

"Mmm, it likes you," said the Pan. How could he be so relaxed? They'd just walked past an invincible six-foot mastodon intent on their immediate demise (whatever The Pan said about her being safe, she didn't believe it) and he was still in the area looking for them.

"It's a machine," said her mouth while her brain trod water, trying to catch up.

"Yes it is, and it only does that to people it likes," he opened the door for her. "Hop in." She did as she was told.

"The ideal move, in a situation like this, is to throw a rug over ourselves and stay here until he's gone. Sadly, since he's already chased us around London, I suspect he'll recognise my snurd. We'll have to revert to plan B." The Pan was jollying her along again. She was so grateful she could have hugged him.

"What's plan B?"

"We get out of sight as soon as possible."

"Oh yes. That has my vote." She was shaking but euphoric. It had never felt so good to be alive. Then again, that was hardly surprising, she doubted she'd ever come so close to being dead. The Pan pressed a button on the dash.

"Fingerprint accepted," said a husky female voice and the engine started.

"Thank you," he said. Instead of driving through the gate he drove to the other side of the car park—putting a row of coaches between them and the café—and turned off the engine. "Alright, if he saw us move, he'll come after us but even if he does we'll have plenty of room to take off first."

"Can we escape?"

The Pan smiled. "I expect so."

"The answer I'm looking for here, Mister Pan, is an emphatic 'yes'."

"Well Ms Cochrane, he didn't get us last time, did he?"

"He destroyed London though."

"Mmm."

"I thought you said you could lose him just like that." She clicked her fingers.

"At home … and to be honest, I was lying."

"This isn't the best time to admit to that."

"Alright. How about this? You know I've outrun him before and I'm pretty sure I'm the only person alive who can, is that good enough?"

She nodded.

"I guess it'll have to do." She hesitated. "How do you live like this every day?"

"You'll get used to it. It's a lot better than being dead." He turned in his seat to face her. "Are you alright?"

"You keep asking me that." And it was very sweet but didn't he understand that it concentrated her mind on the trouble she was in. She didn't want to think about it, not head on, or there'd be more tears. She looked down and bit her lip. He leaned his head down so he could see her face.

"I know I do," he said. "And you keep saying you're fine but," he paused, "if you're not, it *is* allowed."

"Thanks." Oops, a bit of a wobble in her voice there. She didn't want him to think she was about to cry, mainly because if he did anything sympathetic, like put his arm round her, she would. She took a deep breath and tried to sound more relaxed. "I'm not really. But for the sake of my sanity let's pretend." She looked down. "It's not going to help either of us if I lose it." For starters, she didn't want The Pan of Hamgee to think she was a wimp. He reached out and took her hand in his and looked thoughtfully down at her fingers.

"After I was blacklisted, I cried for about three days. Then I decided to end it all. I told you I was an arse—I jumped off a bridge—but although I had every intention of killing myself, when push came to shove, I swam. I guess something in me wasn't ready to die after all." He lifted her hair off her face and hooked it behind her ear so he could look into her eyes properly. "What I'm trying to tell you in my own, awkward way is that I understand how this feels. I realise it must be difficult for you but on the bright side, you may find you are stronger than you think."

"You don't know me."

"No, that's true, but in my line of work, one of the things I have to be able to do to survive is pick out the most reliable person in a crisis. Trust me on this, you are the bona fide archetype."

She knew he meant it. So touching and so serious even if it had been delivered with the habitual humour. They sat there in companionable silence for a moment.

How to answer that?

"Thank you," she said. "That's a lovely thing to say but, at the very least, you're overestimating me and at the worst it's cobblers." He laughed. "I hope I don't let you down."

"Oh, you won't," he said.

She cleared her throat. This was all getting a bit serious.

"I like that we're hidden but how are we going to tell when he's gone?"

"I'm going to go stand on the bonnet and peer through the windows of this bus."

"What if he sees your face?"

"He's two hundred yards away – he's not going to see my face and even if he does he's not going to recognise me."

"What if he uses a portal?"

"Which one of these twenty identical buses are we hiding behind? Even if he can see us through the portal, he can't transport himself to where we are without special equipment and time. He's never been behind this bus so he doesn't know what to imagine and there are twenty of them. If he does recognise me, he'll have to walk over here and I think we might see him coming. Do you have a mirror in your bag?"

Ah yes, good plan. She took out her powder compact and though her hands were still shaking, managed to open it.

"Here."

"Thank you."

He climbed onto the snurd and stood facing her, holding the powder compact out in front of him. She was impressed at the way he got the right angle so fast, straight away, in fact. He didn't need to move it at all. He might be used to this but she suspected he wasn't using the compact. Ruth had no clue whether the average Hamgeean was actually human—even though this one said he was—but was this more evidence that he might, really, have eyes in the back of his head?

She glanced up at him. He was ignoring the mirror by that point, looking straight at her. He clambered down, opened the driver's door, leaned in and spoke to her.

"I think he may have gone," he said. "I just need to top up the water and then we can go and find Sir Robin. There's a bottle under your seat. Could you …?"

She rummaged around, found a full plastic bottle and passed it to him. She was surprised when he walked round to the back of the snurd, opened the fuel cap and emptied it into the petrol tank.

"That'll keep us going for a while," he said as he settled himself into the driver's seat beside her. He handed her the empty bottle. "Please would you put that back?"

"Sure."

"Thank you." He noticed she was distracted. "Are you certain you're alright?"

"I'm fine but you—you just put water in the petrol tank."

"I put water in the water tank, what's petrol?"

"Are you telling me this thing runs on water?"

"Of course. It splits the H2 from the O, all that flammable stuff in water, the thing we use to put fires out. It's kind of ironic."

"Kind of miraculous, I'd say. OK, so I think we have something that splits the components in water and enhances performance, but a straight water-powered engine? No. That is, if you'll excuse the pun, a pipe dream for us."

"Oh." He was surprised.

"Yeh, 'oh', so if you want a new life, get an engine design off your Snurd people and patent it here. You'll be rich in no time."

"I might just do that. Come on then, shall we go and find Sir Robin?"

"Yes. And please, please let him have access to a shower. If I'm stuck with these shoes and this ridiculous outfit I'd rather not smell like an old sock."

"That outfit is far from ridiculous. I like it."

"It's not designed for this sort of thing."

"Perhaps not, but rest assured, it *does* do what it was designed for."

"Which is?"

"Flatter all your best bits."

He smiled at her. Their eyes met and she felt a bit light-headed. There was a long pause. Neither of them wanted to look away and break the moment but he cracked first.

"Come on then," he said. He swiped the reader on the dash with his thumb and pressed the starter. "Let's go and see Sir Robin. If anyone can get you out of the mess I've got you into it's probably him. I need to warn him what I've done, too. Lord Vernon believed he was dead until I waded in, shouting my mouth off."

"You know, I'm intrigued as to how saying 'I'm a little teapot' over and over again could be classed as shouting your mouth off."

"I bet you are. It's a rare skill." A joke but there was a brittle edge to his voice. "When Lord Vernon mentioned that Sir Robin was dead, my reaction showed him otherwise." He stopped for a moment and when he spoke again he sounded more himself. "You know the place written down on that card?"

"The—"

"Yes that," he cut in swiftly. "You said you could direct me there."

"Yes."

"Alright, let's not hang around here then." He made to flick the aviator switch and she put her hand on his arm.

"Wait. We're blending in remember? Pretending this is a car. No wings."

"Ah yes." A hint of disappointment in his tone.

"And one more thing, Mister No-Name. We're somewhere in England now. That means you have to drive on the road, within the speed limits and you have to stop at traffic lights when they are red because, on this planet, green is the one that means go."

"If we fly we won't have to do any traffic lights."

"If we fly we will be the only people, in this entire version of reality—apart from Lord Vernon—in a flying car."

"It's not a car, it's a—"

"Snurd. Yes, I know and it's very conspicuous."

Chapter 34

Deep in the bowels of Scotland Yard, or at least, the basement, DI Philip Softone and DC May Gurney sat in a small, airless room sipping cups of watery tea. He was a small, chubby – if energetic – man of about fifty, dark, greying hair, mischievous brown eyes and with a reputation across the force for being his own man. He was respected by his colleagues but he was not quite so popular with his superiors. May was a little more reserved; slight, dark-haired and one of the rising stars of the force. Clever, analytical and not easily swayed by the opinions of others, she was the perfect working partner for DI Softone. However, unlike him she was a great deal more tactful with the powers that be and therefore a great deal more popular with them, as well as with her colleagues.

The two of them were examining CCTV film of the incident at the Festival Hall and the subsequent carnage.

"OK. Let's start at the beginning," said DI Softone. "What have we got?"

"It looks like a car chase, sir."

"Cars? These things are flying."

"That's true, sir, but they're still cars."

"DC Gurney, you realise two separate groups of religious extremists, the New Improved IRA and something called the Animal Rights Society have claimed responsibility already. Somebody's blown a big hole in the Daily Mail building, knocked the ball off the top of the Coliseum and rendered Nelson's Column structurally unsound—not to mention smashing numerous sets of traffic lights and a couple of speed cameras in-between—and they've put several more holes in other buildings along the way. The tabloids are going to have a field day with this."

"True, sir," said DC Gurney.

"Well, DC, I hope you have something good. Top brass are leaning on me pretty heavily to hand this over to the anti-terrorist squad or MI7," he said.

"It's good, sir. It may not be good enough yet—I need more time to work on it—but this is what I've got. I don't think they're terrorists. The events, so far, bear the hallmarks of a rescue." DI Softone had been a policeman a long time and he didn't think they were terrorists either. He was intrigued by DC

Gurney's alternative explanation. She was a bright girl and she was usually right.

"What's your thinking?"

"It's these guys here, sir." She clicked the mouse a couple of times and brought up some grainy CCTV coverage. It was the inside of the Festival Hall. He watched as the film unfolded frame by frame showing a sea of people lying down.

"That's the young man arriving, is it?" said DI Softone, pointing to the screen.

"Yes, but if you look, the interesting events happen here." She clicked to freeze the film and moved an arrow over to the side of the picture. "There." She highlighted two very tall men, seemingly in some kind of military uniform.

"Who are they?"

"You may well ask, sir. They're up to no good, though, this is one of only two shots we have from last night. They know where the cameras are and they're staying out of sight."

"Your other shot?"

"Here."

Another click of the mouse, a different view, this time of the crowd of concertgoers on the stairs. The Cochrane girl was out at the front.

The footage continued. The window caved in, the vehicle arrived through the fractured glass, a young man leapt out and ran up the stairs. He was wearing a black wide-brimmed hat and a cloak.

"Very theatrical," said DI Softone. "He looks like the Phantom of the Opera. Or there's that port logo—you know—the guy they always put on the label with the hat and cloak?"

They both giggled.

"Got it in one, sir. I hear the girls in uniform are calling him Zorro. Now, if I move this on a bit …" a few more clicks of the mouse. "There you are. Up at the top, it's our two big gents again." They were half hidden by a pillar and the crowd in front of them but one of them held his hands out in front of him in a familiar stance.

"Is he aiming a gun?" said DI Softone.

"I think so sir." As DC Gurney moved the film backwards and forwards through the next few frames, DI Softone could make out a beam of light shining from the hands of the large man in uniform to the ground near the Cochrane girl's feet.

"Laser fire? Is that what melted the stairs?"

DC Gurney nodded.

"Who are these people? CIA?"

"No, sir, we've made discreet checks with MI6, the Russians, the Americans and Mossad. They all assure us they are not in the position to use lasers in the public domain."

"What about the North Koreans?"

"Do they look North Korean to you, sir?"

"Fair point. So who the hell are they?"

"Good question, sir. The vehicles are interesting as well." DC Gurney switched to the film of the exit footage. "OK, here it is, they run and jump in and what you have is a standard classic sports car. Then, there, behind the smoke. See? The wings actually grow out of the sides before it takes off."

"Are you sure?"

"Yes, it's a flying car but it's more than that," she pulled up some more footage. "Here's a shot from a camera on the street. It's outside the Festival Hall heading to the river." She zoomed in. "Wings. Absolutely no doubt, and here," she clicked on an earlier excerpt showing the stranger's car landing. "Ignore the glass, watch this section." She moved the film on, still by still. "There!" she pointed. "A definite outline, wings, morphing into the side of the car. Then there's the train driver's report from Farringdon. It flew into the tunnel ahead of him and he described exactly the same thing, said the metal itself changed shape. It's an intelligent compound, sir."

"A what?"

"An intelligent compound. I've looked it up and I checked with the folks at the labs. We have something like it, sir. It's been around in various forms since the 1930s. There's a conspiracy theory that current versions are reverse engineered from some of the Roswell debris. To start with, it was pretty high-end, used in space and the like—it still is, I believe—but these days there's a fair bit of it around on the streets; braces and glasses frames to name two examples. The metal we use is a nickel titanium alloy called Nitinol and it moves from elastic to rigid and from one shape to another with the application of heat. The changes in our version occur at an atomic level, the atoms slant or stay in a box formation, allowing for two shapes."

"Which means?" asked DI Softone.

"It means that the stuff these people are using is several generations more advanced than anything we could produce here. The memory of their metal extends to several shapes and it can move from one to another, apparently without heat or certainly with less heat than our metal needs. I can't say for sure but it also looks as if their version changes sub-atomically. It may even be able to liquify or solidify when required."

"Oh come on May, it's not the bloody Terminator."

"No, sir, it isn't quite that advanced but you've chosen a good analogy."

Philip Softone blew the air out through his teeth.

"DC, is this an alien abduction?"

"No, sir. At least I don't think so. This car—"

"With the wings?"

"With the wings. It's a variant of a nineteen sixties Lotus Elan. What are the chances of aliens inventing a spaceship that looks exactly like a classic British sports car?"

Round and O-shaped, surely, unless …

"Maybe they wanted to blend in."

"If they wanted to blend in, why use the wings?"

DI Softone scratched his head. "Expediency? Dire need?"

"Possibly, sir. We've another positive ID at South Mimms early this morning. They escaped again but we know a lot more about it. It's an exact facsimile of a 1960s Elan S2 yet the colour scheme is two-tone, which is more like the Elan Sprints from the early 1970s. Most were usually yellow, blue or red, but this one's grey."

"How close are we to finding them? Is that going to help?"

"I don't know, it might. We can't be far off, though. I'd be surprised if there are more than a few hundred left. I'll check but it could be there are few enough grey ones for us to question the owners and eliminate them one at a time. The traffic boys are onto it so if they're trying to pass it off as a normal car they won't get far."

"Do we have the registration?"

"Yes and no, sir. We have a crystal clear shot of the number plate at the Festival Hall but the boys at South Mimms have quoted a different one. I can double-check that, although it probably doesn't make much difference. Both the registrations are dummies. I've already looked them up. I haven't had the CCTV footage from the services, it should be arriving any minute. I do have this, though."

Another deft click of the mouse and a still flashed up showing the rear of the flying car.

"What am I looking at?" asked DI Softone, wishing he was more of a petrolhead.

"The lettering. The sixties Elan had metal letters, L-O-T-U-S, equidistant, centred. It was an incredibly expensive thing to get right. That's why the modern ones had decals until recently. Look at this. What do you see?"

"S-N … Snurd? What the hell's that?"

"Exactly. I've searched all our databases and there's nothing."

"So what is it? A concept car? Some joker building their own?"

"Possibly. What's important is that you and I can read it. It's western lettering."

"More evidence against our friends with the flying cars being little green men."

"Yes."

Not necessarily a case for MI7, not necessarily a case for miles and miles of red tape. DI Softone began to feel a flutter of optimism. At the least, this might be enough to stall any forced handover for a day or two.

"What about terrorism?" he asked as the picture on the screen reverted to a shot of the man driving the Lotus. DI Softone looked at it. He was young, late teens? Early twenties maybe? Not much more than that.

"I don't think they're terrorists, sir."

"No. Me neither. This lad doesn't look right. It's difficult to see but what d'you think? Has somebody roughed him up?"

"It looks that way, sir. We will have a better picture when the film from South Mimms comes in but I'd be prepared to stick my neck out and say that's bruising round his nose."

"Yes and there he is sitting in a piece of technology so far in advance of anything we can throw at him it's laughable and yet he's scared, on the verge of panic, I'd say, wouldn't you?"

"Yes, I would, sir, but he might have been expecting the other one to turn up."

"Hmm. So, if these guys aren't aliens, we'll need to present the powers that be with a plausible alternative. Who are they? James Bond villains?"

DC Gurney smiled.

"I don't think so, sir, although the one in the second car might be."

"Hmm. Our friend, here, looks, to me, like a very frightened young man. Do we know who he is?" asked DI Softone, more in hope than anticipation of any result.

"No, sir. He doesn't crop up on our database or any of the others we've heard from. We're waiting for the Germans and the Australians to come back to us but it looks as if he's a first offender."

"So, our lad flies in through a window, snatches our girl and goes ... where?"

"It's difficult to piece that together, sir. We've a couple of reported sightings along the Thames and then nothing, so far, for forty minutes."

"So the next thing we know they've picked up a friend and they're flying round London trying to kill each other."

"Not each other, that's another interesting factor in this case. I've checked and double-checked all the footage we have and our man with the Lotus doesn't fire a single shot on camera. Not one. All the damage is caused by the second car, in fact I'm beginning to think our man didn't fire at all, maybe the Lotus is unarmed."

"What do you have on the other car?"

"The evidence suggests torpedoes, laser cannon, machine-guns, some kind of pulse weapon—that's what fried all the traffic lights."

DI Softone swallowed.

"I hope he doesn't come looking for us. I mean, is it a version of a real car like the other one?"

"Yes. It's a lot more esoteric but still based on something here. I had to get Barry in traffic—I mean, sorry, Sergeant Onyx—onto this one."

"Is Barry Onyx into cars?"

"The most massive petrolhead, sir —he puts me well in the shade. There's no maker's mark on it anywhere but he thought it was a replica of a 1955 Mercedes concept car. I haven't had time to get much info but from what I've found on the Internet so far, I'd say he's right."

"No letters?"

"No. It doesn't even have a number plate and there are no sightings before or after the chase. It's as if it turned up out of thin air, pursued our man and disappeared again the minute it lost him."

"Maybe it did. What about this girl, Ruth Cochrane? She can't just drop off the grid. She has a mobile phone, credit cards, she'll have to use a cashpoint or she'll starve, she might call her work, her friends ..."

"Yeh, she's called her work but from a payphone. I reckon she rang from South Mimms. Obviously, she called her flatmate from there too."

"Ah the flatmate, the cooperative one?"

They laughed.

"Yeh, her. Can't say I blame her though, she looked at death's door." A pause. "I checked out what she told us. Three months ago, Ruth Cochrane did report being followed. I spoke to the officer who interviewed her, she said Ms Cochrane was clearly agitated and nothing she said made a lot of sense. There aren't many notes from the interview but as far as I can gather, she hid in a hedge and her pursuer was some big gentleman, wearing fancy dress and armed to the teeth who called her 'chosen'."

They shook their heads at each other.

"Oh and he had a static-powered torch apparently."

"Sure, sure, then again, look at these cars. Did you check her history? Any substance abuse?"

"That's it though. There's not a thing. Our Ms Cochrane is squeaky clean."

"Suspiciously so?"

"No. Just fine, upstanding citizen clean."

Damn. He nodded.

"Go on."

"We know where she works so I've got a team working on the last three months' CCTV footage from her commute in. These guys are pros but three months is a long time. Who knows, we might catch a glimpse of them again. As for finding her, we may get some news on her credit card soon. She was wearing evening dress, so if she plans to disappear long-term I could see her buying some casual clothes, or at the least trying to get back to her flat. I'll bet she needs some comfortable shoes—the CCTV footage isn't conclusive but I reckon she's wearing some serious heels."

DI Softone smiled. The woman's perspective. Very useful. DC Gurney was smart and she was going places. Further than him, for sure, and yet she wanted to learn and clearly valued anything he might teach her. He knew he was a fine copper but he didn't suffer fools gladly, especially when he was working for them, and his 'uncooperative attitude to authority'—or at least, his intolerance of idiots higher up the pile than him and his refusal to kowtow to them—had held him back. He knew his career had gone as far as it was going, so the DC's obvious regard for him was touching.

"How long before they are in custody? Your best guess," he asked her.

May shrugged.

"A couple of days at the outside. Do you want me to call MI7?" An unwilling do-I-have-to tone to her voice. So there it was, she felt it too, something wasn't right and she was no more willing to surrender control than he was.

DI Softone rubbed his temples. It'd been a rough night. He'd been called in shortly after the incident took place so he hadn't slept. He'd done nearly a full day's police work on top and he'd dearly like to go home to bed, but … There was a big but. It wasn't the red tape that was putting him off. Something about this case wasn't right. All his instincts were warning him against handing it over to anyone else. He'd been a policeman a long time and the guy driving that flying car didn't look like an alien. He just looked scared and the girl, she'd got into the vehicle of her own volition. That wasn't the kidnapping the press and his DCI believed it to be. And in DI Softone's view, the chase wasn't the terrorist outrage they suspected either. There was more to this and clearly DC Gurney felt it too. He trusted her judgement implicitly. His DCI might believe the arguments that it was a pursuit rather than a terrorist attack but when it came to MI7 the technology was a problem. Philip Softone rubbed the stubble on his chin and wondered how long he could stall, twenty-four hours? Forty-eight? Seventy-two at a push?

"We'll sit on it as long as we can. The fact they're driving replica cars and that lettering thing should help. Anything about the guys the flatmate mentioned?"

"Nothing much, just the footage I showed you. Not much to go on, they knew what they were doing. They stayed to the side, the background, the blind spots," she sighed. "They're certainly big, though, I believe they were armed and …" she stalled.

"You reckon *they* could be aliens."

"Yeh."

"Any evidence, other than the static torch?" DC Gurney gave him a quizzical look. "You are thinking that, too, aren't you? That with the laser guns, Ms Cochrane might have been telling the truth about the torch."

"Yes. The guns were certainly lasers. They're stone steps, sir, and they've melted."

He looked at his watch.

"You want a decent cup of tea?"

"That would be good."

"Excellent. That flatmate made a damn good cuppa. Let's take her some headache pills."

"Is that wise, sir?"

"No, but I'd like to get a message to Ms Cochrane and her friend with the flying car. They need our help and for that, they have to come in. I can't see who else is going to deliver it, can you?"

Chapter 35

The Pan of Hamgee was tired. He hadn't slept for twenty-four hours and he wasn't paying attention. And that was why, when he caught sight of the green traffic light at a busy junction underneath a raised piece of road which, Ruth informed him, was called Westway, he slammed on the brakes. The snurd stopped immediately but unfortunately, a car following closely behind them didn't. There was a loud crash as it smashed into them.

"You idiot," said Ruth.

"I'm sorry," said The Pan.

"What did I tell you about traffic lights?"

"I know, I know, green means go. I was distracted, I hadn't even realised there were lights here, I saw it out of the corner of my eye and …" He stopped, she was on the brink of losing her temper completely and shouting at him. He didn't blame her.

"You're not insured, either, are you? Do you even have insurance where you are from?"

"Of course we do but my existence is treason, remember? It's illegal to insure me and I'd be foolhardy to give anyone my address."

"And you're a petty criminal and so you don't insure your car anyway."

"Don't be stupid! If I was a petty criminal I'd be squeaky clean to avoid any police attention. I'm not though, I'm a GBI and that's different."

"It's all illegal."

"Yes but saying I'm a petty criminal, you're implying I had a choice. And it's not a car it's a—"

"I know it's a bloody snurd, Mister Pan. OK, look, sit there and do not, do not, do not get out, alright? Whatever happens."

"Alright." Now The Pan was angry with her. It wasn't his fault if the stupid traffic lights were the wrong way round, but he was angrier with himself. "I said I was an arse," he muttered as she slammed the door.

He watched as the driver got out of the car behind them. He was bull-necked, tall, wearing a tight T-shirt and, judging by the size of him, he was an all-in wrestler. He looked like the kind of guy whose temper had gone missing on a permanent basis and right now was fully lit—and then some.

The Pan watched as the other driver squared up to Ruth and began to shout.

It was not gentlemanly to sit in the snurd and let this happen, it was cowardly. Not that such knowledge would ever have stopped him from staying exactly where he was before—The Pan was fully able to accept his shortcomings. He had a watertight excuse here, too. Ruth wanted him to stay put, but his respect for her wishes was overridden by his desire to impress upon her that, against all evidence—not to mention the truth—he was not actually a coward. Hiding in the snurd, however much she wanted him to, was not impressive. And he loved her. And nobody worth anything would hide behind the person they loved if that person was taking the heat for something they'd done. And he wanted her to think he was worth something. Yes. It would send her into orbit but he was going to have to get out and confess.

"What in the Prophet's name am I doing?" he said to himself and opened the door.

"You stupid cow!" the other driver was shouting. "What are you? You're a stupid effing bimbo that's what you are! Look what you've done to my new car!" Ruth, and The Pan, behind her, looked. The front was caved in. It must have been going fast, breaking the speed limit, perhaps. It might explain the shoutiness of the other driver if he was being defensive. It was hard to tell, of course. The Pan hadn't felt much of the impact but then, he wouldn't have expected to; the snurd's safety features were designed to absorb it.

"I'm so sorry," Ruth was telling the other driver. "I really am, I'm fully comprehensively insured. Would you like to call the police?"

"I've already called them, you daft myopic bint!" shouted the driver manically waving a mobile phone under her nose. "And do you know what I've told them?" he shouted, poking her in the chest with his finger. "I've told them some stupid, drunk cow has stopped dead at a green light, right in front of me, for no reason and trashed my car. That's what I've told them!"

The Pan took a deep breath and spoke.

"If you had left yourself enough room to stop, perhaps you wouldn't have hit us," he said quietly.

"Oh yeh?" said the irate driver. "I wasn't the one stopping at a green light." Ruth turned round. Strangely she didn't seem angry, the way The Pan had expected, more concerned.

"I told you to stay where you were," she said.

"Yes, you did," said The Pan. "But I'm not a great one for doing what I'm told, so here I am." He stepped past Ruth and stood between her and the other driver.

"You should have taken your girlfriend's advice," he told The Pan.

"Maybe so, but I was driving, not her, so I think your argument, if you have one, is with me."

"No, no—" began Ruth.

"Yes," said The Pan firmly.

"That's good because I do have an argument with you, you stupid ponce!" shouted the man. "Look! Here it is." He gestured angrily at his crumpled car. At that moment there was a sound of tearing metal and the snurd moved forward on its own. That was bad timing, The Pan thought. He watched the polymorphic metal repairing itself. The other vehicle was still crumpled. He waited. Nope. It wasn't going to return to its original shape. Despite the Chosen One's reaction when he'd told her about polymorphic metal, he hadn't really taken in that metal like the bodywork of the snurd might not actually exist in this version of the universe. It dawned on him that the impact might have destroyed the other driver's vehicle. Ah. No wonder he was so angry.

The Pan stopped looking at the vehicles and decided that it might be smarter to focus on Ruth and the other driver. They were staring at the SE2 in amazement but also, in the case of the irate man, as if it was infected with something deadly. Having settled itself into its original form The Pan could hear his snurd announce, in its very sexy voice, that the damage was repaired and all systems were functioning normally. Oh, perhaps talking vehicles were unusual here, too, even if mobile phones for everyone were the norm. Mentally, he berated himself for leaving the driver's door open, at least with the door closed it would have been muffled.

The other driver glared at the snurd. "What the f—" he began. The Pan had an uncomfortable feeling that it was glaring back. It made a strange noise confirming his suspicions. It didn't often growl but since it had, he knew it had definitely been glaring.

"Easy," he said and it stopped.

"Don't you 'easy' me, you plank," shouted the man.

"I wasn't 'easy'-ing you," said The Pan.

"Then who were you talking to, eh?"

Ah, how to find a plausible answer which didn't admit speaking to a machine.

"Look, I'm sorry. I think there's been a bit of a misunderstanding. The traffic lights are the other way around where I come from and—"

"Don't try to pull that crap on me! Traffic lights are the same all over the world and in case you hadn't noticed, that's my car you've just smashed."

"You smashed it yourself, all I did was stop," said The Pan. "I'm sorry about that."

"Not sorry enough," shouted the other driver, and without warning, he hit The Pan hard on the nose. The Pan reeled backwards against the snurd and the man advanced on him shouting, "I bet you're sorry now, aren't you? You jumped up little—"

"Stop it!" shouted Ruth. The other driver waited. Good, thought The Pan as he sat down on the boot lid of the snurd. He didn't fancy being punched again. Shakily, he put a hand to his nose and realised, with alarm, that he was bleeding blue blood. Copiously. Everywhere.

Arnold's bogies.

"Oh brilliant! How much worse can this get?" muttered Ruth as she handed him a handkerchief.

"It can't help it, it's polymorphic metal," said The Pan, "or did you mean the growling? In which case, it was only being protective."

"No, I meant you. Your nose. It's pouring blood. And we humans, him and me," she gestured to the other driver, "we bleed red."

"I'm sorry," The Pan held his hands out, palms upwards, "so did I until recently."

"I see," she sighed. "That *is* blood coming out of your nose, isn't it?"

He nodded. "I'm afraid so."

"So if this isn't normal for you either then what's going on? Are you ill?"

He shook his head helplessly. "I don't know."

"No wonder he doesn't understand traffic lights, he's a fricking alien!" said the irate driver weakly and he went and sat down on the kerb with his head between his knees.

"Don't be silly," said The Pan. "I'm not an alien, I'm Hamgeean."

"No. Stop talking," said Ruth.

The man looked up. "You're what?" he asked.

"I'm—"

"Shut up, no really, please, be quiet," Ruth said to The Pan. "He's Glaswegian," she told the other driver.

"No he effing isn't!" said the man, standing up again. "It may be cold in Scotland but not enough to turn their blood blue."

"They have a blue flag," said Ruth and The Pan laughed. "Shut up," she whispered. "I can't believe this. You utter cretin! It's bad enough having an accident but don't you realise an alien and a Hamgeean are one and the same thing round here? I told you I would deal with this and you have to come wading in and get yourself thumped.”

“Well, I thought that if I didn’t, you might get thumped.”

“For God’s sake he wouldn’t have hit me, Mister Pan, I’m a girl.” Mmm, the Chosen One was fiery when provoked and he liked that in absolutely the wrong way. Arnold, what was he thinking? He dragged his thoughts back to reality.

“That doesn’t usually stop them at home,” said The Pan. She was angry and he had to mollify her. “I’m sorry,” he said, “I couldn’t let you take the blame.”

“It would have been a lot easier.”

“It would also have been wrong.”

As he watched, the other driver crossed the road and started talking on his mobile phone again. And Ruth sighed.

“That’s touchingly gallant of you, even if it’s also a trifle dim.”

“You like gallant, do you?”

“Yes, Mister Pan, but not dim.”

“Well. What now?”

The other driver was still on his mobile phone.

“I think he’s calling the police again.”

He was shouting at them to hurry up.

“Looks like he’s lost it.” The Pan glanced at the snurd. “We can go if you like,” he said. People on the pavement were stopping to watch, other motorists were slowing down. If they were going to run, The Pan knew they’d have to hurry up.

“I’m sorely tempted but I don’t think that would be a good idea,” said Ruth.

“Are you sure?” he held up his keys. “Do you really want them to meet me?”

“It’s not ideal.”

“Then I’m guessing we agree. It’s not so difficult for us to disappear. In this version of the universe I don’t officially exist, the snurd doesn’t exist …” he swung an arm out towards the SE2 blipping the keyring as he did so. The engine started. “Wouldn’t it be easier? Especially now it seems that I also bleed a different colour to the norm.”

“Yeh and you stop at green traffic lights.”

“Yep, I’m afraid I do and Ruth, none of it is going to make things easier with the authorities for either of us.”

“No. But the problem isn’t that you’re invisible, it’s that I’m not. They’re going to catch up with me sooner or later.”

“Then later, on our terms, when we’ve decided what we’re going to say.”

"No," she shook her head. "Now, to get it over and done with. I have to live here after you've gone. The longer I leave it the worse it will look and anyway what about …?" she stalled. "Lord Vernon. We'll be safer in police custody."

"No. We'll be trapped where it's nice and easy for him to pick us off."

"There'll be policemen to protect us, though."

"Which will achieve what, precisely? You've seen enough to know what he's like. D'you think he's going to let a little thing like killing a few policemen get between him and us?"

She was thoughtful.

"No, but we have to ask for their help and you have to claim political asylum."

"I have to what?"

The police had arrived, several of them.

"You have to claim asylum." She was speaking very quickly. "Tell them the truth. Tell them that you are being persecuted at home and that you'd like to stay here and become British."

"Ruth, that's not going to work, they're going to be asking me about kidnapping you, breaking the front of a building, smashing your capital city and driving without insurance."

"It's our only option. Anyway, you're Lucy's speciality, she's a human rights lawyer, she can get us out of this."

"What rights?"

"Yours. There's no time to explain. Trust me, OK? It won't be for long. Please. Just tell the truth."

"How? They'll never buy it."

"Yes they will. This is Britain, not K'Barth. I know you don't believe me but it *will* be OK. So don't get jumpy, don't be afraid, just tell the truth like I said, sit tight and wait for Lucy and *don't* do anything stupid."

"How will I know? I couldn't spot stupid in this place if it jumped up and bit me. I'm more than foreign, Ruth, I'm from another version of reality!"

She wasn't angry any more. Instead she was half pleading, half commanding with, maybe, a dash of desperate. "Trust me," she said.

He looked into her eyes. She meant it.

"Alright." He blipped the key ring again and the snurd switched off its engine.

Chapter 36

Before DI Softone and DC Gurney had even stood up, a uniformed officer popped his head round the door.

"Sir?"

"Yes?"

"There's been an accident near the Westway. Someone stopped at a green light at the bottom of the slip road. Apparently the guy behind ran into him. The car's the one you're after."

"An old Lotus?"

"Yes, sir, there were two people in it, a man and a woman, the man was driving and he's been assaulted, the guy who ran into them punched him on the nose and, I think this might be a joke, sir, but the team on the scene swear his blood is blue."

DI Softone nodded at DC Gurney.

"Thanks officer. Are the officers on the spot going to bring them in?"

"Yes, sir. At the moment they're still on the scene but they'll be taken to Paddington Green."

"What's the e.t.a.?"

"Fifteen minutes, tops, sir."

"Good, we should be with you by the time they're processed. You're giving the driver a blood test?"

"Yes, sir, both drivers."

"OK. Nice work, put them all in separate interview rooms will you? We'll start with the girl while the MO is collecting blood from the others."

"Sounds like we've found our man, sir," said DC Gurney when the uniformed officer had gone.

"If he is a man," said DI Softone. "I want to keep this case but our anti-alien argument is shaky enough. It's going to play havoc with it if he really does bleed blue."

Chapter 37

It was only a few hundred yards to the RAC club and Lucy was surprised at how easily they completed it. Big Merv seemed to know the way, which helped, but the people out and about on the street acted as if they were unaware that there was a six-foot tall, orange Swamp Thing among them. Lucy noticed nothing more than glassy stares and on a couple of occasions a blink or a shake of the head.

"It's amazing, they're completely ignoring you," she said as they walked a quiet stretch of road with no-one on it.

"Yeh, good innit? 'S like they don't wanna believe their eyes. You think they'll talk?"

"No, we're not far from theatreland. They'll probably think you're a bit part from one of the shows having a pre-performance walk. They're doing a musical version of 'The Creature from the Black Lagoon' at the moment."

"Flamin' typical. I'll bet the Creature from the Black Lagoon's a mean mother who looks like I do. Yeh, I bet he's stupid an' all."

"He might be stupid but I don't think you are. Sorry. We're clearly all …" what would the word be? "Thingist."

"Ain't so different back home with Lord Vernon up top." He smiled to let her know it was OK. She paused for thought.

"You know, I don't think this would work outside London."

He laughed.

"Yeh, Sir Robin said that, but he reckoned that round 'ere, with my antennae under a hat, anyone what realises I'm real would just think I was a big bloke with a bad spray tan."

Lucy laughed before she could stop herself. Big Merv's expression was enquiring.

"'S that funny? Only, I can't say as I know what a spray tan is."

"It's complicated but basically, the pink humans on this planet—the ones like me—we change colour if we spend a lot of time in the sun. We like that. We think it looks healthy and we call it a tan. Unfortunately we've broken our planet so now too much sunlight is bad for us, not healthy at all. However, we've still got this daft idea that tanned equals healthy so instead of lying in the sun, endangering ourselves, some of us … um … we paint our bodies."

Big Merv was suitably dumbfounded.

"Blimey. An' this tan thing, it makes you go orange?"

"No, a tan makes us go brown but a bad spray tan makes a person look orange. That's the joke."

"This orange?" asked Big Merv holding his arms out sideways in a classic here-I-am gesture.

Lucy laughed again.

"No. Not quite that orange but nearly."

The concierge at the Royal Automobile Club greeted the two of them warmly, but without shaking Big Merv's hand, Lucy noticed. They were too near the world outside, presumably.

"Sir Robin sends his apologies that he cannot greet you personally," the doorman told Lucy. "He is expecting you and he will return shortly. In the meantime, he requests that you go on up and make yourselves at home."

"Nice one." Big Merv reached down to pick up the bag.

"Please allow us, sir. I will have your luggage taken up. I believe you know the way?"

"Yeh. Thanks mate," said Big Merv. They walked up a short flight of stairs and through a large central atrium lit by a glass ceiling two storeys above. The carpet was a bespoke weave for the space and in the middle of it was a display of historic cars, shiny two-seaters; one dark green, one yellow. The information board declared them to be Lotuses, or was that Loti? Lucy wasn't sure.

"Ruth would approve of that," said Lucy.

"I 'spect she'll be here before long, girl."

'Girl', Lucy decided she could let that one go; it was 'treacle' and 'sweets' that were a bit much. Big Merv took off his hat and ushered her towards the stairs. She followed him, but as they started to climb, her phone rang.

Chapter 38

After the accident, Ruth had been separated from The Pan by a woman police officer who had breathalysed her – clear – then asked her name and date of birth and invited her to the station to answer some questions.

"Do I have a choice?" Ruth had asked.

"You can accompany me voluntarily, or I can arrest you and you will accompany me in handcuffs."

"That's a 'no' then, is it? Thank you, I'd prefer the without handcuffs, voluntary version, please."

The PC looked as if she was thinking better of her offer but eventually said "Much appreciated, madam. This way please." She took Ruth by the arm and put her into the back of a police car.

And here she was at Paddington Green. She was nervous, she didn't want to find herself being questioned by the anti-terrorist squad. She looked around the faceless interview room and wondered how The Pan was getting on. Badly, probably. The policewoman guarding her had offered her a cup of coffee. It came from a machine; presumably one where the pipes were plumbed in wrong and a little bit of everything went into every cup, regardless. The grey watery liquid in front of her tasted as if it could have been anything from chicken soup to tea.

Nobody had offered her a chance to make a phone call but nobody had arrested her yet, either. She wasn't sure of her rights. Did she get a phone call or did the police do it for her? She was pretty sure they were supposed to inform someone of her whereabouts but not sure when she could demand this. She decided she would see what happened when someone came to actually interview her. She was happy to help the police up to a point, but at the same time, she didn't want to say anything unnecessary that might get her or The Pan of Hamgee into any more trouble.

After a short while, a couple of plain-clothes officers arrived, a man and a woman. She was young, he was older, mid-fifties, perhaps? Ruth couldn't be sure. He was quite short for a policeman and a bit overweight, but he had a vibrancy about him. There was an initial kerfuffle when they discovered there weren't enough chairs for both of them and the male one had to go and pinch one from a room down the hall. Finally, the female one pressed the button on the machine by the table and announced that they were DI Philip Softone and DC May Gurney interviewing Ruth Cochrane. They checked her address, her date of birth and then the questions started.

"The young man you were brought in with – what's his name …" he shuffled the papers in front of him as though he'd jotted it down and forgotten where.

"The Pan of Hamgee," said Ruth.

"Thank you, yes, The Pan of Hamgee." He sounded doubtful, as he repeated it, and she realised that the police officers might not actually know The Pan's name and that the whole note-shuffling thing might be a ruse to find out. Dammit. Too late now.

"I was wondering if you would tell me how you met him?" said DI Softone conversationally.

"He flew through a window and landed at my feet," said Ruth.

The officers smiled.

"Why?"

There was a difficult one, Ruth decided that mentioning all the Chosen One stuff was probably a bad idea.

"I'm not sure."

"He didn't tell you?"

"Yes he did."

Bum. No! She shouldn't have said that.

"But you didn't believe him?"

"His reasons were a bit far-fetched."

Or that, damn.

"What did he say to you?"

"'I'm a little teapot', mostly."

"Then how could you understand anything he told you?"

"I couldn't. Not much." This looked much easier on the telly than it was in real life. The policeman's tone wasn't unfriendly exactly, it was just neutral – and he had that quiet confidence of people who were smart. The woman one clearly thought so. She was watching him like someone who is eager to learn and that felt like bad news to Ruth.

"Not much," the policeman repeated.

Why did he have to do that? It was like every detective series she'd ever watched.

"No."

"I see. Then, how do you know his reasons were a bit far-fetched?"

"Because it wore off and …" She stopped. "This whole thing is nuts."

"If it's nuts why did you get into his car?"

"I didn't know it was nuts then, did I? And it's not a car it's a—" Ruth began. Nooo. For heaven's sake what was she doing?

"Why did you get into his vehicle, Ms Cochrane? Were you kidnapped?"

"Of course not. Somebody shot at me! Didn't you see that? Two huge blokes with uniforms and swords and guns. I was standing on the stairs and they fired a laser at me, and the stone step boiled, and you lot weren't anywhere so I had a choice of going with them or him. What would you have done?"

"What I would have done is irrelevant. I'm interested in what you did."

His reply put Ruth on the defensive.

"Yeh. I'm sure you are," she snapped. No. Not like that. She was angry and upset and she was afraid she would say the wrong thing or worse, cry, which would be deeply humiliating.

"I went with him because he didn't have a gun and I didn't expect his car to fly. In fact, the honest truth is; I thought I could jump out and run away at the first set of red lights."

"Why could he only say 'I'm a little teapot'?"

"Because he comes from somewhere …" What to call it? "Abroad and he'd been tortured."

"Tortured?"

"Yes, haven't you looked at his face?"

"After the accident the other driver punched him, madam."

"Yes, once, on the nose, but he has a black eye, too, doesn't he? They gave him drugs to make him tell the truth and he didn't want to so he thought about a song."

"I'm a little teapot short and stout," began DC Gurney, presumably taking the role of Good Cop.

"Yes, that one and until the Serum wore off it was all he could say."

"Serum?"

"Serum. Truth Serum."

Ruth didn't know what The Pan was going to say to the police. She'd told him to say he was persecuted at home and ask for political asylum but she realised, with alarm, that she hadn't actually told him not to say anything else. What in heaven's name would he be telling them?

"And you believe that."

"He bleeds blue. He drives a space car and I think …" She was going to say he had eyes in the back of his head but something stopped her, she wasn't quite confident enough, in her own mind, that it was true and even if it was, less confident he would want it mentioned. It might be a secret. "I need to talk to a lawyer."

"You are only helping us with our enquiries at this stage."

"Yes, I know, but if I'm going to do that I need to discuss what's happened to me with someone sensible."

"Like your lawyer?" asked the male one with heavy irony.

"She's not like other lawyers."

"They all say that," he said drily and for a moment she almost liked him.

"In this case, it's true."

"Fair enough," said the policeman. "You can phone your brief but before you do, one last question. Do you have any idea who would chase you or why?"

To her complete dismay, a shudder went through Ruth and she started to cry. No sobbing; soundlessly, as if the stress and worry of the last three months had built up to such an extent that it was leaking out of her eyes in liquid form. She was alone and lonely and The Pan of Hamgee was the only person who would really understand how she felt. She longed to talk to him, and she wondered where he was, and the tears ran down her face faster than she could wipe them away.

There were many ways Ruth had imagined talking to the police but it hadn't occurred to her that it might be like this. They would be cynical and hard-bitten and used to people crying to get their sympathy. She knew that if she was in the police officers' position, she would be unimpressed. Perhaps it would even prejudice her case.

"Lord Vernon …" Her voice sounded faint, she was going to have to get over this pathetic inability to say his name without turning into such a big drip. She started again, "Lord Vernon is the closest thing I've seen to pure evil. He came to find me, three months ago. He followed me but I hid and he went away and I came to you and you wouldn't help. In fact the person I saw treated me as if I was mad, or on drugs." The tears were still coming, she looked down at them spilling off the end of her nose into her lap. Blimey! Why wouldn't they stop? What must she look like? She heaved a sigh, wiped her face on her sleeve and looked up again. "After that, Lord Vernon sent some of his troops to watch me and they have followed me since then." Her voice sounded bitter and angry but not to the depth she actually was. "I thought I was going mad and I was so afraid and you wouldn't bloody help me. So, perhaps you can understand why it is that now, I'm not bothered about helping you."

The woman, DC Gurney, was pale and couldn't meet Ruth's eyes. The man,

DI Softone, stood up, went to the door and had a murmured conversation with someone in the hall. He came back with a small plastic packet of paper hankies. He pushed the hankies across the table and nodded at DC Gurney. She announced, for the tape, that she was stopping the interview for a moment or two and switched off the machine. There was a knock at the door and DI Softone went and opened it. After a brief exchange with someone in the hall he returned to the table with a telephone handset which he handed to Ruth.

"Dial nine for an outside line. I'll give you three minutes." He nodded towards his colleague. "We'll be just outside."

"Thank you," she said.

"This isn't only about helping us. It's also about doing yourself a favour—and your young man."

"I know. That's why I need to talk to someone."

"You appreciate that you aren't under arrest—" began DI Softone.

"Yes, and I don't want to be, that's why I'd like to speak to my lawyer if it's all the same to you."

"Fair enough," he said. He stood up and he and DC Gurney left the room. Ruth heard them talking to the uniformed officer outside the door. She was glad she could remember Lucy's mobile number. She heard footsteps retreating down the corridor and the voices of the police officers faded away as they moved out of earshot. She picked up the phone and dialled.

Chapter 39

Across London, at the bottom of the stairs in the RAC Club, Lucy glanced at the screen of her ringing phone. The number was not one she recognised. She shrugged and pressed the green button.

"Lucy, I'm really, really sorry, I know you're ill but I need your help."

"Ruth! Don't worry, I'm much better—" Lucy began.

"You are?" Ruth interrupted her.

"Yes," she glanced up at Big Merv who was standing next to her, one hand on the banister rail, looking imposing. And orange. Very orange. With antennae. She took a deep breath. "Um, yes … never mind that now, where are you?"

"There's the thing, Luce," a long pause. "I'm at Paddington Green."

"The police station?"

"Yes," said Ruth, she sounded on the brink of tears. "You're a lawyer and … um … this is my phone call."

"Have they charged you?"

"Not yet."

"Then what are you there for?"

"I'm helping the police with their enquiries. We had an accident."

We, Lucy sighed fretfully. She didn't like the sound of this.

"Ruth, are you hurt?"

"No, we're both fine." There it was again.

"Ruth. Who's 'we'?" asked Lucy.

"The Pan and I."

"The who?"

"The person who was driving. His name is The Pan of Hamgee."

She had to be kidding.

"Ruth, nobody is called The Pan of Hamgee unless they are one, living in a fantasy world, or two, a rap star. Which is he?"

"Neither."

"Then what's his real name—trust me, he has one."

"That is his name, Luce."

"No, Ruth, it isn't. What did he call himself at the police station?"

"I don't know. We've been separated."

"Good. This Pan of Hamgee person sounds like very bad news."

"It's not like that Lucy, honest. Can you come and help us?" Lucy felt a hand on her arm and Big Merv was beaming down at her.

"Sorry Ruth. Hang on a moment."

"The Pan of Hamgee is a diamond geezer, sweetheart," said Big Merv. "And that's his real name. He's the bloke I was telling you about."

"Your getaway driver?"

"Yeh." A positive ID, good in many ways but … she glanced up at Big Merv's antennae.

"Is he …?" No, start again. "Does he have any distinguishing features?"

"Nah. He dresses a bit funny but he's a regular bloke. Human, like you." Well that was a small mercy.

"OK. Ruth, I'm going to get a taxi, it will take a few minutes. In the meantime don't, I repeat, *don't* say anything until I get there. Right?"

"Um …" said Ruth.

"You haven't." Lucy slapped her hand on her forehead. "Why? You've probably stitched yourself right up."

"I hope not. I hardly told them anything. They only wanted to know what happened and they seemed decent."

"Yes Ruth, that's how they do it," she sighed. "Right, don't say anything else, OK? See you in a very few minutes." As she was about to ring off she heard Ruth's voice again.

"Luce?"

"Still here …"

"Thanks."

"It's nothing. Hang in there and from now on, until I arrive, it's 'no comment' straight down the line." She pressed the red button and turned to Big Merv. "Wait here, I won't be long."

"I'm coming with you."

"You can't. Not this time. You're orange and you have antennae. There's no-one else like you on this planet."

"Yeh and no-one'll admit I'm here. It'll be a piece of cake."

"No. This is the police station I'm going to. They have CCTV and you'll be very, very real to them if they see you on that. They're also a bit more suspicious than the average person. If they see you, they'll assume you are there, rather than pretend you're not."

"Lady, there ain't no-one like me back home either. I'm used to being looked at. I'm a freak. Other Swamp Things are green."

"Here there are no other Swamp Things. They only exist in B movies."

"It don't matter. I'm protection. I got a job to do. I gave Sir Robin my word an' that means I go where you go."

"To be honest, I'd quite like it but—"

Quickly, unexpectedly, he grabbed hold of her arm and pulled her close to him.

"You wanna help Ruth?"

"You're going to let go of me right now, aren't you, Big Merv?" She glared up at him.

"Maybe, girl. When you've answered my question." His hand was tight around her wrist and for the first time in his company Lucy felt fear.

"OK, here's my answer. Yes, I want to help Ruth and yes I am going to." The green eyes met hers.

"Well then, you got a choice. We can go to the police station together or you can try and go alone and I'll take you upstairs and keep you there." The grip on her wrist tightened.

"If you try and stop me I'll scream."

"So what?" He put his other arm round her but he was smart about it. To anyone else it would look like a hug. Only the two of them knew different. "You think any of these flunkeys is a match for me?" Suddenly Big Merv seemed larger and more menacing than Lucy had thought, especially with one arm tight around her waist and the other hand gripping one of her wrists. The green eyes stared into hers. No malice, no anger but unfortunately, no sign of giving in, either. She swallowed.

"No."

"'S right. So listen up, lady. I meant what I said. I ain't gonna hurt you but I also made a promise about you and I ain't breaking my word. I can see you got a job to do but so do I. So, you gonna do this my way or am I taking you upstairs?"

She thought about her self-defence. Could she kick him and run? She looked up at him. No, he was pretending to be casual but—always assuming she could kick him hard enough to wriggle free—she had no doubt he would be faster and fitter than she was.

"It doesn't look as if I have much option."

"That's right. You don't." He let go of her and she rubbed her wrist.

"You have a grip like a vice, Big Merv."

"Sorry, girl. An' I'm sorry to get heavy like that. It weren't polite and you deserve more. No hard feelings eh?" An apology. Unexpected and disarming. Lucy was thrown.

"No hard feelings."

"I know I ain't no good at showing it but I promise I got your best interests at heart."

"It's OK. I'm sorry, too. I don't mean to be antsy or difficult. I'm not used to being protected." Now she felt guilty. How had that happened? He was the one who'd grabbed her arm.

He smiled. As usual, it lit up his face.

"You'll get used to it." Kind of reassurance but also, kind of, an order.

"Only if I want to."

"You will, treacle, you will."

"Not if you keep calling me 'treacle' like that."

He laughed and any traces of awkwardness between them evaporated.

"Sorry Luce."

'Luce' again.

"That's better. This won't be easy. There may be points where I'll have to be like the others and pretend you're not there, too."

"'S OK. You do whatever it takes."

"We'll see how it goes, but please, don't say or do anything unless I ask you to."

"Sure, girl."

"And don't take your hat off."

"OK, girl."

"Come on then, let's go." She turned on her heel and walked back across the bespoke carpet, past the cars and down the stairs. The doorman hailed them a taxi and she walked out onto the street and got in, all the while pretending that she was alone. Big Merv sat opposite her and throughout the entire journey she chatted to the taxi driver and behaved as if she was his only passenger. She managed to get some useful information about what the papers thought Ruth had been up to; useful but not good. At Paddington Green, she paid the driver who was so pale that she felt guilty and gave him a large tip.

Chapter 40

Phone call duly completed Ruth waited for the DI to return and handed back the telephone handset.

"Thank you."

"Your brief on her way?"

"Yes."

"Hmm," he nodded curtly. "There's a woman PC coming to stay with you. We also have a trained counsellor, if you need one. Anything you say to her will be in the strictest confidence."

"That's very kind of you, but I'll be OK," said Ruth. "How is The Pan?"

"Your young man?"

"Um … yes."

"I'll let you know. We're just going to talk to him now. Would you like something to drink?"

"A glass of water would be good."

A woman police officer came in as DI Softone went out, and she stood in silence on the other side of the room. A few minutes later the DI put his head back in through the door and handed the officer a glass of water. She put it on the table in front of Ruth.

"I'll see you in a short while, when your lawyer has arrived and you've had a chat. Now then, it's time I found DC Gurney and we spoke to your friend." He nodded at the officer and closed the door.

****

DI Softone reckoned the vehicles involved in the accident should have been recovered by now. DC Gurney had gone to organise the teams who would examine them, and the accompanying paperwork. So he headed for the canteen, to get some real tea and have a think. As he strode down the hall the Medical Officer was hurrying the other way. DI Softone put out an arm to stall his progress.

"Hey, did you …?"

"Your bloods?" said the MO.

"Yes?"

"The first one was over the limit, not much but a snadge over."

"Good. We'll be throwing the book at him then. The other one?"

"Very interesting. I've had the lab run everything and anything I can think of."

"Find anything?"

"Nothing obvious. It's normal human blood. O negative, if you want to know, nothing out of the ordinary, no trace of drugs, nothing recreational, anyway."

"But?"

"But I think there may be traces of something else. I've no idea what it is, it's nothing I've seen before but it's similar to something I've heard of—a compound the Russians used in the Cold War. Some sort of truth drug. There was a lot of it by the looks of things but either it was administered a while ago or it's broken down very fast. I'd have to conduct further tests to be certain."

"Then go ahead. When will you get the results?"

"Tomorrow morning."

"Damn." DI Softone blew the air out through his teeth. "What about the colour? Do you know what's making it blue?"

"Oh no. There's absolutely no explanation for that. In every other respect it's normal blood. Absolutely what you'd expect from the man in the street."

DI Softone gave him a nonplussed look.

"There's nothing else unusual about it?"

"Other than the colour? No. And even that's impossible to trace—I was expecting a vegetable dye but it's so subtle it's as if the stuff is actually natural."

"Could it be?"

"Natural? I doubt it, there's no medical or chemical precedent; unless he's from another planet, of course. Is he from another planet?"

"I don't think so," said DI Softone but, deep, deep down, he wasn't sure.

"Whatever it is, it's a great trick. Can you ask him how he did it and let me know?" said the Medical Officer.

"Will do," said DI Softone. "Although I'm not sure he'll be able to tell you," he muttered at the Medical Officer's receding back. He went to find DC Gurney.

Chapter 41

The Pan was put in a police car with no choice, but—a plus—without handcuffs. Upon arrival at the police station his personal effects were taken from him. With growing dismay he handed his hat and cloak, his snurd keys, the thimble and the snuff box to a dour police officer who bagged and catalogued them. Next he was taken to see a medical officer who took some blood from his arm. They told him this was to check for 'chemical intoxicants'. In the dim fluorescent light he watched the officer and his assistant as they handled the glass phial of dark blue liquid. Their impassive expressions were rigid and clearly taking some effort to maintain.

Finally, he was led to an anonymous room containing a table with a chair either side, the table and chairs were blue, the lino on the floor was blue, and whatever the original colour, the paintwork was now that unappealing shade of beige caused by years of cigarette smoke.

After a moment or two, a man carrying another blue chair came in, with a woman. They were making every effort not to wrinkle their noses but The Pan noticed their exchanged glances. Clearly the room hummed. No wonder. He had spent three days in a state of perpetual fear. Apart from an ineffectual sloosh and a change of shirt, that was a lot of cold sweat and no bath. He looked down in the direction of one armpit and sniffed. Arnold's pants yes. BO that could knock out a gorilla. He winced. Social embarrassment aside, there's no point being the best escape man in K'Barth if everyone within thirty feet of you can smell where you're hiding.

The woman police officer sat in the chair opposite The Pan and the man placed his chair beside her. He didn't sit down though, he merely leaned on the back of his chair. What to do? Ruth had said to trust her and to tell them the truth. He had no difficulty trusting her but could he trust these people? He cocked his head on one side and looked at them thoughtfully, probably. But would they trust his sanity? Mmm. Possibly not, although the snurd might make them more open to the truth if it was as exceptional, in this version of reality, as Ruth's reaction to it suggested. Then again, they might not have it, it wouldn't surrender itself without a fight; most likely it would be on the run.

There was a recording machine on the table and the woman pressed a button.

"Dee-Cee Gurney and De-yigh Softone interviewing …" a pause as she checked her notes, "The Pan of Hamgee." She gave the date and time.

"Good afternoon, sir," said the man. "I'm De-yigh Softone and this is my colleague, Dee-Cee Gurney."

"Yes, I heard your colleague saying," said The Pan. What strange names.

"Even so, I thought it would be polite to introduce ourselves formally. Do you understand why you are here?"

Oh dear. How to answer that one? It was vital they took him seriously; he had to be calm, collected and self-contained, but at the same time, not to the point where they took it as animosity or arrogance and he alienated them.

"I think I might be in a bit of trouble." Arnold. That was not a good riposte, it was leaning dangerously towards frivolity. The Pan had learned never to use humour with people in authority, unless he wanted to wind them up, of course, in which case it was guaranteed to do so. But he didn't want to wind up this Softone person.

"A bit of trouble," said De-yigh Softone. "Yes, you could say that." He sounded severe, like someone who brooked no argument, but there was the merest hint of a twinkle in his eyes. Not one to cross, but a good man who might even respond to humour, despite his position of authority. The Pan felt a little less frightened.

"What sort of trouble do you think you're in?" asked the woman.

"Well, I'm not a hundred per cent certain. Let's compare notes. You start."

Oops, too glib. Silence from both officers. Yes, definitely.

"This isn't a joke, son," said De-yigh Softone.

"Yes, I can imagine. I'm sorry, that came out wrong. I'm from somewhere else and it's different." How lame did that sound?

"We are prepared to believe that. We've seen your car," said De-yigh Softone.

"It's a—" The Pan began and stopped.

"Snurd?" asked the woman, "have I pronounced it right?"

"Yes, snurd is correct." By The Prophet, how had she known that? No, wait a minute, they would have been talking to Ruth while he had the blood test. Arnold, the blood test. Did they have the results yet? Of course they did. That would be fun to explain. He tried to think about something else. He watched De-yigh—yep, that was a strange name—flicking through his notes. Both police officers were quiet for a while and The Pan had an idea that they were using the silence to unsettle him, hoping he would jump in and fill it. He was tempted to do so but he decided it was wiser to wait and let them do the talking.

"So, sir," said the man eventually, "I gather from my uniformed colleague's notes …" he held them up briefly, "that you are having difficulty answering some of our questions."

"I didn't notice," lied The Pan, "I think the difficulty arose when your officer tried to believe my answers." Well, that bit was honest and put with the lie made a half-truth, sort of; a reasonable start.

De-yigh and Dee-Cee exchanged oh-no-it's-a-wise-guy glances.

"You do realise, sir, that you are going to be charged with driving an unlicensed vehicle without documentation. However, if you agree to stay in the area, we are prepared to release you," said Dee-Cee.

"Then … am I free to go?"

"Not yet, sir, no."

Mmm, the police could do half-truths too.

"So, I take it further charges are pending?"

"That depends on you, sir. They could be but what Dee-Cee Gurney here and I have to decide, is whether we should press them. At the moment, you are in serious trouble. I have my misgivings as to whether or not you are at fault but unless I can uncover the facts, that's the way it will stay. I am going to ask you some difficult questions and I would appreciate some honest answers. I want to help you but if I am going to, you will have to help me."

The Pan waited, thinking carefully about what he should say. The Chosen One had told him to tell them the truth but snurd or not, were these people going to believe him? A lot depended on whether or not they did. He would have to pick his words with care.

"As you know I'm not local. I don't have any instinct as to how you do this here. It doesn't matter what happens to me but I want to make things right for Ruth. What do I do?"

"Only you can decide that, sir."

Oh great. A helpful steer was clearly out of the question. The Pan leaned his elbows on the table and tried to think. They watched, so he took his time. Eventually he leaned back and gave the man one a cool, appraising look, or at least he hoped it was.

"Fair enough. Then, if it's all the same to you, I'm pretty pushed for time so maybe you should start asking me some of these difficult questions you mentioned," he said.

"OK," said De-yigh Softone. "Would you confirm your name, for the record?"

"I'm The Pan of Hamgee."

"Yes, son, and now you can stop messing about and give us the real one."

"That is my real name, what is it with this place? Why are you all so up-tight about what I'm called? The Pan of Hamgee is perfectly sufficient where I come from, and I don't see how you can talk, De-yigh and Dee-Cee. The only difference is I'm not banging on about your names, am I?"

"De-yigh?" said De-yigh Softone and he began to chuckle.

"No, those are our titles," Dee-Cee cut in. She smiled with surprising kindness. "DI is his job title, just the initials, it stands for Detective Inspector and I'm DC as in Detective Constable, my actual name is May and his is Philip."

The Pan was embarrassed.

"Arnold."

"Your name's Arnold?"

"No." He put his hands out emphatically in front of him, palms forwards, in a stop-you're-absolutely-wrong gesture. It was hard to play it cool when every move seemed to be making him look a bigger and bigger fool. "I'm afraid that was swearing. My name is The Pan of Hamgee, which I think, in your language, roughly equates to 'Hamgeean'."

"OK," said DI Softone slowly. "Well, Mister Hamgeean, where are you from?"

The Pan felt the verbal equivalent of a giant crater opening up in front of him. He took a deep breath and stepped into the void.

"Hamgee. I don't mean to sound as if I'm being sarky about this," he said quickly, "even though I'm aware I do. Hamgee is a place, as well as my name, it's in K'Barth which is the country I'm from." He floundered to a stop. The Pan had never knowingly helped the police with their enquiries; more the opposite. He wasn't sure how to go about it. Even so, he realised that there was a strong possibility it wasn't done like this. They were looking at him as if he was nuts. "I wasn't lying when I told your colleague I came from out of town."

"Would out of planet describe it more fairly?" asked DI Softone.

"No. It's this planet," said The Pan. "But a different version of reality—parallel but not the same. I'm here to help Ruth although I haven't been able to tell her the half of why. I don't know all of it, myself. She told me to tell you the truth and ask for political asylum. Otherwise, to be frank, I'd have made up something a bit more plausible than this." He shrugged and gave a self-deprecating smile.

"That's interesting."

Interesting? Why, The Pan wondered nervously.

"Why does Ruth need your help?"

"Because the Grongles are after her, because Lord Vernon wants her and I'm the only person who can keep her from him." Many things frightened The Pan, but hearing that bald statement of fact out loud was scarier than most of them. He could feel the sweat pricking at his temples and the clamminess returning to his palms.

"Aren't you forgetting about us?" asked DI Softone.

The Pan made eye contact and the calm of his voice surprised him when he said. "No. You saw his snurd and you saw what he did to your city. You're not enough."

"And you are?"

"Yes." Too arrogant; too obviously bravado. Qualify it. "I'll have to be, I can drive better than anyone else in K'Barth and I'm all she's got." Arnold, that was still cocky, not to mention inexact. In a choice between himself and these police, The Pan was merely the least useless of the two.

"Okaaay," said DI Softone slowly. He hadn't bought it. Well, he was a policeman, he probably knew the sound of cobblers when he heard it. "And what about Ms Cochrane? Does she want you to keep her from Lord Vernon?"

"Fervently. She's almost as scared of him as I am." He laughed nervously and the police officers looked at him quizzically.

"This Lord Vernon, who is he?" asked DC Gurney. There was no reason why they should know but it was a fraction of a second before The Pan was able to shut down his expression. Only a tiny moment but long enough for both officers to see the beginnings of a look of stunned surprise, not to mention jealousy, at the thought of living in a world where Lord Vernon didn't exist.

"Lord Vernon is the Lord Protector, supreme ruler of all K'Barth. He's not my number one fan but then, I suppose if I had guts enough to do hatred, I'd feel the same way about him." Excellent answer and entirely true. "It seems that wherever I go and whatever I do, I'm destined to be in his way. People who get in Lord Vernon's way tend to die, so the situation is not doing a great deal for my long-term prospects." The Pan was sweating in earnest.

"Interesting," said DI Softone. Why did he keep saying that?

"No. Not interesting, frightening," The Pan corrected him.

Another pause. DI Softone made eye contact, presumably to check whether that was more bravado or had been a real joke. The Pan wondered what conclusions he had reached but his expression was unreadable.

"Is Lord Vernon a Grongle?" asked DC Gurney.

"Yes he is."

"Then, perhaps you should tell us more about the Grongles," said DI Softone.

"What's to tell? They invaded K'Barth before I was born, imprisoned or killed all our leaders and, while the rest of us were too busy bickering about who would replace them, the Grongles stepped into the power vacuum and took over. Anything else you want to know?"

"Would you describe one to us?"

"They're big, about …" The Pan wasn't sure how these police officers would measure height. The legs of his chair screeched across the lino as he pushed it back and he stood up. He put his hand up above his head, yes, he could just about reach, "About so high." He sat down again. "At home they're pretty distinctive, they have green skin and red eyes. If the ones I've seen here are anything to go on they've changed their skin colour somehow. Here, they merely look unhealthy and they wear sunglasses all the time so you probably wouldn't know about the eye colour. I think they've been following Ruth for a while which would fit because that's what they told me, too."

The police were attentive.

"When did they tell you that, sir?"

"Lord Vernon told me yesterday evening while I was in their custody, just before I came here."

The statement hung in the air but DI Softone didn't pursue it.

"Could you identify a Grongle if you saw one, sir?"

"Could you identify another human being? Where I come from there's more than one intelligent species. Not knowing what a Grongle looks like is like not knowing what air is for." He stopped and the two officers regarded him impassively. "Sorry, don't mind me, that's a yes."

"Thank you, Mister Hamgeean," said DI Softone calmly. He nodded at DC Gurney who slipped a photo from the back of her notes and passed it to him. "Are these Grongles?" he asked and when he flipped it round The Pan saw it showed a grainy image of the two guards from whom he had rescued Ruth.

"Yes," he said.

"Hmm," said DI Softone with a curt nod at DC Gurney. She raised her eyebrows. Did they believe him, The Pan wondered. Did these police believe what he, a blacklisted outlaw, was saying?

"So you say these Grongle people had malicious intentions towards Ruth Cochrane and you came here to rescue her."

"Yes," said The Pan. "This place was my only shot at a new start and a normal life, I'd hardly come here and mess it up this badly unless I was acting on some pretty concrete information."

The sarcasm washed over their heads.

"Which did not include the position of the Festival Hall's windows, it would seem, sir," said DI Softone.

Before he could stop himself The Pan rose to the bait.

"I had one and a half minutes to get to her before they did. You saw—" he began angrily and stopped. He realised he was standing up. What in The Prophet's name was he doing? Yeh, don't be sarcastic if you can't take it back. He took a deep breath and sat down. He tried to compose himself and looked across at the police officers. They were good people and he knew he was being tested but he wished they would just level with him. Maybe he should level with them but would they understand? Not in a million years, except The Pan had promised Ruth. Yes. A promise is a promise. He'd give it a go, the abridged version, of course. "There are people, from my world, here, in hiding. Lord Vernon wants them, as well as her. He wanted me to go and find them for him. If I escaped I had to rescue her or he would have … she was …"

"Lord Vernon's insurance?" asked DC Gurney.

"If you like." The Pan was fidgeting. Arnold, this was going badly and he wanted to be calm and collected – on the outside, at least.

DC Gurney exchanged another glance with DI Softone who said, "That's interesting."

By the Prophet, it didn't take much to interest this bloke. He must have a rubbish home life. No, he was talking about something else. What did he actually mean? A pause and DI Softone asked another random question.

"What do you do for a living, sir," a glance at the notes, "in K'Barth?"

The Pan could feel more sweat pouring off him and his shirt was beginning to stick to his back. He must reek; he wished he could have a shower and change his clothes and he hoped Ruth knew what she was doing about this honesty thing.

"I don't have a job in the conventional sense. I'm a GBI."

"A GBI, could you tell us what that is, sir?"

"A Government Blacklisted Individual, my existence is treason so it's illegal to employ me, ergo no job."

"Then how do you survive?"

"That's the point, I'm not meant to."

"But you have?"

The Pan shrugged.

"Yes, I have. I rob, I lie, I cheat, I steal." A little too much self-hatred in the way he'd listed those things. "And," he looked over at them. Should he say this? No. But he'd made a promise to Ruth. "I drive."

"You drive," said the DI, yep, he knew exactly what The Pan was talking about, that was clear but he asked anyway. "What kind of driving?"

Why hedge around the obvious? Just say it.

"I chauffeur bank robbers."

"So you're a getaway man."

The Pan coughed.

"You could call it that."

DI Softone gave DC Gurney an ah-that-explains-it smile. At least, The Pan thought that's what it was.

"Is that why you're on a government blacklist?"

"No, the blacklist happened first. I drive because, as a GBI, it's the only way I can survive. I'm not on the blacklist because of what I do—well, I probably am by this time but—"

Digging another huge hole. Stop. Now.

"I think we understand what you are saying," said DC Gurney.

"As a GBI I have no insurance, no driver's certificate, I'm about as illegal as it gets but I'm also invisible so …" The Pan held his hands out sideways. "If you wanted to let me go, I think you would find I disappeared without trace."

"I'm sorry to say it's not that simple," said DI Softone. His manner had changed. For the first time the DI sounded ominous. "I can believe you drive, but you and your friend have caused a considerable amount of damage."

"Lord Vernon—who is not my friend—caused the damage. I drove and nothing else—or do you mean I caused it because I dodged his fire and let it hit London instead of me?"

The officers exchanged glances again. There was a hidden agenda here but The Pan couldn't divine it.

"You expect us to believe you didn't shoot back?"

"Of course I didn't shoot back! I drive and that's all I do. I don't kill. I never have. I never will and that's the truth—though I don't expect you to believe it." The Pan wanted to keep his voice calm and neutral, without emotion, but the statement came out with more forcefulness than he had intended.

DI Softone took it as fighting words, clearly.

"Sir, you do realise, don't you, that if you're lying we will find out? We have extensive CCTV footage of everything you did."

"Good. Then I humbly suggest you have a look at it and come back when you know the facts."

"You sound very confident."

"I am because I remember what I did. And can I remind you, that a few sentences ago, I offered to disappear."

"That won't be possible, the damage will still be there to remind us, long after you've gone."

The Pan looked up at the police officer; coolly, he hoped, but it was a difficult stunt to pull with a flop sweat on.

"Trust me, the bunch behind me are going to cause a lot more damage and compared to me they'll be *very* memorable."

"The Grongles?"

"Yes."

"Is that why you're so afraid?"

"Yes." No harm being honest answering that one. "Lord Vernon is already here, looking for us and in this place," he made an all-encompassing gesture to his surroundings, "I'm … Well, I think you call it a sitting duck."

"You're safer here than anywhere else."

"No, that's where you're wrong. You haven't met these guys. I have and believe me, if I'm here and Lord Vernon decides he wants to come in and get me, you're in deep poop."

"We'll see about that."

"I like your style but trust me on this, I'm telling the truth and that's not something I do often."

DI Softone looked him up and down.

"I see …" he said. Another brief exchange of glances with DC Gurney. "Can you explain what they want you for, Mister Hamgeean?"

Should he spill everything? No. Not unless he had to, it would make it too complicated.

"I told you, I'm a GBI, I'm committing treason by existing."

"Yes, sir. DC Gurney here and I, are wondering, what did you do to become a GBI?"

The Pan shrugged. By The Prophet, they really wanted to know.

"I have a big mouth and I said the wrong thing to the wrong guy." A bit like he was doing now, very probably, but he couldn't be certain.

"Who was that?"

"Lord Vernon. He was a nobody then but now he's the law. He controls everything. He likes things his way and unfortunately, as I told you, I keep standing in it. That's enough to make you a public enemy where I'm from and that's why he's after me now."

"Why is he looking for Ms Cochrane?"

Arnold, they'd already tried this one from a different angle. The way the K'Barthans chose their Architrave was clearly a novel idea in this version of reality. Explaining it to Ruth had shown The Pan that much. How could he answer the question in a way that was truthful and yet, would not make them think he was lying? Tricky. The Pan's thoughts turned to Lord Vernon, despite his best efforts to point them the other way. Where was he? The Pan had been in this room, with these policemen for some time. Too long. If Lord Vernon had found him and Ruth at the café then he might already have found them here. How close was he? Outside? Or was he going to materialise at the table with them any minute? More sweat ran down The Pan's face and he wiped it away with his sleeve. He had to get this over with and Ruth to safety. No time to make the truth palatable then. He answered the question.

"She's the Chosen One. You know I said there were people from K'Barth here, in hiding?"

"Yes, sir." Both officers were looking sceptical.

"Well, it's complicated but someone Lord Vernon wants has chosen her and she doesn't have any way of getting out of it—at least not until we've found him. Then, I think she intends to have words and try to persuade him to pick somebody else." He laughed bitterly at the thought. She hadn't a hope. "In the meantime, she's the only link between the guy who has chosen her and Lord Vernon. Lord Vernon wants the guy so that means he wants Ruth." To the point but was it a step too far on the honesty front? Please Arnold, don't let them stuff him in a padded cell and throw away the key. He was pretty sure Ruth had talked about telling the truth and asking *for* asylum rather than getting himself locked up in one. Too late now.

There was a long silence. The two police officers exchanged looks. Not surprising, as that hadn't been the most articulate explanation. Quick though. Bonus points for speed. The Pan took a surreptitious glance at the clock.

"So where do you fit into all of this?" asked the DI.

Gulp. Did they have all day?

"I think we've covered the salient points."

The two officers looked at him enquiringly and The Pan sighed. The short version then.

"Lord Vernon captured me and he wanted me to find this guy, the Candidate—that's what we K'Barthans call the person who has chosen Ruth—and betray him. If I didn't, then as I explained …" He stopped. "Look,

I'm no hero, I'll do any number of despicable things to save my own arse but even I can't live with causing another person's death. I've done that once and …" As he thought about his family, his voice almost broke. He paused to compose himself. "I know I can't do it again. So I had a difficult choice. I couldn't betray the Candidate but I couldn't refuse because if I did Lord Vernon was going to …" Nope, he couldn't put the words 'Ruth' and 'harm' in the same sentence. "I had to come and find Ruth, I had to get to her before they did. I didn't have time to think or plan or worry about breaking a window or your precious capital city. Arnold knows it's unlikely I'll get her out of this but if I stand any chance at all it's because I reached her before Lord Vernon's troops. I only had a few seconds to judge it in and I messed up." He held his hands up and let them drop, "I'm sorry about the damage but that's the truth. I'm here to protect her and that's what I did. If I'd had more time to plan I might have been less stupid about it."

Another pause, no reaching for the handcuffs, no obvious signs of doubt. Strange.

"And afterwards?" asked DC Gurney.

"We ran. That was my fault and yes, I know it was stupid too, but I was hoping we would have time to hide and decide what we could say."

"Concoct a plausible story," said DI Softone wryly.

"No it was more a case of … how can I put this? Finding a way to make the truth believable."

There. It was done and in a bizarre way it felt kind of good. The two police officers across the table said nothing to each other or him.

"What happens next?" asked The Pan. "Can I go? Only, Ruth and I are a little pressed for time."

DI Softone looked enquiringly at DC Gurney and she shook her head.

"Not quite yet."

"Do you believe anything I've told you?" asked The Pan.

"We might not have done but as we've already stated, there's your car—" DI Softone began. DC Gurney leaned over and whispered something. "Sorry," he corrected himself, "snurd. And of course, there's this."

He took a familiar glass phial of blue liquid out of his jacket pocket and put it on the table.

"Mine?" asked The Pan. No harm in checking. Putting aside his fears of Lord Vernon's imminent arrival, he was beginning to feel more comfortable in the company of the police, not relaxing, exactly, but there was a minute reduction in his tension levels.

"Yes, it's yours. It's normal blood; Group O negative, nothing unusual, nothing out of the ordinary except the colour. Is that natural?"

"I think so. I'm not sure."

"How can you not be sure? It's your blood."

"Well, it used to be red."

"What turned it blue?"

The Pan shrugged.

"You have me there. I don't know. If you could tell me, I'd be a very happy man."

More looks between the two officers.

"What about Truth Serum?" asked DC Gurney, more to DI Softone than to him.

What? It sounded as if they were going to give him Truth Serum. The Pan hadn't expected that and he was angry. This honesty thing was harder than it looked. Emotionally, it had cost him and now, when he was on the point of liking these police they'd reverted to the behaviour he was used to. He laughed humourlessly.

"You can try it if you like but you'll find I'm immune."

They turned to face him abruptly.

"No, you misunderstand, there's no such thing as Truth Serum here," said DC Gurney. "I was suggesting it might have turned your blood blue."

The Pan shook his head.

"Only if it can do it retrospectively."

"Your friend, Lord Vernon—"

"Be advised he is not my friend," said The Pan, coldly.

"My apologies. It was just a turn of phrase. I would assume he fits the general description of Grongles ..." again a quick check of the notes. "Tall, sunglasses, red eyes underneath?"

"No, not his eyes. They're grey, like a human's. That's a disability to a Grongle so he usually wears sunglasses to hide them back home. He should be green but like the others he's pale at the moment because he's done the same thing to his skin. He's tall, even for a Grongle and he wears a uniform; black jacket lined in red, with a stand-up V-neck collar, brass buttons up the middle, short tails at the back, black trousers, red stripe down the side, waistcoat, white shirt with a kind of scarf—we call it a cravat—"

"So do we," said DC Gurney.

"Black, suede, knee-length boots. He sometimes wears a long coat, also black, red lining—then there's the weaponry; he carries a sword, a gun, a laser pistol, knives—perhaps I should leave it at armed to the teeth. He has a mobile phone—that's notable where I come from—he wears black suede gloves with rings on the outside and he drives the Interceptor; the most lethal vehicle ever constructed. Oh, and not forgetting," The Pan put on his best impression of Lord Vernon's soft, evil voice, "he talks like this."

For the first time, DI Softone cracked a smile.

"Sounds like a nice guy. You obviously know how to pick your enemies."

"Yeh, I'm a total prat."

DI Softone said nothing but gave DC Gurney a look.

"I wouldn't be so sure about that, sir," she told The Pan and announced, for the tape, that the interview was finished.

"Thank you, Hamgeean. It's time for us to have another chat to your girlfriend. Be patient," said DI Softone kindly, "we won't be gone long."

"Thank you," said The Pan as the two police officers made to leave. "Please be as quick as you can. Lord Vernon is tracking us and if we stay in the same place for long, he tends to find us." He wanted his voice to sound calm but he couldn't suppress the fear in it. The idea of Lord Vernon catching up with him … no, don't think about it. The officers noticed and again, they exchanged glances.

"You are safe here but we will be as quick as we can with your girlfriend," said DI Softone. DC Gurney knocked on the door and a constable in uniform came into the room.

"Wait! Before you go, there's something else you should know," said The Pan.

DI Softone paused at the open door with a questioning expression.

"She's not my girlfriend."

"Is that an issue?" asked the DI.

"It might be for her. If you call her my girlfriend to her face, you may find she's unimpressed."

Chapter 42

Before going to see Ruth again, DI Softone and DC Gurney took a moment to discuss their findings.

"Well Detective Constable, what do you think of our young friend?" said DI Softone.

"I can't believe I'm saying this, sir, but I think he was telling the truth—he certainly believes it is, anyway."

"Yes, and it's bad news."

"Why is that, sir?" She always called him 'sir' but sometimes it felt more intimate than his name might have done.

"Because God knows I must have lost the plot but I believe him too and it would be easier for us if he was lying." He smiled. "It didn't come naturally to him did it, honesty?"

She laughed.

"No."

"In my whole career, I've never heard a taller story but there's no doubt he believes what he's saying."

"Yes, and this Lord Vernon, sir …"

"Hmm." He nodded. "Sounds like a right charmer, doesn't he? I've seen few people so frightened of anyone." DI Softone took a moment to sip the watery substance in a paper cup which the machine down the hall classed as tea and wished he'd had time to get a second cup from the canteen. "Except, perhaps, for his girl. Quite the hero, isn't he, giving Lord Vernon the slip and coming here to save her?"

"Yes. Although I don't think they'd met before yesterday, sir. I think that's why he was so keen for us to know they aren't an item."

"But he loves her, doesn't he? Anyone can see that."

She thought for a moment.

"Yes, I think he does."

"So what do we do with him?"

"He mentioned political asylum, sir."

"Yes, but nothing about a lawyer or a phone call."

"Maybe she didn't have time to explain that, sir. He said she told him to ask for asylum."

"Hmm." He nodded. "Or perhaps there's no-one to call. I think he should see a lawyer, though."

"I'll get someone to explain his rights to him, shall I?"

"Excellent idea, much good may it do him."

"Sir?"

"His blood is blue and he drives a car-shaped space rocket, I'm surprised MI7 aren't crawling all over us."

"Give it time, sir."

"More time, I hope. There's more to our friend than meets the eye and I don't like giving him to them until we've got to the bottom of it. Talking about the car-shaped space rocket, where is it?"

"It's in Neasden."

"Neasden? What's it doing there?"

"Uniform tried to get it onto the back of a tow truck. Apparently, it went for one of them and then drove away. They've got it cornered, sir, but it keeps growling at them."

"Without anyone at the wheel?"

DC Gurney pulled a notebook out of her pocket to double-check the facts.

"Yes, sir," she said as she read through the pages. "It seems to have a will of its own."

"So, are you saying that you think we may need to enlist our Hamgeean friend's help to catch his car?"

"There is a possibility, sir."

He chuckled.

"Do we have much to hold them on?"

"No, sir. If we do charge him with the traffic offences we can let him out on bail. The girl is here, safe and sound, he clearly hasn't harmed her and she shows no fear, not of him anyway. If the Festival Hall press charges that's up to them but I don't think we will."

"What about the terrorism issue?"

"The CCTV evidence is unequivocal and it's backed up by eyewitness reports. All the damage was done by the other one. MI5 might try to scare our lad to get access to his snurd but they've nothing concrete. Of course, add his blue blood and MI7 are the ones most likely to want him."

"We can't have that. If what I've heard about them is true they'll kill him and cut him up to see how he works."

"Yes, sir, I believe they do have a tendency to do that."

"Hmm. The one we really want is this Lord Vernon. He did all the damage, what do we know about him?"

"Very little so far, sir, but I'll keep digging. I *have* managed to confirm what

Barry said about his car. It is a copy of a Mercedes; the Uhlenhaut. It was based on their F1 chassis at the time so they only made a handful. What's more only two were ever modified road use." She took a picture out of her file and slid it across the table.

"Have you contacted Mercedes?"

"Yes, sir. Nothing to do with them. In fact, they were unimpressed that I'd asked."

"I'm not surprised. What the hell is it? What's it doing here? What's the Hamgeean lad doing here? He can't really believe all this 'chosen' cobblers can he?"

"I'm not sure he does, sir. The trouble seems to stem more from the fact that the K'Barthans themselves do believe it. If I've read this right, the K'Barthan Candidate is like some kind of Dalai Lama. That makes Ms Cochrane, potentially, their queen."

"I bet she's happy about that," said DI Softone. "It sounds pretty crazy to me."

"Well here's something crazier. Someone claiming to represent the incumbent K'Barthan government has rung and asked for extradition."

"That was quick."

"Yes, sir. Suspiciously so."

"How the hell did they know?"

"I suppose if their listening devices are as advanced as their vehicles they probably heard it from us."

"Hmm." DI Softone nodded. "Do we even recognise the K'Barthan government?" Why was he asking that? It was bound to be a 'no'.

"No, sir."

"Any contact name for the lot in K'Barth?"

"General Moteurs, sir. First name, Ford."

"You couldn't make this stuff up."

"Very true, sir. You know what they say, 'truth is stranger than fiction'. If it is truth."

"Yes. Every time, in my experience. Yet another reason to suggest it's all real."

DC Gurney smiled.

"Tell you what. Why don't *we* explain the Hamgeean's rights to him? I'd like an informal word with this lad. I want to get to the bottom of this and if we want to know the truth, I think our young friend, The Pan, is the one to ask."

Chapter 43

In the foyer at Paddington Green, Lucy stood at the reception window while she explained the purpose of her visit to the goggle-eyed desk sergeant and introduced Big Merv as her assistant. Within minutes, a detective constable opened the security door.

"Good afternoon Ms Hargraves, I'm DC Barnes, DI Softone sends his apologies." Lucy was aware that DI Softone's failure to greet her in person could be construed as insulting. Yes and it was probably meant to be. Never mind.

"Good afternoon," said Lucy and she shook hands with DC Barnes regardless. His gaze travelled up, past her. He put his hand to his collar and adjusted his tie. Nervous, definitely. Big Merv must be glaring at him. "This is my assistant, Mister Merv."

"How do you do, sir?" The detective grimaced, clearly Big Merv packed a bonecrusher handshake.

"Shall we go and see Ms Cochrane?" said Lucy.

"Sure. The DI says she's free to go. We have no further questions for her at the moment," he said, as he led Lucy and Big Merv to a small anteroom to sign in. "So, we'll be releasing her into your custody. The DI would rather she didn't leave the city for a day or two, if that's all the same to you. We may need to speak to her again."

That was a relief. The detective constable led the pair of them upstairs.

Chapter 44

After DI Softone and DC Gurney had gone, Ruth sat in the interview room and sipped the glass of water they had left her. It seemed like ages before the door was opened by a plain clothes officer who ushered Lucy into the room. Then the officer went out into the corridor, along with the constable who had been in the room with Ruth, and closed the door behind him.

"Luce!" Ruth stood up, intending to run and hug her friend but then she noticed she had an escort and stopped. With Lucy was a man. He was dressed in a flash but tailor-made suit—a dark charcoal grey with a light blue stripe—he wore a black leather trench coat over the top of it, also made-to-measure by the looks of things, and the whole ensemble was topped with a black trilby hat. He was built like a nightclub bouncer, except with a neck, and from the look of his face he lived like one, too. His nose was crooked, presumably from being broken at some point and his expression severe. He had green eyes that were not a strictly natural shade and were far too piercing for comfort. Ruth wondered if, perhaps, The Pan of Hamgee had his own lawyer. Whoever this person was, he was wearing the worst spray tan Ruth had ever seen. He was orange. Truly orange. There wasn't even a nod to it being brown.

"Blimey," she said before she could stop herself.

"This is Big Merv," said Lucy. "He's here to protect me."

Ah yes, that made sense. Ruth thought for a moment. The Pan had mentioned a Big Merv, who had sounded pretty frightening. He had also been going to throw The Pan into a river, as far as she recalled, with concrete boots on. Yikes. Ruth looked up at the man standing beside Lucy. He was tall as well as big, over six foot, built like the Incredible Hulk and yes, scary was an apt description. This was the kind of guy who wouldn't think twice about chucking someone into a river. He was menacing. No, that was the wrong word. It wasn't evil menace, like Lord Vernon. He was a little sinister but mostly formidable and stern. He had presence. Yes, that was it. Quite a lot of it and those green eyes didn't help. At the moment they were looking straight into Ruth's with a weighing-up kind of expression. Yeh and they weren't missing much. She cleared her throat.

"Big Merv. The Pan of Hamgee's boss?" she asked him cautiously.

"Not no more, girl. I'd like to think he's a mate, now."

"I see. Well, thank you for not throwing him into the river, then. I think he might have saved my life."

They both looked down for a moment.

"He ain't the kind of bloke I'd ever chuck in the river."

"You did a pretty good job of convincing him you were going to."

"Yeh but, see, that's the whole point innit?" said Big Merv. "You ain't got nothing to worry about, girl and neither has he." He put out his hand. "You gonna say hello?" He smiled and his whole demeanour changed. It was amazing. Suddenly, Ruth found it difficult to believe he would hurt a fly. Despite having been firmly convinced of the exact opposite only a few moments earlier.

"Wow," she said. Crass or what? She shouldn't have said that. Approaching him carefully and cautiously, because it looked as if it might be clammy, she shook his hand. "Uh … how do you do, Big Merv?"

"Wotcher cock," he said, vigorously returning her handshake. Once he'd let go, she turned to her friend and hugged her.

"Luce, thank you so much."

"It's OK," said Lucy. "Anything I can do to help."

"Um …" she looked sideways at Big Merv. "When you say Big Merv here is 'protection' d'you mean …?"

"Big Merv is a retired businessman," said Lucy. She said the word 'businessman' carefully.

"I thought he was a bank robber," said Ruth.

"Not right now, sweets," he said. Sweets? She smiled.

"What happens next?" Ruth asked.

"You go and sign for your things and we go home, or at least we go back to Sir Robin who is very kindly putting us up at his club."

"What about The Pan?"

"What about him?"

"We can't leave him here."

"Yes, we can."

"No, Luce, we can't. Didn't you hear what I just said? He saved my life."

"You think? You nearly got done for terrorism and he may well be—"

Big Merv guffawed.

"He's no terrorist. Sure he's on the blacklist but that ain't the same."

"The blacklist? What's that?" asked Lucy.

"His existence is treason," said Ruth quietly. "The way his police see it, he's forfeited his right to exist by being—well, from what he said, I think he might have been a bit of an idiot—but he was the son of a dissident, which can't have helped. His family are all dead, he's classed as vermin and he can be shot on sight. He was going to start a new life here and he gave it up to save me from those big scary guys. You know, the ones who've been following me around.

They wanted to take me back to their leader, Lord Vernon."

"Lord Vernon?" Lucy turned to Big Merv. "The man in the uniform who turned up at the flat?"

"Yeh. That one."

"Oh." Lucy shivered.

"You've met him then. Luce, I know this probably sounds insane and I promise, when we get back, I'll explain, but if you can get them to release The Pan of Hamgee then I think I owe him that much."

"Yeh an' Sir Robin wants all three of you, so we ain't goin' without him," said Big Merv sternly, wading in on Ruth's side, much to her surprise. She looked pleadingly at Lucy, who was weakening.

"OK. I probably owe anyone who is willing to save you from this Lord Vernon person. However, this isn't wise because he could be in a lot of trouble and I don't really want it washing off on you."

"I think it might be too late for that," said Ruth. "And you know it's the right thing to do."

Lucy heaved a sigh.

"OK. I'll go and get him. You go with Merv and get your things and I'll meet you both downstairs in reception, right Merv?"

"Right."

"With The Pan?" asked Ruth. Lucy still looked worried.

"Yes, with The Pan. But, Ruth, I should warn you that while, as your friend, I completely understand your viewpoint, as your lawyer, I don't like this."

"Lucy, you're a star."

Chapter 45

The Pan waited and tried not to wonder where Lord Vernon was. It was one of the most difficult things he'd ever done. A guy in uniform came and stood just inside the door, legs slightly apart, hands linked behind his back and a bored expression. After what felt like an interminable amount of time, the two officers returned.

"I have your car keys," said DI Softone.

"Thank you but," The Pan hesitated, the whole it's-a-snurd-not-a-car thing was beginning to wear thin and he decided to leave it at 'thank you'.

"I believe we are going to need your help."

"I thought I was helping."

"Yes, sir, you are but we need somebody to catch your car. A couple of the boys from traffic have it cornered in Neasden but it's growling at them and I thought if you and I went up there and spoke nicely to it, it might let you drive it here to the station."

"It probably doesn't want to come here."

"It's evidence, it doesn't have a choice," a pause, "and before we go find it, I want to explain your rights. You don't seem to know what they are."

"I don't."

"Hmm. I thought so." The DI passed The Pan's keys to him across the table.

"Do you have the rest of my stuff?"

"Don't push it, lad."

"I don't mean to but it's important I have those things. They are of …" How to explain? "National significance."

"Let's get the car, first, shall we?"

"Alright then." The Pan grabbed the keys. This was wasting time, he had made a monumental hash of saving the Chosen One and he needed to find Sir Robin, fast, before Lord Vernon did. He couldn't escape. He'd promised Ruth he wouldn't. So he would have to content himself with letting the police tag along on his search, and finding some way to persuade them to let him bring Ruth, too. He held up the key ring.

"If you want my snurd then I suggest you tell your people to back off. We don't need to go and get it. If I press this button it will come to us." He jangled the keys. A picture of the wall of Lord Vernon's office blowing out flashed into his mind. "If your people have been baiting it long we should probably go outside or it may decide to come into the building." If they were expecting him to try and escape they might construe his suggestion as an unsubtle attempt to get into the open. "Does this place have a flat roof?" The police officers exchanged more looks. "Trust me, it'll be fully lit, it's arsey at the best of times and it doesn't do doors," said The Pan.

"Yes," said DI Softone.

The Pan stood up.

"Excellent. Show me the way."

Before they could move, the door of the interview room opened and a blonde woman walked in. She was dressed in jeans and a jumper but still managed to look smart and, more to the point, formidable. She strode into the room as if she owned it, with a flustered police officer in her wake. It was all very impressive until she saw DI Softone and DC Gurney and then her face coloured in a deep blush which slightly ruined the effect.

"Sorry, sir," said the uniformed police officer. "I did say you were interviewing a suspect."

"That is not a suspect, he is my client," said the woman.

DI Softone and DC Gurney both turned to The Pan who raised a quizzical eyebrow and spread his hands out sideways.

"Don't look at me. I've never seen her before in my life," he said.

"I'm Ruth's lawyer and upon her insistence, I'm yours Mister … Thing," said the woman in a tone that brooked no argument.

"Mister Thing?" The Pan stifled his smile but not before she'd seen it. She clearly wasn't happy about her brief. "Well, Ruth tends to call me 'Mister Pan' or 'Mister Hamgeean'. I suggest you take your pick. Who are you?"

DI Softone stepped in.

"This is your lawyer, Ms Hargraves." He pronounced the 'Ms' carefully. "While appearances may suggest otherwise, she is on your side and is here to protect you from us." DI Softone was clearly making a joke, possibly at this woman's expense. The Pan wasn't sure what to do and smiled weakly.

"It's good to see you well again, Ms Hargraves," DI Softone went on. "At least, I assume you have made a full recovery."

"Yes I have."

The Pan wondered what that was all about.

"I found a flu cure that worked. Are you pressing any charges?"

"We may charge your client for driving without documentation and driving an untaxed and unlicensed vehicle. These are offences he, and you, should take seriously. There is a complication in that I gather he's," the DI hesitated, "a foreign national. He has asked for political asylum. Your area of expertise, I believe. The incumbent government of his home nation," he glanced down at his notes, "K'Barth, is demanding extradition but surprise, surprise, since we hadn't heard of them before today and can't actually prove they exist, we don't have a treaty with them. Technically, we should keep him in, but on this occasion, Ms Hargraves, we will be releasing him into your tender care. I'm sure you understand that a number of parties will be unimpressed if he disappears."

The Pan watched as the woman narrowed her eyes. He switched his attention to DI Softone. Stern words, but his expression suggested he would like her to ensure that her charge disappeared forthwith.

"Then I assume you will be releasing him straight away."

DI Softone threw an any-more-business glance at DC Gurney who nodded. "Yes."

"Good," said The Pan's lawyer. "Shall we get on with it then?"

"Yes. Let's," said The Pan with relief.

Before they could release The Pan he had to collect his things and sign for them. They were escorted down the hall to the place where he had handed in the gold thimble and Sir Robin's snuff box. She walked beside him.

"How do you know Ruth?" he asked, more to make conversation than anything.

"I don't think that concerns you," she snapped. Ah. Not keen, clearly.

"Where is she?"

"Ruth?"

"Yes."

"Downstairs in the foyer." The Pan's stomach lurched.

"On her own?"

"No, she's with your boss, Big Merv. There is no way on God's earth I'd be here, with you, if she—and he—hadn't insisted."

"Yes, I picked that one up," said The Pan. "I'm not as thick as I appear."

"Well that's a blessing. But you still smell like a mad tramp, which is definitely not. It's bad enough having to act for you, without you stinking like the rankest rubbish dump on earth. When did you last have a wash?"

"You know there are a lot of people who want to kill me, right now, but I reckon most of them like me more than you do."

"You kidnapped my best friend and you've smashed up London." Ah, so she was Lucy the flatmate.

"No. I saved her life and somebody else smashed up London, by mistake, while they were trying to smash up us. I think you'll find there's a difference."

"Whatever, you still might have had a wash."

"You're right, of course. I'm absolutely at fault. It's dangerous to get too smelly when you're on the run but finding the time to have a shower can be tricky." Lucy glared at him and luckily, before the conversation could deteriorate any further, they reached the place where The Pan had handed in his possessions.

"Here we are, sir," said DC Gurney.

"Thank you," he said. The DC gave him a sympathetic smile and cast a fleeting glance at Lucy. The Pan raised an eyebrow. "Mmm," was all he said. A burly policeman appeared at the window.

"Name?" he asked.

"The Pan of Hamgee," said The Pan.

The policeman glanced at DC Gurney who nodded.

"Takes all sorts," he said and consulted a clipboard for a brief moment before he bent down and ferreted about under the desk. The Pan stood fidgeting nervously. He had a growing sense of unease about Ruth and this was taking longer than he wanted.

"Sign here," said the policeman as he swivelled the clipboard round and pointed to a printed box next to The Pan's name. The Pan did as he was told and received his hat and cloak, which he put on and a plastic bag containing the thimble and Sir Robin's snuff box. With trembling hands he ripped it open, put the box in his pocket and looked into the thimble.

There was Ruth, with Big Merv, but their faces were all wrong. There was someone with them, although he couldn't hear or see whoever it was they were talking to and most of the view was just a grey blur. He turned to Lucy.

"They're in trouble. You shouldn't have left them alone," he said as he put his thumb into the thimble.

Chapter 46

Ruth was escorted through the security door into the foyer to wait while Lucy negotiated The Pan's release.

There was a hole-in-the-wall style reception desk with a bell to ring for attention. An officer was there when she and Big Merv arrived and explained that Lucy would not be down for ten minutes or so.

"I'm about to make a cuppa love, d'you want one while you're waiting?"

"No thanks," said Ruth.

"What about your friend?" he said in a slightly quieter voice that suggested he wasn't certain that Big Merv was really there. Well, Big Merv was very unusual. And orange. So Ruth could forgive the policeman for that.

"Nah mate, I'm good," said Big Merv.

"Take a seat and make yourself at home then, I'll be back in a few minutes," said the officer and left the desk to go and make the tea. Ruth listened to the sound of the kettle and muted voices in a back office somewhere.

"I dunno about you girl, but I'm gonna do what the man said." Big Merv went to the group of seats in the middle of the room and sat down. The lobby was at the side of the building and the windows looked out onto the access road leading round to the car park at the back. The view across the road presented nothing more than the wall of the next building: windowless black slabs of pebbles set in concrete. There wasn't much light getting in and Ruth felt sorry for anyone who worked on reception full-time. Presumably they didn't or they'd get SAD. Yeh, and health and safety would have a lot to say about that. Her eye took in the bedraggled plants and past-its-best decor. The place could do with a lick of paint. She sighed and went and sat beside Big Merv. She hoped Lucy would hurry up.

The main door swished open and closed as someone else came in. Ruth looked up suddenly. It was somebody tall. Immediately she feared the worst and stood up. No, not here, surely? Nobody would dare to come looking for her here. Not even *him*.

"Good afternoon, Ruth," said a voice, quiet-yet-carrying and super-malevolent.

"No …" stammered Ruth.

"Oh but yes. And Big Merv." The Swamp Thing stood up and put himself between Ruth and Lord Vernon. As one, Ruth and Big Merv began to back away. She wondered if she could get to the reception point but Lord Vernon anticipated her idea.

"I advise you not to call for help or you will only have yourself to blame for the death of an unarmed police officer."

"You wouldn't …"

"No? Are you prepared to bet on that, Ruth?" No-brainer, of course he would.

"No."

"'S OK girl," said Big Merv.

"Not for you, vermin," said Lord Vernon. Slowly, he began to walk towards them. "I have waited a long time for this." He pronounced the s of 'this' with a hiss. No way. No way on God's earth was Ruth going to let him anywhere near her.

"What do you want?" As he advanced, Ruth and Big Merv kept moving backwards.

"You, Ruth …" he stopped to look her up and down, taking his time, watching her fear take hold. "And believe me, when I want something, I always get it."

"Oh no you don't. Not this time," she warned him.

"You'd better leave her alone, sunshine," said Big Merv.

"Alas, I cannot. Ruth is the Chosen One." Mock sad and no attempt to hide the smugness underneath it. Ruth stepped sideways from behind Big Merv.

"If I am, then you should show me a little more respect." No harm in trying to pull rank, even if she didn't believe it. He did.

Lord Vernon raised his eyebrows. He seemed more amused than discouraged. "I take it you appreciate who you are."

"I know who you think I am."

"That is not the same answer."

"No, it isn't but I mean what I say. Stay away from me," she said.

"Yeh, you come any nearer, buster, and there'll be some choice action," said Big Merv, stepping in front of her again.

"Big Merv," sneered Lord Vernon. "You're going to try and protect her are you?"

"'S right. If you want her, you're gonna have to come through me."

"I doubt that will take long. It seems you are unarmed whereas I …" There was a long metallic scraping sound as Lord Vernon drew his sword. He waved it casually a couple of times and then, with lightning speed he flipped it straight so it was pointing towards Big Merv's chest. "There is nobody else here. Do you think the pair of you can overcome me and escape?"

Big Merv stood his ground even as Ruth stepped out from his shadow.

"I ain't afraid of you, Lord Vernon," he said, pushing Ruth behind him again. He was though. She could see beads of sweat on the back of his neck.

"You lie, Big Merv. I only wish I had the time to do this with my bare hands. If somebody goes to the effort of standing up to me, I do like them to feel it is appreciated. Sadly …" he flicked the sword upwards and down again.

Together, Big Merv and Ruth stepped backwards again. Lord Vernon was closing in but slowly, his eyes alive with malicious glee. He had them cornered and he knew they were afraid so he was taking his time, drawing it out, making them suffer.

"I do so enjoy these moments. Any last words, Big Merv?"

Ruth felt the solid wall behind her and stopped. She couldn't get into the building again, it was a security door, she'd have to be buzzed in by the policeman at the desk. He was still away out the back, making his cup of tea and she couldn't call for his help. She had no doubt Lord Vernon would do as he threatened and kill him if he reappeared.

Somebody whimpered and Ruth realised, with more embarrassment than horror, that it was her. Lord Vernon smiled, savouring his moment of victory.

Big Merv took her hand, keeping himself between her and him.

"Don't," she said and tried to pull him backwards.

"You should listen to her, Big Merv. You can't save her."

"Maybe not but I'm gonna try."

"Then you will force me to kill you and take the Chosen One at the same time. How delicious." He flicked the sword up and down again. "Such gifts are rare. And it's not even my birthday."

There was a loud sucking sound, like bathwater going out, followed by a pop and The Pan of Hamgee appeared out of thin air.

With alarm, he noticed Lord Vernon and grabbed Big Merv's hand.

"Quick!"

Big Merv swept one arm round Ruth's waist and held her tightly as the sucking noises started up again. Lord Vernon's reaction surprised her. He didn't make a lunge with the sword or try to stop them, he simply stood there. With a sinister smile he pointed at Ruth and then at himself.

"You are mine."

"Not yet," said The Pan firmly as the bathwatery sounds increased in volume and intensity. There was a second pop and Ruth was back upstairs, landing in a tangled heap on the floor with The Pan of Hamgee and Big Merv while DI Softone, DC Gurney and Lucy jumped back in shock.

"What the hell's going on?" asked DI Softone.

"Long story," said The Pan.

"What happened? Where's Lord Vernon?" asked Ruth.

"For the moment, downstairs on his own," said The Pan as he helped her to her feet. She threw her arms round him and hugged him tight.

"Thank you, oh thank you," she was almost sobbing with relief. Ignoring the others she hung onto The Pan, who, at that moment, seemed to be the only constant thing in a shifting world. Ruth couldn't explain what but something about him seemed to have changed—or was it in her head? He was different, softer round the edges. Maybe it was fear, adrenaline or perhaps pure relief. Whatever it was, almost on autopilot and without fully realising what she was doing, she kissed his neck. It wasn't a straightforward peck either, it was something soft and lingering and a great deal sexier than she meant it to be. He breathed in sharply and gripped her a bit tighter, for a fraction of a second too long, before he stood back, still holding her hands. He raised one eyebrow and flashed her a small, confident smile that made her eyes widen and her heart flutter. Something about the way he was looking at her made her catch her breath and everything slowed down. No, no nooo. What was she doing? She was flustered and embarrassed and didn't know what to do.

He laughed and hugged her again, breaking the mood. On the edge of her field of vision, she noticed Lucy, with folded arms and an expression of extreme misgiving. Then everything came back into focus and The Pan was suddenly serious. He held up his keys.

"Come on everyone. We have to fly. Last night Ruth overheard Lord Vernon talk about tracking portals. If he can, he'll be coming right after us so we don't have much time. Our friends here tell me we can take off from the roof so I suggest we go there, very quickly."

"Gets my vote," said Big Merv. The Pan turned to the police officers who were obviously trying not to stare.

"What happened just then?" asked DI Softone. "In the last twenty-four hours I've questioned a man who bleeds blue blood and drives a flying car, I've also met this Thing," he waved a hand at Big Merv. "I didn't think I could top that lot until I saw what you just did."

"It's only a portal."

"Which doesn't tell us anything," said DC Gurney.

"Quantum mechanics …" The Pan shrugged. "There's no time to explain, Lord Vernon has one too and the odds are he'll use it any minute to follow us. We need to go and anyway, my snurd will be looking for me."

DI Softone raised his eyebrows at DC Gurney.

"This way," she said and ran off down the corridor.

The rest of them followed.

The lift had an out-of-order sign on it.

"Don't worry, it's only three flights," said the DC as they began to climb the stairs. Ruth was buoyant. She was alive and not with Lord Vernon and it felt good. On the other hand, she was out of breath and lagging behind and far more worryingly, she'd kissed The Pan of Hamgee in a way that was definitely going to give him The Wrong Idea and she didn't regret it one bit. Oh dear. Her shoes cut into her and her feet ached. She slowed to take them off and several yards ahead, The Pan stopped, came back down the stairs and took her hand.

"Here, have a tow," he said. They started after the DC again.

"D'you really think Lord Vernon can come and get us by portal?" Ruth asked as he hauled her along.

"Yes, but not straight away or he'd be here. We may not have much of a start but it will make the difference if we hurry."

"What if he runs faster than us? He's not wearing four-inch heels."

"Neither are you any more."

"You know what I mean."

"So long as we get to my snurd before he does we'll be fine." The Pan was fit, they were running up stairs and he wasn't even out of breath. Then again, he spent a lot of time running away, so Ruth supposed it was only to be expected.

"And if we don't?" she asked, rather more breathlessly than she'd wanted to. He turned to her as he pulled her along.

"We will."

There was a loud bang, downstairs, followed by shouts and a pinging sound.

"What was that?" said Ruth.

"Lord Vernon," said The Pan.

"Laser fire. Hurry it up mate," Big Merv shouted down from ahead of them.

The six of them burst out of the door onto the roof to find The Pan's snurd with its engine running and its wings in position. It seemed, to Ruth, to be crouching, ready to run. No, it wasn't crouching, it was a machine she told herself as she watched the metal roof melt and liquify into the bodywork. Yes, of course it was a machine and quite a small one … Blimey. She looked at Big Merv. There wasn't going to be much room.

"Quick, get in," said The Pan. Big Merv and Lucy ran to the snurd and jumped in but DI Softone and DC Gurney hung back. "All of you," The Pan told them.

"No, your Lord Vernon and I need to have a little chat," said DI Softone. The pinging noises and shouting were sounding closer.

"You won't get a chance before he kills you. Come on," said The Pan.

DC Gurney looked from The Pan and Ruth to DI Softone.

"I can make him believe they escaped from us," she said, ran to the door and shouted down the stairs. "Quick, they're getting away, where the hell is the armed response unit?"

"Right, lad, Ms Cochrane. On you go."

"We can't leave you here," said Ruth.

"Yes you can. The DC there is a bright girl. I think we can make it stick."

"No you can't," said The Pan. "Go and get in," he told Ruth but she waited. The shouts and the laser fire were getting louder, Lord Vernon would be arriving any second. "It isn't right to leave you but I have to save the others above all else. We can't wait any longer. This is your last chance. Ms Gurney, Mr Softone, please come with us."

"That's DC Gurney and DI Softone to you." DI Softone winked. "Much as I'd love a ride in that nifty vehicle of yours, the answer's no. Get out of here."

"Come on then, Ruth." The Pan grabbed her hand and they ran to the snurd. He jumped in and pulled his seat forwards, Ruth scrambled in behind him. There wasn't much room because Big Merv was in the passenger seat and a lot of the small space behind the seats was occupied by Lucy. She wedged herself in as best she could, next to Lucy's feet. "Heads down and hands off the sides, everyone," said The Pan, as he pressed a button on the dash. The metal roof morphed into position above them. He lost no time, put the SE2 into gear and drove off the side of the building. It sank a few feet before The Pan took full control and it rose up again.

"We shouldn't have left them there," said Ruth.

"I know," said The Pan. "And now we have to make this real or Lord Vernon will kill them." He flung the snurd round and buzzed low over the roof. DI Softone and DC Gurney threw themselves to the ground just as Lord Vernon, followed by a number of police officers, spilled out of the doorway into the daylight. Lord Vernon turned and fired a few shots at the police pursuing him before leaping over the prone forms of DI Softone and DC Gurney, running into the middle of the roof, taking aim and firing at the SE2. It bumped as the armour absorbed the red bolts of laser fire. The Pan circled and turned to make a second pass and again, everyone on the police station's flat roof threw themselves onto the concrete. Lord Vernon was the first to stand up again. After aiming a few more shots at the police officers pursuing him he turned his attention back to the SE2, and pointing the laser gun skywards, he fired. The Pan avoided most of the shots with some furious weaving and a roll but once again the snurd juddered as the armour absorbed a hit. In Lord Vernon's other hand Ruth could see what appeared to be a set of keys.

"Look …" she pointed.

"Do we have to?" said Lucy. Big Merv leaned round in his seat and took her hand.

"'S OK, babe, we're safer than houses up here," he said.

"I don't feel it," said Lucy.

"Trust me girl, I done this a hundred times, even Lord Vernon can't touch the boy here. He's red-hot." He spoke to The Pan. "What's he doing, mate?"

"He's summoning the Interceptor," said The Pan. "I wonder what's keeping it. It should be here by now."

"Looks like it ain't coming," said Big Merv. "Can't say as I'm too sad."

They buzzed the roof a third time but as The Pan flew in, Lord Vernon put his gun back in its holster and took something out of his pocket. With a last look up at the SE2, he vanished.

"Mmm, I think that's done it," said The Pan. He made one more pass, higher, to be sure the police officers were OK. Ruth sighed with relief as DI Softone waved them away. Good, no worries there then. The Pan flipped the snurd downwards, round a couple of buildings and onto an empty side road where he landed and pressed a button on the dash. With a quiet metallic whine it changed back into a car. "No wings, as promised, Ms Cochrane," he said.

Mock formality again. Ruth was grateful for the opportunity to laugh.

"Thank you," she said.

"My pleasure," said The Pan.

She smiled and then grinned at Lucy who was still wearing an expression of concern, mixed with a dash of bug-eyed shock.

"Is this what you've been doing for the last twenty-four hours, Ruth?"

"Yes. It's OK Luce, we're safe now."

"Maybe, but I think we should go back to the—" she began.

"Don't say it out loud," said The Pan from in front.

"Why not?"

"Because we think Lord Vernon is probably listening," said Ruth. "It's OK though and Mister Pan, before you ask …" She leaned forward. The feeling of being so close to him made her slightly giddy. She spoke into his ear. "I know the way. Let me direct you."

"Go ahead," said The Pan. He glanced sideways, checking the road behind him and as she watched his reflection in the wing mirror, he closed his eyes for the briefest second and smiled to himself.

Chapter 47

Something had happened to the Interceptor. Lord Vernon pictured the place where he'd left it in his mind's eye and put his thumb into the copper thimble. The problem was apparent immediately; a metal immobiliser fitted to the front wheel, rendering it helpless, unable to move. He could feel its distress and that made him angry. Kneeling down he examined the yellow plate. It was padlocked on.

Who had done this? He stood up, his eyes searching the street for the perpetrators. No-one. Only a few people who were clearly innocent bystanders. Tempting as it was to kill them in a fit of pique, he didn't wish to draw attention to himself. He swore under his breath. Whoever was responsible for this had allowed The Pan of Hamgee to escape yet again. They would pay. He would find them and make sure of that. It would be the last time they meddled with someone else's vehicle. Lord Vernon took out his laser pistol, slid the power setting back to low and fired. The metal smouldered. He increased the power a notch and fired again. The metal appeared unchanged but Lord Vernon kicked it savagely and it disintegrated into ferrous shards.

He pressed the button on his keys as he vaulted neatly over the bonnet, no need for the Interceptor to duck, Lord Vernon had this off pat. As the gull-wing door opened he slid into the seat. Something was obscuring the windscreen. A plastic bag with a piece of paper in it. He opened the window, reached a hand round and removed it.

He read the warnings on the bag. The human savages in this version of reality had dared to give him a parking ticket.

"I think not," he snarled as he ripped it to pieces and threw the shreds out of the window.

The Hamgeean would be long gone now and the Chosen One with him. Lord Vernon gripped the steering wheel and stared ahead. The muscles in his jaw clenched as he closed his eyes, channelling his rage, feeding on it. The Chatterton-Dix creature had better deliver or Lord Vernon would find some other way to manage his anger.

"And you will not like it, Nigel," he said.

Chapter 48

The Pan drove Lucy, Big Merv and Ruth to a large building in the centre of London with a flag hanging from the front of it. It was cramped and uncomfortable in the snurd but he managed to complete the journey without serious incident. The Pan was glad, for all their sakes, that it wasn't a long journey.

Ruth's position behind him involved her leaning between his seat and the doorpost with her head distractingly close to his. As instructed, she was giving him the sparsest of directions: 'left,' 'right,' 'straight on,' 'get out of the bus lane,' 'stop it's red,' – those kind of things.

However, in an initiative of her own, presumably so it was difficult for any listening Grongles to hear what she said, she was speaking in a low voice, pretty much into his ear. Simple 'left's' and 'right's' were having such an effect on him he wondered what would happen if she whispered something more provocative. He then had to spend the rest of the journey trying very hard not to.

When the SE2 drew up outside the RAC everyone was relieved. Once they had all climbed out of the snurd, they went inside, where the staff on the door appeared to know they were coming and greeted them as Sir Robin's guests. The others went ahead while the doorman gave The Pan directions to an underground car park, and a token to get in free, but when he reached the entrance the SE2 stalled. It wanted to park elsewhere. He sighed.

"No, I wouldn't want to sleep in there either. Alright then, but not a word to anyone and don't do anything I wouldn't do."

He drove it round the corner, got out and blipped the keys. It pulled out into the traffic and headed off into the gathering dusk.

The Pan returned to the club and tried to hide his glee when, once again, they let him in. He climbed a flight of stairs to an oval atrium, where he found a set of wheels very similar to his snurd.

"How come these get to park inside?" he muttered. Close to him, someone laughed.

"You really should stop talking to yourself. It's not parked. It's a display you dolt, it's a car—a Lotus to be precise."

He couldn't keep the smile off his face. She'd waited for him. Surely that meant something?

"Ruth, why aren't you with the others?"

"Because I wanted some time to myself and this is about the only place where I'm safe to wander round on my own. Besides, one of us has to show you where we are staying. Oh and I can't have a shower yet because Big Merv is using one bathroom and somebody called Trev is in the other one."

No way.

"Trev's here?" The Pan was laughing.

"Yes."

"And Gladys and Ada?"

"So I hear."

"You haven't met them?"

"Not yet. Where have you been? I've been waiting ages."

"Sorry, it took longer than I thought."

"You got lost?"

"No …"

"You didn't park it, did you? You let it go off on its own."

"It argued …"

"What am I going to do with you, Mister Pan?" she said.

"Mmm … I could think of something."

"Stop flirting."

Uh-oh. She sounded stern.

"Are you angry with me?"

She shook her head and smiled.

"No. Although I don't know why not."

He nodded at the car.

"Nice."

"Yeh, expensive too. I always wanted one of these but just as I'd scraped the money together they got trendy and the price shot up."

"It looks like my snurd," said The Pan.

"Yes, I suppose it does." Ruth took his hand and led him up several flights of stairs to a door marked 'service'. She pressed the dot of the i and it opened with a click.

"Service?" He gave her a quizzical look.

"Service," she said flatly but she was trying not to smile. "I hope you're paying attention, Mister Pan."

"Of course."

"Good." Behind the door was a large cupboard. Along two sides were shelves. Dusters neatly folded, tins of polish, dishcloths, rubber gloves, sponges and green scritchers were all lined up carefully, each in its allotted place. Leaning along the other wall: brooms, mops in buckets, vacuum cleaners and hanging on a peg, several pinnies. She turned on the light and shut them in. The Pan raised one eyebrow.

"Did you mean to lure me into a cupboard or are we lost?"

"I would never be so foolish as to deliberately lure you into a cupboard. I know exactly what you'd try to do."

"Yet here we are. What happens next?" he asked her.

She giggled.

"Will you behave?"

"I take it we're lost then."

"No, Mister Pan, we are not lost." She pushed one of the brackets holding up the back shelf and the entire wall opened slowly into a room. On the far side of it was a large water tank. Large, in this case, meant big enough to accommodate the quantities of water required to service the entire club and probably top up the swimming pool downstairs. It was the size of a double-decker bus or thereabouts. She turned a light on, switched the cupboard light off and the wall began to swing slowly back into position. The Pan stepped smartly through to join her in the space beyond. He glanced at the tank and raised the other eyebrow this time.

"Are we here about the plumbing?"

She laughed again.

"Will you be sensible for one moment?" On the side of the water tank was a tap. She turned it but no water came out. Instead the front of the tank swung open. "Apparently, the Underground has quite a lot of money and the RAC are very accommodating. Sir Robin says the apartments here were built some years ago when the Grongles first invaded K'Barth. The Architrave was going to flee here but he never did ..." Well, The Pan thought, he'd got beheaded, which might have made travel difficult.

"Sir Robin says they are portal proof. Apparently you'll understand what that means, heaven knows I don't." She leaned back against the side of the tank and gestured him past her. "There you are, Mister Pan. Welcome to Free K'Barth."

He moved closer to her and peered in. The tank contained a flight of stairs at the top of which was a short corridor and a perfectly normal door.

"Arnold in the skies. Now that's impressive." He chuckled. "Shall we?"

She took his outstretched hand.

"If you insist."

Ruth and The Pan climbed the stairs but as they moved towards the door at the end of the corridor, he noticed a shift in her mood. She slowed and eventually stopped a few feet away.

"I think we've come up a bit short," he said as he leaned forward, theatrically pretending to reach for the handle. She didn't laugh. Oh. "Are you alright?" he asked her.

"Sort of …"

"Sort of. Mmm, that sounds like a 'no' to me. Care to elaborate, Ms Cochrane?"

She looked down at her feet.

"OK, I feel really bad saying this but I went in there while you were parking and there are people inside and they're not … They're from … They don't …"

"You mean, it's full of K'Barthans."

She was relieved but at the same time embarrassed. About as embarrassed as she'd ever been by the looks of it.

"I'm supposed to be the Chosen One and I feel like a circus freak."

It was easy to appreciate her point of view. As far as he was aware, The Pan was the only man in existence with four eyes in either of the realities he'd visited. There were many reasons he kept quiet about the extra pair, but his fear of standing out, of being branded weird, was high on the list. Neither he nor Ruth had any way of telling whether or not the K'Barthans behind that door knew she was the Chosen One. But if she was anything like him, The Pan could understand her fear that they might. He tried to put himself in her place. How would he feel? Under pressure? Conspicuous? Did she feel that everyone was watching, wondering what would happen next, and worse, pinning their hopes on her?

"It's understandable. I feel like a circus freak myself, sometimes," he said.

She smiled gamely, but the 'you-are-one' quip he was expecting never came. The Pan waited while she stood there, deep in introspection until something seemed to resolve itself.

"I'll get used to it. I'll have to, won't I? But I feel out of place."

"Even with Lucy?"

"She seems completely unfazed but she's on the phone to her work. She's busy organising an emergency week off, she's calling it 'personal reasons' but I think she wants to look after me. Anyway, it's OK for her. She hasn't been chosen by one of them."

He raised an eyebrow.

"I thought you said you weren't chosen. I thought we were here to find the Candidate and have strong words with him about picking someone else," he chided with a smile.

"I did, but what if …" she stopped. "There are people in there who are …" she stopped again. "OK, the person who greeted us was very polite and everything but he was about three feet tall, orange, furry and he looked like a guinea pig and—"

The Pan burst out laughing. Arnold's snot! She was feeling nervous and awkward and it wasn't tactful at all but he couldn't help himself. Oh well, nothing to do about it now but try to make the joke stick.

"Ms Cochrane, are you worried you've been chosen by one of them?" He was surprised and delighted when, instead of being cross, she seemed relieved and broke into genuine laughter.

"I'm so embarrassed. I'm sure I'm being a racist or a speciesist or something. I bet you're not bothered, are you?"

"It depends … We consider ourselves intellectual equals but certain species are just biologically incompatible. I'm not sure what a guinea pig is but if the Candidate was a Spiffle, which is what I think you're describing, he would probably fancy someone a bit less humanoid. Another Spiffle, for instance—or possibly a Blurpon. Physically, they're a bit more like each other." Should he go into the emotional differences, the most laid-back species on the planet versus the most uptight, violent, Olympic-standard launderers? No.

"OK, OK Mister Pan. Could you possibly be a little more sarcastic about this?" asked Ruth. She was laughing properly now.

"I doubt it. I'm sorry." He hugged her. "If it helps, I will be with you every step of the way, alright?"

"That's not necessarily going to be an advantage."

"No." He smiled but the elation he'd felt only minutes before had evaporated. That had smarted more than he'd expected. Suddenly everything felt a little lacklustre. She looked into his eyes and took his other hand.

"That was a joke, Mister Pan," she said gently. "I'm sorry if I hurt you, I'm a bit wired and I expect my comic judgement is totally off."

"No, I'm not hurt." Arnold, why did he have to be so crazy about her? She was going to take him apart.

"Do you mean that? Only you look—"

"You're fine." He pulled her towards him to give her another hug. This time, she hugged him back. Properly. There was a lot of contact, almost as if she was melting against him. She put her head on his shoulder, in no hurry to let go. The Pan's spirits soared skywards again. He closed his eyes and held her tight. "You are more than fine," he whispered.

She looked up suddenly, smiling.

"I didn't catch that, Mister Pan."

He looked into her eyes.

"I think you did."

"Oooh, you're a cool customer," she said and she was laughing and hugging him and he was flying. "Honestly, I didn't."

"It was nothing worth repeating," he said. She gave him a measured look so he qualified it, "Alright, nothing worth repeating … yet."

"Really?" she said flatly.

"Really." They stood there, gazing into each other's eyes, for a moment that seemed to last a long, long time. If he tried to kiss her, The Pan wondered, would she scream? On the face of it, it appeared not. She lifted her chin and he took a breath. He leaned in and stopped. Nothing he'd ever done in his life had ever taken so much willpower as not kissing Ruth, right there. But, tempting as it was to seize the romantic initiative, the entrance lobby to the K'Barthan Underground HQ was patently not the time or the place. More to the point, if he actually started kissing Ruth, The Pan wasn't sure he'd be able to stop. And a gentleman would wait until she was more comfortable in the company of his K'Barthan compatriots before making a move.

"Ms Cochrane," he untangled himself and linked his arm through hers. "It's high time you met my friends. I think they're going to like you." She smiled and his heart did a backflip. "I'm hoping you'll like them, too. I know this isn't easy but I meant what I said. I'm here whenever you want me."

She squeezed his arm.

"Thank you, Mister Pan."

"A pleasure, as ever. Shall we go inside?"

She took a deep breath.

"Why not? If only to have a shower."

"Ah, so The Chosen One needs a wash. I thought something around here smelled a little fruity."

"You are so damn cheeky, Mister Pan. You're the one who really honks. Lucy thinks you smell like a tramp."

"She's right. I'm sorry. I'm so rancid it's dangerous, they'd sniff me out if I was hiding on a rubbish dump." He laughed, and opened the door.

Chapter 49

Ruth's second visit to the Underground's secret headquarters did little to improve the impression made by her first visit several minutes earlier. It was exactly as she would have expected a busy diplomatic building to be—maybe that's why it felt so wrong—because the strains of familiarity to the scene only accentuated the bizarre nature of the K'Barthans. She didn't want to appear prejudiced, but there was a world of difference between seeing a blue-skinned alien woman snog the Captain on GalaxyTrek and actually meeting one in the flesh. It made her nervous. She held onto The Pan who put his arm around her waist and gave her a reassuring squeeze.

"Don't worry, you'll be fine," he whispered as a large, roughly humanoid thing ambled towards them. It looked a little like Big Merv—and it had the same antennae—only green and yes, Ruth thought, it probably was a lady.

"Sorry, I can't stop, there's a lot to do," she held up a sheaf of papers and then, despite her words she did stop; dead in her tracks. "Wow, you're the guy who outran the Interceptor, aren't you?"

"Yes," said The Pan, surprisingly shyly.

"You have no idea how cool that is. We all watched it on the news. Lord Vernon must so hate you! You're the toast of Free K'Barth." She looked down coyly and shifted from one foot to another. Was she flirting with him? Yes, it looked like it, although The Pan didn't seem to have noticed.

"I think Lord Vernon hating me is situation normal," he smiled politely. "Though I doubt our escaping has improved things." The green (yes, she had to be) lady scribbled something across the corner of the sheaf of papers she was carrying, tore it off and pressed it into The Pan's hand. "If you need anything, here's my number ..." The Pan raised his eyebrows.

"Your ...?"

"My phone number ..." she stopped as The Pan and Ruth exchanged bemused looks. "You *are* single, aren't you?"

"Er ... yes ... at the moment." He looked at Ruth and every nuance of his expression said, "Help me!" She stifled a giggle, but even so, she moved a little closer. The green thing clocked it and then, probably from pure embarrassment, snapped back into businesslike mode.

"Sir Robin knows you're here. Please take a seat and I'll get someone to attend to you."

"Thanks," said The Pan casually and sat down on one of a row of chairs along the side of the corridor. Ruth sat next to him. He looked into her eyes. "What was all that about?"

"You tell me, Mister Eligible. But I'd say she just hit on you." She smirked. "How big is Free K'Barth?"

He scratched his head.

"I don't know, but they're obviously very short of men."

"Maybe they like idiots." She giggled. "Smelly ones at that."

Together they watched the green lady moving away down the corridor. He took a deep breath. Ruth could see him visibly dropping his guard and relaxing.

"It's good to be home," he said.

"I had no idea how tense you were until we came in here."

"Yes, well," he smiled and raised an eyebrow. "Meet the calmer, smoother me. I hope you like it."

"I guess it'll pass." Ruth liked The Pan, full stop.

A door closed in the corridor.

"Ah, someone's coming." He moved in his seat and waved one hand in the general direction the sound had come from. It just happened to involve moving closer to her. It was far from subtle, which was endearing. She looked down to hide her smile.

A blue man with a surprisingly long neck and strange protruding ears walked past in the direction from which the Swamp Thing lady had come. He carried a bundle of files and was reading one of them as he walked. He was almost past them when he suddenly noticed they were there, stopped and turned to address them. This one spoke mainly to Ruth.

"Good afternoon. Welcome to Free K'Barth. Are you really the Chosen One?" he asked her. She glanced helplessly at The Pan.

"I don't know, I don't feel very chosen …" she said.

"Is it true this guy outran the Interceptor?" asked the blue thing.

"Yes, it's true," Ruth smiled. The blue thing regarded the pair of them thoughtfully.

"You're not the Candidate then?"

They both laughed.

"I think that's highly unlikely," said The Pan.

There was a pause, during which Ruth reckoned the blue thing was searching for a tactful way to say 'but you like her don't you?' Instead he moved on to safer ground.

"Sorry, I shouldn't be waffling on. Has anyone offered you a drink?"

"Not yet," said The Pan.

"How remiss. I do apologise. What can I get you? Tea, coffee, or if you prefer, we have a nice range of herbal blends from the north of K'Barth."

"Coffee, strong coffee; white, no sugar, please."

"I'll have the same," said Ruth. She was less nervous now but leaned back a tiny fraction, anyway, to feel the reassuring warmth of The Pan's arm.

"I will be back directly," said the blue man.

"What kind of milk is it?" asked Ruth tentatively when he'd gone.

"The animal?" She nodded. "Ah, it's a big thing, leg at each corner, horns," The Pan put a crooked finger up either side of his head, miming them. She was disappointed that he'd moved his arm. "It eats grass. I'm not sure if animal names are the same in your strain of Grongolian but our lot call it a 'cow'."

That was a relief!

"So do we."

"That's good." He smiled into her eyes. "Would you like to know about the blue guy?"

"Yes please."

"Well …" he leaned back, more or less assuming his original position except now he put his arm round her shoulders. She leaned against him. "The blue chap is a Blaggysomp. They hail from Smirn, in the centre of K'Barth. Their capital city is called Driesch. It's a mountainous region and not many of them bothered to venture down before the Grongles came."

"So why now?"

"It's remote, so people on the run used to go up there to hide. The Blaggysomps were kind enough to shelter them at first. So now, if anyone on the blacklist escapes the Grongles, Smirn, well, Driesch mainly, is one of the first places they look. Things are too hot for most of them up there now so they've started to come down. Unfortunately it's also too hot for them down here but in a different way. They have to shave off their fur and according to Gerry, the guy I used to deal with at snurd, who is also a Blaggysomp, they are martyrs to sunburn."

Ruth tried not to but she couldn't help laughing.

"They're not blue because it's cold up there?"

The Pan seemed nonplussed.

"No. They're blue because they just are, up there in the cold or down here in the warm. When they are sunburned they go dark blue."

More footsteps now. Two female humans skittered up the corridor faster than was safe on such high heels.

"Are you the guy who escaped from Lord Vernon?"

"Mmm-hmm." The Pan smiled. "Twice."

Ruth nudged him in the ribs.

"Big-head."

He chuckled and the girls tittered coyly.

"Are you the Chosen One?" the taller of them asked Ruth.

"Mmm-hmm," she said, aping The Pan.

"Are you two an item?" asked the other one. Blimey. Nothing like cutting to the chase. "Um—" Ruth began.

"Not yet, but I'm working on it," said The Pan. God he was cocky. He winked at her and raised an eyebrow.

"Stop that," she said, and she laughed.

Several more K'Barthans appeared, including the small furry orange thing that had greeted Ruth earlier, all of them wanting to know the same things; whether The Pan had really outrun the Interceptor, whether Ruth was actually the Chosen One and if the two of them were an item. After a few minutes there was quite a crowd gathered.

"Excuse me, but what's the big deal about us going out?" Ruth asked the Spiffle who had greeted her originally when she'd arrived with Big Merv and Lucy. He was the most friendly and approachable as well as the nearest, although talking to him was a little surreal, like conversing with a highly intelligent cat. Nooo not like a cat. Ruth didn't want to think things like that, in case she said them because she was sure it would be rude, not to mention un-PC.

"You're the Chosen One, you belong to the Candidate. If you've fallen for someone else it means something."

"What though?"

The Spiffle shrugged.

"Search me. Unless he's the Candidate. Some people think he might be. Is he?"

"I don't think so and he definitely doesn't. Would he know if he was the Candidate though?"

"Oh yes, he'd know."

Ruth turned her attention to the rest of the conversation. A tall, beautiful, raven-haired woman at the back currently held The Pan's attention, too much of his attention, Ruth thought, until the dark-haired beauty wrinkled her nose in distaste and said, "Does the smell help you to blend in?"

Ruth began to giggle but The Pan was taken aback.

"No, I just haven't been able to have a wash."

Ruth leaned over and whispered in his ear, "Now who's the circus freak?"

"Mmm … I'm merely sacrificing myself to divert unwelcome interest from you."

"Of course."

On the edge of the crowd Ruth noticed another of the human K'Barthans was wearing a T-shirt. Stencilled on the front of it, in a heart shape, was a reproduction of the grainy CCTV pictures she'd seen in the newspapers of herself and The Pan of Hamgee with the legend, 'Is he or isn't he?' written above it. It was bizarre to see that it was in English, although, she supposed they would say it was in Grongolian. The picture was from the Festival Hall as they were running hand in hand down the stairs. There was no sign of the snurd parked at the bottom, though. Maybe they'd airbrushed it out. Ruth felt uneasy. She was stuck in a world full of people and things that were so out there they made the extras in the weirdest sci-fi movies look normal. She and The Pan were supposed to be in hiding and instead it looked as if, in a small way, they were celebrities. Keeping a low profile was going to be difficult.

Ruth noticed a door opposite them marked 'private'. There was a rattling of keys and it opened. The Pan stood up. Ruth followed suit and again he put a protective arm around her. A well-built man of about forty opened the door, carrying a tray with two cups and a plastic box on it.

"Oi! You lot. Hop it," he said. There was a general mumbling and shuffling of feet. "Go on. Git," said the man as he stood in the doorway. Suddenly something streaked past him. A parrot, Ruth thought, but it was difficult to tell. Surely, only a victory of willpower over the laws of physics could get a bird that bald airborne.

"Air biscuits!" it shouted as it circled over the heads of Ruth and The Pan's crowd of admirers. "Bombs away! Bombs away!" With mumbled see-you-laters and nervous glances upwards they went swiftly about their business, presumably to avoid being spattered with any of the parrot's. Finally it landed on The Pan's shoulder.

"You never told me you owned a pet," said Ruth.

"Hello Humbert," said The Pan. "I don't." He let go of her for a moment and stepped forwards, arms out sideways. "Trev! I thought you were on holiday."

"Bite my winky!" shouted Humbert and to Ruth's alarm he flapped over to her shoulder. She could feel his claws digging into her as he hung on. She looked at him out of the corner of her eye. Her evening event clothes weren't totally ruined yet, but she didn't hold much hope for them if they were covered in parrot poo. She thought about the pigeons living in the rafters at Farringdon Station. Or more especially, what they tended to do, from a great height, on the unwary commuters below. Please let parrots have better control, she thought.

"I am, mate!" said Trev to The Pan. He hurriedly put the tray down and ran to The Pan's outstretched arms. The two of them hugged, clapping each other on the back and laughing.

"Thank you, I thought they were never going to leave us alone."

"Yeh. There's nuffin' clears a crowd quicker than a brush with Humbert," said Trev.

"Very true," said The Pan. "He's Ada's parrot," The Pan explained to Ruth.

"Wipe my conkers please," said Humbert, quietly, into Ruth's ear.

"And it seems he likes you," The Pan added.

"How can you tell?"

"He said 'please'. Trev, this is—"

Trev wrinkled his nose.

"Blimey mate, you don't half pong."

"Yes, yes. I smell like an unwashed warthog but—"

"Nah mate, it's far worse than that."

"Thanks, Trev, a picture of tact as ever. Ruth, this is Trev," said The Pan.

Yes. Ruth had got that but it seemed easier to pretend she hadn't so instead she put out her hand and smiled.

"Hello Trev, how do you do?"

"Wotcher, Ruth. Here, let me take that." He held out one arm and Ruth tried not to show too much relief as Humbert obligingly flew over and settled there. "I've brought yer coffee an' some buns. You got plenty of time to get sorted before supper."

Chapter 50

After a shower, Ruth found Lucy and they caught up properly on each other's news. Lucy told her how she and Nigel were no longer an item. Ruth duly commiserated with her friend, even though she was secretly relieved that Nigel, who had always treated Lucy so shabbily, was off the scene.

Then Lucy told Ruth all about her adventures with Big Merv, how she'd met Lord Vernon and Ruth gave her the full story about The Pan, except that she studiously avoided mentioning that she fancied him. Judging by the look of concern Lucy wore, she'd either guessed there was something going on or feared there might be. Never mind.

As they sat in the room they were to share, Ruth took in her luxurious surroundings. There was a large double bed and a lounge area with comfy chairs and a coffee table. It was a bit like a hotel, except instead of the minibar, kettle and other self-service arrangements, there was simply a large red bell pull.

"That's posh," said Ruth, giggling. "Have you tried it out?"

"Not yet," said Lucy, putting something in her mouth. "Ugh ..." she shuddered.

"What's that?" asked Ruth.

"Another of Mrs Poldark's Gnissoids."

Ruth laughed.

"That sounds like a medical condition."

"You may be my flatmate but if it was a medical condition, I doubt something called Mrs Poldark's Gnissoids is the kind of thing I'd admit having, not even to you. I had flu this morning and Big Merv got me some stuff to make it go away. These are part of the cure," she held up the box. "So long as I suck a gnissoid every four hours I won't notice I'm ill."

"Wow! That's brilliant."

"Yes, almost, but I swear they taste of Satan's bile. I'm supposed to keep taking them for two weeks but I can see myself giving up on them way before that and opting for the flu instead."

"They taste that bad?"

"Yes. And some!"

"Ugh. Poor you."

Ruth's mobile phone began to ring. As she saw the number on the display she was filled with dismay.

"Hang on a moment," she said to Lucy, unplugged the phone from the charger and slipped out into the hall.

Chapter 51

A few miles east, in a flat in the Barbican, Nigel Chatterton-Dix waited for Ruth to pick up the phone. If this was going to work, he would have to give the performance of his life. He thought himself into 'tortured soul' mode accordingly. The phone rang a surprisingly long time before, finally, Ruth answered.

"Hello?" she said.

"Ruth …" he began, with a sob.

"Bye-bye, Nigel."

"No wait! Don't hang up."

"One good reason? You vile, snivelling crapbag."

"I've made a terrible mistake—"

"You bet you have," Ruth cut in. "And Lucy certainly did when she fell for you."

"Please, Ruth, I have to talk to you. I've been a fool and I need your help. I can't be without Lucy. I have to get her back."

"Yes, Nigel, you have been a fool and if you really love her that much, perhaps you should have thought before treating her like a doormat."

He relaxed and concentrated on quelling his irritation. He wasn't going to get what he wanted from Ruth without a sanctimonious lecture. And she was going to make him grovel, too. Never mind, things would be different when he introduced her to Lord Vernon. Yes, that would cut her down to size. He waited for his smile to fade before speaking, in case she heard it in his voice.

"I understand you hate me, I understand why you are making me crawl but I've changed, Ruth. I need Lucy." Well, that wasn't a lie, he just didn't need her the way Ruth would be thinking. "I have to talk to you."

"You could always talk to her."

So sarcastic. So irritating.

"She won't talk to me!"

"Have you tried?"

"No, but why should she? You said yourself, I've treated her badly and it's true! But there are reasons—I need to explain. If you knew, you would understand and then maybe if you spoke to her, she would listen."

"Why should I help you? You've been nothing but trouble since I refused to shag you on the grounds that you were dating my best friend." She wasn't biting.

"Ruth, I've said I'm sorry. What more can I do?"

"You can leave her, and me, alone for ever."

He had to do something radical to change her mind, now, or she was going to hang up.

"Please Ruth. I'm begging you, I'm dying here." He thought about what would happen when Lord Vernon returned and before he could stop himself, he burst into tears. "Help me. Help me, please."

"Nigel, you are so full of it," said Ruth, but her voice had softened. Perhaps she knew genuine desperation when she heard it, even if she didn't understand the real reason why. "OK. Where and when?"

"It needs to be somewhere we can talk openly. What about my place? Can you be there at seven o'clock?"

"I won't be staying for dinner, Nigel."

"I'm not asking you to, that's when I get back from work, usually. I tell you what, I'll leave early. What about six o'clock or just after? I don't want to be your enemy, Ruth, and I want to do what's right by Lucy."

"Yeh, well in my book the best thing you could do for Lucy would be to leave her alone." A sigh. "Luckily for you I think she may disagree. OK then, your place, ten past six."

"Ruth."

"Yes."

"You won't tell her, will you? Not until I've explained everything to you."

"No, Nigel. I won't tell her."

"Thank you. Thank you so much."

"Yeh. Goodbye Nigel."

She hung up.

Nigel breathed out slowly. On one level, bursting into tears had been humiliating and unexpected. He was badly shaken by the depth of his fear. On another level, it had been lucky that he had because it had probably changed Ruth's mind.

"Genius," he began to laugh, "pure genius!" He stood up and danced across the room, and threw himself onto the sofa. "Once again, Nigel, you have pulled it out of the bag! God I'm good!"

He took the business card Lord Vernon had given him from his pocket and dialled the number.

Chapter 52

Washed, dressed and a great deal more relaxed, The Pan strolled through the private apartments in the Underground's secret HQ, exploring. They were spacious and extensive, though not quite extensive enough for everyone to have a bedroom each. He was to share the largest room with Big Merv and Trev, Gladys and Ada had another room, Sir Robin had a camp bed in the study and Ruth was sharing with Lucy. The Pan knew Ruth and Lucy would have lots to catch up on so it seemed tactful to leave them to themselves while he familiarised himself with his new surroundings.

In the dining room, the table was laid for dinner—dinner for nine. Strange. That would be Sir Robin, Gladys, Ada, Their Trev, Big Merv, Lucy, Ruth, himself and someone else. Another member of the Underground? He put it to the back of his mind; his subconscious could mull it over while he carried on with his exploring. Big Merv and Trev were playing backgammon in a large drawing room. It seemed an unlikely pursuit for either of them but they were clearly enjoying themselves and The Pan, who didn't feel like either watching or talking, left them to it. There was a kitchen, the study Sir Robin was using, the bedrooms and the two bathrooms. He found a smaller, less formal sitting room and even a library full of ancient K'Barthan volumes. It looked like a fascinating and comfortable place but he moved on.

The Pan was tired but unsettled. He was anxious to talk to Ruth and leaving her to spend some time with her friend was taking every ounce of his self-restraint. Ruth liked him. He knew he wasn't imagining it now. What were she and Lucy talking about? Him? He had the impression that Lucy wasn't his biggest fan, and he hoped she wouldn't be trying to put Ruth off. Chemistry aside, there were a lot of practical reasons for the Chosen One not to start a romance with someone who had no future, came from a different version of reality, oh, and who wasn't the next Architrave. The Pan had never been one to let that sort of thing deter him, but Ruth was down-to-earth and sensible. She'd hold no truck with the Architrave thing but might be daunted by inter-reality romance.

He searched for Gladys and Ada to thank them for bringing his clean clothes, they'd brought his pyjamas, too. However, after following the heavenly smell of supper cooking to the kitchen, he discovered they were not there but, instead, were closeted in the study with Sir Robin, talking Underground business. He guessed that confirmed his suspicions then, the extra guest was another Underground member. He decided not to disturb them. Everyone seemed to be busy and settling in nicely. Everyone except him. He stood in the hall wondering if he'd given Ruth and Lucy long enough to catch up when he noticed a door he had not yet opened.

That might kill a few minutes. Behind it, he discovered a flight of stairs leading up to the roof. It was all garden, the whole thing, barring a massive glass dome which illuminated the central atrium of the main building below. He whistled.

"Arnold," he said as he looked around him. It was well established. There were small trees, mostly fruit-bearing varieties, raised beds of flowers and vegetables, decking with loungers, deckchairs, tables and umbrellas and there was even a small swimming pool. As he wandered through the garden, he felt curiously at home, as if he belonged. Yeh, well, it was the Underground headquarters, a slice of the old K'Barth. It would be marked out by a general ambience of his home, so similar and yet so different to the version of reality he was in. He walked along the path from the stairs to the other end of the roof, turning the occasional slow circle as he went, in order to admire his surroundings.

As he walked, right into his ear, someone said, *Cluck*.

He span round but there was no-one there.

Cluck, said the voice again. He relaxed. It was just a chicken. By The Prophet that was cool. The Underground 'grew' their own eggs as well as vegetables. He wondered where the chicken coop was. Nowhere immediately obvious. He listened out but the chicken didn't cluck again. Never mind, he'd probably happen upon it by chance if he carried on exploring. Or perhaps he'd imagined it.

He couldn't wait to show the roof garden to Ruth. She would like it, he was sure. At the end of the path in the furthest corner, he found a smaller area which was lower than the rest, on the roof of a newer extension. Tucked away down a flight of steps it was secluded and private, protected on two sides by the walls of the original building. As he descended the steps he realised they continued down into the apartment. At the bottom of the next flight he could just make out a door. A private entrance? Maybe. Perhaps this part had been reserved for the Architrave. He looked around him. This area was square, and half roofed in — the roof, a smaller square, in one corner. There was a strip of balcony along two sides. The Pan reckoned it was directly above the dining room and the kitchen. He peered over the balustrade and found he had guessed correctly.

Behind him, in the corner under the roofed part, was an area of decking, with a low bed, the mattress covered with a crisp, white, fitted sheet. There was no other bedding, instead it was piled high with large cushions. More of a daybed, perhaps. Other floor cushions and beanbags were strewn decoratively about the decking. There were also tables and some reclining chairs. Tastefully positioned lanterns hung from the rafters or stood on the tables.

"Mmm … very nice," he said as he took it all in. He walked over to the cushions and tried them out. "Very comfy, too." Only to be expected he supposed. He moved to the bed and lay looking up at the timbers of the roof above. The sounds coming up from below were muffled. It felt quiet, safe and private. Big Merv and Trev could have the room, he would sleep up here: dozing in peace and tranquillity, while the chaos and buzz of life in a huge city continued around him. Perfect. He got up and leant on the edge of the balcony, breathing in the balmy evening air. Beyond the street, stretching out into the distance was London. It was beautiful, even with a few bits missing.

Cluck. Sometime, The Pan realised, he would have to find these chickens.

"Later."

The chicken clucked again but in a desultory way, this time, as if to say, 'suit yourself'.

The balcony ran beyond the half wall, opening out into another secluded area. There were two doors which he opened. They contained a bathroom and a small kitchen.

"Handy," he said aloud. The bathroom was luxurious and equipped with soaps, toothbrush and a seemingly limitless supply of large towels. Clearly other people had stayed up here, people who didn't want to share a bathroom and didn't fancy the idea of trekking all the way back downstairs if they were caught short in the night. He peered into the kitchen, checking the fridge and cupboards. Both were stocked with treats—olives, smoked salmon, dips, biscuits, strawberries and raspberries, not to mention some chilled half-bottles of champagne in the fridge, and in the glasses cupboard, a bottle of Gladys' home-made Calvados.

The Pan helped himself to a raspberry and then scraped a cracker across the surface of a bowl of hummus. Arnold's pants he was hungry. Better stop—it'd be a pity to ruin dinner.

Back to the balcony again and as he leaned over and looked out at the view his thoughts turned to Ruth. Round and round they went in an endless loop, but The Pan wasn't bothered. He was safe for the moment and happy to relax, let his guard drop and enjoy the novelty of dwelling on his favourite subject.

After some time spent in pleasant reverie, he realised he'd been there too long. It was time to go inside. He hadn't said 'hello' to Sir Robin. Gladys and Ada were cooking, which usually meant supper at seven, or maybe eight because of the meeting with Sir Robin. He glanced at his watch; nearly five o'clock. Perfect, there was a strong chance they'd be starting to cook dinner in earnest by now so they were bound to have finished their meeting. He would see if they needed a hand.

He retraced his steps and emerged into the hall, opposite the kitchen. From behind the door he could hear the clatter of pots and the hubbub of voices. Mouthwatering smells wafted into his nostrils. Yep, Gladys, Ada and Their Trev were back in there now and cooking up a storm. He decided he would join them and help but as he took a step forward, something caught his eye.

At one end of the hall was the entrance door to the apartment, at the other was a large window. It was getting on for evening now, the light had acquired a golden tone and the shadows were lengthening. The sun lit up the leaves of a London plane tree outside, its greenness showing the first tints of autumn. Framed against this leafy magnificence stood Ruth, with the light illuminating her, like a halo.

The Pan caught his breath. She was oblivious to him, her freshly charged mobile phone clamped to her ear. As he watched her, she turned round to face him, unseeingly, and stood with her back to the window, leaning against the sill. She was looking a little punk – all the more interesting after the restrained nature of her business-function-friendly evening clothes. She wore purple canvas jeans, dark blue, pointy, suede ankle boots with kitten heels and zips in the side, and a dusky blue top with a zip up the front which flattered all her best bits. Wonderfully, it seemed something had distracted her while she was zipping up the top, because she'd left the neckline tantalisingly low. Everything went into slow motion as The Pan imagined taking her in his arms and slowly, teasingly, undoing that zip. His mouth went dry. He swallowed. He tried to collect himself and prayed his thoughts hadn't shown on his face.

Oh dear. She didn't look happy. Please Arnold, let it be because of the phone call and nothing to do with any inadvertent mental undressing on his part. More to cover his confusion than anything he spoke to her. Despite looking straight at him, it appeared she hadn't realised he was there because she started, as if he had made her jump.

Chapter 53

Ruth leaned against the sill of the open window, watching as the backlight on her phone faded. Bum. Nigel could never have seen the error of his ways. It was a ruse of some kind and now she had to go and see him. Why hadn't she just told him to get stuffed? Too late now. Ten past six, his place. She looked up.

The Pan of Hamgee was a lot of things but not, in Ruth's estimation, the kind of person who could stand in front of her, unnoticed, while she made a call. Even so, there he was looking sheepish.

"How did you do that?"

"What?" he asked.

"Creep up without me realising?"

"I didn't creep up! I came through that door there a few seconds ago and you were on the phone so … I just stood here. You weren't listening out for me, that's all."

Her favourite top was having a marked effect. He was flustered and making a miserable failure of not looking at her cleavage. One glance at that face and his true emotions were anybody's. It was endearing and engaging. Well, quite a lot about The Pan was engaging. Best think about something else.

He cleared his throat and waved his hand at her mobile. "Bad news?" he asked, dragging her back to reality with a bump.

"I don't know. It was Nigel, Lucy's ex. He chucked her by voicemail and now he says he's haunted by remorse. He wants to speak to me about it. He wants me to help him persuade Lucy to take him back." He came and stood beside her, at the window.

"But …?" His eyes scanned her face.

"What, apart from the fact he's a vile, odious prig and I don't want them to get back together, you mean?"

He laughed.

"Yes, apart from that."

"It doesn't really ring true. Nigel would never be haunted by remorse."

"I see …" he was thoughtful. "Anything else?"

"Am I that easy to read?"

"Yes. So come on, out with it."

"He told me not to tell anyone he rang and he wants me to come alone."

"Mmm." He leaned on the windowsill next to her and although he was looking at Ruth, his mind seemed to be elsewhere.

"Is that all you can say?"

"Sorry, I was thinking. Ruth, I know we're not in K'Barth but I don't like the sound of this. Why do you have to be on your own?"

"He didn't give a reason."

"Really? That would be enough to ring my warning bells."

"Mine too, if I'd remembered to ask him but I forgot."

"Then phone him and ask. If you don't like his answer don't go."

"I have to, I said I would."

He looked at her, his expression still thoughtful—and serious—which was alarming because there was nearly always a hint of a smile in The Pan's eyes, somewhere. She expected him to crack a joke, try to lighten her mood, but he didn't.

"You don't have to. You're on the run and that policeman asked your friend Lucy to ensure we disappeared."

"Not in so many words."

"There were enough for me. Let's recap. This Nigel bloke has asked you to come alone, you're suspicious and you don't think he loves her, anyway. Looks straightforward enough to me, you stay here."

"If only it were that simple."

"It is."

"No, it's not. OK, I don't think Lucy getting back with Nigel is too likely. I mean, there's a chance because she's in love with him but she can still see he's a git. I think she knows breaking up's the sensible thing to do, even if it's painful but …" she stopped.

"This is like milking blood out of a stone, Ms Cochrane. But what?"

"But firstly, from Lucy's point of view, I don't want to rake it up unless I have to. What with rescuing us and being followed everywhere by your friend Big Merv she seems to have forgotten about Nigel for the moment."

The Pan chuckled.

"Ah, yes. Big Merv is difficult to miss. I can imagine he's quite distracting."

"Larger than life."

"Mmm."

"The problem is, nothing's distracting Nigel. He cried. I've never heard a man cry. He didn't treat her as if he was in love but on the phone he sounded desperate. I have to go, if only to break it gently."

The Pan took her hands in his and looked at them for a moment.

"Do you want me to come with you?"

No-brainer—of course she did—but she had to do this. It wasn't about danger, she was pretty sure of that, it was about confidence; hers. He was worried, and as usual, despite his best efforts he was failing, dismally, to hide it.

"No. It'll be OK."

"Are you sure?"

"Yes. It's Nigel, he's rank and I loathe him but I'm pretty sure that's all he is. He's not going to get involved in something like this. Anyway, two days ago I wouldn't have thought twice."

"Two days ago, Lord Vernon hadn't chased us across London."

"He was still watching me, though. The only difference was that I didn't know his name. Nigel is from London, not K'Barth. He has nothing to do with any of this. OK, so I'm surprised because I didn't think he cared one jot for Lucy and that's probably why I'm worried. But I could easily have misjudged him. I expect it's my paranoia that's doing the rest."

"You don't think it is, though, do you? Or we wouldn't be having this conversation."

"Yes I do. I'm just exorcising my doubts."

"Mmm. I listen very carefully to doubts like those and I firmly believe it's the reason why I'm not dead."

"Yes, but you're a criminal and a getaway driver, not to mention a loon, and therefore extra specially paranoid. *I'm* just being stupid."

"I'm happy to accept that I'm paranoid but you could never be stupid. Not by any stretch of the imagination. When are you meeting him?"

"Ten past six or as near as." She was nervous about leaving but at the same time she didn't believe she was in any real danger. She had something to prove not just to The Pan, but to herself. He seemed to understand because he didn't press her.

"Alright. How about a compromise? You have until six fifteen, tops and then you have to ring Lucy on your mobile phone.

"She'll want to know why I rang her."

"Then tell her the truth; that you went out without saying where you were going, that you want her to know where you are and that you're alright. Otherwise, if we haven't heard from you by then, I'm going to come looking for you."

"Thank you."

"It's a pleasure. Are you sure you don't need a lift? I could run you—"

"No," she said firmly. She looked at her watch. "It shouldn't take long, I should be on my way back by twenty to."

He looked at her with an appraising clarity that unnerved her. "I'll hold you to that."

Then he walked with her to the end of the corridor and she opened the door. Side by side, they went back through the 'public' areas of the Underground HQ, down the stairs, through the secret doors in the water tank and the back of the cupboard and down the real stairs of the club proper to the foyer and the street entrance. There, they stopped. He turned her round to face him.

"Ruth, are you sure you don't want me to come with you?" he asked. Now he was getting over-protective.

"No. This won't take long. Really. I'll be back in time for supper."

Chapter 54

Despite the Chosen One's tiring proclivity to keep escaping, Lord Vernon felt relaxed and at ease. He was confident that she would soon be in his power. In the meantime, General Moteurs had returned to discuss the results of his latest meeting with Sir Robin Get. The General was not relaxed, although he was calm enough, if pale. One of the Palace servants served fruit smoothies and finally, glasses filled, mats and a plate of bar snacks just so, the servant withdrew.

"General. How did Sir Robin and your friends at the Underground react to the news that my installation will take place next Saturday?"

"They are foolish enough to be delighted, sir."

"Excellent. When will they be ready for collection?"

"Tomorrow morning, sir, as scheduled."

"Good. And when they are in the cells, where they belong, I shall make the date of my installation public."

"Sir."

Lord Vernon raised his glass.

"To the annihilation of the Underground in K'Barth. What a pity I cannot wipe out their Grongolian colleagues at the same time."

"I believe it is just possible that you can do that, sir," said General Moteurs.

"Do you? How?"

The General took a sip of smoothie.

"Sir. As of tomorrow, the Underground here will cease to exist. This is their plan. To roll over and play dead until such time as the Candidate will rise up and vanquish you."

"The Candidate, this boy who does not know who he is or what he is for?"

"The same."

"Perhaps they are confusing roll over and play dead with roll over and be dead."

"Perhaps so, sir."

"Have you met the boy?"

"No, sir. Not yet."

"But if required could you find him and … decommission him?"

"No, sir. That is why I have not delivered them to you before now. Sir Robin assures me that I will meet him. Tomorrow."

"Good. After that I assume you will be able to remove him, if required."

"Sir. However, the longer he lives without realising his identity the greater the chances firstly, that he will never do so and secondly, that the chain of succession will be broken. Indeed, Sir Robin believes that if he does not realise before Saturday, he is lost."

"Interesting, but we digress. You were going to explain how I might terminate the Grongolian Underground."

"Sir. They are working in tandem with their brothers and sisters here. They are planning to stage a coup."

"What a surprise. When?"

"Sir, the best, the only opportunity for them is when the High Leader is out of the country. It has occurred to me that we have a bona fide means of achieving that by inviting him to your installation."

"Naturally, I would appreciate his presence." Oh yes, to rub his nose in it. "But it is academic since my office tells me his diary is full for the next six months."

"Yes, sir. However, I have taken the liberty of exploring the matter further and he has expressed an ardent desire to attend." Lord Vernon viewed that as unlikely but said nothing. "Should you announce a date for your installation I am reliably informed he will make it his business to be here."

"How fortunate. However, the security measures alone would be substantial. I doubt even you can arrange them by next Saturday, General."

"On the contrary, sir, they are all but taken care of."

Lord Vernon raised his eyebrows.

"Excellent. Continue."

"The coup will fail, sir. The Underground in Grongolia are compromised completely. My operatives there, who are, after all, your operatives, will expose the traitors around them. You will be very popular in the Home Nation."

"And the High Leader will be in my debt." Lord Vernon smiled. That would be most amusing.

"Sir. I believe you may appreciate that."

"Yes, Moteurs." Lord Vernon regarded the General with a penetrating stare. As usual the red eyes met his with equanimity. He was speaking the truth, that much was plain and Lord Vernon was pretty sure he knew how it was being spun. "If you can achieve that, then perhaps I shall have need of a Field Marshal," he said slowly.

"I will look forward to it, sir."

"I am sure you will." Lord Vernon checked his watch. It was time to visit Mr Chatterton-Dix. "And now, General. I am required elsewhere." Lord Vernon stood up. "We will resume this conversation upon my return. You are available at seven thirty?"

"Sir," said General Moteurs. He bowed, clicked his heels and was gone.

Chapter 55

As soon as he turned his back on the street and started to head back to the RAC, The Pan began to worry. Despite Ruth's reassurances, his instincts began to gnaw at him. At the top of the stairs to the atrium, he stopped. Above him was the glass ceiling. He stood next to the club's display of pretend snurds and looked up. It was as if just thinking about the tranquillity of the garden up there gave him enough headspace to clear his mind. His doubts crystallised into certainty. He'd done the wrong thing. He should have insisted he went with her or at the least followed her. Instead he'd let her go outside, alone and unprotected. Arnold! What a plank!

He turned and ran, jumping down the stairs and hurtling at speed, through the doors onto the street. Which way had she gone? He turned round in a circle, looking for her. There! In the distance. He sped after her. It was rush hour. The traffic on the street was backed up in a jam and there were a lot more pedestrians on the pavement to impede his progress. Ruth was walking fast and she had nearly reached the tube station by the time he caught her up.

"Ruth." He grabbed her arm. "Ruth, wait." He was out of breath from running. She turned round angrily, though there was a hint of relief there, too. Unfortunately, cross won out.

She fixed him with her sternest glare and said, "Let go of me, please, Mister Pan."

He removed his hand at once and she started to walk again. He fell in step with her.

"I'm sorry."

"Good, now go back to the club …" She kept walking and The Pan stayed right beside her, ducking and diving round the people coming the other way as he spoke.

"How can I? I made you a promise that I'd keep you safe and that means not letting you go out on your own."

"No, it means not stifling me. This is my city, I've lived here a while and I think I can be trusted to make a tube journey, in broad daylight, without protection." She upped her pace.

"I fully understand that and I don't mean to stifle you," he said as he ducked round a woman with a pushchair, "but this isn't a simple tube journey. You have a git to meet at the end of it." They arrived in a ticket hall with barriers. She stopped. The corners of her mouth twitched but she suppressed her smile and turned and faced him.

"I'm serious, Mister Pan. Your insistence is very touching but you are not coming." He knew from her eyes that she was frightened. It was taking all her willpower to refuse him and that made him all the more anxious to go with her.

"Try stopping me," he said.

"I don't think that'll be a problem."

He raised a sarcastic eyebrow.

"You think? As the best getaway man in K'Barth, I'm a difficult man to ditch."

"For all your cockiness, Mister Pan, I don't doubt it but I think you've forgotten something." Before he could reply she stepped forward and kissed him on the cheek; a soft lingering kiss that was completely unexpected and sent his blood pressure soaring. "This is London."

He had to hand it to her, she timed her response to perfection. Without a backwards glance she swiped her Oyster card across the reader and nipped through the barrier. Disarmed, undone, The Pan didn't move fast enough; didn't get close enough to slip through with her. The barrier closed with a slam. "See you later, Mister Pan," she said and was lost in the crowd.

The Pan made a mental note that the dominant male approach only worked for, well, dominant males. Yeh. Bin that one. Now what? Ruth had made it clear his presence wasn't required and yet he couldn't ignore her eyes, her voice and most of her body language, which were, frankly, begging for help. And he had let her get away.

How could he have allowed this to happen? With no money for a ticket, he couldn't even follow her. Anyway, she'd be long gone and he had no clue where to. There was only one thing for it. He was going to have to go and speak to Lucy. That's right, the scary one who really didn't like him. She was probably with Big Merv. He turned and ran back the way he had come.

When he reached the Free K'Barthan Embassy again, The Pan burst through the main door into the corridor and almost collided with Lucy and Merv as they came out of another. They both looked concerned. Lucy spoke first.

"You," she said. Her tone was not friendly.

"Me," said The Pan. "Or at least, I was last time I looked."

"What have you done with Ruth?"

"Nothing—that's the point—" began The Pan but Lucy spoke over him.

"We were talking and then her phone rang and she got up and disappeared.

I've been looking all over. It's as if she's gone out, but with this Lord Vernon person after her, I know she wouldn't be that stupid."

Oh. How to answer that?

"Actually, she has gone out."

"And you let her?" said Lucy incredulously.

"No. I mean yes and you're right I shouldn't have but it's not always easy to stop Ruth from doing the things she wants to do. I was looking for you because I need your help."

"Wotsup?" asked Big Merv at the exact same time that Lucy said,

"What have you done to her?"

Oh dear. Never mind. It wasn't as if Lucy could loathe him any more than she already did and at least Big Merv was there. He might listen to reason.

"Lucy, there's no time to explain but you're right, Ruth shouldn't have gone out but she has, and I think she might be in trouble."

"You were supposed to be looking after her."

"Yes, I was but she was very adamant about going. If you must know, I tried to stop her but she ditched me at the tube." Big Merv stifled a laugh and The Pan was irritated. "Give it a rest, Merv," he snapped. "Actually Lucy, Ruth has gone to talk to someone called Nigel. Your boyfriend, I believe."

"Nigel is not my boyfriend. He binned me. By voicemail. By answerphone message—"

He could hear the anger rising in her voice and cut her off.

"I know what voicemail is."

"Then you'll also realise he's a cruel, heartless, sh—"

"Yes and it doesn't reassure me. Lucy, forget whose boyfriend he is, or isn't," he added hastily. "The point is that he rang Ruth, in tears and declared his undying love for you."

"I don't think Nigel could love anyone."

"No? Well he told Ruth he does and he thinks it's you, and she has gone to his flat, for ten past six, so he can bend her ear about how much he wants you back. She wasn't supposed to tell anyone but she told me and I'm not supposed to tell anyone either but I'm telling you because I'm worried that I shouldn't have let her go. All that stuff about Nigel, Lucy, I need to know, does it ring true? Only if it doesn't I have to be there in time to stop her from going in, and unless you help me, that's going to be tricky because I don't know where he lives."

"In the Barbican but he won't be at his flat by then, he doesn't usually get home before seven at the earliest."

"And here we are at the root of the problem. If he's not there, who is?"

"Mebbe he's come home special," said Big Merv.

"Yeh right. Or maybe there's someone else in his flat, waiting for Ruth. We still have time to get to her if we need to but first, I want to check I'm not overreacting. Am I?"

"I don't think so," said Lucy slowly.

"Fine. Then I have to find where Nigel is, quickly, and see what he's doing."

"I'm sure you can use your superpowers or whatever it is you do."

Big Merv wisely stepped in.

"Nah sweets, it ain't that easy."

Lucy gave Big Merv a sideways look but whether it was on account of what he'd said or because he'd called her 'sweets' The Pan couldn't be certain.

"Merv's right." The Pan held up his thimble. "This one's traceable so it's for emergencies only. If I use it to move, I'm sure Lord Vernon knows. But I can look through it to see what Nigel's up to. If he's genuine and he wants to speak to Ruth, let him. I'm probably being paranoid and over-protective and I don't want to go chasing after her if there's nothing wrong. You know how it is with the love thing. I don't want her to think I'm a control freak …" No, no no. Where had that come from? 'Love thing?' Bad, bad, bad. Big Merv and Lucy fixed their attention on him. Big Merv wore a leery smile and Lucy a steely glare.

"Love thing?" she said.

"It doesn't matter. Forget I said that. It was a mistake! There's something more important—"

"Have you got your hooks into my flatmate?"

"No."

"But you think she's in love with you, don't you?"

"No, I meant more that I'm in love with—"

"Did she say so?" Lucy spoke over him without listening. The Pan thought about the way Ruth had kissed his neck at the police station, the hug they'd had just before they'd come into the embassy and that top—with the zip. He doubted she was wearing it for Nigel's benefit. He wasn't imagining this. It was real. He was sure. And she wasn't the kind of girl to lead a man on, not one she knew was interested, and she did know or she wouldn't have fazed him with that kiss at the station.

"Not in so many words. Listen, there's no time for this, we—"

"She's way out of your league. You know that, don't you?" Lucy interrupted him. This was taking too long.

"Yes," The Pan looked her in the eye. "I know."

She seemed surprised he'd admitted that. Who on earth did she think he was? Big Merv chuckled and The Pan turned on him in exasperation. He was in a hurry and now the conversation had veered off at a tangent.

"Merv, mate, shut up. You're not helping."

"If you do anything to hurt her you'll have me to answer to—" began Lucy. Yes, fine, a lovely sentiment and he liked her for it but there was no time for it now, The Pan glanced at his watch, Arnold no.

"Alright, I get the picture. I'm not worthy of her," he broke in. "You know it, I know it, he knows it," he swung his arm at Big Merv. "More to the point, Ruth knows it, but this is more her business than any of ours. I suppose I have saved her life a couple of times, so that might have swayed her, and what I'm trying to do here—if we could put aside your extensive investigation into why she could possibly be attracted to me, if she is, until we've found your errant beau—is work out whether I need to do it again."

She bridled at the word 'beau'. Arnold's armpits he should have called Nigel something else.

"Nigel isn't my beau."

"Yes, yes—" Arnold's snot. He ran his hands through his hair.

"In fact, if you must know, Nigel is a slimy, no-good, snivelling—"

"Alright. Enough," said The Pan angrily. He put his hands out, in front of him, in a stop-right-there gesture as he spoke. Lucy didn't like it, he could tell but at least she shut up. The Pan began to wonder if he would make more conversational headway with Big Merv. No. She was angry and smarter than both of them and interrupting her in full flow was bad enough; talking over her head would be a very dumb move. He took a deep breath.

"Lucy, Merv, please help me. The one thing we all agree on is that we care what happens to Ruth. We can sort out the rest when I get her back. I think she might be in trouble and right now, whatever you think of me, we need to work together." He held the thimble out to Lucy. "All you have to do is imagine Nigel while you hold this. Then, have a look inside it and tell me where he is. If he's in his flat, fine. He and Ruth can get on with it. If he isn't I need to get her out of there."

Lucy's eyes met The Pan's. They were a different shade of brown to Ruth's but her expression was equally direct. There was no hiding place from a look like that and he was surprised at how easily he could return it with confidence. Then again, however much Lucy distrusted him, his concern for Ruth was as genuine as hers. Common ground.

After the briefest of hesitations, Lucy took the thimble from The Pan's outstretched hand and closed her eyes. Almost immediately she opened them again.

"If I'm thinking swear words, will it—?" she began and stopped.

The Pan smiled encouragingly, or at least he hoped he did.

"It doesn't matter what you think, exactly. So long as Nigel's in there somewhere."

Big Merv started chuckling again.

"Yeh. Trust me, girl. If it were fussy about swearing it'd never work for this plank."

"Very true, Merv. Lucy, I'm sorry, I'd do it, myself, but I have to be able to picture the person I'm looking for and only you know what Nigel looks like."

A few moments passed.

"What a bastard," said Lucy. "He's in a restaurant."

"Are you sure?"

"Of course I am, I've been there with him myself."

"What's he doing?" asked Big Merv.

"Eating, presumably," said The Pan.

"No. Far too early. He's having an aperitif." Lucy's tone was acid.

"On his own?" asked The Pan.

"Of course not. He's supposed to be meeting Ruth about getting back with me and he's sitting calmly in a restaurant, in Clerkenwell, with someone else." Someone female, The Pan presumed, if the disgust in her voice was anything to go by.

"That's all I need to know," he said grimly as she handed back the thimble.

"What's going to happen to her?" asked Lucy anxiously, her cool, business-like manner cracking for the first time.

"Nothing," said The Pan firmly. "I'm going to go and get her." He glanced at his watch. Twenty minutes. Speed was of the essence but the thimble was too dangerous. He would have to use the SE2 in aviator mode; there would be no time to blend in, not if the traffic he'd seen outside was anything to go by. He blipped his keys. "I can find her but if I can avoid using the portal …" he held up the thimble. "Do you have Nigel's address?"

"Yes," Lucy rattled off something incomprehensible. The Pan rephrased his question.

"Can you tell me how to get there?"

Lucy nodded.

"Good. My snurd should be on the roof by now. If you come up there with me you can explain before I go." The Pan headed up the stairs with Big Merv and Lucy following. The snurd was already there, engine running, doors open. As the three of them approached the top began to retract.

The Pan slipped into the driver's seat.

"Alright Lucy," he said as he rummaged around in the glove compartment and took out a pen and a dog-eared pad to take notes. "How do I find Nigel?"

Without hesitating Big Merv got into the front and Lucy climbed into the space behind the seats.

"What are you doing?" The Pan asked them.

"What's it look like?" said Big Merv.

"You're not the only person who loves Ruth, you know. She's my best friend," said Lucy. Kind of an olive branch, The Pan noticed as the remark flashed past. "We're coming too."

A glance at Big Merv, next to him, showed that the pair of them were in agreement. Oh well, no time to argue and anyway, it was a bit of a relief. Three of them had much better odds of rescuing Ruth than one, even if it meant The Pan had two extra people to look out for.

"Fair enough. And thank you. Which way?" he asked as he took off.

"Over there." Lucy put her arm through the space between the seats, over his shoulder, and pointed. "You can drop Big Merv and I off at the restaurant. It's only round the corner from Nigel's flat so it won't take a minute for us to catch you up once we have his keys. It'd be a pity if you turned up to save the day and couldn't get in."

It was the sort of thing Ruth would say and despite his worry The Pan almost smiled. They were flying over Trafalgar Square by this time. He noticed that the column in the middle was surrounded by scaffolding and swathed in police tape and green netting.

"Good point. What if Nigel won't give you his keys?"

"Oh I think he will, don't you Merv?" said Lucy breezily.

"Yeh. If we ask him nice," said Big Merv.

The Pan was even more relieved to have Lucy and Big Merv's company, despite the worry of what he might be getting them into.

"Go easy on him," he said. "Remember we've just got the police off our backs."

Big Merv chuckled. "We'll take care of him, mate," he said in a tone of voice that suggested he was going to enjoy his part of the task. The Pan almost felt sorry for Nigel and hoped Big Merv wouldn't chuck him in the river.

"Nobody will be throwing anyone into any rivers, with or without concrete boots," said Lucy firmly. Arnold, she knew. Big Merv must have told her. That was amazing. Or then again, perhaps not. Big Merv smiled and shrugged.

"If that's the way you wanna play it, lady."

"Well, well, well, I do believe Lucy and I have found something else we agree on," said The Pan and she gave him a thin-lipped smile. "It's a start."

Lucy pointed downwards to a long frontage of decking furnished with tables and chairs, a hedge and clipped, standard box trees in pots, and the odd customer sitting out.

"That's it," she said.

"Good," said Big Merv as The Pan searched for a quieter spot to land. "Hurry up and park it so we can go find Nigel, you Hamgeean pranny. Then you can go get yer girl."

'Your girl.' Not technically correct and worse, guaranteed to get Lucy's back up. The Pan risked another glance at her. Mmm, definitely. However, as she explained how to get to Nigel's flat she was calm, even civil, as if it had slipped her mind that she was meant to be utterly ill-disposed towards The Pan.

Chapter 56

In the street, outside the restaurant, Lucy peered through the gap between two window boxes. There, in the bar area, she could see Nigel and Sabrina sitting at a table enjoying a pre-dinner drink.

"Git," she said.

"He there?" asked Big Merv.

"Oh yes, he's there. With his new girl." She realised she sounded bitter. He squeezed her arm.

"You're worth better than 'im," he said, which threw her a little.

"Thank you," she said.

"'S OK. You ready?"

"As I'll ever be."

"'S good." A curt nod. "I reckon it's time this Nigel bloke learned to show some respect." He smiled but not the usual way. This was a grim smile with no warmth and it made Lucy nervous. He stepped up to the door and opened it. "After you, girl."

Halfway past him, she stopped and looked searchingly into his face.

"You're not going to punch him, are you Merv?" The felt-tip green eyes met hers.

"Depends on 'im, donnit."

"Merv …"

"Nah. Shouldn't take that."

"Good. All you have to do is stand there and look threatening."

"No problemo."

No, thought Lucy as she looked him up and down. No problemo at all. Not for Big Merv.

As they stepped inside, their path was professionally blocked at once by the maitre d'.

"Can I help?" He was polite but firm; then he recognised Lucy, who had been there often enough with Nigel. "Why Ms Hargraves, are you and …" he did a double take and expertly concealed the beginnings of a pained expression, "your friend joining Mr Chatterton-Dix tonight?"

Good recovery. Lucy was impressed. Big Merv wasn't the usual customer. He could hardly be classed as one of the jet-set eating fashionistas who usually used this restaurant. He was way too scary for that and of course, where she saw orange skin the maitre d' was seeing a bad spray tan; Lucy glanced at Merv and back at the maitre d'—very bad. No proper glitterata would be seen dead with such a sub-standard cosmetic enhancement. At the same time, Big Merv was a formidable presence; all of it, despite the suit, pure gangsta.

"No, we won't be joining Nigel for dinner," said Lucy. "He doesn't know we are coming. It's a surprise."

"Then I'm sure he will be delighted to see you, Ms Hargraves." He was clearly, if discreetly, relieved they weren't stopping. "A drink?"

"Not for me but perhaps you'd fetch one for Nigel and his date," said Lucy. "That vintage cognac he likes."

"As an aperitif …?" the maitre d' began but his voice faltered when he noticed the way Big Merv was staring at him. "They are drinking an excellent champagne, perhaps more of the same …?"

"No thanks. When he sees us, he will appreciate the cognac," said Lucy. She watched the maitre d' walk away and smiled. She was worried about Ruth but at the same time, bits of this were going to be fun. Nigel was sitting at a table in the bar, with his back to the door, talking animatedly. Sabrina was facing them but she was too busy hanging on his every word to notice their arrival.

Lucy turned to check that Big Merv was following her. He was. He smiled, not the scary humourless one, the real deal this time, for her. Then he adjusted his hat and winked. Reassured, she turned and walked the rest of the distance to the table. A waiter arrived at the same time as Lucy and Big Merv and she stood behind him, waiting until he had placed the glasses of cognac on the white linen cloth in front of Nigel and Sabrina. Nigel looked up in surprise, his mouth framing the first words of complaint, and noticed Lucy.

"Hello darling," she said.

"I thought I told you to stay away from me," he said coldly as the waiter made a swift exit.

"Big mistake," said Lucy. She felt the formidable presence of Big Merv as he stepped closer to her and watched the dismay register on Nigel's and Sabrina's faces as they noticed that Lucy was with someone. Someone about the same size and shape as an immaculately tailored rhino, only orange and, by the looks of his expression, rather less adept at anger management. Big Merv's right hand was deep in his overcoat pocket and he was holding it slightly outwards away from his body. It was suspicious-looking, that pocket; lower, as if weighed down by something heavy. Please no. Not a firearm, thought Lucy. She was a solicitor, for heaven's sake, she had standards and there were rules and if her protector pulled a gun—even on Nigel, who, God knew, deserved it—it was still a step too far. Nigel went pale. Lucy realised he must have drawn the same conclusion as her and despite her own misgivings about firearms, she was unable to suppress a smile at Nigel's fearful reaction.

"Evening," said Big Merv, nodding at Nigel, who ignored him and addressed Lucy.

"Bringing your work home with you Lucy?"

"No Nigel—" Lucy began.

"Whoever he is, it makes me even more glad I got rid of you," Nigel interrupted her. "What do you want?"

"Oh … nothing much, just a quick word," she said breezily and she smiled at Sabrina. "Alone, if you don't mind."

Sabrina clearly didn't appreciate being snubbed but then Lucy didn't appreciate being two-timed. Sure it wasn't Sabrina's fault, Nigel would have been the one who pursued her, but everyone at the ad agency knew he and Lucy were an item. Lucy waited but Sabrina stayed put, so she fixed the other woman with the kind of glare she only usually reserved for commanding the attention of jaded, cynical—and more to the point, obstructive—police officers and said, "Any time this century is just fine, Sabrina."

Big Merv fixed Sabrina with his own green felt-tip version of Lucy's expression and under the foundation and well, yes, Lucy had to admit, that was a very tasteful and probably very expensive spray tan, she went a little pale.

"The lady wants to talk to your boyfriend in private, so if you know what's good for you, you'll make yourself scarce; go powder your nose or something, treacle. Anything so long as you go where we ain't."

"That's no way to talk to a—" began Nigel, belatedly standing up for Sabrina.

"Shut it," said Big Merv, gesturing with the pocket.

There was a pause while Nigel weighed up the situation, looking from Lucy to Big Merv to Lucy before turning to address Sabrina.

"Do what the …" he hesitated, his eyes fixed on Big Merv, "man says, darling. This won't take long." Without a word Sabrina stood up and took her tiny handbag from the table.

"Uh-uh-uh," said Lucy. "Leave your phone where it is."

With a scowl, Sabrina put the bag back and sashayed across the restaurant to the ladies. The three of them watched her go and waited until the door swung closed behind her.

"What do you want, Lucy?" Nigel shot her a sneering glance as he spoke.

"A little assistance, darling," she said glibly.

"What if I don't want to help?"

"Oh I'm sure you will," Lucy glanced at Big Merv and back at Nigel. "This is Mister Merv, but you can call him 'sir'. If you don't cooperate with me, he's going to be very upset. You wouldn't want to upset my friend, would you?" There was a pause during which Big Merv's size and presence did the talking and then, as if he wasn't already looking menacing and scary enough he moved round, half behind Nigel and put one hand heavily and suddenly on his shoulder. Nigel flinched and Lucy almost laughed but managed to contain most of her inner glee as Big Merv leaned down so his face was close to Nigel's.

"You heard the lady. You ain't gonna upset me, are you, sunshine? See, when I get upset I do things people regret."

Nigel went white.

"Yes, it would be a pity if someone got hurt," said Lucy, "but I'm sure Mister Merv will be able to contain himself if you cooperate. It's your choice, of course, but as I said, we do need a little help from you. We want to find Ruth and we think she might be in your flat."

Nigel looked at his watch.

"Not yet," he croaked.

"Great. Then you have time to warn her and undo whatever it is you're up to."

Nigel shook his head, "I can't."

Lucy let her gaze flick briefly from Nigel to Big Merv.

"Actually, Nigel, I think you'll find you can." Lucy glared at her ex.

"No."

Lucy had never seen anyone this frightened. Sweat was running down the side of Nigel's face and dripping off his chin, his hair was lank with it, sticking to his forehead and he was shaking. She knew he was afraid of Big Merv but clearly someone else was scarier. That had to take some doing.

"Are you sure about this, Nigel?"

He cast his eyes down. "I can't," he said in a low voice. "Really, I can't."

"That's unfortunate for you," she said.

"You don't understand," Nigel was so scared he could hardly speak. "You haven't seen this man."

Over the top of Nigel's head, Lucy and Big Merv's eyes met. Lucy raised her eyebrows in a way that she hoped said, 'Do you know something about this?' He nodded.

"I think Mister Merv here might have met your friend," she told Nigel.

"Yeh," Big Merv chuckled but again, with such a conspicuous lack of humour that it merely increased the tension. "I reckon I know 'im so well I gotta picture in my wallet. Want me to show you?" He took his hand off Nigel's shoulder and put it slowly inside his coat, removing a wallet, which he opened with one hand. In a single, practised movement, he slid out a banknote and closed the wallet, putting it back in his coat. Still one-handed, he pulled the note taught between his thumb and fingers so it cracked, and flipped it up in front of Nigel's face. "See, I gotta hunch you been talking to this bloke on 'ere."

Nigel swallowed.

"Yes." His voice was little more than a whisper.

Lucy almost felt sorry for him. Nigel hated being manipulated but this time, it was somebody important and powerful enough to appear on money. Not on the back, either, but on the front of every single denomination of note, where the Queen should go in her own reality. She thought of the man who had come to the flat and asked about Ruth, and was unable to suppress a shudder. Poor old Nigel. Stuck between a hard place, she glanced over at Big Merv, and a hard nut.

"Yeh, we understand your reservations. You upset Lord Vernon and things ain't gonna be pretty." Big Merv nodded. "'S natural you're afraid. But it leaves you with a problem, see? Coz we're here and he ain't and we can make things pretty ugly an' all."

"That's right," said Lucy. "You have a choice, Nigel. You can walk out of here now and help us find Ruth, which might make the scary man on Mister Merv's money very angry. Or you can stay here and make us angry."

Nigel laughed weakly.

"I don't think so. He's not some small-time crook." Big Merv tensed but said nothing. "He's going to kill me if I cross him. What are you going to do?"

Lucy raised her eyebrows. She was enjoying herself far too much for somebody who was, after all, supposed to be a pillar of society.

"That's the million dollar question, Nigel. Mister Merv, how ugly will things get?"

Big Merv jabbed the pointy end of the suspicious pocket against Nigel's ribs.

"Pretty ugly," he growled.

"There you have it, Nigel. Like Lord Vernon, Mister Merv is from out of town and that's helpful because, in many ways, it puts him beyond the viable reach of our justice system. So, here's what's going to happen. You're going to do exactly what I say and if you don't I'm going to let Mister Merv express his anger. I've never seen him angry but he's a well-known public enemy where he's from. Even Lord Vernon can't touch him. So, I'd imagine it's pretty spectacular. It's your call, Nigel. You can play nicely with us, or Mister Merv will be forced to redecorate this lovely restaurant in brain and red."

"You'd never—" began Nigel

"I'd never, but, Mister Merv here has been known to, if provoked … Are you going to take that chance?" Without breaking eye contact with Nigel she inclined her head slightly, towards Big Merv. "What's it to be?"

The silence seemed to stretch for ever until eventually, Nigel spoke.

"Lord Vernon will kill me. You'll have my blood on your hands."

"I have a difficult choice here, Nigel. Unless I'm very careful, there will be blood on my hands whatever I do; my only choice is whether it's Ruth's, or yours. Perhaps if you weren't a cheating slimy scumbag it'd be harder to decide. As it is, if you agree to help us now, we will try and keep you safe."

There was another long pause before Nigel spoke.

"What do you want me to do?"

"Get up and walk slowly to the door."

"No tricks, son, or I'll have to do something you might regret," said Big Merv.

Nigel rose slowly to his feet.

"Oh no," said Lucy as he made to walk towards the exit. "Not so fast. May I?"

She put her hand inside his coat and removed his wallet from his pocket.

"You wouldn't leave Sabrina to pay the bill, would you?" she pulled out a large sheaf of cash and put it on the table.

"Let's go, you little scrote," said Big Merv. Lucy took a tight hold of Nigel's arm and guided him out of the restaurant.

"He'll be back in a minute." She smiled sweetly at the maitre d', "We just need to pop outside for a quick word."

Once in the safety of the street Lucy held out her hand.

"Your keys, please, Nigel."

"Is that it? You've dragged me out here to rob me?"

"'S right pal," said Big Merv quietly. "Give 'em to the lady."

"No—no—"

"I said, give them to the lady, you tart or I don't care what The Pan said, I'm gonna put a slug in you and take 'em."

"Merv—" began Lucy. His eyes met hers with a look of warning.

"'S only a borrow, sunshine. When we've finished you can have 'em back." He smiled nastily. "If Lord Vernon don't get to you first."

Sullenly, Nigel put his hand in his pocket, took out his keys and handed them to Lucy. "Sweet," said Big Merv. "We gonna find Ruth, girl?"

"Yes. Must dash, be seeing you Nigel."

"B-b-but Lord Vernon! You can't—" began Nigel.

"Shut it, shazzbutt," said Big Merv. "You heard. Hop it."

Nigel looked from one to the other of them with an expression of total horror on his face.

"Don't do this, you have to take me with you—"

"We don't have to do nothing," said Big Merv and without warning he hit Nigel hard in the face. For a moment Nigel stood still and straight, his eyes bulging, then he fell over backwards, out cold. "What next, girl?" asked the Swamp Thing casually.

Lucy turned on him angrily.

"We have the keys, why did you do that?"

"Coz if I don't he's gonna hang around an' cramp our style … or he's gonna squeal to Lord Vernon and where'll that get the Chosen One?"

"She's not the Chosen One."

"Listen, sweets and listen good. You and her are in denial. She's chosen and there ain't nothing anyone can do."

"OK, OK. Maybe you're right. I suppose I should thank my stars you didn't shoot him."

"Nah. Couldn't 'a' done," Big Merv took his hand out of his pocket, thumb up, first finger pointing outwards and held it up. "I got big mitts." Lucy stared at him and he began to chuckle at his own joke for a moment until he noticed her expression and stopped. "You didn't think I was packin'?"

"If you want my honest answer, yes, I did."

He laughed outright.

"You're crazy, girl. I'm a businessman, I don't kill no-one."

"No?"

"OK lady, I understand you got this thing about honesty so I'll level with you. There's a few blokes who ain't around coz of me but I don't wanna kill no-one, that's the truth. I told you. A life's got value and I respect that. So the way I play, is that I don't do nothing untoward unless I gotta."

She knew she was staring at him with her mouth open but couldn't quite manage to close it.

"'S the way it is, treacle. Life's cheap where I'm from. You said the flat's just round the corner." He glanced down at Nigel lying prostrate on the pavement.

"We oughta be there sharpish."

"What about him?"

"He'll be alright." Big Merv hauled Nigel up and slung him over one shoulder, strode over to the restaurant's outside tables, which were currently empty, and dumped him in a chair. Swiftly, he arranged his legs and arms so he looked as if he'd dropped off, while sitting casually.

"Whadda you reckon?" he asked her.

Lucy was doubtful. "Should we leave him?"

"Yeh. He'll be out long enough for us but not so long as Lord Vernon'll get him. I was gonna see if he had a mobile phone but he can keep it. We'll have Ruth safe an' sound well before he wakes up. Tell you what, if you're worried things'll get hot for him we can swing by and pick him up on the way back, when we've got Ruth."

"OK." She shrugged.

"C'mon then. Let's go," said Big Merv.

Chapter 57

In the street, outside Nigel's flat, Ruth's mobile beeped. Nigel had sent her a text.

'Ruth. V sorry, milk is off. Am at shop. Buzz service to get in. Flat door on latch, coffee on. Back soon. Please wait.'

Oh.

She checked the time on her phone. Six o'clock.

What would The Pan do now? Scarper. But The Pan came from K'Barth and he had every reason to be cautious. This was London, England, Earth, and Ruth's very existence was not a crime. That Nigel wasn't in his flat gave her a momentary flutter of nerves but he was still around, ergo …

Tentatively, she pressed the service buzzer and when someone answered she explained about Nigel and the milk. Yes, Nigel had been in a few minutes earlier, yes, he had mentioned her and the milk and yes, she was to go on up, said the voice. He reminded her of the floor and flat number and the door opened with a click. Ruth put the door on the latch, just in case she needed to get out in a hurry. It closed with a bang.

She looked round the foyer. This being where Nigel lived, and therefore some of the most expensive real estate around, the communal areas were furnished as if they were private, too; fresh flowers, sofas, a coffee table with magazines, thick carpet, artworks, no expense spared. It left her with a feeling that she was going to trespass into someone else's apartment on her way to Nigel's. In the corner was a Victorian-style desk with everyone's post on it. Nothing for Nigel, she noted, which she took as confirmation that he'd been in and collected it—or that he had no mates. She was too nervous to use the lift—she didn't want to feel trapped. Anyway, the entrance to the stairs was the other side of the hall. This way, if anyone was waiting by the lift doors to ambush her as she arrived she'd see them before they saw her. She'd have a head start—as long as she remembered not to make too much noise coming up.

"What am I doing?" she muttered as she began a stealthy ascent. "Five flights and it's only Nigel, for heaven's sake." Nobody was going to have got to him. "You mental bag, Ruth, *five flights*. What are you like?" she muttered as she climbed. Even in more practical, comfortable footwear, five flights was a fair hike. But she couldn't persuade herself to take the lift.

The smell of fresh coffee wafted enticingly down the stairwell to greet Ruth as she went up the last flight of stairs. Quietly she peeped into the fifth-floor lobby. It was every bit as plush as the one downstairs. Behind her, evening sunlight streamed in through a large picture window at the top of the stairs and the doors separating them from the lobby, which were also glass. It painted everything golden.

The fifth-floor lobby, like the one at the entrance, was deserted. Ruth saw nothing untoward. Thank heavens for that. Clearly, The Pan was overcautious after all, and she was an idiot. Well, she was happy to take that over the alternative.

Five flats led off the lobby, which was, essentially, square. The staircase exited next to the lift shaft and together, it and the lift doors took up one wall. The other three walls led to the flats. The doors to a pair of two bedroom flats were set in the wall to Ruth's left and two more in the wall opposite led to cheaper one bedroom flats. In the wall to Ruth's right was a single door which led to a penthouse three bedroom apartment; Nigel's. As the largest and most expensive flat on the floor it took up a good quarter of the space, essentially, the entire end of the building on that side.

Nigel's door was ajar, as he'd promised. It had two locks, both on the latch. Timidly, Ruth ventured into his apartment and found herself in an entrance hall. It was quiet, apart from the muffled sounds of cars and people in the street. She followed the noise into the sitting room. The sound was coming in through sliding doors onto the balcony, which were ajar. White muslin curtains rose and fell in the breeze as if the building was breathing. Most of the balcony was still in sunlight, lit from the side by the evening September sun, although the curtains made the view fuzzy and indistinct. Another wall of the sitting room was made up of glass windows, with the same white muslin curtains. The balcony looked inviting.

Ruth went back into Nigel's hall and, following the smell of coffee this time, she put her head round the kitchen door. A filter machine was finishing its work, reaching the final crescendo of a noise not unlike the sound of a chain-smoking vagrant's regular early-morning coughing fit. Two cups were set out beside it. Ruth usually took coffee with milk but Nigel's smelled so good that she decided she would help herself to half a cup without it. Then she could sit on the balcony and ring Lucy.

Coffee in hand, she moved cautiously across the sitting room. This interview was not going to be easy and she didn't want to complicate things—by spilling coffee all over Nigel's white carpet for instance. It looked and smelled new, too. Concentrating on holding the cup steady she pulled back the curtain and pushed the sliding doors further apart with her foot. They glided easily. Well, they would. This was all state-of-the-art stuff. Lots of modern art and design house furniture. Very Bauhaus, very high quality and very expensive. It was smart and sophisticated but hardly homely. In fact, to Ruth it seemed intimidating and unfriendly; a style of decor which seemed to state clearly that guests were not welcome; cluttering up the place sprawling on the sofas, creasing the leather and generally making it look untidy. Yeh. Just right for Nigel, then. The thought made her giggle. She was feeling a lot more relaxed now, confident that everything was normal and OK and that Nigel would be back soon with the milk.

A playful gust of wind rustled the curtains and there were two loud bangs, one after the other, as the front door, followed by the door of the room Ruth was in, blew closed. She jumped, slopping burning coffee over her hand.

Ow! Perhaps she wasn't so relaxed after all. And now look. Bum. There were several splashes of dark brown coffee all over that wretched carpet. Who in their right mind would have a white carpet, anyway? She considered it unlikely that Nigel did his relaxing at home. Still, it was his flat, and since she was there to tell him he was dumped it was probably bad form to trash it. She'd have to get a cloth. She glanced round for somewhere to put the cup and then she heard it; a tiny noise in the entrance hall, inside the flat; a click. Nigel? Possibly, except this person was trying to be very quiet and since she was expecting Nigel it seemed unlikely that he'd go to the trouble of stealing silently up on her unawares.

Ruth strained to hear above the whisper of the traffic but she could only feel, rather than hear, someone approaching the sitting room door. As she watched, slowly, silently, the handle began to turn. Where to hide? There was only one suitable sofa and it was the other side of the room. Then she noticed the loungers outside on the balcony, two of them, made of wickerwork with white cushions and valances round the bottom. Very trendy, even if they reminded Ruth of the 1970s beds she'd stayed in at her grandparents' house when she was a child. She scuttled outside, flung the coffee cup over the balcony—please let no-one be underneath when it landed—and wriggled under the nearest lounger.

She heard the balcony doors hiss as someone opened them further. Peeping through a gap in the valance she watched the end of someone's boot prodding at the coffee stains on the carpet. Then the boots walked onto the balcony, towards Ruth's hiding place. They were suede, black suede, but unlike The Pan's they were immaculate. There was no elastic at the sides and they were knee length. At the top of the boots, a brief glimpse of black, military-style trousers, with a red stripe at the side. Oh no. She held her breath. The boots came to a standstill. It seemed Lord Vernon was listening. Her heart beat so loudly in her ears that she was afraid he would hear it. She watched his feet as he turned and addressed the whole apartment in a voice that managed to be quiet and yet carrying at the same time.

"You can hide, Ruth, but you cannot escape." He waited but she stayed silent. He might be bluffing. "As you wish. I notice you have sampled Nigel's excellent coffee. I will wait here with the rest of it." Again he paused to listen. Ruth lay still, hardly daring to breathe. The boots moved towards the door and stopped. "If you do not join me within the next two minutes, I will take this place apart." He let his words sink in, and then, "I suggest you accept your fate. Be assured, if you force me to search, I will not be so ..." another pause as he sought the right word, "courteous when I find you." Ruth heard his footsteps go inside. He was going to get a cup of coffee. She imagined him walking to the kitchen. She was going to have to go over the balcony. It was her only chance.

She slithered quickly from her hiding place under the lounger, ran to the edge of the balcony where it met the wall and climbed over the railings.

Standing on the outside of the railing was different to looking over it. The ground seemed a long way away. Even so, Ruth saw no other option. It was simply a question of which was the greater; her fear of heights or her fear of Lord Vernon. Absolutely nothing to worry about, there. Her fear of Lord Vernon trumped anything. This should be a piece of cake. Yeh, right. With a speed of thought that only comes with fear, Ruth examined her options.

The building was modern and mostly red brick but the outsides of the balconies were clad in beige concrete, with a red metal railing running a few inches above the top. She held onto the railing and searched for another handhold lower down. The concrete was applied in panels moulded with a wood-like grain and arranged with horizontal grooves in-between, like planks of real wood. But as soon as she tried she knew she could not use the grooves as handholds. The fake planks were nothing more than a cosmetic enhancement; the grooves were shallow and barely wide enough for her fingertips. Maybe if she moved fast she would be strong enough, transferring her weight before her fingers slipped.

No.

She would need the grip of a mountain climber or a flair for parkour, neither of which she had. Ruth had completed the London Marathon once. Admittedly, she had done so in a fluffy duck costume and she'd walked most of it but she'd had to complete another long-distance run, in a reasonable time, to demonstrate her fitness to enter. Over a year later though, she knew she lacked the kind of hard-core strength and endurance required for a descent like this, not to mention the confidence.

She checked her other options. There was a gap of about two or three inches at the bottom of the panel, at floor level, into which she had placed her feet. However, Nigel's balcony was floored with stone tiles, burnished smooth. If that floor was to be her first handhold, she would have to slip her feet out and drop, which would involve a sudden transfer of her weight to her hands. Could she grip that shiny stone hard enough to avoid falling, she wondered.

No.

Nothing doing there, either.

There was a drainpipe but it looked more ornamental than functional and she wasn't sure it would hold her weight. In theory, it might hold her long enough to swing off it; except that if she did, she'd need to get enough purchase on the brickwork with her feet, to swing herself back towards the building again. The blue suede zip-up boots she was wearing were comfortable to walk in and they looked good. However, they weren't designed for climbing and she wasn't confident enough of their grip to stake her life on it. Once again, the move, though possible, would require a level of climbing ability, not to mention confidence, that Ruth didn't have. Would raw fear conjure it up for a few seconds though? Possibly.

Clinging to the wrong side of Nigel's balcony, desperately trying to think, the unthinkable happened. As she realised how high up she was and how narrow her options were, her fear of falling overcame her fear of Lord Vernon and she froze.

"Why can't I do this? I'm going to die," she whispered.

"No, you're not," whispered a voice which was not Lord Vernon's.

She steeled herself and looked down. The Pan's face appeared below her. He climbed out from the balcony of the flat beneath and up the wall to her, casually, without a second thought, like a piece of Velcro taking a stroll. Ruth could imagine that shinning up and down buildings would be a mundane skill for someone whose very existence was a crime; like walking for normal people. Even so, blimey.

"What are you doing here?"

"Rescuing you." He held out his hand.

"No! Don't let go! It makes me feel nervous to watch."

"It's fine, I do this quite a lot. Come on, you'll be alright. Use the drainpipe."

"I was going to, but I can't, I'm not strong enough. Please go or he'll get you too."

"No."

She glanced over into Nigel's sitting room. Still no sign of Lord Vernon. He was taking his time.

"It's no good. I can't do parkour." She realised he might not know what parkour was but thankfully he seemed to have guessed the problem.

"But I can, so you don't need to. Climb down me."

"What?"

"Climb down me. Hold onto my feet and swing onto the balcony below. But for Arnold's sake, hurry up." She looked down at the ground five floors away. Why did it have to be so high? She glanced through the windows into the sitting room. It was too late. Lord Vernon was striding towards them, flinging aside his cup. When she saw his face, she almost screamed. He was green, really green. In his natural shade he radiated more evil, more malevolent intent than Ruth could believe possible. He crossed the sitting room in seconds, ripping the curtains out of his way as he went and, with one swift movement lunged for the railing. His hand locked around Ruth's wrist and she let out a cry of pain as he lifted her into the air and flung her into the corner behind him. Bruised and humiliated she leapt to her feet.

Before The Pan had time to move Lord Vernon grabbed his collar and forced him outwards.

"No," she screamed. The Pan fought, as with his other hand, Lord Vernon prised his fingers from the railing and, still holding him by nothing more than his coat, extended his arm. The Pan, his feet planted on the bottom of the balcony, grabbed Lord Vernon's sleeve and then his wrist with one hand while he frantically reached for a hold with the other. But he wasn't as tall as Lord Vernon, his reach lacked the length and his efforts fell well short. Lord Vernon kicked the toes of The Pan's boots so his feet slipped from the balcony.

"Stop it!" shouted Ruth. Lord Vernon turned his head and the slate grey eyes met hers.

"No."

Ruth leapt at him but, supremely unruffled, he ducked, bumping her sideways and over the top of him with one elbow. She landed in a tangled heap on the floor. Lord Vernon turned his attention back to his victim. As The Pan struggled to claw his way along his arm, deliberately, slowly without breaking eye contact, Lord Vernon pulled back his free hand.

Ruth staggered to her feet again, casting about her for something to use as a blunt instrument. She had to save The Pan but her hands were shaking uncontrollably and as she fumbled to lift a stone planter Lord Vernon smashed his fist into The Pan's temple. It made contact along the hairline with a crack and Ruth could see his grip on Lord Vernon's arm was weakening, his hand slipping.

"No," she shouted again, except that this time, it was more of a sob.

Lord Vernon delivered a second blow, to the side of The Pan's face. His eyes rolled. He made one last woozy attempt to grasp the railing. A third punch and The Pan's hand finally slid from Lord Vernon's arm. He stopped struggling, dangling suspended over nothing, his arms hung loosely by his side. Lord Vernon held him there for a moment.

"Goodbye, vermin." Coolly, distastefully, as if he were dropping someone else's litter into a bin, he relinquished his grip on The Pan's collar, pushing him outwards as he did so, and at the same time stepping smartly back to make doubly sure he left nothing, not even his own arm, within reach. Ruth watched, powerless, as like some horrible slow-motion dream, The Pan's eyes closed, his head lolled back and he fell off the building. The sickening thud as he landed somewhere, below, came remarkably quickly. Lord Vernon moved towards the rail to inspect the results of his handiwork but was distracted by a noise. It came from inside the flat; a loud bang and then another one. He turned to Ruth.

"How fortunate that I remembered to bolt the door. It seems someone is trying to break in."

Ruth stifled a despairing sob but she could not stop the silent tears. She thought she was going to be sick.

Lord Vernon pulled a laser pistol from his belt. "These are beginning to annoy me," he said, and vaporised Nigel's cool glass doors and chic muslin curtains. "Stay," he commanded her, like a dog. She wiped her eyes and nose on her sleeve.

"No," she managed. Maybe she could climb down to the flat below while he was busy at the door. He registered her glance towards the railings with a look of sneering contempt.

"Oh, you won't be going over there. If you had the courage for that you'd already be gone and your friend would still be alive." He was right. She could never climb down safely, not now. Lord Vernon smiled a sinister smile as he read it in her face. "What a disappointment. I thought you were a little more …" the contempt in his expression intensified, "spirited than this." There was another loud bang. "You are mine. And now, I will deal with your friends. This won't take a moment." He left her and strolled into Nigel's sitting room.

Ruth ran to the balcony rail. Whatever Lord Vernon thought and whatever she feared, she was going. Now, or The Pan would have died for no reason. The bangs from inside intensified in volume as, blinded with tears, she climbed quickly over the railing, skidding and sliding and trying to avoid looking down until she absolutely had to. But her shaking legs found no purchase and she slipped. Her arms jarred as they took her weight and in her shock and pain she nearly let go. Desperately, she held on but felt her grip slowly failing. For a few seconds she hung precariously, her feet scrabbling to get a purchase on something, anything that would hold her weight long enough to renew her grip. Then her fingers slid off the rail and she fell.

She felt the air rushing past her and in that brief millisecond, pictures of all the people she cared about flashed through her mind. No. She couldn't die. Not now. She didn't want to leave them behind.

Her feet hit a hard surface and she was struggling with somebody until she realised they were trying to hold her and stop her falling. She stopped fighting and felt a steadying arm around her waist.

"Easy tiger," said a voice. A hundred feet above the ground she was standing on the bonnet of The Pan's snurd with him beside her. She threw her arms around his neck and for a brief moment, she clung to him.

"I thought you were dead."

"So did I."

"I'm so sorry I—How did you—?"

"Later, I promise—there's no time now. Sit down, fast," he said. Briefly, his eyes met hers and despite the serious expression on the rest of his face, they were smiling. Hand in hand they bundled over the windscreen together into the seats. She settled herself and did up her seatbelt. He stayed standing.

From inside the flat came a final loud bang and the sound of a door hitting a wall very hard. As the snurd rose above the railing and stopped, Lord Vernon came into view, standing in the middle of Nigel's sitting room, with his back to them. On the far side of him, framed in the doorway, were Big Merv and Lucy. Lord Vernon took aim at them with the laser pistol.

"Hey, greenie gills," shouted The Pan.

Lord Vernon hesitated, laser pistol poised to fire.

"Oi! Snot face!" That was too much, and he turned angrily towards the balcony. "Look who's sitting in my seat." The Pan pointed downwards, towards Ruth. Behind Lord Vernon, Big Merv nodded and disappeared, taking Lucy with him.

"Not for long." Lord Vernon made to fire but then shoved the laser pistol back in its holster and bounded towards the SE2. The Pan was too quick for him this time. Dropping swiftly into his seat he flipped the snurd round and away just as Lord Vernon was gathering himself to leap onto the bonnet. Ruth watched as Lord Vernon stood on the red metal rail for a moment; perfectly balanced, hunkered down, ready to pounce. Then he leapt nimbly back to the balcony floor and ran inside the flat again.

"He's after Merv and Lucy," she said.

"I know, hold tight. If I can make this turn fast enough we'll get to them before he does." The Pan rounded the corner of the building and landed the SE2 on the street. Tyres squealing, the snurd slid to a halt at the bottom of the steps leading up to the front door at the exact moment that Lucy and Big Merv tumbled out.

Yeek! Just in time, Ruth remembered that Big Merv wouldn't fit in the back. She scrambled into the cramped space behind The Pan, and Big Merv leapt into the front. Lucy jumped in and squeezed down behind him, opposite her. As the roof slid into position The Pan red-lined the engine, speeding away just as Lord Vernon ran out of the building behind them, laser gun in hand. Green-skinned, on a London street, he raised the gun and fired.

The shots pinged off the armour of the retreating snurd and sparks ricocheted onto the nearby buildings. Through the back window Ruth saw the Interceptor arrive and just as Lord Vernon wrenched open the gull-wing door, the SE2 left the ground and took off.

Chapter 58

The Pan flew more or less at street level, a few feet above the cars but not quite above the buses. It was a strategy that was going to get them noticed, but since the police had let them go and Lord Vernon already knew they were there, it probably didn't matter. There was no time for blending in and if he landed the snurd they'd be easy to pick off in the stationary traffic. At least this way, the SE2 would be harder to pursue and be more difficult to target from above, even if it was clearly causing a bit of a commotion below. The others were silent, whether through relief, shock or the somewhat white-knuckle nature of street-level travel he wasn't sure. Well, he supposed it probably felt pretty fast to them but The Pan feared he was not going fast enough.

Unlike Big Merv's MKII his SE2 was only designed to carry two people, three at a push. With four on board, the handling wasn't as tight and responsive as usual and the acceleration was significantly lacking. He tried to hide it but he was nervous and he suspected that Ruth, close behind him, could tell. His head ached, too. He put a hand up to his temple, checking the bruises there and along the hairline. Lord Vernon punched hard. The whole area was tender and as usual, the rings had gouged the skin, although luckily, only under his hair which was matted with dried blood. Dry was good. He checked the mirror. The hair was oddly rigid but the colour didn't show. He checked behind. The Interceptor was closing. He'd been expecting this but even so his spirits sank a little. He knew he could outrun Lord Vernon, but a lot depended on luck, and more disturbingly, his wits.

"Here he comes. Are you all strapped in?" said The Pan.

"Will he catch us?" asked Lucy. The Pan turned round to her.

"There are a lot of us on board but he wants Ruth alive. That should even the odds." He paused. "I apologise, in advance, if things get bumpy."

The Interceptor bore down on them from above and fired a volley from its laser cannon. A nearby street light exploded.

"What was that?" shouted Lucy in alarm.

"A warning shot," said The Pan.

"Are you sure?" squeaked Lucy. Lord Vernon fired some more. He was trying to drive them lower. The Pan had to take evasive action, rolling the SE2 repeatedly.

"Do you have to do that?" Lucy squealed.

"This doesn't look like wanting me alive!" said Ruth, as Lord Vernon fired again. "And he nearly murdered you in cold blood …" she was calm, unfazed by the idea or the snurd's erratic manoeuvres. The Pan could only admire her cool-headedness.

"He did, didn't he?" he said, trying to mimic her calmness. He stopped speaking while he flipped the SE2 on its side to fit through the gap between a double-decker bus in front of them and another coming the other way. Both Big Merv and Lucy covered their eyes but when he glanced briefly at Ruth, she was staring fixedly ahead. That worried him.

"But back in Nigel's flat, he didn't shoot at me with you in the snurd."

He banked sharply, heading between two buildings and threading the SE2 between another double-decker and the underside of a railway bridge. "I expect he didn't want to risk my lifeless body falling on one of the buttons and causing a disaster," he said. He was trying to sound less afraid than he really was because he was the getaway man, he was supposed to know what he was doing and the others would be relying on him. He flipped the snurd on its side and slalomed through a set of traffic lights. He was good at this, he knew that, but every time Lord Vernon chased him, he wondered if 'good' was going to be enough. The Interceptor wasn't going away. More fire and another lamp post bit the dust.

"He's wrecking London again," Ruth shouted. The snurd juddered as its armour absorbed some of the blast and The Pan rolled to avoid a second burst.

"Can you stop doing that?" said Lucy, her voice sounding weak. She had gone very pale.

"Sorry Lucy. Merv, can you pass her a bag?" Big Merv pulled a plastic bag from the glove box in front of him and handed it to Lucy. He wasn't looking too good himself. "I'm sorry, it's because he's trying to drive us down," said The Pan.

"Then please can we go up?"

"At the first opportunity," said The Pan, as at last, a chance to do so arose. The snurd hurtled skywards with the Interceptor in pursuit. However, it seemed that The Pan was right about taking them alive. With a clear target Lord Vernon stopped firing.

"He's up to something, this ain't right," said Merv.

"Mmm," said The Pan. "I've an idea what he might be planning but I'm hoping I'm wrong. With four up he might just succeed. We're a bit sluggish."

He accelerated, but the heaviness of the SE2 was telling and the Interceptor easily won the contest of straight-line speed. It came alongside them and for a moment it stayed there. The Pan turned sharply. The menacing form of the

Interceptor moved closer so he swung the wheel again. His reactions were faster but the SE2's response time was a fraction slower than usual, long enough to give Lord Vernon the opportunity to match each of The Pan's attempts to evade him.

Slowly, inexorably, Lord Vernon manoeuvred the Interceptor closer.

"Do something, mate," shouted Big Merv as the Interceptor's black wing inched ever nearer to the SE2's grey one.

"He's too close, I can't risk any damage at this speed," said The Pan. Even if the snurd self-repaired they'd be toast.

The Interceptor was now so close that the wings of the two snurds were almost touching.

"By The Prophet's sandals! He's gonna tip us," shouted Big Merv.

"Not if I can help it," said The Pan.

Ruth and Lucy were pale and wide-eyed in the back.

"What's tipping?" shouted Lucy.

"He'll put his wing under ours and turn us."

Sure enough, there was a metallic grating sound as the wing of the Interceptor made contact and it jerked upwards throwing the SE2 sideways. The Pan rolled it and levelled out. Immediately, the Interceptor moved in again.

"He's going to try and land us," said The Pan. He could see where: on a high-rise office block ahead with a large flat roof. Figures on the concrete formed a reception committee. "Listen, we can't outrun him but I think I've an idea. Merv, I need your help."

"How?"

"Put all your strength behind the wheel when I say." The Interceptor locked wings with them again, lifting the snurd and pushing it downwards towards the roof. "Now!"

With Big Merv's strength added to The Pan's, the SE2 levelled out. The wings creaked and groaned under the strain as, locked together, the two snurds flew across the London sky. They were losing speed and for all The Pan and Big Merv's efforts, heading where Lord Vernon wanted: downwards, towards the roof.

"Alert! Alert! Excessive loading on wing," said the husky voice of the snurd.

"We can't hold it, he's gonna bring us down," shouted Big Merv.

"No, he's not," said The Pan. "Not on there. He's already thrown me off one building today and trust me, once is enough."

The metallic creaking increased in volume and a klaxon under the dash started to sound.

"Hang on," said The Pan and nobody could really tell if he was talking to them, or the SE2. Together, he and Big Merv were still hauling on the wheel with all their might. "Merv, let go when I tell you," said The Pan. "I warn you, everyone, this is going to make all of us pretty nauseous. Hold it Merv, hold it …"

Despite Merv and The Pan's efforts, the Interceptor continued to force the SE2's wing upwards turning it and at the same time, pushing it towards the building. The block loomed closer and closer; a hundred feet, thirty feet …

"NOW!" Big Merv let go and The Pan spun the wheel. The snurd flipped over and plummeted downwards, rolling wildly as it went.

The sudden absence of resistance took Lord Vernon by surprise and destabilised the Interceptor. It rolled, righted itself, and as Lord Vernon tried to level out, he overcompensated, sending it skidding sideways across the roof in a giant power slide, all screeching tyres and billowing smoke. For a second he regained control but then the forces of nature won out. The Interceptor reached the other side of the roof and slid straight off the edge.

Meanwhile, still spinning, the SE2 hurtled downwards towards the street until, at last, The Pan was able to control it. They were about level with the fourth floors of the buildings, when, dizzy and exhausted, he was able to flip it straight and speed off, skimming the roofs of the cars at street level. Ahead he caught a glimpse of a wide stretch of water. Brilliant! The river! He bumped the SE2 over the concrete waterside walkway, turned in what he hoped was the right direction for the K'Barthan Underground HQ and as they passed under a bridge he dipped the nose, flicked the submariner switch and drove beneath the waves into the brown underwater world beneath the Thames.

"Arnold! It's murkier than the river Dang," said The Pan. They were safe for now though, and as usual he couldn't quite believe it. He breathed a sigh of relief and turned on the low-vis guidance system. At once a head-up display, showing the riverbed, appeared on the windscreen. It was detailed, as if it was a film – only in green, like a world of darkness illuminated by infra-red. "Right," said The Pan, deftly avoiding a wrecked car with a bedstead on top of it. "I think that should have got rid of him. Anyone know where we are?"

His passengers sat in stunned silence.

"You know mate, that weren't bad. Ever thought of doin' it for a living?" asked Big Merv weakly.

The Pan cracked a watery smile.

"Very funny, big man."

Lucy and Big Merv laughed, Ruth stayed quiet.

"I reckon we done good," said Big Merv.

"Mmm," said The Pan. "I think you and Lucy did a bit better than me. I'd never have found Nigel's place without you two."

"Nah. You saved the Chosen One, and our bacon an' all."

"Yes! I can't believe we're alive!" said Lucy. "Ruth. Don't you ever, ever do that again, will you?"

"Yeh, girl, it weren't too fly."

"I'm sorry," said Ruth. Her voice sounded small. With his extra eyes, The Pan watched her crane her head round away from the others so she was looking out of the window. She was very pale, her mouth set in a thin line and through the back of the seat he was pretty sure he could feel her shaking.

"Go easy, you two, she had a tough time back there and she was only trying to do the right thing. Anyway there's no harm done." He sighed and leaned back in his seat.

Poor Ruth. He hoped she would be alright. He almost jumped when she slid her arms around his neck and leant her cheek against his. Arnold The Prophet, it was good to feel the warmth of her skin against his, alive, vibrant and close, when she had so nearly been torn away from him. He revelled in this secret moment of intimacy stolen in front of the others. Or not. Big Merv and Lucy were watching them closely.

"I'm sorry," said Ruth again. Her voice was a bit wobbly.

"Please don't be," said The Pan. Oh dear, was she going to cry? She wouldn't want to. He tried a joke. "I know you leak when you're stressed, Ms Cochrane, but if you do it in here it'll fill up and we'll all drown."

Pathetic.

Ten out of ten for effort but still pathetic. Oh well. He put one hand up and squeezed her arm, leaning his head a tiny bit as he did so; not so much the others would see but enough for her to feel the increase in pressure. He felt her eyelashes brush against his skin as her eyes closed for a moment. And then she sat back a little and smiled. Not an almighty guffaw, not even a laugh, but progress.

"I'm glad your driving is better than your jokes or we'd be stuck on that roof with Lord Vernon," she said. "I mean it though, I'm really, really sorry to be so stupid and thank you for coming to get me."

"What else would we do?" said Lucy.

"Yeh. 'S right. An' I'll tell you something else, sweets, it's not easy being the wrong side of the law. Takes time to learn, an' it ain't like you've had that," said Big Merv. "Not like this little scrote."

"Mmm," said The Pan. Ruth put her head close to his again. He hoped she wasn't going to do anything rash. For a moment he felt again that lingering kiss at the tube station. Arnold! He wanted some more of that but not here, not now or he'd probably crash. Being hugged this way was … mmm … very nice but it was also highly distracting.

"Shouldn't we surface and see where we are?" she said, instantly grounding The Pan's wandering thoughts.

Ah yes. Good idea. Her voice sounded croaky. As he drove to the surface she leaned even further forwards, craning her head to see through the windscreen. "Anything look familiar?" he asked.

"Yes. You need to go that way." Her face was perilously close to his again as she pointed and the shivers ran down his spine.

"Alright then. Let's go," he said.

Chapter 59

Nigel woke up. His head hurt.

"What the …?" he muttered. Why was he outside? It was getting dark and the other diners had gone indoors … and where was Sabrina? He remembered the visit from Lucy and some other person, hired muscle, he presumed. Clearly one of her human rights cases from the wrong side of the tracks. This one had been pretty well-heeled, all tailor-made suit and made-to-measure elegance, but way too flash, like a premier league football player and with the worst spray tan Nigel had ever seen. They'd taken his keys and … Oh no. He thought he might be sick. It wasn't concussion. He was almost paralysed by fear at the idea that he might have failed Lord Vernon. Lucy and her companion had gone to Nigel's flat where Ruth was waiting. And if Lucy and her friend had got there in time to rescue Ruth it meant that Lord Vernon would not find her. And if Lord Vernon didn't find her, he was going to come looking for Nigel to ask some questions about why she hadn't shown up.

"Arrgh!" He put his head in his hands. OK, no point in panicking. Stay calm, think this through, then act.

Best case scenario: Lucy and her scary friend had arrived too late and Lord Vernon had got his woman. That was not a good thought but he could live with it.

Worst case scenario: Lucy and her muscle had saved Ruth. If that had happened, Lord Vernon would be angry but maybe he would be mollified if Nigel refused the gold, gave him back his diamond and offered him more on top. Everyone had a price. Sure, Lord Vernon was powerful enough to appear on his local currency but that didn't necessarily mean he was loaded. No. The diamonds … it did. It would cost Nigel a lot of money to buy him off; it might cost everything he had, but if Nigel had made one fortune he could make another and if he promised something else … maybe he could find another way to deliver Ruth, with Lucy and her friend, as well. Yes, that might get Lord Vernon off his back.

Then there was Lucy and what was his name …? That was it, Merv, Mister Merv. They wouldn't be happy if Lord Vernon got Ruth but they would be easier to neutralise than Lord Vernon. Merv had punched Nigel. That must fall into the category of Grievous Bodily Harm and Lucy hadn't tried to stop him—which must make her an accessory. Nigel had lawyers, powerful ones, and Merv and Lucy had threatened him in the restaurant. It would be enough to get Merv convicted. As for Lucy, a word from Nigel to the right people, not to mention the media, and her career would be dead in the water. And Nigel would sue the pair of them for damages on top, of course. Although if Lord Vernon found them they probably wouldn't be around to cause any trouble.

The best that could happen would be if Lucy and her Mister Merv friend arrived at the flat while Ruth and Lord Vernon were still there. Nigel swallowed. That would mean two bodies on his couch—possibly three—but Lord Vernon had said he wanted Ruth alive. Not a good scenario but Nigel understood that if he could find a way to dispose of the evidence without involving the police, it might be better for him. So long as the arrival of Merv and Lucy didn't make Lord Vernon think Nigel had double-crossed him. If that happened, there'd be some uncomfortable explaining to do, but in theory, as long as Lord Vernon bought his story, Nigel might be able to draw a line under it there. *If* Lord Vernon bought his story. That was a big if and Lord Vernon hadn't struck him as a particularly reasonable individual. He grimaced at the thought.

Ouch. He rubbed his jaw—it felt as if he'd been punched in the face with an anvil—and wondered what to do next. It was the potential worst case scenario that was worrying him. Should he disappear for a while and wait to see what happened? Maybe. He had plenty of money salted away in a Swiss bank account. He could fly out tonight. Then he could arrange for a private investigator to find out what had gone on and, depending on the results, he could come back or stay disappeared. He had a few shady contacts of his own, people who knew people who could get him a false ID. He'd need some face-altering surgery but there were discreet clinics in Switzerland and his contacts could arrange that, too.

Only one stumbling block—Nigel would need his passport. He would also need cash. If he had to go into hiding, it would be foolish to leave a trail of credit card transactions behind him. He had several thousand pounds in his safe, along with the diamond Lord Vernon had given him. He could use that money to pay for the air fare and to pay for a hotel. Could he get back to his flat though? Should he even try?

He checked his pockets in the forlorn hope of finding his phone and was surprised to find that it was still there. He stood up. For a moment he thought of returning to the restaurant to say goodbye to Sabrina, but decided against it. He rang the caretaker at the flats and began to walk. Yes, Ruth had been in, yes, of course he would check and, after a suitable period of small talk while the caretaker climbed the stairs there was a long pause.

"Mr Chatterton-Dix," began the caretaker. "I—I—"

"What is it? Is she there or not?" snapped Nigel, who was now waiting in a nearby side road until he had word that the coast was clear to go home.

"No, there's no-one here but your flat has been turned over, the door has been broken down, there's coffee all over the carpet, your balcony doors are all smashed …" a pause, "in fact, they're gone. I'll call the police."

That was the last thing Nigel wanted.

"No! I mean, no," he tried again, more calmly. "I will do that when I get there. I'll be at the building in a few moments, can you buzz me in? Only I've been mugged. That's why I'd rather speak to the police, I may as well report both crimes at once." Yes! Nigel realised his brain was as sharp as ever and began to feel better. He would build another successful life, he could do it. He was Nigel Chatterton-Dix, Nigel slicker-faster-quicker-and-invincibly-luckier-than-anyone-else Chatterton-Dix. Then he would come back. He thought, with regret, of Sabrina. Perhaps he'd even give Lucy and her friend some payback for wrecking that one.

"I'm sorry to hear that, you've done well to keep your phone."

"I told them it was in my car and luckily they believed me. They got my keys and my cash …"

The caretaker met Nigel at the front door. Nigel brushed aside his sympathetic enquiries with a brusque 'thank you'—he was only being nosey anyway—and left him in the lobby. Taking the spare keys with him, he went up to his flat.

When Nigel had gone out he'd left the door on the latch. Someone had bolted it and it had been forced, but the latch was still up and the deadlock still intact. Good, he would be able to secure it. Which reminded him—he flicked the latch down and closed the door. Then he put the key in the deadlock and turned it.

The smell of coffee pervaded the hall, still just the right side of stewed. When he went into his sitting room, he realised the caretaker was right. There had clearly been a fight. In the middle of the room, a cup lay on the carpet, the coffee spattered around it, almost as if it had been thrown. The balcony doors were gone, along with the curtains from that side of the room. Nothing was left of either apart from the odd piece of charred, twisted metal. What on earth could have done that? It looked post-nuclear, the remaining metal lumpy in places as if it had melted. All the more reason to be quick then—the evidence suggested Lord Vernon had got Ruth, at least. However, until he knew for certain, Nigel didn't want to be there long. If Lord Vernon was coming back he doubted he had much time.

He hurriedly opened the safe, grabbed his passport and the cash. Then he went back into the hall and through to the bedroom where he threw a few essentials into a holdall and ran into the hall again.

"Going somewhere, Mr Chatterton-Dix?" said a voice—a particularly quiet, yet carrying, evil voice that Nigel had hoped he would never hear again.

Leaning against the closed front door was Lord Vernon, but this time he looked very different. So different that for a moment, Nigel hoped against hope, that he was a hallucination. He was no longer pale, unlike Nigel, who was rapidly going white. No. This time, Lord Vernon's skin was bright green. The colour seemed to suit him and accentuated everything about his face and notably his eyes, those merciless, ice-cold eyes that already scared Nigel witless. Who the hell was Lord Vernon? An alien from outer space? A little—no, make that big—green man.

"I—I locked the door," said Nigel. Lord Vernon smiled with obvious relish but without a molecule of warmth, like a snake mesmerising its prey.

"Yes, you did." He held up the caretaker's bunch of keys. In his haste Nigel realised he had left them in the lock. No! How could he have been so stupid?

The keys jangled as, without breaking eye contact, Lord Vernon casually put them in his pocket and took a step forward. Nigel dropped the holdall and stepped backwards.

"Then how did you get in?"

Lord Vernon glanced over at the balcony. He'd come up the side of the building. He must be super-human, or maybe just not human, Nigel thought, with trepidation.

"You promised to give me Ruth."

"And I delivered."

"I beg to differ. She did not come alone." Lord Vernon's voice was even but there was an underlying anger which sounded like bad news. Especially for Nigel trapped in his flat with him. No, don't think about that, this was not the time to panic. He took a deep breath. He was petrified but he had to stay calm. He was a good negotiator. He usually got his way with charm, tact and a little bit of iron. Heaven knew he needed every ounce of those right now, but he'd beaten this monster once before. He could do it again so long as he kept a cool head and stayed positive.

"I assure you, I had no choice. It was that or be murdered in a restaurant.

They had a gun. All I could do was stall them." Nigel was aware that he hadn't
stalled them at all and hoped it didn't show in his face.

"Them?" Lord Vernon snorted. "I am not talking about them, I am talking
about the Hamgeean."

Nigel was genuinely perplexed.

"The who?"

"The Pan of Hamgee." This time the heat in Lord Vernon's voice was
unmistakable.

"The Pan of Hamgee?" Nigel stepped backwards again and Lord Vernon
followed. He had never heard the name, didn't even know if it belonged to a
man or a woman, so why did it sound familiar?

"I don't know who you're talking about," he said. With nowhere else to go,
he stumbled into the wreckage of his sitting room. Lord Vernon came after
him, purposefully.

"Oh, but I think you do."

Nigel's heart sank as he remembered that yes he did, obliquely. Back at the
restaurant, at the very end, just before knocking him out, Lucy's escort had
threatened him and said 'I don't care what The Pan said I'm gonna put a slug
in you and take 'em.'

"OK, so they mentioned 'The Pan' but I swear that's all I heard," said Nigel,
offering up what he knew, in the hope that it would do his cause some good.

"And you think I will believe that, Nigel? I wonder what else you are holding
back. You humans always stick together."

'You humans'? There'd been plenty of hints but this was the first time Nigel
fully appreciated that he was talking to a different life form. One that regarded
itself as supreme and other beings as inferior with the same arrogant
condescension the human race showed animals. Only, unfortunately, Lord
Vernon spoke from what could well be a position of considerable superiority,
not to mention height. Nigel looked fearfully up at him. Now what? Same as
the previous time; argue of course, but politely.

"Humans don't stick together on this planet. We fight," said Nigel.

"Really?" Lord Vernon's tone was the very essence, probably distilled
several times, of sarcastic. Nigel continued to back away as Lord Vernon
advanced on him.

"Yes. We're the only intelligent life form here." Lord Vernon said nothing
but he stopped. Nigel took one more step backwards and stood still. If only
Lord Vernon was female, he'd have given more for his chances. Even so, he
still believed that if he kept his head, he had guile enough to negotiate his way

out of this. "OK, we're m—" Nigel stopped just short of saying, 'men'. As descriptive epithets went, it was unlikely to be the right choice. "We're both pragmatic p—beings. I don't know where you are from but I know you have power—more than me. Why would I attack the bigger guy? Why would I do this to my own flat?" He pointed towards the vanished balcony doors.

"I believe I did this to your flat, Nigel," said Lord Vernon coolly.

"Yes but I let it happen."

"Of course," Lord Vernon laughed mirthlessly. "As if you had a choice."

"OK, so I did my best. I got Ruth here, when you wanted, I told her not to tell anyone and she blabbed. I don't know how Lucy found out where I was, but she did, and she turned up with some hired thug who knocked me out and then they came here to find her. That's all I know. I swear."

Lord Vernon locked eyes with him. Nigel hadn't believed he possessed a soul, and was quite sure that no-one had ever looked into it before. He wasn't positive that was happening now but he couldn't help thinking, that if it ever did, this is exactly what it would be like. He wanted to turn his head away but he couldn't. Something powerful in those eyes drew him in. It was as if Lord Vernon was taking the energy, the fight, the life out of him and revelling in every moment of the process. Cold fear held Nigel, his pulse quickened, his breath came faster and he began to wonder if he would pass out, when Lord Vernon abruptly shifted his attention. He began examining the ends of his fingertips, or at least, the black suede fingertips of his gloves: Nigel had never seen Lord Vernon's hands.

"Interesting. It seems you are telling the truth. Clearly, you have no knowledge of the Hamgeean. In this respect, you are luckier than I."

Well, yes. Nigel was luckier than most people. Had the famous Chatterton-Dix lucky streak finally come to his rescue? Would he, could he get out of this alive?

"Perhaps I shall spare your life." Yes!

"Naturally, I will have to think about it." Then again, maybe not. There was a long, long pause.

When he spoke, Nigel could only whisper.

"Please … I would give anything."

"Anything?" Lord Vernon raised his eyebrows. "How very generous of you," he sneered, "but I think I would prefer … everything."

"I don't understand—"

"I am sure you do. I would rather like to kill you but I am offering you a chance to persuade me otherwise. Perhaps if you can provide me with sufficient … incentive to overlook your failure I will let you live.”

Nigel was silent.

“How much are you worth?”

“I can’t tell you.”

Lord Vernon drew his gun.

“I think you’ll find you can.”

“No—I promise—I don’t know, I have assets, stocks and shares, their value fluctuates …”

Casually, Lord Vernon flicked the safety catch off.

“Perhaps you misunderstand me. Let me clarify, I know you, Nigel. I know who you are. I do not think someone who is willing to surrender an acquaintance to me—even one they do not like—for that much gold would be so vague. I’ll wager you *can* tell me the extent of your fortune, down to the last decimal place.”

“Three million,” croaked Nigel.

“Three million is not quite enough unless there is … a little extra? If there is, I would strongly advise you to confess. Now.”

Lord Vernon took aim.

“N—no, wait. Alright, there’s another million in a Swiss bank account, I can give you the number.”

Lord Vernon tutted.

“You would withhold a whole million from me Nigel? That is very greedy of you. And the rest?”

“There’s no more.”

“Are you certain?”

“I promise you, I am telling the truth. You have to believe me.”

Lord Vernon smiled, once again with a spectacular absence of warmth.

“I do not have to do anything, Nigel. Not if I do not want to.”

“Lord Vernon, I promise I will give you four million in cash, if you will just spare my life and give me another chance to get Ruth. I tell you what, I’ll get you the other two—Mister Merv and Lucy—and I’ll throw in the Bentley as well.”

“That’s an improvement, Nigel, but given enough time I will have them all. And I find myself wondering, if you have four million in ready money, how much more you have in …” he glanced around him, “assets?”

So. It had come down to this, as Nigel feared it might. Bastard. He wanted the rest too. Nigel took another deep breath. He could do this. He could sacrifice the flat, his car, his artworks, his possessions. His job was still there, and so was Sabrina. He could, he would, start again.

"Take it then. You have the keys. Take it all. I'll leave it and go. Here." Carefully, he stepped forwards, taking his phone from his pocket as he went, and placed it on the glass coffee table. "I'll even leave you this."

Lord Vernon laughed mockingly and cast a disdainful look around him.

"I'm afraid that is not sufficient. I am not some savage you can buy with a few brightly coloured beads. Do you think these baubles, this … hovel you inhabit is enough? I own an entire nation, with everyone and everything in it. Half a planet is mine to use as I see fit. You are not going anywhere, Nigel."

Lord Vernon's finger tightened on the trigger.

"No! For the love of God! Please …" Nigel fell to his knees and wrung his hands.

****

Lord Vernon sighed. He was suddenly and heavily tired of this place—these wheedling humans and their worthless trinkets. Who did Nigel think he was? It had been enjoyable to make him suffer and ruining him would have been amusing—but for such a paltry sum it wasn't worth the effort. No, he had served his purpose and since Lord Vernon could see no further use for the little slimeball, this really wasn't worth his time. The human still seemed to be talking, but it was just noise, now. He squeezed the trigger. With its usual easy motion, the laser pistol fired.

****

The last thing Nigel heard was an electronic pinging sound. There was a flash of red light and he disappeared. An unpleasant smell of burning pervaded the flat, mixing with the aroma of, now, stewed coffee. Lord Vernon put one hand on the barrel of his laser pistol. It was only a little warm to the touch. He rubbed it in his hair to boost the charge and put it back in its holster. Throwing Nigel's keys dismissively to the floor he pressed the button on his key ring, strolled out onto the balcony and climbed casually over the wall into the Interceptor, which had come to his summons. The gull-wing door closed.

Anyone watching would have seen it accelerate for an instant before it disappeared in a flash of light.

Chapter 60

DI Softone rubbed his eyes. He'd managed to snatch an hour's sleep, just enough to make him feel even worse when he woke up. It would do though.

When he'd seen the body, for the first time in many years, he'd nearly thrown up. Strange that such an effect should be wrought by the fact that there was no body, to speak of; nothing but a pile of grey dust and a shadow. It was the shadow that got him, a greasy stain across the carpet in the outline of someone on their knees, arms outstretched in supplication. Just thinking about it made him start to feel queasy again.

"You OK, sir?" asked DC Gurney. He gave her a weak smile. She was impossibly fresh and bright-eyed. Clearly the brief kip had done her good. Then again, she had a few years on him. He rubbed the stubble on his chin.

"Do we know what happened?"

"The flat's owner is one Nigel Chatterton-Dix. I've been talking to the caretaker. Mr Chatterton-Dix returned in a state of some agitation just after six thirty. He said he'd been robbed and lost his keys so the caretaker gave him his set. Then he went upstairs and according to the lady in the flat below him there was a lot of banging about and she heard him arguing with someone, although she couldn't hear the other person. The next thing, she smelled burning. It was so strong that she went up to complain and when Mr Chatterton-Dix didn't answer she thought he might have set the place on fire and she went and got the caretaker. The pair of them came up here and found the door locked and the smell as bad as ever. That's when they called the emergency services."

"Us?"

"And the Fire Brigade. They broke down the door, sir, and found this."

"And you think that's our Nigel, do you?" said DI Softone, as he watched a member of forensics sweeping the ash into a plastic bag.

"I'd say so. We'll have it tested but it looks that way, sir, because—"

"It's a human-shaped shadow."

"Yessir."

"So, have you any idea what kind of weapon can do …" DI Softone suppressed an urge to gag, "this?"

DC Gurney made a face.

"It seems to be some kind of laser, sir."

"Our friends from the Festival Hall?"

"Very possibly, sir."

"What about Ruth Cochrane and the Hamgeean lad. He has a flying car. Any reason why he shouldn't have access to a laser?"

"Could be, sir, but reports suggest he was heading in the other direction at the time Mr Chatterton-Dix arrived home."

"We have a confirmed sighting?"

"Several, sir. He chose to fly a few feet above the traffic. It caused quite a stir."

"I can imagine. What about the other one? Lord Vernon? Any sign of him?"

"Yes, he turned up again and chased the Lotus up over the rooftops. We're not sure what happened after that. We have a confirmed sighting of the Lotus going into the Thames and another confirmed sighting of the black vehicle flying this way."

"The Pan of Hamgee said Lord Vernon and the two at the Festival Hall were all the same species. There must be a connection."

"There is, sir. Mr Chatterton-Dix was dating Lucy Hargraves, Ruth Cochrane's flatmate."

"Ah yes, our friendly neighbourhood lawyer. She didn't like our Hamgeean friend much, did she? Perhaps Nigel felt the same."

"Possibly, sir. I checked with Ms Cochrane's mobile phone company and Mr Chatterton-Dix did call her this evening around five-ish."

"There's a thought. What if Lord Vernon came here after Ruth?"

"Do you think Mr Chatterton-Dix was working for Lord Vernon?"

"I'm not sure. It's plausible, though, isn't it? And the Hamgeean lad said Lord Vernon wants Ms Cochrane."

"There's only one body, sir and comparing descriptions of Mr Chatterton-Dix with the shadow, I'd say it's the same build and height as him but too tall to be Ms Cochrane."

"Agreed, I'd say it's unlikely to be her but that doesn't necessarily make it Nigel. What about the Hamgeean lad or Ms Hargraves?"

"The boys are checking the most recent CCTV footage of the Lotus now but it looks as if there were four up when it was travelling away from the scene. We believe that Ms Cochrane, along with Ms Hargraves and her assistant Mister Merv, were in it with him, although we can rule Mister Merv out from the shadow, it's clearly someone a great deal smaller than him."

"Hmm." DI Softone nodded. "Putting the rest aside, we're agreed that Lord Vernon did this?"

"I'd say so, sir. The labs are going to analyse the dust to try and confirm whether or not it really is—" her voice caught.

"Mr Chatterton-Dix."

"I was going to say, 'organic' sir. I doubt there's enough left to confirm anything more than that."

"D'you think Ms Cochrane is still alive?"

"It's difficult to tell, sir. No witnesses have come forward who saw the car come out of the river."

"Right. We'd better get a frog team to check just in case, and put an APB out on her and our Hamgeean friend. If they're still around, of course."

"They seemed sensible, sir. I should think they're long gone."

"I hope they are." DI Softone shook his head. "This'll be one to tell the grandchildren, eh?" Both police officers laughed weakly. He walked out onto Nigel's balcony and leaned against the railings. The smell was less pronounced out here and he began to feel less sick. He felt rather than saw DC Gurney come and stand beside him.

"You OK, sir?" she asked.

"Yeh. Just thinking. This is all new ground to me. If they are alive then I think we need to speak to those young people again." He heaved a sigh. "If I thought it would do any good I'd take them into protective custody but after what Lord Vernon did to the station I'd rather not risk it. It's a miracle there were no fatalities last time."

"Yes, sir."

"Tell you what. I bet her lawyer has her phone switched on."

"I'll give her a call shall I, sir?"

"Yes. Someone has to let her know what's happened to her man."

"Sir."

"Then again, she's probably screening her calls."

"Yes, sir."

"Of course, if she's worried about him, she might answer a call from her boyfriend …" he walked back into the sitting room and picked up Nigel's mobile.

"Forensics will kill us."

"Better that than Lord Vernon killing again."

"We don't officially know it was Lord Vernon."

DI Softone said nothing and let the silence speak for itself.

"OK we might."

"We have enough evidence to lock him up for several years."

"Yes, but not for murder."

"Give me time. I'll find something."

Like everyone else on the crime scene, he and DC Gurney were wearing latex gloves. It was difficult to persuade the touch screen to work. He handed it over to the DC who was able to call up Lucy's number at once. She pressed the green 'send' button.

"You want me to—?"

"No, I'll handle this." He took the phone and held it as close to his ear as he could without allowing the screen to touch his hair or face. No point sending forensics ballistic unless he had to.

Chapter 61

The Pan parked in a side street behind the Free K'Barthan Embassy and he, Lucy, Ruth and Big Merv decamped from the snurd. He bipped the keys and it drove away. His head ached less now, but the gouges Lord Vernon's rings had made in his scalp smarted. The Pan experienced renewed surprise at being treated with courtesy by a doorman. The one at the club welcomed the four of them with a polite 'good evening' and made no attempt to stop them from going upstairs. Once they were finally through the secret doors they were greeted with enthusiasm by Sir Robin.

"My boy!" he headed straight for The Pan. "I have never been more delighted to see you." He stopped shaking The Pan's hand energetically when he saw his face. "I say, you have been in the wars."

"Mmm."

"Never mind, you're here now, that's all that matters. Better late than never, I think it's high time we all had a chat, don't you? There was someone I'm very keen for you all to meet, but sadly he's had to go. Let's have a chat anyway."

The Chosen One stepped decisively forward.

"Sir Robin, can I look at The Pan's head first?" she said. Her voice was quiet when she added, "As you can see, Lord Vernon hit him but the rings cut him too, in his hair."

"Ruth," The Pan took her hand. "Thank you but it's alright. There'll be time for that later. Right now what's worrying me is Nigel."

"What're you worrying about him for?" asked Big Merv.

"Because he may be in danger."

"Yeh well I ain't so upset about that. Not after what he done. Aren't you forgetting that we've been in danger and all, thanks to him?"

"Alright, perhaps he does deserve a bit of comeback—but not from Lord Vernon," said The Pan.

"Why, yer daft Hamgeean spanner? It ain't like we owe him? I reckon we should leave him. If he can pull a bright bird like Lucy here, then he ain't daft. He'd have known the score."

"No he wouldn't. And we can't leave him. It's not ethical."

"Indeed," said Sir Robin smoothly. "My boy, you're quite right. However—"

"No, he ain't," Big Merv interrupted him. "I'm not going back. Nigel's the nonce 'ere and it ain't our problem if he gets what's coming to him."

"Merv, you don't have to go back, but I do," said The Pan. "Arnold in the skies, I wish you'd brought him with you."

Big Merv shifted uncomfortably.

"I'm sorry mate, I left him at the restaurant. I knocked 'im spark out so I dumped him at a table outside. I was gonna say something but when things got dangerous I clean forgot."

"Then I have to go and get him," said The Pan.

"You would be very unwise to do that," said Sir Robin.

"Lucky I'm short on wisdom then, isn't it?"

"Don't be bleedin' mental," said Big Merv.

"I have to. We can't just leave him to Lord Vernon. No-one deserves that. It's not the K'Barthan way."

"That is true," said Sir Robin. "However, as I was about to say before Big Merv interrupted me," he gave the Swamp Thing the kind of gimlet stare that would probably stop Lord Vernon himself from interrupting again. "Nigel is beyond our help."

"So long as he's alive I have to try," said The Pan. "If I can find him."

"That is my point." Sir Robin stepped forward and put his hand on The Pan's arm. "Let it go. This time there is nothing you can do."

The Pan's eyes met Sir Robin's and he couldn't remember seeing such sadness or weariness in another person's face, ever.

"You look how I feel," he said and was surprised when Sir Robin came back with a gentle joke.

"I think that may be better than feeling the way you look." As he smiled the gold tooth caught the light. "You have done all you can. More than Nigel might have deserved or expected." He was going to continue but Lucy's phone started ringing. She took it out of her pocket and looked at the screen.

"Oh my God! It's Nigel!" she cried and everyone gathered round her as she pressed the answer button. The Pan wasn't convinced and when his eyes met Sir Robin's, the old man shook his head. Lucy was speaking.

"Nigel. This is important. Don't say anything, just listen. We've got Ruth and that means that any minute now, Lord Vernon is going to come and get you. And although you're a vile, two-faced, two-timing sod and therefore deserve it, I really won't be able to live with myself if he finds you. So you need to come here right now, or hide somewhere and wait for us to collect you ..." She paused for breath and stopped. There was a long silence while Nigel spoke.

The Pan could almost make out the words but not quite. He moved closer. "Are you supposed to be using his phone?" asked Lucy weakly. The Pan moved closer still. "What news? No, I can't come in." Another pause. "He's dead, isn't he?" said Lucy and this time The Pan was close enough to hear a male voice.

"We can neither confirm nor deny that at the moment, Ms Hargraves."

"He *is* dead, though, isn't he?"

"I am very sorry, Ms Hargraves, the evidence would suggest that to be the case," said the voice, followed by something The Pan didn't catch.

"Yes, she's here," said Lucy.

"Who is it?" asked The Pan.

"Could you hold on a moment?" Lucy pressed the mute button. "The police."

"Anyone we know?"

"DI Softone."

"What does he want?" asked Ruth.

"He rang to tell me he thinks Nigel's dead, but he's not sure," said Lucy. She spoke calmly but she looked tearful and The Pan felt sorry for her.

"Do you want me to talk to him?" he asked, and to his surprise, Lucy held out the phone.

"Yes please."

The Pan had never held a mobile phone before.

"Don't press it against your face too hard. You'll probably cut them off with your cheek or something," said Ruth.

"Do you want to hear?" asked The Pan, beckoning everyone in.

"Here." Lucy pressed the screen. "Now it's on speakerphone. Let me just unmute it and … there."

"DI Softone?" said The Pan.

"Mister Hamgeean. You're not in the Thames then?"

"No."

"Good. That'll save me the cost of a frog team. I hope you are looking after Ms Cochrane and Ms Hargraves."

"I'm doing my best."

"Glad to hear that. I am doing my best to find one Nigel Chatterton-Dix. I don't suppose you've seen him in your travels, have you?"

"Not personally."

"Anyone else you know might have done?"

"I believe he may have been …" how to put this? "having a sleep outside a restaurant earlier this evening."

"What about Lord Vernon—have you seen him?"

"We ran into each other."

"Lord Vernon and these Grongles of his, would you say they are capable of murder?"

"I'd say capable is understating it, for them it's more like a hobby."

"I see. What sort of weapons might the Grongles, or Lord Vernon, use?"

"Pretty much anything that comes to hand. Why?"

"I've found a pile of ash and a greasy stain—"

"And you want to know if it's Nigel," said The Pan. He felt ill, almost too ill to speak. "I—" he stopped, mainly because if he carried on trying to talk he'd throw up.

"I am afraid that is very likely," said Sir Robin stepping in. "Although we may never know for certain."

"Who is this?" said DI Softone.

The Pan concentrated and managed to contain his nausea.

"An expert, his name is immaterial. Did you hear what he said?" he asked.

"Yes," said DI Softone. "Is there no way of knowing definitively?"

The Pan's eyes met Sir Robin's, who again shook his head.

"No."

"I see, but would you say …?"

Sir Robin nodded.

"Yes. I'm sorry, but I think that probably is Nigel you have there."

"Then we need to find your Lord Vernon."

"No. Trust me on this, you don't. He'll go away eventually."

"That may be, but in the meantime I'd like to question him about a murder. I take a dim view of murder and no-one does it on my patch without proper retribution. If he's involved, I want to know and if he isn't, I want to rule him out."

"If Lord Vernon's involved you don't want to know. He does whatever he wants wherever he likes."

"Not on my patch, he doesn't."

"Listen, DI Softone, seriously, drop this. It isn't your problem and I am sorry I've brought it here. We have to sort this out on our own but I promise, you'll be the first to know when he gives up on us. I give you my word, we'll be in touch."

Ah. How to ring off? He looked at the buttons on the screen and pressed the green one. No, wait a minute. Green meant go here. That wouldn't be right.

"Is he still there?" said the disembodied voice of DI Softone.

"Looks like it, sir," came the voice of DC Gurney.

The Pan pressed another button and the screen flashed a message, 'call on hold'. No. That wasn't right. He pressed it again. 'Unhold' said the screen.

"Still there, Mister Hamgeean?" said the tinny voice of DI Softone.

"Yes. I think you might have to ring off," said The Pan.

"No can do. We're triangulating your position."

"Arnold's snot." The Pan looked up helplessly.

Ruth took the phone from his hand and pressed the screen. Ah yes, the red button. It would be.

"Thank you."

"It's a pleasure, Mister Pan."

Ruth handed the phone back to Lucy, who took it, turned abruptly and walked away down the hall. The Pan suspected she was crying. Ruth's eyes met his in a moment of mutual understanding. It was only right that she should look after her friend but clearly she was also worried about the wounds under his hair. He nodded when she gave him a quizzical look and pointed to her temple. It was lovely that she cared, but it was only a scratch. He smiled and waved her away, and so, taking Big Merv with her she followed Lucy. The Pan and Sir Robin watched them go into the drawing room and close the door.

"Well, my boy, you've had quite a day," said Sir Robin.

"Yeh. You could say that." He was tired and sick at the thought of what had happened to Nigel and could find no words to express the way he felt. "Listen, Sir Robin, I need your help. Ruth … I have to get her out of this mess."

"Indeed, my boy. Once again, it's time we had a talk. How about a pre-dinner drink to pep you up? I'm sure there are some excellent roasted almonds somewhere and the club does a very nice amontillado. They were kind enough to let me have a bottle and it really is very good."

What in the name of The Prophet was amontillado?

"It's a type of sherry. Sherry is a fortified thing they make with grapes. Anyway, it's splendid stuff." The Pan couldn't help smiling and Sir Robin took this favourable reaction as a 'yes'. "Marvellous, I'm so glad I've twisted your arm. Come along then." All The Pan really wanted to do was get Ruth alone, but she and Big Merv would be busy looking after Lucy for a while. Anyway, The Pan realised it would be good if, the next time he saw her, he was able to explain how Sir Robin was going to help her get her life back. Yes. Talk to Sir Robin first. The Pan watched him walk down the hall and disappear into the study, leaving him no choice but to follow.

Chapter 62

Lord Vernon returned to his apartments in K'Barth in a resigned frame of mind. He had hoped to be closely questioning the Chosen One by this time, but once again, it was not to be. Patience. A single night was of little importance. He could wait until tomorrow. They would all be in his power then, Ruth, Sir Robin and the Hamgeean. The corners of his mouth turned upwards in a malicious smile at the thought of the Hamgeean at his mercy. That would be a treat.

His first action on arrival was to enquire as to the whereabouts of General Moteurs but it seemed he had not yet returned from his meeting with the Underground. Lord Vernon poured himself a drink and retired to his balcony to wait. He held out his hand and admired the ring, worn by all forty generations of Architraves. There would be no more of them now. He would be the last and for him the position would be a stepping stone to yet greater things. He intended to found a dynasty; he was confident he could persuade the Chosen One to provide him with an heir, one way or another. She was not of his species but since she came from a parallel reality, her non-Grongle nature could be overlooked. Yes, she was a suitable enough female, which reminded him, he had been highly focused the past few days. He wanted something to ease his tension but a visit to the cells would not suffice. This evening he desired a more intense form of relaxation. His thoughts turned to the blonde K'Barthan human from the laundry and he let them linger. She would make the most delicious reward for his patience. He glanced at his watch. Seven o'clock, General Moteurs was due to report at half past. Half an hour would not do justice to such a prime specimen, but later …

He flipped open his phone and dialled. If General Moteurs was a weapon of finely honed precision, then Captain Snow was the bluntest of blunt instruments. But in his own way, he was equally effective. Especially in areas such as this, where the General's old school morals precluded his full cooperation.

"Captain," said Lord Vernon.

"Sir."

"I would like to relax with a female. You have some … fresh meat." He licked his lips. "Human, blonde, long legs, blue eyes. They were foolish enough to send her to collect my laundry."

"Yes, sir."

"Tell me, does she have an aptitude for her work?"

"No, sir."

"How surprising." It was as he suspected. She was Resistance. He could do anything he liked to her and she would have no recourse. "Bring her to me."

"Yes, sir, right away, sir."

"No, Captain. Not right away. Make her presentable first: bathe her, dress her in something appropriate, feed her—I want her to have stamina—see that nobody touches her and deliver her here at nine thirty." He rang off without waiting for Captain Snow's reply.

Good, that should allow plenty of time to discuss his next steps with General Moteurs before spending the rest of the evening in indulgent pleasure—Lord Vernon closed his eyes, relaxed back into his chair and allowed his imagination free rein—how luscious.

Chapter 63

The study was a small snug room lined from floor to ceiling with bookshelves, apart from two notable gaps. A chimney breast and an open fireplace were on one wall and, behind the desk, hung a picture and the shelving only came halfway up the wall. The volumes on the shelves varied from thrillers and modern works to some of the rarest and most finely bound books The Pan had seen. The carpet was a rich dark brown, the curtains a chintzy patterned velvet and there was a Chesterfield three-piece suite in that ubiquitous leather upholstered style favoured by this kind of club. The suite was very battered, and as The Pan discovered when he sat, very comfortable. He wondered how much of this taste was down to Sir Robin. All of it, probably. Apart from the books, there were few things that The Pan would have picked out but at the same time, if it were his office and he found it like that, he wasn't sure he'd change anything. The room had a familiar, worn, homely feel that put him instantly at ease. The suite was arranged around a low glass coffee table, which The Pan was tempted to put his feet on, but his good manners won out.

The curtains were drawn and the room was lit with concealed lighting along the tops of the bookcases, which illuminated the ceiling, and a number of reading lamps, one on a table by the window, one propped precariously on a shelf in front of the books and one on the desk. The desk itself was an old one—a couple of hundred years old—and seemed curiously familiar.

"Nice desk," said The Pan. He wondered where he had seen it before.

"I thought you might notice that," said Sir Robin. "It used to belong to the Architrave." He retreated behind it and past a leather swivel chair which was as battered as the suite.

"Which one?"

"All of them after it was made," said Sir Robin absently. The section of shelving beneath the picture was mostly obscured by the desk and Sir Robin disappeared from view as he knelt down and rummaged about on these shelves at floor level. After a few moments he resurfaced with two glasses. Not all books then. Sir Robin returned to the shelves for another rummage and The Pan looked at the picture above him, a large painting of a man in Architraval robes holding a hen. That would be the Eighth Architrave—the one with the thing about chickens.

"Interesting painting," he said.

Cluck, said Sir Robin.

"What?"

"Sorry," said Sir Robin as he straightened up with a bottle of rich golden-brown liquid. "Did you think I said something?"

"Didn't you?"

"No," said Sir Robin at the exact same moment someone else said, *Cluck*?

Arnold. That wasn't good.

Sir Robin poured the brown liquid into the glasses.

"It must have been something outside," said The Pan weakly. Mmm. Was this a test? Either that or he was cracking up. In the absence of any positive plan of action The Pan decided to ignore the clucking. Who knew, if he ignored it long enough, it might go away. He glanced up at the portrait of the Eighth Architrave. What was his name? Nope, no idea.

Cluck, said a voice and The Pan got the impression that it was telling him, if not the name of the Architrave, then at least the name of the chicken. Unfortunately, as a non-chicken speaker, he was unable to translate it. The Pan's recollection of his history lessons was sketchy at best but he thought the Eighth Architrave's tenure had been short. Yeh. Only ten years or so. The Pan could recall several paintings of him and was convinced in his own mind that the same chicken featured in all of them. He tried to scrape together any other facts he could remember. There'd been a bit of an upset at the end of his reign when he had suddenly abdicated. Perhaps the chicken had died and he didn't want to go on without it. Then again, pictures of the Eighth Architrave were always different to the others. There was a look that the rest of the Architraves had; a kind of thousand-yard stare, as if they carried the entire world on their shoulders or as if most of their headspace occupied an entirely different level.

Now The Pan looked closely, he couldn't help thinking that if anyone in this painting had that Architraval 'look' it was the chicken. What if the chicken was the Architrave, The Pan wondered—blasphemously, he suspected. Yes, and maybe the man was just some chap it hired to carry it about. His naughty thoughts amused him and he chuckled.

"You like it?" asked Sir Robin as he brought the two glasses over to the coffee table between them.

"What? The picture?"

"Yes."

"It's alright." Sir Robin went back to the desk and ferreted about in the drawers.

Cluck. Arnold, no. Why wouldn't the chicken shut up? The Pan felt he had enough on his plate right now without suddenly hearing chicken noises. He concentrated on the picture and on the conversation he was having with Sir Robin, a real, live individual, who *did* exist. And wasn't a bird.

"I'm not sure I'd be too keen if I was the Eighth Architrave. I bet that painter and him didn't get on," The Pan said.

Sir Robin dumped a bag on the desk—the kind of heavy-duty fabric bag used for carrying money—and looked over at The Pan with a thoughtful expression.

"You think so? Why?"

"Well, to me, the chicken looks like the intelligent one."

With a gargantuan effort of will The Pan concentrated his mind and discovered he was able to blank out the ensuing cluck. He was sure the imaginary chicken was still there, pecking away at the edges of his consciousness, but he couldn't hear it any more. Good. Long may it stay that way.

Sir Robin chortled.

"Intriguing that you should notice. Not surprising, of course, but interesting." More ferreting about and as he searched he continued. "The chicken in that picture is the Architrave, of course, but I assume you knew that?"

"No," said The Pan because it was easier than explaining how surprised he was that his naughty, blasphemous thoughts had turned out to be … neither blasphemous, nor naughty.

"Everything has to happen once," said Sir Robin, with a chuckle. "Ah! At last." He finally found the item he was looking for and with a triumphal expression held up two packets of roasted almonds. "These are very out of vogue here, but I rather like them." Without warning, he threw a bag at The Pan who caught it.

"Nothing wrong with your reactions, I see."

"Thank you."

"Now then," Sir Robin picked up his packet of almonds and the fabric bag. He came and sat down in the second comfy chair, dropping the almonds on the table and putting the fabric bag on the floor by his feet. Closer to, The Pan recognised it as the one the Mervinettes had stolen and given to him. It had been full of strange items, mostly used in the Looking, and he had been forced to surrender it to Sir Robin the first time the two of them had met. It had also contained the gold thimble which Sir Robin had let The Pan keep and the ring, worn by forty generations of Architraves. The Pan tried not to think about what had happened to that. He'd been a fool and he should never have sold it.

Sir Robin sat down. "Chin chin!" he raised his glass and drank. The Pan followed suit. "You like it?"

"It's not bad." An acquired taste, The Pan thought, but one he could get used to pretty quickly.

"Now then, I expect you have some questions," said Sir Robin.

"Yes, I wanted to ask you—"

"Indeed. All in good time."

"But these things—" The Pan put the snuff box, the one Sir Robin had sent to Ruth via Lucy, on the table.

"Oh, leave those where they are for a while. Let's relax a little first," said Sir Robin, raising his glass and stuffing a couple of almonds into his mouth with evident relish. The Pan was not to be deflected. Sir Robin was, after all—or at least had been—the High Priest of K'Barth, the old Architrave's right-hand man. And The Pan did have a lot of questions and he was pretty sure Sir Robin had the answers.

"Is the Candidate here?"

Sir Robin paused for a moment and then resigned himself to talking shop.

"Interesting question …" he said. He leaned back in his chair and made eye contact with The Pan, which was scary because as usual it made the full extent of his intelligence—or at least the extent to which it was greater than The Pan's—blindingly clear. "I believe so."

"Cryptic as ever, I suppose a straight yes or no would be out of the question?"

"For your own protection, I'm afraid that is the case," he smiled. A fond smile though. "The Candidate is here but since he has not yet realised his purpose he is not exactly with us."

"What?"

"I do understand that it's a difficult concept to grasp. I suppose you could say we've reached a kind of halfway house. The world is seldom black and white—there are many shades of grey and this situation is no exception. At least I can be confident of your ability to grasp that sort of conundrum. You are a man who appreciates grey."

"I appreciate grey?" The Pan didn't like the underlying implication. "Because I'm lukewarm and generally unable to commit to anything, I assume?"

"Not at all, you are decisive and incisive. I mean this: first, you appreciate that not every situation is cut and dried, that there are shades of grey; and second, while you have chosen to pursue a life of crime—a profession which some might perceive as bad—you are, essentially, a good man."

A sarcastic guffaw escaped The Pan before he could stop it.

"We've done this one, Sir Robin. I'm not. As we both know, or we should, my presence is merely the next stop on from what you previously referred to as 'ogling a girl'."

"Ah yes. The Chosen One." Sir Robin smiled indulgently.

"Are you going to make a move on her?" he asked, congenially.

Blimey! Talk about out of the blue! Not to mention underhand. Old people aren't supposed to think about stuff like that, it's young people's territory. Then again, Sir Robin must have been young once. The Pan thought about how Gladys might have ended up with a Trev and then immediately tried not to.

"Possibly." Arnold. That hadn't worked. He'd been aiming to play it cool but there was too much emotion and too much seriousness in his voice.

A pause. A kindly smile. A flash of that gold tooth again.

"I had an idea you might be keen on her. She's certainly got the hots for you."

"Mmm I hope she has. Although, sadly, I doubt it'll make much difference. It's more complicated than simple attraction, isn't it? Even if she does like me, it's about heart versus brain and she's strong-willed. She's from a different version of reality and she has a bright future ahead of her. I have nothing to offer her and I'll probably be dead by next week."

"Do you love her?" asked Sir Robin. There was a pause while The Pan wondered how to answer and decided to be truthful.

"Oh yes. Arnold! I know this sounds pathetic but I want to grow old with her. When I fantasise about her it's not just about …" he whistled, "you know *being* with her." He hesitated. "Well … quite a lot of it is, but it's also about living with her, sitting in the garden at my parents' place reading, walking along the beach, talking to each other. It's all academic, though, isn't it? For a start, growing old is not a luxury I am likely to enjoy and then there's the fact she belongs to the Candidate. According to Lord Vernon—who told me a lot more than you did, by the way—her fate and the Candidate's are intertwined. She will love him and no-one else, so when he turns up, I'm dumped."

"Bunkum!" said Sir Robin with some force. "I wouldn't listen to Lord Vernon. He's a smug, self-satisfied oaf who knows less than he thinks he does." The Pan smiled and raised an eyebrow.

"I heartily agree, but he might be right on this one. I'm not a gambling man but I'll bet my life I'm not the Candidate. So if all this chosen thing is true I would be a fool to get involved with her. I'll only end up heartbroken when he turns up and whisks her off."

"Oh, I don't know about that. You can never be sure how these things are going to turn out. They have a saying in this reality, 'faint heart never won fair lady'. I wouldn't mess about. If I were you, next time you and Ruth are alone, try kissing her."

The Pan felt he could do without the relationship advice.

"Thank you. The thought has crossed my mind on numerous occasions. Moving on, there's something important you should know."

"I assume you wish to tell me that Lord Vernon knows I'm alive."

"He's searching for you as well as us."

"Yes. It had to happen sooner or later. I'm not surprised." No trace of fear, a calm statement of fact. By The Prophet, the old boy was an ice-cool operator.

"You don't seem too worried," said The Pan.

"Worrying won't help."

"I know. My father used to say that—it's one of the few things we agreed on. Easier said than done though, isn't it?"

Sir Robin smiled and inclined his head.

"Indeed. Your father was a wise man."

"Yeh, and a better one than I am."

"You've changed your tune."

"I've found out who he was. Pity it's too late." Suddenly The Pan realised how weary he felt, not just physically but mentally, with the whole tawdry business of blacklisted existence. Sir Robin's expression was difficult to fathom: sympathy, concern and possibly a bit of disgust. "Were you friends, you and my dad?"

"Yes, we were colleagues."

"In the Underground?"

Sir Robin's eyes met his.

"Yes. In the Underground and on the Council of the Choosing. Your parents took a lot of risks. All those luminaries who came to stay—"

"Yeh, we were pretty busy; there were all sorts."

"Indeed—quite a wide variety for a lecturer in Random Mathematics, wouldn't you say? Did you ever wonder who they were?"

"Not at the time. Now, I can guess. Some were on their way into hiding, right?"

Sir Robin nodded.

"The platinum thimble was your mother's. She was always rather better at that sort of thing than your father was."

"What?" The Pan was afraid he'd cry. He stood up, walked across the room and leant against the bookshelves for a moment. He shut his eyes and took a few seconds to compose himself before he turned round to face Sir Robin. "I'm sorry that—my parents, all this—I've been an idiot."

"Yes, you have."

Oh, don't pull any punches. It was the truth but not expressed with quite as much tact as The Pan would have liked; he felt bad enough already.

"But you were young and ill-informed. Your foolishness is understandable and forgivable. I doubt I would have acted differently myself at your age and even since our last meeting I can see a change in you. You are a quick learner and it seems you are growing up."

OK, a sly compliment in there, although The Pan doubted it was true.

"As usual, you flatter me. Shall we get real now? I've been so stupid you could almost call it a skill. If this was a game it would be my special attribute."

"No. For a man thinking on the hoof, it wasn't too bad."

The Pan shook his head and started pacing the room. Somehow, moving about made him feel better.

"Lord Vernon wanted me to get close to you and find out who the Candidate is."

"I see. And is that why you're so interested?"

"No." The Pan stopped walking. "I just want you to understand why I blundered in through that concert hall window and stuffed it all up. You see, if I didn't do what Lord Vernon wanted, he was going to …" The Pan ran out of words because, once more, he couldn't put the ones he needed in the same sentence as the word 'Ruth'. He tried again. "His troops were watching Ruth, they've found some way of changing colour and they've been following her for months. Lord Vernon said he would hurt her if I didn't do what he wanted. I only had a few seconds to get to her before they did and I wish I'd made less of a mess. It hasn't done any good either. I seem to be bugged. And worse, I could have called his bluff and avoided all of this. She's the Chosen One and I can't see him touching her."

"On the contrary, Lord Vernon is not one to take chances, not over a matter of such importance. Even if you had agreed to his demands he would have taken Ruth into custody, which would have been grave news for us. As for being bugged, I'm afraid you may be, some of the time. Not here, of course. Like the old Palace—which is now the Security HQ—this place is portal proof. If you try to get out of here with a portal it will simply bring you back, unless you switch off the field first. I believe you discovered that the hard way."

"Mmm," agreed The Pan.

"There is only a narrow margin between genius and madness; usually it's failure. You showed a remarkable capacity for lateral thought. A little more spring in your step and you might have cleared the field."

"Yeh right, you're too kind," said The Pan.

"Not so. Now, portal proofing. You should know about this. If you are outside this building and wish to use a portal to find somebody inside, it will be difficult. I believe you also recognised that for yourself when you and Big Merv planned your mission to rescue me. However, once inside the field, you can use the portal to find and view people both outside and within its confines. You can also use the portal to move about within the field. However, getting out is a little more difficult." He smiled. "That is why the Grongles made the Palace their Security HQ. They have reverse engineered our technology since. Well enough to produce other fields of their own—there is one around the Bank of Grongolia, for example—which is why you and your friend Big Merv had to run that little errand for me. Am I making sense?"

"Yes."

The Pan threw an almond up into the air and caught it in his mouth.

"So, you realise that, here, you may speak freely," said Sir Robin.

"What about outside?"

"You are also safe, if you carry your portal with you. If you stay within five feet of one portal it will cause too much interference to the signal for you to be visible to another one."

Interesting. Was that how Lord Vernon had tracked them down at the police station? The Pan's thimble would have been far enough away from him to make him visible. Or had he simply listened to the police? Difficult to tell.

"I'm assuming you have managed not to lose your portal?" added Sir Robin and The Pan smiled to himself.

"It's here."

"And your mother's platinum one?"

"In my snurd."

"Stealing that from Lord Vernon was a flash of genius, too. What a pity he had a spare."

"I think you're confusing genius with desperation. There wasn't a smart plan behind it. I was trying to stop him following me."

The thought of Lord Vernon's frustration seemed to amuse Sir Robin like nothing else.

"It was quick thinking, though; you nearly succeeded."

"Yeh. Nearly. Instead I've led him here where he's broken London and destroyed most of a police station, along with anything else in his path and some things that weren't. Except Ruth's life, of course, I've managed to wreck that for her all by myself."

"Indeed, I wouldn't call you a subtle operator, but you are effective. The Chosen One is here where she is safe."

"For now. Ruth heard Lord Vernon mention portal detection. Apparently they can tell where a portal has been used, that's how they traced us. How he almost …" he shook his head. "I went home."

"That was foolish," said Sir Robin gently.

"I know, but it's not just you. He knows about Gladys and Ada. I had to warn them."

"And you took the Chosen One?"

"No—even more stupid. I left her."

"I see. Where?"

"On top of a building. Arnold! How could I have been such an arse? I thought she'd be safe there. I didn't want to take her to K'Barth and then K'Barth came to her while I was off …" He ran his hands through his hair. "I am bombing in flames here. Everything I do to try and sort things out just makes it worse."

"So it would seem," said Sir Robin slowly, "but not from any lack of action or intelligent thought on your part. You have merely been unlucky."

"Or up against a superior brain."

"You are every bit Lord Vernon's equal," said Sir Robin with sudden anger. "Never forget that. What you lack is confidence. A little of that and you will achieve a great deal."

"I need the money, Sir Robin. At least then I can get the concert hall off her back."

"Is that what you would do with one million Grongolian dollars?"

"Yep. I'd take it home, buy jewellery, gold or something which is valuable anywhere, bring it back here and sell it. I'm hoping, that way, I'd have something left for when I go back."

"Gracious. You *are* smitten."

No point denying it.

"Yeh. I told you. I am."

"I seem to recall I promised you a new life and a new identity."

"Yes, but I'm assuming that was here. My face will be all over every wanted list on the planet."

"I'm afraid so."

"So I'm screwed."

"For the moment, my boy, but if you can hang on until next Saturday, I think a new opportunity may present itself."

"If I live that long."

"Never say never, eh? May I have the box?"

The Pan pushed it across to him. Then he took his thimble from his pocket and put it on the table.

"Thank you," said Sir Robin. "She's a bright girl, the Chosen One."

"Yes she is, but I wouldn't call her that to her face, 'Chosen One', I mean—she'd probably like 'bright'—but as far as being chosen goes, she's in denial."

"So are you, my boy, if you think you can buy her life back. I'm afraid even twenty million Grongolian dollars wouldn't be enough to restore the status quo for her. Lord Vernon will not rest until she is in his power. Her only choice is to join him—"

The Pan laughed humourlessly.

"I don't think she'll be doing that any time soon."

"Then she will be on the run until he falls and the Candidate becomes Architrave."

"Of course. And those events are *so* likely to happen before the end of time."

"As I have already said, everything is possible."

"Look, unless we can find the Candidate in the next few days and change his mind about who he's chosen, she's going to be running for the rest of her life, you know that, don't you? And it's a short life at that."

"It doesn't have to be. It could be a long and happy one."

"If only," sighed The Pan, "but none of us can face Lord Vernon, not even you. He's too powerful."

"And on the brink of something close to omnipotence—he must be stopped."

"Who's going to stop him? Who can?"

"The Candidate will. And Ruth."

"No. No way. Not her. It's not fair. She's not K'Barthan, she doesn't understand our customs and I made a promise I'd try to get her out of this."

"My boy, it's far too late for that."

"Then hide her. If I can't have a new identity now, I'll leave it. Give it to her, instead and I'll take her place."

"And now you're really talking bosh. Brave bosh but—"

"I'm not brave, just desperate. Sir Robin, if you know who the Candidate is, talk to him, in the name of The Prophet I'm begging you. Talk to him and tell him what he's doing. I'll do anything you want—no matter how dangerous or stupid—if you will just tell me where to find him so Ruth and I can go to see him, together, and persuade him to pick someone else."

"You can't expect the poor boy to do that any more than you could. He's in love with her."

"How can he be? He's never met her."

"On the contrary, the two of them are very close."

"I don't think so."

"Oh? How can you be so sure?"

The Pan glared at him, "Because I can."

"So you know all her friends, do you? You've met each and every last one of them?" Sir Robin's voice was hard. "Jealousy is an ugly emotion and it does not become you."

"Alright, you've made your point. Please, Sir Robin, if you have a heart, just tell me." Too much like begging, but he couldn't help it.

"I cannot possibly. The laws of K'Barth, of the Choosing, of our society itself, forbid it. Anyway, he has no idea who he is. Before anyone can suggest he attempt the frankly impossible task of convincing himself he no longer loves Ruth, he must understand his calling for himself."

"What if he can't? What if he never knows?" asked The Pan.

"He will."

"How can you tell?"

"I can't, but I believe in him and it's a chance I'll have to take. If it reassures you at all, I am almost certain that he will appreciate exactly who he is and what he is for. Soon."

"It doesn't. Is this about trust? D'you think I did a deal with Lord Vernon? That he let me go so I would lead him to you?"

"No. I know where your loyalties lie. I am simply forbidden to tell you who the Candidate is. The unfortunate irony of this situation is that if I could, you, the only person I categorically cannot tell, might well be the only man I would. The information is too dangerous to share with anyone else, even Ruth." He eyed The Pan. "You understand that she will need protection, the protection of someone she trusts."

The Pan sighed.

"Lord Vernon will find her eventually."

"Yes, but he will take longer to catch her if she is with you. Stay with her, keep her safe for as long as you can."

"I intend to, if she'll let me. But she has a mind of her own and what can I offer her? A life with no pride, no dignity and no hope. She's worth more than that."

"Yes. She is and so are you." Sir Robin rubbed his eyes and for the briefest instant he looked his age. Then he rallied, changing the subject abruptly. "I expect you'd like to know what these are," he said, hefting the bag of things onto the table. He fished about in the bottom and brought out the thing which looked a little like a gyroscope, only not. "Shall we start with this?"

Chapter 64

The laundry was closing now. Everyone had gone for supper except for Snoofle, who was responsible for locking up, and Deirdre, who was helping him. They had received a warning from one of Snoofle's sources elsewhere that Captain Snow was looking for her. Whether on his own behalf or that of Lord Vernon no-one was sure, but Snoofle had agreed that the mission was compromised and that Deirdre must be smuggled out of the old Palace forthwith. Deirdre would be sorry to say goodbye to Snoofle as well as to Mrs Pargeter and the 'girls', but she was happy to go and prove her humble origins somewhere else if the alternative was being murdered, or worse, by Lord Vernon.

Not that escape would be easy. Snoofle had warned her that she might have to hide inside the building until her three-month work stint was up.

Glancing cautiously round, Snoofle led her into the supply cupboard, switched on the light and closed the door. The pair of them sat down, he on a pile of washing powder cartons and she on a drum of bleach.

Snoofle didn't look happy.

"Why did you go? You know Room A is a Blurpon-only route."

"I didn't, actually, and the corporal who rang said that unless someone went up there, Lord Vernon would come down here. What else could I do?"

"You should have come to the kitchens and found me."

"It would have taken too long. This place is like a rabbit warren. It was hard enough to find Room A."

He looked up at her.

"Denarghi's not going to like this."

"I know that," she snapped and regretted it immediately, but she would be demoted for this and it hurt. "Sorry." She didn't usually apologise.

"It's OK."

"Snoofle, have you briefed him?"

"Yes."

"Not good?"

"Not at all."

"D'you think he'll send help?"

"You're the Candidate so he might, but he's got it in for you." He heaved a sigh.

"I know." She sighed as well. "OK. Let's do this."

"Good luck," he said. He took a mobile phone from a pouch on his belt, dialled Denarghi's secure line and handed it to her.

"Lieutenant," said Denarghi. No niceties, he cut straight to the chase. "We are engaged in a battle for freedom against a tyrannical regime. You are the Candidate and your orders were to keep out of sight, gather information discreetly and await more orders, yes?"

"Yes, Your Majesty."

"And now I have Snoofle bleating on to me about your immediate extraction. Do you realise how difficult it is to remove a worker before their three-month tenure is over?"

"Yes, Your Majesty, I do. If you remember, I raised the question when you ordered me here. I would not have disturbed you but I have come to the notice of Lord Vernon himself and he is looking for me to—"

"Is your cover compromised?"

"Yes."

"He said so?"

"No, but he looked at me and—"

"He thinks you're pretty," Denarghi cut in, "but that doesn't mean he knows who you are."

"I think he does."

"But he hasn't said. Unless you can give me concrete proof that Lord Vernon knows your identity you will stay exactly where you are."

"But I cannot sustain this 'Rosa' deceit! I'm a fighter! The laundry is—"

"Beneath you. Yes. You said."

"No I didn't! Don't put words in my mouth, sir." A touch too much irony on that 'sir'. She must be careful.

"You implied it strongly enough. I sense a lack of resolve in you."

"Never! I—"

"There is no room for the cowardly or the weak-willed in this organisation."

How dare he? In the kinds of quick-strike operations Deirdre normally conducted neither fear nor lack of resolve was an option.

"I am no coward and you know that," she said through gritted teeth.

"No? Yet you are begging to be extracted on a whim. If that isn't weak-willed cowardice I would ask you, what is?"

"You ordered me to stay alive. I am merely following your command. I am wholly committed to the Cause, you know that."

"Then if you are following my command it will be easy for you to obey your other orders, Lieutenant. You will serve K'Barth and unless you can prove that you have been positively identified as a member of this organisation you will endure whatever Lord Vernon or any of the others subject you to."

"But—"

"I fail to see the problem. What is the worst that can happen? I know what you get up to with the males here. He'll hardly be deflowering you, will he?"

Deirdre had never been so angry, which was a handicap because it was difficult to compose a cogent counterargument through all that red mist.

"Are you calling me a tart? Because nobody smecking calls me a tart, Denarghi sir, not even—"

"That is my last word, Lieutenant."

"Your Majesty, this is unjust! It goes against everything we stand for."

"Yes, Arbuthnot. It is unjust, but it is expedient and as a loyal member of the Resistance, I know I can rely on you to take one, or several if required, for the team."

"I have shown unwavering dedication to the Cause again and again. You, yourself, have held me as an example to others. You appointed me Candidate. How can I serve the Cause if I'm dead?"

"At the moment Lieutenant, you are precious little use alive. Let me give you some new orders. You will continue as you are, unless your fears about Lord Vernon are founded in fact, in which case you will make sure you get close to him, very close, and assassinate him."

That was a little more like it, except that Lord Vernon would require more than a one-woman team, even a woman with combat competence like Deirdre's. She had an idea.

"Your Majesty, if you send me an assassination cell I can plan a proper hit—"

"No cell, Lieutenant. You have your orders."

The line went dead.

"That wasn't too bad," said Snoofle.

"What the hell do you mean?"

"He wouldn't have liked being threatened or your use of the word 'smecking' but at least he can't have you shot for insubordination. Not from there."

"No, Lord Vernon's going to do that for him."

"And he didn't demote you."

"You're scraping the barrel, Snoofle."

She glared at him for a moment. It was time to go. She stood up suddenly, banging one of the shelves and knocking an open carton of washing powder onto his head. The two of them looked at each other in silence and then he started to laugh.

"It's not funny," she said. He shook himself, the way dogs do, creating a blizzard of powder. It made both of them cough and then suddenly, she started to laugh, too. Maybe it was nerves, because nothing about the situation was amusing but the two of them sat there giggling, anyway.

"Keep the faith," he said. "There is another way, but first we must finish locking up." Deirdre didn't dare hope but it sounded as if Snoofle had a plan.

Chapter 65

The Pan was beginning to adapt to Sir Robin's tangential conversational style, and as he had such a tentative grip on what was going on, any information had to be useful. He glanced at the machine the old man was holding up.

"Why not?" he said.

"Excellent. Tell me, what do you know about it?"

"Nothing much. Lord Vernon said it shows the significance of people."

"He really is a blind fool. He's right, of course, but it's so much more than that. It is a confibrulator, although most of us informally call it an Importance Detector. It can be used to determine the extent of a person's effect on world events. You, for example—"

"Score zero," said The Pan. "Well, it varies but mostly it's zero."

Sir Robin smiled.

"My boy, that is simply not possible," he said as he set up the machine.

"Yeh, I realise I should score one or two, but I don't," said The Pan.

"Really?"

"Really." The Pan gestured to the machine. "Help yourself."

Sir Robin moved it so the red pointer was pointing at The Pan, flipped the lever and started it spinning. As before, it gave off flecks of blue light and the needle fluctuated wildly from one end of the scale to the other.

"That is interesting," said Sir Robin. "I hope you don't mind my saying but your interpretation is well off the mark, isn't it? I'd call that a ten."

"Well, usually, I would class myself as a glass-half-full kind of man but to me it just looks broken. If any of the dials on the SE2 did that I'd be straight round to Gerry at Snurd to get them looked at. But I wondered if, perhaps, it's impossible to obtain my reading?"

"That is a very plausible explanation."

"Why would that be?"

"Why do you think?"

"Who knows? Maybe I'm a freak. After all, I can resist Truth Serum." Sir Robin took a sharp breath.

"Can you now?"

"Yes, so perhaps if I don't want to know my reading I'm able to … I dunno … block it somehow."

"That has been known to happen."

"Does it mean anything?" asked The Pan.

"Only that you are somewhat recalcitrant—I might go so far as to say pig-headed. Nothing we don't already know. Of course, there may be a grain of truth in Lord Vernon's view. He thinks you are a nobody who is about to do something important, yes?" The Pan nodded and Sir Robin continued. "When I first came to see you, I believe we talked about reality theory."

"The idea that small things can have big consequences?"

"Yes. I believe one of those small things is about to happen. Someone will make a decision soon which could have momentous repercussions."

"Could have?"

"Yes, if it is the right decision. It all depends what you decide."

"What? No-no-no! Not me."

"My boy, you must face up to the truth. You are irrevocably caught up in this. You cannot escape the fact and I'm afraid that, yes, there are certain aspects of all our futures which hang on you. If you are bold enough, if you make the right moves, there is every chance that you, all of us, will come out of this smiling."

"Thanks, no pressure then."

Sir Robin chuckled, which annoyed The Pan. From where he sat there was nothing funny about his situation.

"So, this decision, do you have a little more info?"

Sir Robin laughed outright. "Oh, I don't think you'll need it. I may not be around but when the time comes I am confident you will do the right thing. The prophecies are very clear upon this point."

"The prophecies. You're making it sound as if I get a mention."

"Perhaps."

"Perhaps? Is that it? A riddle? Is that all you can give me? Seriously, if what you say is true then how will I know what to do?"

"Because you are you and you will follow your heart. I know you do not understand it but trust me, the answers to all your questions are hot-wired into your personality. We are not talking tactics here, my boy, simply whether or not to stand your ground or run."

"I tackle that one every day and as you know, I always run."

"You oversimplify. You do not run, not always."

"I never stand my ground."

"You will."

"No. Trust me. I'm made of the wrong stuff for that, Sir Robin."

"I disagree," said Sir Robin firmly. "I doubt you fully understood what I am talking about."

"Then you could always try ditching the secret code and making yourself clear."

"I cannot. If fate is to play itself out in our favour, if we are to defeat Lord Vernon, your choice has to be spontaneous."

The Pan was irritated and he didn't want to be. He threw another almond up into the air, caught it in his mouth and decided to change the subject.

"Lord Vernon took Ruth's reading, she scores seven."

"Yes, she would. As I said before, the Candidate is very taken with her."

"Oh, I'm sure he is." The smecking git. Sir Robin was eyeing him with concern. Time to move the conversation along before the subject of seething jealousy cropped up again. "Sir Robin, if you can answer this question, I was wondering, how does a snuff box prove someone's the Candidate?"

"Ah, well, first of all, let's check it's the real box. Do watch this—it's a splendid trick." Sir Robin wound up the gyroscope and set it spinning again, "I just need to alter the field like so …" He moved his hands backwards and forwards over the machine, while The Pan watched carefully.

"That looks like magic but Lord Vernon did something very similar with my thimble and he assured me it was science."

"Indeed, all magic is science—just because we don't understand something it doesn't mean there isn't a scientific explanation. Although in this case, the explanation is that we've kept a lid on this particular branch of science so that it looks like magic to everyone else."

"Is that ethical, Sir Robin?" asked The Pan.

"Interesting question," the old man paused. "Probably not—but portals for all would be chaos, it would only be a matter of time before two people materialised in the same place at the same time and died horribly. And, my boy, you can't run a stable theocracy without a dash of smoke and mirrors. If you want people to look after themselves it's no good telling them the naked truth because they'll ignore you. You can't lie but if you couch the truth in terms of a story or a nice illustrative parable you can make it more palatable. Of course, it is very tempting to just lay down the law. That is where the last Architrave went wrong. He was really very lazy."

"How so?" asked The Pan. He threw another almond skywards but, with a surprising turn of speed, Sir Robin reached forward and snatched it out of the air.

"My boy, would you not do that? It's very irritating."

"Sorry."

"Not to worry," said Sir Robin as he popped it into his mouth and sat down. The Pan was disappointed to lose it. The almonds really were very good.

Sir Robin took a sip of his drink and continued. "I'd be interested to know. What did you think of him?"

Clearly a loaded question so The Pan took a little time to mull it over. The last Architrave's most obvious flaw was his cowardice. He never seemed to stand up to the Grongles. Everyone could see he left that job to the High Priest; Sir Robin.

"It's difficult to criticise him when I doubt I'd do much better, myself," said The Pan, painfully aware that, as a fellow coward, he was in no position to cast aspersions. "He seemed to be a bit snooty. As if he reckoned he was above us. Then again, that might have been me being chippy. I'm not very good with authority. I got the impression he had a bit of a hotline to The Prophet though."

"On the contrary, when you say 'snooty' you have him off pat. He thought he had a right to the people's respect so he didn't bother to earn it. Consequently, they would not listen to him or follow him. However, he was canny enough to see that if The Prophet lays down a law telling us all to wash regularly or avoid eating fungi, most of us will do what we're told. If the Architrave explains that it's insanitary not to wash or that some of the fungi—which look very like the edible ones—are deadly, most people will tell him to mind his own business and enjoy a short, scrofulous existence abruptly terminated by mushroom poisoning."

The Pan laughed.

"Give the guy some slack. The truth can be pretty ugly. It's not surprising he didn't know how to tell us. He must have realised no-one liked him and it wasn't as if he had any good news to give us, ever. He was caught between his people and the Grongles. I can see how the Arnold hotline thing happened. I doubt I'd have been any different."

"What would you have done?"

"Cheat. No-one listens to me, so if I had to do a job like that, I'd find someone people do listen to and get them to do the talking. In fact, if I was in his position I'd just get you to make the edicts, or I'd command you to teach me some of your management skills." He put on an imperious voice for the 'command you' bit and Sir Robin chuckled. "Come to think of it, how come he didn't do that? Didn't you get on?"

"No, we got along perfectly well, he simply lacked your humility and intellect."

"Steady on."

"You have given me a very good answer," said Sir Robin. "And I am flattered you think I would be able to help. However, I might not be as cooperative as you'd like."

"I can believe that."

"So, if I refused and you had to do it yourself?"

"I guess I would try to be as truthful as I could." The Pan shrugged, "I doubt it's possible to be completely honest in politics but I would aim to omit the things I couldn't say rather than lie. If nobody listened to me, I would be asking myself why and trying to fix that. If all else failed, then I'd pull rank on you."

"And when I am gone? I am older than you, I would not be around as long."

"Good point. In that case, I'd have to make certain I milked you dry for everything I needed before you pegged it."

"I don't doubt you would, you scoundrel! However, there is a great deal of wisdom in your view. Of course, good government isn't so much about being truthful as about being as truthful as you can—there's a big difference—and education. A well-educated populace is less likely to die of mushroom poisoning but is more likely to question the logic of your decision-making. Very much easier to govern in some ways, almost impossible in others. And, the last Architrave did rely rather heavily on the last three books of The Prophet, which was a mistake. All that 'shall' and 'shan't'. I doubt Arnold had much to do with them."

"Are you serious?" said The Pan.

"Absolutely, surely the authenticity of the books is academic, isn't it? If you're anything like the average K'Barthan I doubt you take much notice of the prophecies at all. Have you read any of Arnold's works?"

"No."

"Good. Unless you are considering a theological career then there is really no need to. I'm confident you can manage to be decent without them. Although the sayings are rather good, I assume they still teach those by rote at school."

"They did, when I was there."

"You remember any?"

The Pan smiled.

"A few."

"Capital. Good lad—but I digress. My argument is that I have studied them all, in detail, and the other books, so people like you don't have to, and I can assure you, the last three books are not The Prophet's style at all. If you ask me, they're written by a bunch of stuffed shirts. They're made up of well-meaning diktats, from subsequent Architraves and over-zealous disciples, which were added after Arnold died."

"But that's blasphemy," said The Pan.

"Yes," said Sir Robin equably. "But I think I can get away with it. As the High Priest, who can be better qualified to interpret the will of The Prophet than I?"

"That's not exactly his will, is it? More his authenticity."

"Indeed, but he made it very plain that he wished us to concentrate on his central commandment above all else."

"That's what most of us do."

"And that's where the last Architrave went wrong. He concentrated on all the petty details. He did a great deal of damage to the credibility of The Prophet and our creed. That's the trouble with religion. It's so tempting to keep tweaking the rules. But if one gets too bogged down in the minutiae of dogma one tends to lose sight of the actual point. If I doubt the provenance of some of Arnold's writings it is because they are laid down in a manner that is simply not His way."

"What about smoke and mirrors, keeping a lid on science? That's no different, surely?" said The Pan glancing at the Importance Detector, still spinning on the table.

"Smoke and mirrors obscure the truth but they do not hide it from an astute and open mind. Laying down the law is tempting—"

"I can imagine, especially when you're in a hurry."

"Yes, but it is very foolish. As the High Priest, I am one of those who are expected to interpret the will of The Prophet, but even I would never be so arrogant as to declare I know it. The average K'Barthan is contrary and strong-willed but many of us, uneducated or not, are reasonably intelligent given time to understand the nature of a situation."

"Yeh, thinking about it, I guess that's why he seemed stuck-up. I know crowds of people do dumb things without thinking but he used to talk to us as if he thought we were all stupid, all of the time."

"Exactly. To manage K'Barthans, you must find a way to speak to them individually even when you are addressing large numbers at once. The mistake many people in authority make is to treat a crowd as an unintelligent organism rather than a collection of intelligent individuals."

There was an extra authority in Sir Robin's voice and he was expounding his theory so earnestly, as if he wanted to impress this important information firmly in The Pan's mind. The Pan pulled the Importance Detector towards him and moved the lever to stop it. Then he turned the pointer towards Sir Robin and set it spinning again.

Chapter 66

As Lord Vernon sat on the balcony of his penthouse rooms, he was glad to see General Moteurs tap at the glass door. The mere presence of the General served to remind him that the Chosen One would not escape. As usual, two glasses of fruit smoothie were placed in front of them, just so. Lord Vernon smiled. Tomorrow morning he would have all the renegades who had tried his patience for so long; the General did not make promises lightly. For now though, there was something else he wished to discuss.

"Good evening, General. Please sit," said Lord Vernon. The General sat. "You are early. Your business with the Underground was swift?"

"Sir."

"And successful?"

"Sir."

Lord Vernon raised his glass and took a sip of smoothie. General Moteurs followed suit and was unable to suppress a grimace.

"Not to your taste?"

"I usually add a little sugar."

Lord Vernon got up and strode over to the glass doors which were opened by one of the palace servants as he approached. He clicked his fingers and pointed to the table.

"Get some sugar for the General, if you please," said Lord Vernon and he returned and sat down. "I have been thinking about your plan to destroy the Grongolian Underground."

"Sir."

"Specifically, your suggestions regarding the High Leader."

"Sir."

"If I save his life you believe he will owe me?"

"He will be greatly in your debt, sir."

"Yes, General. However, I am wondering if we can take matters a little further than debt."

"Sir?"

"You mentioned that Sir Robin believes the Candidate will stroll into my installation and take power."

"That is unlikely, sir, although he may try. It is possible that the Resistance might also attempt a coup but neither party will gain entry into the temple."

"What if we were to make it possible? What might the consequences be for the High Leader, for example, if something went awry?"

General Moteurs seemed bemused.

"Nothing would go awry, sir. Security is my remit. At least I assume you will be entrusting it to me."

"Do you? I might assign it to someone else."

Moteurs buried his reaction, but he would take any attempt to remove his responsibilities as a deliberate affront and a sign of Lord Vernon's displeasure.

"I think that would be unwise, sir."

"Really? Let us examine this from a different angle. You have told Sir Robin you are dissatisfied with affairs both here and in Grongolia."

"Sir."

"I am wondering if that is true."

"Sir?"

"I know your technique, General." He paused. The General stirred his smoothie with studied calm but under that impassive facade, Lord Vernon sensed an increasing tension. He continued. "So, if you tell Sir Robin that you are dissatisfied. I would say that means you are."

"No, no, sir, I—"

"You would be wise to stop talking, Moteurs," said Lord Vernon ominously.

"Sir." The General must be wondering where the conversation was going. He sat straight and unmoving. His features were still composed, collected and inscrutable but now as Lord Vernon leaned back in his chair and steepled his hands, he could detect the General's fear.

"Have you lost faith in those who lead you?"

"No, sir. Not in you," blurted the General and stopped.

Oh, he was not so inscrutable now. There was a great deal of tension in his voice. Perhaps he was afraid he had fallen from grace. Lord Vernon smiled, which did not seem to help the General relax. Rather the opposite.

"I am not talking about myself."

A long, long pause.

"You refer to the High Leader?" said General Moteurs. He had retained an astonishing amount of composure and kept his fear from his voice, but now, Lord Vernon noted, he failed to hide his relief.

"Yes."

Again, Lord Vernon made eye contact. The General held his gaze.

"I would be unwise to comment, sir."

"Naturally, you are a stalwart of the state. However, I can read your heart, Moteurs."

"Sir."

"I am Lord Protector of K'Barth, General, it is my job to know and anticipate the political landscape."

"Sir."

"Many of our colleagues would happily see the High Leader supplanted by someone a little more ruthless in getting what the Grongle nation wants. I want to know your view. You may be honest with me. This conversation is off the record." Except, of course, if the General crossed him, in which case it would suddenly be very much on the record.

"Then, sir, yes. I believe there is an argument for someone stronger, more dynamic, more forceful at the helm." General Moteurs was very pale now. He was taking a big risk. The words he had just uttered were a capital offence.

"Do you?" said Lord Vernon. "So … if the High Leader were involved in an accident; something for which outside agencies—the Underground or the Resistance—could be held responsible; and was supplanted by someone with a little more … charisma …?"

"I would not necessarily oppose it."

There was a knock at the balcony door. The servant had returned with sugar in little sachets and spoons. General Moteurs opened one of the packets and tipped it into his drink. He stirred it, tried it and opened another. With uncharacteristic clumsiness, he ripped it from top to bottom. The contents spilled over the table. He swore, also unlike him, and the servant, who had not yet withdrawn, took a small dustpan and brush from the pocket of his apron, rushed forwards and swept the sugar away. Pleased at last to disturb the General's air of supreme calm, Lord Vernon slowly drew his knife. The General's eyes widened for a moment.

"Your hands seem unsteady this evening, Moteurs. Perhaps you should use this." Lord Vernon flicked the knife round and held it out, handle towards the General.

"Thank you, sir." General Moteurs proceeded to open another four sachets, handling the razor-sharp blade carefully. He tipped them into his drink. When he had finished, he gave the knife back to Lord Vernon, who dismissed the flunkey with a nod and continued. The General stirred his drink and took a sip.

"So, Moteurs," Lord Vernon leaned forward. "I wonder, just for the sake of argument, if you, personally, were asked to arrange for something to happen to the High Leader, how might you achieve it?"

The General inhaled his mouthful of smoothie and choked. Lord Vernon watched him try and fail to suppress a prolonged fit of coughing.

"Is this some kind of test, sir?" he asked eventually.

"No, General. This is not a test. I merely wish to explore an idea. Shall we kick it around and see what happens?"

"As you wish, sir." General Moteurs seemed a tiny bit less tense after Lord Vernon's reassurance.

"Good. So, General, as I understand it, correct me if I am wrong, the Underground has been kind enough to arrange a coup in the Home Nation. You have infiltrated their ranks, so, if the opportunity arises and they successfully take control, you will control them or, since I control you, I will."

"Sir."

"You are handing me the Home Nation on a platter. Tell me, if you were put in such a position, would you pass it back to the High Leader?"

"I fear not, sir."

"Then I have made my point."

"You … you wish to seize power, sir?"

"I am toying with the idea."

"Sir." General Moteurs was silent for a while, stirring all the sugar he'd ladled into his drink through the liquid. He took a sip and grimaced again.

"A little too sweet?" asked Lord Vernon.

"Sir."

"You require another?"

"Thank you, but no."

Lord Vernon raised his eyebrows.

"As you wish. So, General, since we are agreed. I ask you again, if I want to …" he waved one hand while he sought the right word, "dispense with the High Leader. How might I make it appear accidental?"

Again, General Moteurs sat in silent thought, stirring his drink. He looked up and his eyes met Lord Vernon's. His gaze was cautious, guarded as if checking what he had heard was true.

"Put me in charge of security, sir, or his bodyguards will be suspicious."

"Who will effect the coup? Not the boy, surely?"

"No, sir. Using the boy would gain us nothing. We have the K'Barthan Underground. We should use the Resistance."

"Go on."

"Even if the Candidate escapes decommissioning and arrives he will not stand a chance against you or them. The Resistance know this. They have their own Candidate. She is no more the genuine article than you are, sir—if you will pardon my frankness. However, I believe the Resistance may seek to have her play out the people's dream; ride in, vanquish you and 'save' her nation."

"The whole concept is laughable," Lord Vernon chuckled.

General Moteurs smiled.

"I agree, sir. However, the Resistance candidate is a trained assassin. I doubt she will have any qualms about dispatching the High Leader."

"Naturally, after such an outrage, we would retaliate," said Lord Vernon.

"Yes, sir. The Resistance's Candidate will be exposed as a fraud—"

"And we will execute her and wipe her colleagues from the face of the earth."

"Sir."

"The entire world will be in my hands." Lord Vernon sat in silent thought for a while. "You have excelled yourself, General."

"Sir."

"I can leave it to you to misinform the Resistance in the correct manner."

"Yes, sir."

"And your tryst with the Underground tomorrow morning?"

"Sir. My troops are standing by, but if you wish to command the attack with your own, I am at your disposal. I will send word when it is time."

"Excellent, I am looking forward to taking these vermin at last. But General?"

"Sir."

"A friendly warning. If your plan fails, if you disappoint me, I will not be as … indulgent as last time."

"I thank you for your patience, sir, but you have nothing to fear on that score."

"No, General. But you do."

The General did not falter.

"They will be yours by eleven o'clock tomorrow morning, sir. You have my word on that."

Yes. And the entire world would follow them in the space of a week. How exquisite. Lord Vernon kept his features composed but guffawed inside.

"Thank you, General. That is all for now. You may go."

Chapter 67

Deirdre and Snoofle left the laundry in companionable silence. "I'm sorry," he said as they closed the door.

Not as sorry as Denarghi would be when she next saw him.

"You tried." She resisted the urge to be sharp. It wasn't Snoofle's fault. She noticed the height of the lock. "D'you want me to lock it?"

"No, thank you. This is my responsibility."

He gathered himself to jump but hesitated.

"Bunk?"

"Thank you."

She knelt down on all fours. Snoofle jumped lightly onto her back and then there was a crackling sound. He let out a startled cry and fell to the ground next to her, unconscious. As she moved to help him she felt something cold against her neck.

"Go on, give me an excuse." She stayed still.

"Why did you do that?" said Deirdre angrily. Slowly and carefully, she looked up. Captain Snow. It would be. "We're not doing anything wrong, sir." The 'sir' was a bit of an afterthought.

"That's right. Just locking up, aren't you?"

"Yes, sir." How she hated calling him 'sir'. He prodded Snoofle with his foot.

"He's only stunned. He'll survive." Deirdre realised Captain Snow wasn't alone. There were five others with him. They were all wearing black and red uniforms, variants of Lord Vernon's. "Take him back to his quarters." Two of them picked up Snoofle and dragged him away down the hall. "He'll come round soon enough. It's you we've come for, sweetheart. Get up."

"No."

He held a long metal pole against her neck, a crowd control stick. There was a trigger at his end and if he pulled it, there'd be a lot of electricity at Deirdre's.

"Hear me, underling. Your little friend is only stunned, but you're bigger so I've increased the charge. If you don't get up nice and easy and turn around, I'm going to make your life very, very painful."

She did as she was told. All the while Captain Snow held the control stick to her neck.

"Get that thing out of my face," she snapped, batting it out of the way.

"We've been looking for you, haven't we boys …?" He swung the control stick back.

"And if you don't get that thing out of my face, you'll wish you hadn't found me," said Deirdre. "So, I'm going to give you a chance and start by playing nicely—"

"I'm not," said Captain Snow. He pulled the trigger. There was a flash of unspeakable pain and Deirdre's world went black.

Chapter 68

"Does this make any sense to you at all?" Sir Robin asked The Pan. He had the air of someone who is a little put upon. He didn't seem to realise that The Pan, though fiddling with the Importance Detector, was still listening.

"Mostly, but I think you might have misjudged the depth of my intelligence … or my education."

"Or perhaps you have."

Nice backhander again, The Pan noted. Untrue of course, but that didn't make it feel any less good. Sir Robin continued.

"Remember this, it's absolutely essential. Liars never succeed in government. Not in K'Barth."

"Yeh, like Arnold said: 'The words of the dishonest man are cheap'."

"Well done my boy, I didn't expect you to know that."

"Oh, I'm full of surprises," said The Pan drily. He held the Importance Detector up to the light for a moment.

"He was absolutely spot on," said Sir Robin. "Once people realise you are a liar they cease to value your words. Indeed, they become cynical and cease to believe anything you tell them—even if it's the truth. When you need them to listen to what you have to say, they will refuse. You can omit matters or keep things obscure but you *must not lie*. You can tell the people that the depth of the problem is too politically sensitive to share publicly or you can make up a story and explain it is to illustrate the truth but you must not lie. Ever. I cannot stress this enough. Treat them as you'd like them to treat you. Show them respect and you will earn it."

"And this is relevant to me because …?"

"Because it is good advice, my boy, and one day you and the people around you may be in a position to need it."

"I think that's unlikely but for what it's worth, I get what you're saying, hand them any old crap and they'll see through it, right?"

"Exactly."

"Mmm." While he and Sir Robin talked, The Pan held his hands above the Importance Detector and absent-mindedly, without particularly thinking what he was doing, because the bulk of his mind was trying to follow the conversation, he attempted to replicate the moves Sir Robin had recently made over the top of it, in reverse. After a few goes, he decided he'd probably done them as accurately as he ever would, so he set the pointer towards Sir Robin and started trying to reproduce the moves Lord Vernon had made to take Ruth's reading. "I suppose that's one of the biggest problems between us and the Grongles," said The Pan as he attempted, without success, to make the Importance Detector detect Sir Robin's importance. "I mean, on paper, they've done some good things for K'Barth; they're organised, methodical, they've made things work that we never could."

"The trains again?" said Sir Robin. He chuckled, though The Pan wasn't sure whether at what he had said or what he was trying to do.

"Yeh, the trains, not to mention Vite K'Barthan, but the Grongles think we're inferior and they treat us like it. They lie to us because, in their eyes, we're not worthy of the truth. We obey them because we're scared of them but that's not respect. If they treated K'Barthans as their equals we'd probably welcome them with open arms ..."

Sir Robin raised his eyebrows.

"Badly put, but you know what I mean," said The Pan hastily.

"Unfortunately, I do." Sir Robin stopped and waited as The Pan made a third attempt to take his reading. The machine pinged and the green pointer swung round to the figure eight. The Pan looked up, smiling.

"Mmm. It seems you're quite important. Doesn't eight make you The Candidate?"

"Certainly not! However, that," he gestured to the Importance Detector, "is no mean feat. Well done, my boy. You really will make a marvellous—" he stopped. The Pan made eye contact and held it.

"A marvellous what?" he asked. Sir Robin was flustered.

"We digress. Now then. The box. How about you put that confibrulator back to where it was?"

The Pan glared at Sir Robin.

"How about you tell me what's going on here?"

"How about you hark back to the point in this conversation when I explained, categorically, that I cannot?"

"Why don't you bend the rules? You're pretty liberal with your interpretation of Arnold's writings. Anyway, I can resist Truth Serum, it's not as if I'm going to give anything away."

"There are some rules which cannot be broken and you may be able to resist

Truth Serum but you would be wise to remember that others cannot." Sir Robin stopped the Importance Detector, gave it a booster wind and stood it next to the box.

"Not even you?"

"Not even I."

They sat eyeing each other and The Pan recognised that he was not going to change Sir Robin's mind.

"Alright, alright," he said, his desire to show off finally overriding his desire to sulk. He reversed the movements he'd made over the Importance Detector and pulled the lever.

Sir Robin clapped his hands and jumped up.

"Capital! Absolutely capital, my boy! If you would be kind enough to move the box a little closer?" The Pan did as he was told. "Marvellous! Now watch this." Sir Robin walked to the door and turned out the main lights. In the relative darkness, the box gave off a faint green glow.

"Very nice," said The Pan, his annoyance forgotten as he was caught up in the simple joy of getting something right. Sir Robin turned the lights back on.

"It is rather pretty, isn't it? It also proves that's the real box, should you ever need to know, because it's green." Sir Robin returned to the table and sat down. "No glow, no show. The real box will only ever glow brightly, unequivocally green."

"Any reason I should know that?"

"Not yet."

"Don't tell me. Later I'll understand."

"Indeed. The future is not set. I do not know how long I will be here for and I must equip you with as much knowledge as I can. It will not all be relevant but I hope the greater part of it will stand you in good stead."

"Mmm." He pulled the bag towards him and took out the jar labelled 'prunes'. "What's this?"

"Ah, that's a pirate portal," said Sir Robin. "Making one of those is a lost art. However, I am proud to say it was rediscovered recently by your inimitable landladies." Sir Robin beamed. What with Trev, The Pan had always wondered if Sir Robin and Gladys were old flames but now he saw the pride in the old man's eyes he knew for sure. And the flame clearly hadn't gone out. Mmm. Best stop there.

"That's quite something," he said.

"Isn't it?" said Sir Robin. "Once the Grongles began to experiment with detection systems we had no choice but to reinvent these. A few months ago Gladys and Ada succeeded and now we have resurrected the Escape Programme. We can't hide the fact portal use has occurred but if we use one of these and smash it on arrival the Grongles will not know where we have travelled to. So we have a volunteer who brings a group of GBIs here once a week to start a new life."

"Like the one I've irrevocably stuffed up."

"Just so," Sir Robin gestured to the jar. "That would be one of a pair. Most people cannot use a portal to go somewhere they haven't already been to. Indeed, I might venture to say that you are the only one who can. They therefore have to be escorted by someone who has been here and who is willing to return to K'Barth. After the loss of your parents the original programme suffered greatly on that account." He stopped. "Only Trev is prepared to make the dangerous trip on a regular basis."

"So … Mum and Dad. Why didn't they just stay here?"

"Because it would have aroused the Grongles' suspicions if a distinguished academic and his family, who were known and watched by the security forces, suddenly disappeared. It could have jeopardised the entire enterprise. As we discovered when we tried to replace them; few people would have the courage to turn their backs on freedom. Your parents did. Not once or twice, but many times. They were K'Barthan and Hamgeean and they didn't want to leave. They wanted your brother and sister to be proper Hamgeean K'Barthans; and you too."

Arse.

"You know, I don't feel too good about that."

"I should imagine not."

The Pan ran his hands through his hair.

"They loved you, my boy, I can assure you that."

And now they were gone, The Pan thought. His last words to them had been in anger and it was too late to seek forgiveness or make amends.

Sir Robin did not comment but The Pan could see he understood. Blinking back the tears he quickly stuffed the idea of his parents to the back of his mind. He didn't want to cry in front of Sir Robin. He turned to the bag for a distraction and took out the last of the things inside; the sewing kit.

"This one's self-explanatory."

"Indeed, a useful blind to hide your thimble."

'Your thimble', The Pan noticed. Good. Sir Robin wasn't about to ask for it back then. The Pan handed him the case and he opened it. Inside, where the thimble had been, was a ring, The Ring, worn by forty generations of Architraves. The Pan watched in stunned silence as Sir Robin took it out and held it up.

"You didn't really think I'd allow this to fall into Lord Vernon's hands, did you?"

"But I—"

"Sold it. Yes, and I'll have you know that your fence charged me double what he paid you."

"But you said—"

"I lied."

"You blackmailed me."

"Yes, I did. If you're interested, it went against the grain. Here, catch." He flicked his hand and The Pan only just caught the ring as it whizzed past his head. Sir Robin continued. "Lord Vernon is wearing a fake. We fed him all the right information to make him believe and he wants to, of course, so he does."

Arnold's pants.

"Smoke and mirrors?" said The Pan weakly.

"You are learning."

The Pan examined it carefully. As before when he held the ring, he was overcome with an irrational desire to put it on. Like the last time, it seemed too big for him. He glanced at Sir Robin and when the old man nodded he slipped it onto his finger. Suddenly it was the perfect size. He held his hand up, fingers pointing downwards.

"Shrinks to fit?" he asked. Sir Robin eyed him meaningfully. "Why?"

"The honest answer is that I have absolutely no idea. It just does for certain people."

"Doesn't Lord Vernon know about the shrinking thing?"

"No, we tend to keep that quiet."

"If he sees this, the whole fake thing is never going to stick."

"Then you'd better make sure he doesn't."

"What?" squeaked The Pan.

Sir Robin was, apparently, oblivious to the bomb he'd just dropped. "The fake he wears is fabulous. It'd take anyone in unless they'd seen the original. Your job, young man, is to make sure he doesn't."

"I can't do that."

"You can and you will. There is no-one else."

The Pan did what he always did when given an order. He argued.

"How?"

"That's obvious, man! Hide it."

"Where?"

"Oh, you'll think of somewhere."

Did Sir Robin realise how irritating he was, The Pan wondered. Yes, almost certainly. Never mind, this time he would bite his lip. He knew he was useless at hiding things, the fact Gladys and Ada used to dust the stash of stolen goods he kept in their cellar told him that. On the other hand, he had regretted letting go of the ring from the moment he'd sold it and it was good to have it back. At least he could look after it, until the Candidate turned up. And on current form, The Pan reckoned that meant the ring was his forever so long as he kept clear of the Grongles. He could settle for that.

Once again, Sir Robin abruptly changed the subject.

"Ah … Yes. While you are looking at that sewing kit, I meant to say there should be something else in there, a piece of paper."

The Pan was still in shock at being given the ring and stared at it on his finger.

"Sorry, did you just say something?"

"Yes. There was a bit of paper … in the sewing kit."

"What?"

"Oh, do concentrate."

"You gave me the ring. It's your fault I'm distracted."

"Yes, it does that. That stone is exceptional. That's why the fake took so long to make, of course we spent years finding a stone of comparable quality."

"Whoa, whoa there, years?"

"Of course, this ring is part of our national psyche. We didn't want the Grongles looking for the real one so we decided to make a replica. You know, to put them off the trail. In point of fact we only just got it done in time. That's why we had to pay your man so much. We wanted him to delay the sale but he knew he was selling it on to a Grongle and he didn't want to."

"Yeh, well, they don't like to be kept waiting."

"Absolutely not."

The Pan looked at the ring on his hand, it was difficult not to, the gold looked antique and there was something mesmerising about the blood-red stone. He turned it round so the ruby faced inwards. The band of gold still had that old yellow glow but it wasn't quite as conspicuous, facing outwards, as the ruby.

"The Prophet was given that ring, ironically, by the then ruler of Grongolia. She wasn't a Grongle, of course." That figured. There had been all sorts of different species in Grongolia to start with. Like K'Barth. It was only in recent history that some had fled to K'Barth and the ones who'd stayed had been exterminated by the Grongles. Sir Robin continued. "It has no real power. It is just a reminder to the Architrave and those around him that he is part of something bigger; a way of life, of thinking. The embodiment of a tradition, yes, but not the be all and end all."

He was lying.

"Are you telling me the Architrave doesn't call the shots? There's a surprise," said The Pan.

"You realise that every one of them, since Arnold himself, has worn that ring?"

"Even the chicken?"

"Even the chicken."

And not forgetting Arnold, too.

"Look after it for me, will you?"

"I'll try, but if you really want it looked after you'd probably be more sensible entrusting it to someone else."

"Perhaps, but I doubt it. Now, where was I? Ah yes, the paper …" he seemed fixated with it. "Just a scrap shoved in that sewing kit. Do you still have it? It's nothing immensely portentous, you understand, just some mathematical jottings. I have never been a master at algebra, though, so I would like to recover them if I can, rather than have to calculate them over again."

The Pan marvelled how anyone who was such an abysmal liar as Sir Robin had contrived to survive longer than he had, while on the government blacklist. To say it was a miracle was understating the case, even if he had clearly spent a large part of the time in the safety of the apartment they were in now. The Pan thought for a moment. The paper was important, obviously, but was it important enough to risk admitting he'd opened the box? Technically, it was reneging on the deal. Then again, Sir Robin had made the deal with Big Merv, not him.

"Well …?" Sir Robin eyed him quizzically.

Arnold. His expression must have given him away again.

"OK, look, I'm sorry, it's in the box. I know I shouldn't have opened it and—"

"Impossible," he laughed, "you really are a lying hound! There's absolutely no chance you can open that yet."

"No, honestly," said the Pan apologetically. "It was inside the thimble originally and I'd put it in my pocket. After you'd taken the rest of the stuff away I realised I still had it. I'd been carrying it about but it was beginning to get a bit dog-eared and I thought it might be important—or useful—and I couldn't think where else to put it," he shrugged. "Once we'd got the box I put the paper inside."

"Indeed?" Heavy irony.

The Pan was nettled.

"Indeed," he said aping the way Sir Robin said it, before he thought better of being bullish. "I'm sorry, I shouldn't have done it. Big Merv said he'd made a deal with you not to open it but it just seemed the smart option, before it got torn or I lost it."

"Yes," said the old man, smoothly. He picked up the box and handed it to the Pan. "If you put it inside, I'm sure you wouldn't mind opening it for me now, would you?"

The Pan shrugged and popped the lid open one-handed.

"Here." He removed the paper, unfolded it and pushed it across the table. The room was silent, the kind of silent that is far louder than actual noise. Something was wrong. Sir Robin was very still, staring at him. It wasn't a reassuring stare. It was a perfect mask, all emotion and reaction hidden. Nothing in his expression hinted at trouble and yet, the staring was taking place and it was going on too long.

Sir Robin shook his head, apparently in wonderment and whispered something unintelligible.

"I'm sorry, I didn't hear that," said The Pan, just to check.

"Nothing, nothing, merely the mutterings of an old man. Don't take any notice of me."

"Have I broken it, then?"

"No," said Sir Robin. He turned the paper over and laughed. "When did you write that?"

"A couple of nights ago, before Big Merv and I came to get you."

"Was that the first time you opened the box?"

"Yes."

"Gracious! This is marvellous news."

"Why?"

"It means our chances of defeating Lord Vernon are greater than I thought."

"Really." The Pan was the one doing the heavy irony this time. "That would suggest you have some kind of plan."

"But of course."

The Pan made eye contact and gave Sir Robin the benefit of a highly cynical stare. It worked, the old man shifted uncomfortably in his seat.

"Well, Sir Robin?" He drained his sherry and waited. "Are you going to let me in on it?"

"Soon, my boy, but not yet."

"Naturally. Any pointers as to when?"

"Tomorrow," said Sir Robin breezily. "I need a little more information from my colleagues on the ground first." The Pan's misgivings must have shown in his face because Sir Robin added. "Trust me, my boy, trust The Prophet, and try to trust yourself. You are safe here and for now there is nothing to fear. May I suggest you take advantage of the short respite you have to relax, enjoy some time with your friends and have a good night's sleep?"

"And tomorrow, are you going to tell us what this is really about?"

"I would dearly like to, but it does rather depend on you. If matters remain the way they are then, alas I cannot."

"Listen, Sir Robin, I am truly flattered that you think I am …" The Pan shrugged, "a better man than I do but surely even you can see I'm in over my head here. You're the only person who can help me and I have to stop this. Ruth and I can't run for the rest of our days. Well, I can but she can't. We have to find a way to sort her life out and put her back in it. This isn't about me, I can look after myself. This is about her. This is her world. She belongs here and it's where she wants to be. I appreciate that you can't say where the Candidate is but please, for the love of The Prophet, give me a pointer; a hint …" he held out his hands. "I promised her I would help her. I have to find him. He has to come out of hiding and speak to her or choose someone else. Where should I look?"

"In your heart."

"What?"

"In your heart."

"Are you mental? What sort of an answer is that?"

"The truth. Everything you need to enable you to know the identity of the Candidate, for yourself, is right there in your heart. You simply have to understand what you see and hear and believe. Unfortunately, until you do, I am permitted to tell you nothing. Indeed I have already let on far more than I ought."

By The Prophet, this was the pits.

Sir Robin noticed The Pan's anger and changed the subject again. "My boy, is that blood in your hair?"

"Don't worry, it's only a scratch."

"Maybe, but I suggest we go and find Gladys and Ada, I am sure they have some antiseptic and a dressing if required—"

Uh-oh, they'd see the blue blood.

"No." The Pan stood up. "It's alright. I can fix myself up," he said.

"Are you quite sure?"

"Yes. Thank you for the amontillado. Nice stuff."

"A pleasure," said Sir Robin.

"Later then," said The Pan and without giving Sir Robin time to answer he walked out of the room, into the corridor. It was a little churlish of him and not very polite but he was too angry to stay there, and sad—lonely, even.

He felt betrayed. He had believed Sir Robin would trust him, explain everything and the reality was still hard to take. How much lower could a man sink when, even among the blacklisted, he was an outcast? No, no. This was silly. He was being melodramatic and maudlin. But he had pinned his hopes on Sir Robin and while he had gleaned a lot of interesting information, some bits more useful than others, he had not gained the answer he sought. Sir Robin was not going to wave a magic wand and fix everything. The Pan would not be able to solve all Ruth's problems for her. Her life, her friends, everything she valued and loved, was gone forever. He had called in the cavalry and it seemed they were busy elsewhere.

"Bastards."

Mmm. Let's get real. The Pan was reasonably self-aware and he knew the driving force underlying all his good intentions was a simple biological urge regarding himself, Ruth and the shedding of clothing. He had hoped to do the knight-in-shining-armour thing, click his fingers and make her problems vanish. Naturally she would then fall, swooning, into his arms before the Candidate got a look in. No chance of that now.

"Idiot," he muttered to himself.

As he stood outside the kitchen he heard the sounds of high-pressure cooking; pots banging, last-minute chopping, sauces bubbling, and through it all Gladys, Ada and Their Trev chatting and laughing. As he put his hand up to knock on the door, he realised he was still wearing the ring. He couldn't hide it. The very idea was a joke. He should go and give it back to Sir Robin. He glanced down the corridor. No, he couldn't face Sir Robin quite yet, not after making such a sharp exit. He knocked on the door and remembered that Humbert, Ada's foul-mouthed parrot, was excluded from the kitchen during cooking. Sure enough, with the eyes in the back of his head he saw Humbert bearing down upon him at speed. Forget waiting for an answer. The Pan opened the door and slipped swiftly inside.

Chapter 69

Ruth and Big Merv had taken it in turns to cheer up Lucy, until she was sufficiently recovered from the first bout of grief to accept Big Merv's challenge to a game of backgammon. It was a blatantly obvious ruse to take Lucy's mind off things, while giving her an opportunity to talk if she needed to. However, Lucy and Big Merv realised how worried Ruth was about The Pan and so she only put up token resistance when they sent her off to find him. Her brief search ended when she heard his voice and Sir Robin's in the study. Ruth decided it was best not to disturb them. She headed for the kitchen. Gladys, Ada and Their Trev were in there so she would offer to help prepare supper and spend some time getting to know them. As Ada opened the door Ruth felt a slight draught, as if someone was rushing up behind her, and only got as far as 'hello' before the old lady pulled her roughly into the kitchen and slammed the door.

"Conkers on the table! Conkers on the table!" shouted a voice from the hall. Ruth had forgotten about Humbert. Something hit the closed door with a loud bang. "Arse!" shouted the parrot, only rather more quietly.

"I'm so sorry, dear," said Ada fussing round her. "We don't let Humbert into the kitchen while we are cooking."

"Too right. He eats stuff," said Trev.

"No more 'an you do," said Gladys. "You is a gannet an' all. I is always having to buy extra to make up for all the stuff what you scoffs while you is pretendin' to help us cook."

"No I don't, it's coz you tastes so much of it." They all laughed and Ruth joined in.

"Is you alright, lass?" asked Gladys.

"Yeh, I'm OK," said Ruth.

"And your friend, dear? Lucy?"

"Lucy. She's a bit cut up but she'll get over it."

"I am glad," said Ada.

Gladys was very much in charge, allotting tasks and looking after the main course, some kind of chicken curry by the looks of it. They called it a Quaarl. Soon Ruth was sitting at the table chopping the contents of a salad while Trev sat opposite her preparing a marinade for some things that looked like squid. It smelled heavenly, all ginger, chilli and coriander although they assured her that nobody, other than The Pan, would touch it with a barge pole.

"I think Lucy and I might," she told them.

"You eats squid?" Ruth nodded. "'S disgustin'," said Gladys. "They has got tentacles."

"Yer," said Trev. "And they is smart."

"Yer, they talks to each other. I isn't risking eating something that'll ask me not to," said Gladys. There was a slightly uncomfortable pause and she added. "Though I'm not saying as I minds if you does."

Ada, who was busy washing up, changed the subject.

"How are you getting on with that nice young Pan of Hamgee?" she asked, and Ruth blushed. For heaven's sake! What was with the blushing? Could she not grow up? They'd only mentioned his name.

"Yer, I hopes he has been polite," said Gladys.

"He's very much the gentleman; the picture of decorum." Probably a bit more decorous than necessary Ruth thought.

"That's only to be expected. He's a very dear man, so thoughtful and polite and always kind to parrots."

"Humph. Even if he eats squid. Them's the ones you wants to watch," said Gladys. She squinted thoughtfully at Ruth over the top of her reading glasses for a moment and returned to her cooking. "If you wants to, mind."

They all sensed Ruth's awkwardness and the conversation moved on. They asked about her life, where she was from, what she did and then the three of them regaled her with funny stories about some of the characters who frequented the Parrot and Screwdriver. After a while, as Ruth finished chopping the salad, someone knocked on the door and stepped quickly into the room, closing it smartly behind them. Once again the loud thunk of parrot hitting wood reverberated through the room.

"Hello," said The Pan. He looked pale and tired but that didn't stop him flinging his arms round Gladys, Ada, in turn and then Trev, again, just for good measure. "I thought I'd never see you again," he said.

"Yer, well, we thought the same about you an' all," said Gladys dourly.

"You know Lord Vernon's after you then?"

"I doubt that will change the status quo, dear."

"Yer, he's got no evidence, see? He can think what he likes but he ain't sure."

"I think he is, now," said The Pan.

"We can always stay here, dear," said Ada.

"Yer, but I 'spect he'll leave us at large. See, he'll think we is going to lead him to the Candidate," said Gladys and she, Ada and Their Trev laughed.

"Don't say I didn't warn you," said The Pan. Light banter, but to Ruth he seemed so tired and downcast, and when she smiled at him he couldn't meet her eyes. Uh-oh. Was he angry with her? He had every reason. She had swanned off on her own and just about got him killed, not to mention nearly getting herself killed and actually succeeding in the case of Nigel.

"Are you OK?" she said. "Your head—"

"It's fine, just a scratch." His tone was sharp, almost brusque. "Gladys, do you have any antiseptic?"

"Yer, that cupboard there," she pointed. Ruth got hurriedly to her feet.

"Maybe I should have a look at it," she said. Out of the corner of her eye she noticed Gladys, Ada and Their Trev exchange glances.

"No." A very firm 'no'. "It's alright. I'll be back in a minute," said The Pan and grabbing the bottle of antiseptic he ducked out into the hall. No crash of parrot hitting door. Perhaps Humbert was elsewhere. No, he was probably waiting for Ruth, a soft and unfamiliar target, to follow The Pan. She wondered if she should. Gladys handed her a plastic bowl while Ada opened a drawer full of towels and tea towels and gave her a flannel. Clearly she wasn't the only one wondering.

"Here you are, dear. Off you go."

"He wants cheering up," Trev explained.

"Yer, and since you has chopped up that salad so fast and we is all still busy, I reckons it's your job."

"Yes dear, I think he'd much rather see you than one of us," said Ada.

As Ruth dashed into the hall, slamming the door just in time to stop Humbert getting into the kitchen, she glimpsed The Pan going into one of the bathrooms. He didn't close the door and she could hear the tap running. Even so, she approached with caution, aware that, whatever Gladys and Ada thought, he might prefer to be alone.

Chapter 70

The Pan leant on the basin and looked at himself in the mirror with something approaching hatred.

"Can I help? I'll go away if you'd rather but …" Ruth stood in the doorway.

"No, it's alright," he said.

"I wish it was," said Ruth.

She seemed cowed, humble and it tugged at his heart. His self-loathing was quickly replaced with concern for her. She pulled a square stool with a cork top into the middle of the room. It was the kind of thing often found in bathrooms, usually with a lifty lid and a cargo of spare loo rolls. "Sit there and stay still, Mister Pan, and tell me if it hurts." He obeyed with something like relief.

Gently, she cleaned the cuts, washing a worrying amount of blue blood out of his hair as she did so.

"You don't have to do this," he said.

"Actually, I think it's the least I can do." Her voice was quieter than usual and he realised something was up. He waited for her to continue. "I'm sorry I ran off."

"It was a little …" he stopped, he wanted to think of a way to put it politely, "underhand."

"I know." She sprayed disinfectant on the cuts.

"Ouch."

"I'm sorry."

"That's alright."

"No. I mean I'm sorry."

"What for?"

"Running off."

Ah. He smiled.

"Yes, you said. It's alright. Your distraction technique was a bit of an eye-opener, though."

She turned away for a moment and he could see she wanted to say more. He looked up at her expectantly.

"It wasn't very nice," she said.

"No, trust me, it was. Extremely nice."

Not the smallest hint of a laugh.

"Thank you for coming to get me," she said.

"It's a pleasure, although I would never have found you without Lucy and Big Merv, and I doubt I'd have got there in time if they hadn't kept Nigel busy so he couldn't call Lord Vernon."

"While you're here, though, thank you anyway." She hesitated. "I keep thinking what might have happened if—"

"But it didn't," said The Pan firmly. She misread his tone.

"I thought so. You're angry with me, aren't you?"

He laughed.

"Why should I be angry? You tried to save my life."

"If I'd listened to you, you wouldn't have been there. I wouldn't have gone to Nigel's flat and neither would you. I could just about bear knowing I'd dragged you over there, I suppose, if I had been a bit less pathetic and cowardly about escaping over the balcony."

"You're not pathetic, or a coward—those are my jobs."

She smiled sadly.

"Not today."

"Oh I think so—today and every day."

"Being brave isn't about being scared, Mister Pan, it's about not letting your fear stop you."

"Well, I admit you have me there, my fear never stops me. I run much, much faster when I'm frightened." He made a stupid face at her and despite herself she started to giggle. "At last, Ms Cochrane, finally I get a laugh, I've been dying on my arse here for five minutes." She seemed to relax. "Seriously, Ruth, you're the lionhearted one. You attacked Lord Vernon. That has to be the bravest thing I've seen anyone do." He stood up.

"It didn't work though, did it?"

"That doesn't matter. Don't be down on yourself. It's the thought that counts. Anyway, I'm here, aren't I?" He put his arms round her and hugged her tightly. "And so are you."

"For now."

"That's better than nothing." Unwillingly, he disentangled himself, picked up the bowl and emptied it down the sink.

"How am I going to live like this?" she asked.

Her voice broke. No, no, no. Those big brown eyes were pregnant with unshed tears. She wouldn't want to cry.

"You'll be alright. I told you, you get used to it after a while."

"I don't think I can."

"Ruth," he turned to face her and took her hands in his, "even with the life I lead, few days come tougher than this."

"I guess," she sighed.

"I know."

"What did Sir Robin say?"

He let go of her. He felt bitter at the thought.

"Nothing." No point lying. "Alright, there is something. I'm not sure he can sort your life out."

"Are you kidding?"

"Sadly not. Look, I know I—"

"He promised, well OK he didn't promise but he oozed confidence, as if he was just going to click his fingers and fix it. He invited me to tea." She was seriously angry, but to The Pan's absolute delight, with Sir Robin, not him. "And you. I thought you believed in him as well." Oops.

"I thought I did but looking at it, it was more a case of hoping, praying and denying my arse off. I've been a prat."

"I guess that makes two of us then."

"It may not be so cut and dried. He did say he'll tell us all more tomorrow morning when this other Underground person turns up. Apparently we're going to have a meeting and …" Should he say this? On a personal level, no, but now it came to it he loved her too much to withhold any information she might use. "He said that you've already met the Candidate and apparently he's in love with you."

"Mister Pan, I work in the arts. I've only met a handful of men in the last six months and I'm absolutely certain they're all gay bar one. None of them can possibly be in love with me unless the Candidate is very, very camp and I've had a gaydar failure of epic proportions."

"So what about the one?"

"He's you, numbnuts."

"Ah."

"Yeh. So what does *that* mean?"

She was winding him up.

"Nothing." He waved one hand and she was distracted by something.

"Wow! Is that yours?"

Ah yes. The ring.

"No," he said. He held his arm out so she could have a better look. The ruby glowed and the gold shone against the inside of his hand.

"Why are you wearing it inside out?"

"Sir Robin wants me to hide it."

"Well, your current location isn't exactly subtle," she laughed.

"No, but I've only had it a few minutes. Concealment is a work in progress."

"Can I see it?" He took it off and dropped it into her hand. She looked at it carefully. "It looks like the box and the thimble. Are they a set?"

Arnold, she was smart.

"Yes. This is the ring worn by every single Architrave," he said. "It's the ring I sold. I thought Lord Vernon had it but it turns out Sir Robin got to my fence before the Grongles, and Lord Vernon ended up buying a fake."

Ruth tried it on but it was huge, hanging round her finger.

"Blimey! How come it fits you? I didn't think my hands were that small but it seems to be made for a giant! Either that or you have the chubbiest fingers in the world."

"On the contrary," he said wryly. "It should shrink to fit."

She burst out laughing and spun it round her finger.

"Or not," she took it off. "You are such a spanner, Mister Pan. Jeans shrink to fit, rings don't." She grabbed his hand and slipped it onto his ring finger. It looked enormous on him, too, but gently, as the pair of them watched, the band shrank until it sat snugly around his finger.

The two of them stood there in silence for a moment.

"That is the weirdest thing I've ever seen," she said.

"Yeh. You and me both."

"So … what does that mean?"

"It doesn't have to mean anything," he said.

"Oh yeh?" She was winding him up again.

"Oh yeh." He looked into her eyes for a moment, dark brown, full of mischief and smiling. Did she not know how much doo-doo she was in? Or maybe she just didn't care. Or perhaps she was a complete and utter nutter. Whatever she was, she was lovely. He took her arm. "Come on, Ms Cochrane, it's nearly supper time and I wouldn't want to keep you from Gladys' food. Let's go and eat."

Chapter 71

Supper was a noisy, friendly meal and after her recent adventure with Lucy, Big Merv and The Pan, Ruth was becoming more at ease with the K'Barthans. The time spent with Gladys, Ada and Their Trev had helped, too. They were a normal, everyday family unit—albeit a quirky one—that not only looked human but actually was. She sat with The Pan on one side and Lucy on the other. Opposite her was Big Merv, who was getting on very well with Lucy, she noticed, and at the end of the table was Sir Robin who had swapped so Ruth could sit with her friend. Lucy was quieter than usual which was not really surprising. It's one thing to be chucked but quite another to discover your ex is now so comprehensively ex that they have ceased to be. Lucy had been upset and angry and, having called Nigel a few choice things while she bent Ruth's ear, she was now feeling guilty about speaking ill of the dead. And even Nigel didn't deserve to be dead. Not really, although he was a four-star git.

There was a brief delay at the start while the ninth place setting was cleared away; the clean cutlery, plates, glasses and place mat were stowed safely back in the kitchen by Trev.

Ruth couldn't help staring at Big Merv's antennae every now and again when she thought he wasn't looking. Except that he kept noticing and then they would all tease her about it. It was making Lucy smile so Ruth was playing the fool a bit more than she might have done. Eventually Big Merv said,

"You wanna closer dekko?"

"Um … if it's not insensitive."

"Nah, you're set," he stood up and leaned across the table, bending his head down.

"Would it be OK if I touched one?"

"Yeh … go on."

Very gingerly, Ruth reached for the end of the nearest antenna, she was careful, in case she hurt him. Once again, she was surprised that his skin wasn't clammy to the touch. Lucy giggled and Ruth was so happy to hear her friend laugh that she almost whooped. Big Merv looked up at Lucy who was still smiling. "You wanna cop a feel an' all, Luce?"

Luce? Ruth had never heard anyone but her call Lucy that.

"Can I?"

"Help yerself."

Lucy reached out and as her hand hovered over one of Big Merv's antennae, he flicked it backwards suddenly, hitting her fingers with it. She screamed and jumped back.

"Watch it, big boy."

Everyone laughed. Big Merv's good humour was infectious and by the end of the meal Ruth felt that Lucy was going to be OK. Not only that, but Ruth was starting to adjust to the strangeness of his presence and the notion that K'Barthans came in a varied selection of sizes and a kaleidoscope of colours. She was even beginning to like the idea of a world so filled with variety.

Gladys was a fantastic cook. The Quaarl was aromatic, hot and incredibly tasty. Ruth was glad to discover that vegetables in both versions of reality looked and tasted the same. The squid was one of the best things Ruth had ever eaten. Gladys, Ada and Their Trev forbore to have any but everyone else indulged themselves. The old ladies believed in feeding people up so the portions were huge, but Ruth didn't mind; breakfast had been a long time ago and being questioned by the police, not to mention scared out of her wits by Lord Vernon, had given her a large appetite. There were jugs of water as well as wine or beer to go with it all, and sitting next to The Pan, Ruth felt safe for the first time in months, as if being in his shadow would protect her. It was only now that she realised how anxious she had been.

There was no reason to relax. It wasn't as if everything was fixed. She didn't know what she was going to do about the Festival Hall, how she would get herself un-chosen or what to do about her job. But right now, in this moment, with this group of friends and benign strangers she felt better. It was going to be OK. Somehow, they'd work something out.

At the end of the meal, Sir Robin stood up and banged his glass with a spoon.

"Ladies and gents; a word, if I may," he said. "I understand that you might be anxious and that most of you have, at the very least, many unanswered questions. However, I do not think it prudent that we try to answer them now. It has been a long day. We are all tired and now that we are relaxed may I suggest we avail ourselves of our secure surroundings and have a good night's sleep. What say we reconvene tomorrow morning at nine thirty in the study?" Except that, to Ruth, this sounded less of a suggestion and more of an order.

There was nothing peremptory in Sir Robin's tone exactly, he simply exuded the kind of casual authority that caused others to do as he suggested. "There are drinks and some splendid chocolates if anyone is interested, but I am afraid I am no spring chicken. I need my sleep so I must leave you and go to bed."

After he'd gone Ada said, "I too must away to bed, dears."

"Yer, after we has done the pots," said Gladys.

Ada disappeared to the kitchen and returned with a large trolley. Everyone helped stack the dirty dishes onto it and then the two old ladies headed off; one wheel of the trolley screeching for oil and trying to go in a different direction to the others.

After they'd gone, Big Merv picked up a bottle of brandy from the sideboard.

"I'm gonna have a bit of this an' watch some telly. Anyone wanna join me?" Lucy grabbed some glasses.

"I'm in. Ruth, are you coming?"

"In a minute."

Lucy headed off with Big Merv.

"Don't forget the chocs, mate," said Trev as he followed in their wake. Ruth could hear the sounds of conversation receding along the corridor until a door closed and they were muffled.

The Pan touched her arm.

"Are you going to bed?"

"Not just yet."

"Good. Can I talk to you in a minute?"

"Aren't we talking now?"

"Yes but I mean really talk to you, which I can't do right now because I need to give Ada and Gladys a hand with the washing-up."

"Wow! They've got you house-trained."

"Mmm. Up to a point. When I'm done, where will I find you? With the others?"

"Why don't I tag along and help? Then you won't have to look."

So it was that Ruth ended up drying the dishes with Ada while Gladys washed and The Pan did the putting away. The kitchen was spic and span remarkably fast. Then, the two old ladies excused themselves. Ruth and The Pan were alone. She folded her arms.

"Well, Mister Pan. What gives?"

"Want to come and see the roof garden?" he asked her.

"There's a roof garden?"

"Yes, I found it just after we arrived, while you and Lucy were catching up." He hesitated. "Would you like a tour? There'll be nobody around but us two."

"That's a very good reason to say 'no' right there."

He put out his hand and she took it. She let him lead her through a door in the wall up some stairs to a rooftop eyrie overlooking the city.

"This is amazing," she said. The lights of the city glittered below and beyond them: phosphorescence on an urban sea. She looked around her, taking in the lanterns, the furnishings and the second flight of stairs. He noticed where she was looking.

"Shall I show you where those go?"

"If you like."

He took her hand again and led her upwards. As they reached the top the roof garden lit up automatically. It was low-level lighting mostly, along the edges of the paths, in the sides of the flower beds, shining onto the ground to light the way. At intervals, groups of clear glass wands glowed with light from a source under the soil.

"This is fantastic," she said.

"Yeh. Not bad, is it?" He let go of her hand and gestured to the rooftop around them. "This is Free K'Barth, like the old K'Barth, I suppose – peaceful and calm. I doubt it was idyllic by any means but when I see this …" he stopped and when he continued his voice was emotional. "I think it must have been wonderful."

"Don't you remember?"

"No. Before my time. The Grongles arrived before I was born."

"Yeh, I guess we're lucky here. We've got plenty of countries suffering a police state but there are also others, like mine, where people are free to live their own lives. Where they're treated as well as … well, as well as people are able to treat each other."

"Yeh. You don't have any Grongles anywhere, either," said The Pan.

"We have our own versions, they just haven't achieved world domination yet."

"I envy you that. I have since I first looked through the thimble and saw you."

She put her hand on his arm. She didn't know what to say.

"It's alright," he said. They turned and made their way back towards the stairs. "Talking about K'Barth, how are you acclimatising to my compatriots?"

"To the …" how to put this politely? "Differences?" she asked.

"Mmm."

"It's like GalaxyTrek. " He was nonplussed. "Sorry, we have this TV programme about this spaceship that goes to other planets. The aliens fall into two types. Group one: weird. Group two: really beautiful human women, only with skin that's blue or green or a colour people aren't here on earth. If it's the second type the Captain always gets to snog one."

He laughed, "Are you telling me K'Barthan truth is stranger than Earthan fiction."

"We call it 'Earthly', not 'Earthan' and yes, Mister Pan, I am."

They reached the flight of stairs. She ran down the first three and jumped down the last five. Oh, the joy of wearing trousers and comfortable footwear. Not to be outdone, he slid down the banister, successfully leaping off before he hit the knob at the bottom, and landing lightly beside her.

"Do you want a drink?" he asked. "I think there's a bottle of Gladys' Calvados round here somewhere."

"Go on then …" she waited. "You wanted to talk to me."

"Yes." He walked over with two glasses full and put one in her hand. She sniffed it. Blimey.

"But you want to get me plastered first?"

"No, Ms Cochrane and you know it."

"OK, so before you start, there's something I wanted to ask you about Big Merv. If the lady who hit on you was a Swamp Thing, how come she's green and he's orange? Are boys and girls different colours, do they just vary the way we humans do or what?"

"The truth is, I don't know. Don't ever mention it to him because he's quite sensitive about it, but Big Merv's a bit of an anomaly. A one-off, in fact, so if you're still feeling like a circus freak, now you know there are two of us who understand your plight."

"Your freaky secret's out, though, Mister Pan. I'm not the only one to have seen your blue blood and it's bound to be mentioned on your police record. Or do you have something else to hide?"

"Apart from my existence, you mean?" He chuckled. "And if I do, I'm going to tell you because …? The point of a secret, Ms Cochrane, is that nobody knows about it."

"But my point, Mister Pan, is that I think I do."

He took it well, returning her gaze with absolute confidence. It was alarmingly sexy. He paused to consider his options.

"You do, do you?"

How on earth was she supposed to play aloof and hard to get when he kept smiling at her like that? Then again, it was difficult to play hard to get anyway, when she was rather hoping to be caught. She wasn't sure of the protocol with an attraction like this. There was more chemistry than either of them knew what to do with, it had been pretty instant and it was clearly mutual. But she didn't want him to think she was easy.

"Well, Ms Cochrane? What are you thinking?"

"All the wrong things," she said before she could stop herself. "But you're trying to change the subject. You can't wriggle out of this, Mister Pan. You're going to have to tell me."

"Mmm, clearly there's no deflecting you. Well, since you've got me where you want me ..." He put his glass down on the parapet, took off his hat and handed it to her. It was heavier and better quality than she'd expected.

"This wasn't what I was going to tell you now, but as you've asked so determinedly ..." He put up one hand in a wait-a-minute gesture before turning his back to her. He linked his hands behind his head and slowly moved them upwards, lifting his hair out of the way.

There they were. Eyes: the same dark blue as the ones at the front, looking at her, smiling. She'd expected the eyelids and the area around them to be bald. It wasn't, although the hair was finer and shorter. Conversely, the eyelashes were longer than average. Yeek. Weird. She could feel herself going pale. Despite her suspicions, seeing the spare pair for real was profoundly shocking. Having a hunch was all very well but judging by the way she felt now, she hadn't really believed. He turned round to face her again and she handed him back his hat, which he put on a nearby table.

"Doesn't your hair get in the way?"

He burst out laughing.

"Is that all you can say? At the very least I expected 'I knew it!'."

"Sorry, I—I'm a bit lumpy, socially. I meant to thank you for trusting me but that came out before I could stop it." He raised an eyebrow.

"I see." The dark blue eyes looked straight into hers. Gulp. How had he taken control like that? He was the one with the guilty secret, the one who should be on the defensive. But while their words concerned the trivialities surrounding his extra eyes, something different was being said. Ruth realised that The Pan of Hamgee was going to try and kiss her, any minute probably. What she had to decide—and quickly—was if she was really going to let him.

"I'm sorry," she said. "That was crass."

"Possibly. But it was also very lovely. I have never done that before so I doubt either of us could know what to expect. And … in answer to your perfectly reasonable question … yes, my hair gets into my eyes but I don't feel it the way I would if it got into the ones at the front. The eyes in the back of my head are different I think. Even with all my hair there, in front of them, I can see. Perhaps it's because it's so close."

"Mister Magic Eyes," said Ruth, trying to lighten the conversation because she didn't know what else to do with it.

"I sincerely hope not." He looked at her intently. "Nobody's ever noticed before. Why did you?"

"I don't know. I suppose it was because I didn't have a clue what to expect. I wasn't sure if you were human. I'm still not sure, even if you are human-shaped."

"You mean there were no preconceived ideas to cloud your judgement, then?"

"I guess."

He smiled and looked down at his hands. "I don't know whether to be nervous or happy."

"Meaning …?"

"Well, on the one hand, nobody else knows and the very fact that you noticed means someone else might and that makes me nervous. On the other, it's rather nice that you're interested." He changed position so he was leaning with his back against the parapet looking at her. It just happened to mean moving closer as well. He was encroaching on her personal space but she liked it, so she let him. "I am human, by the way."

"I'm glad to hear it."

"Well … I say human but we Hamgeeans are a bit of a mixed bag. So, I suppose a few generations ago there might have been a bit of goblin in there somewhere but it would be a long way back. It's thousands of years since they died out."

"Please tell me I didn't hear you say that."

"It's nothing to worry about. I think the current theory is that goblins and humans interbred. They reckon the goblins disappeared because goblinism is recessive to humanity. So in theory we're all a bit goblin except that we don't really know because apart from fossils and cave paintings goblins don't exist … Even if it is there, it's too diluted to count properly, I'm no more goblin than you are and we've no evidence that—" he stopped. "Shall we forget about the goblin thing? I was just trying to be honest."

"I think you might be trying a bit too hard."

"Possibly." He moved closer and took both her hands in his. "Listen, Ruth, there's something else you should know, too."

"And that is, Mister Pan?"

"My name." He hesitated. Clearly it was easier to own up to goblin blood or bidirectional vision than to tell her what he was called. She looked coolly into his eyes, at least, she hoped she did but it was more difficult than she expected. They were dark and limpid, and now an important part of her brain, a part she needed, seemed to have wandered off.

"Go on then."

"It's Defreville."

"Defreville."

"I'm afraid so. In every generation of my family some poor swine gets lumbered with the name Defreville. I am that unfortunate creature."

"You know, it's a lot better than 'the'."

He laughed.

"You don't like it, though, do you?"

No, or at least, not as names went, but yes, because it was his. Oh dear, this felt more and more like the L word. Did she really have it that bad? After, what was it? Twenty-four hours? Less?

"It's quite exotic. Foreign."

"Not at home."

"Good thing you're stuck here then, isn't it, Defreville?"

"Mmm …"

"Thank you for telling me."

"It's alright," he said. "The thing is …" They stood gazing at each other, dreamily. His eyes were deep blue, almost black, and intense, and she was, well, if she hadn't known she was far too pragmatic and sensible to contemplate such a thing, she'd have suspected she was drowning. "I want you to know who I am," he said, "because …" he moved even closer.

"Because …?"

He pulled her towards him and slid one arm round her waist. It made her stomach turn over in a very dangerous but comprehensively lovely way. She wanted to laugh. She should not be doing this, she should really not be. Except she had led him on abominably and anyway, at that moment she knew, more certainly than anything, that she loved him and it was all she wanted to do.

"Because …" he said. He ran one finger slowly down the outside of her jaw and under her chin, tilted her head up and kissed her; a gentle shy kiss with enough electricity in it to spark up the national grid.

"Defreville …" she breathed.

"Ruth …" He smiled, moved his hand round to the back of her head and kissed her again. Blimey. He knew how to kiss a girl. She felt fizzy and liquid almost, as if the two of them were melting into each other and she was shaking. She closed her eyes, put her arms round his neck and hugged him for a moment. He held her close. His shirt was soft and warm against her cheek and it felt familiar and comforting, like coming home after a long trip away. He kissed her neck and she looked up into those eyes and yes, no doubt about it, she definitely was drowning. So this time she kissed him, with a great deal more enthusiasm than was ladylike or proper.

"I expect we shouldn't be doing this," said Ruth.

"No, I should imagine not." He didn't seem to be able to stop smiling. "Things might get complicated."

"I think they're pretty complicated already, Mister Pan."

"Mmm … they are, aren't they? I don't know about you but, in this instance, I have to say I like complicated."

He glanced over to the bed.

"Shall we mess things up a little more?"

Ruth knew exactly what to say at this point. 'No'. Strong women have willpower and they don't put out on the first date. Then again most strong women are smart enough to draw the line at inter-reality romance. Anyway, most strong women would have a greater probability of surviving until the second date than Ruth. And technically, this wasn't a date so it didn't count.

"I'll have to think about that …" she said and waited just long enough for the first hints of disappointment to register in his face before adding, "and now I have. Yes."

He laughed and then he was kissing her again—another few million megawatts—and when at last they stopped it was she who stood back, took him by the hand and led him to the bed.

Chapter 72

Deirdre lay on the ground pretending to be unconscious. Arnold knew she was exhausted, so she didn't need to pretend too hard. Lord Vernon knelt beside her, one knee, the one carrying his weight, across her chest, one hand pinning both of her wrists to the floor above her head. He growled, an animal rumble like a big cat, but she did not move or show her fear. She might be rubbish at playing Rosa Trampleasure but she could fake loss of consciousness. It was the most basic technique for combatting Grongle methods of information retrieval, and Deirdre had passed that module of her training at the top of her class. She felt the cold sharp edge of a knife as he put it against her throat. It took all her concentration but Deirdre did not react.

"I know you are not asleep, my darling."

He waited. She lay still.

He increased the pressure on the knife and she felt a tiny sting as the tip of the blade broke the skin. Only a scratch but she felt the warm blood on her neck. She concentrated on remembering her training.

"I really shouldn't fraternise with my enemies like this and I must confess that usually, at this point, we would say a very final goodbye. But you ..." he leaned down and spoke quietly into her ear. "You have brought me immense pleasure. You are the ripest and juiciest of forbidden fruits. And that you have tried so hard to kill me ..." he pressed his face against her neck and inhaled deeply. "Oh, that just makes you taste sweeter. I want a second helping of you." Once more, he waited but with an immense effort of will, Deirdre kept up the pretence of unconsciousness, kept her breathing regular and her face and limbs relaxed. Focusing, concentrating on the Ninja Nimmist techniques she had been taught, she retreated into her inner self; cutting off her surroundings and clamping down on her screaming imagination, which was far harder to control than the pain of the knife. "So ... I will entrust you to the care of Captain Snow." She felt his weight shift as he moved backwards. "And when you are a little more ... yourself ... we will do this again." Finally, he took the blade away from her throat, let go of her hands and stood up. She lay with her eyes closed, taking advantage of these few moments to gather her strength. She could not kill him now. This time she was beaten, and since he had spared her life she must accept defeat, no matter how much it rankled, and think of her mission. He knew she was Resistance but he hadn't realised she was the Candidate, that was certain, or he would have killed her. She listened as he moved about the room tidying up his appearance, smoothing his hair, adjusting his clothing. After a few moments he walked to the door and spoke in a low voice to the guard outside.

Someone put their hands under Deirdre's arms and dragged her roughly out of the room. She was dropped onto the tiled floor in the hall, which was painful, but Arnold knew it didn't hurt as much as her pride. She kept up the pretence of unconsciousness.

"Captain," said Lord Vernon.

"Sir. The female met with your approval?"

Lord Vernon laughed. Possibly the most chilling thing Deirdre had ever heard, even on top of his version of pillow talk.

"She fights like a tigress, Captain. I'll wager she is more at home in combat than the laundry."

"You are done with her?"

"No. See to it that she makes a full and speedy recovery. I want her again, soon."

"Sir."

Captain Snow sounded doubtful and Deirdre realised she must look every bit as bad as she felt.

"Do not be deceived by appearances, Captain. She will return to health soon enough," said Lord Vernon.

"Sir."

"And you will reserve her for my personal pleasure. No-one else is to touch her."

"Sir."

"That is all."

Deirdre heard a door slam and she was dragged to the end of the corridor and dropped a second time. She wished they wouldn't keep doing that and was just debating whether it would be prudent to act as if she was coming round, to save herself any more bangs on the head, when they threw a bucket of cold water over her. She wanted to scream and leap to her feet. Instead, she rolled over slowly, groaning as she pretended to wake up.

"Good, you're awake. Get up." Captain Snow hauled her to her feet and she was marched into a service lift.

It was warm, but even so Deirdre felt cold. Then again, she was dressed to entertain Lord Vernon in a short ivory-coloured silk slip and it was soaked, clinging to her body with a clammy embrace. She swore she would kill him for this because if she stopped being angry she would be wretched. She imagined stabbing a knife deep into his heart; if he had one. After what he'd just subjected her to, she thought that unlikely. Maybe she should just slit his throat, although she'd already tried and failed to do that. As soon as she was brought to his rooms, as soon as he had made his intentions clear, she had grabbed a letter opener from his desk, tried to assassinate him and had failed spectacularly. She could almost match his speed and skill in combat, but he was fully armed and seemed to be able to read her thoughts in her face and eyes almost before she had them.

She had fought for her life and her dignity until she was too exhausted to defend herself any more. She bit back the tears. He would pay for what had happened next. She shivered and pulled the nauseating slip about her. It was ripped and the bucket of water had made it transparent. Captain Snow and his guards were having a good look. That's right, get an eyeful. Pigs. She glared at them. It would have felt good to punch them for their disrespect, but it would get her nowhere. Two hours of fighting Lord Vernon had sapped too much of her strength. She must save herself. She was bruised and aching and she must keep alert, watch for a chance to escape and keep the last shreds of her energy for that.

The lift descended to the next floor down and stopped. One of the guards swore and pressed the button marked B for basement but the lift obdurately went about its duties, announcing in a tinny female voice that the doors were opening and then opening them, slowly, to reveal an empty hallway.

Deirdre saw her chance. She let her head loll to lull them into a false sense of security and then, as the doors began to close she kneed the nearest guard in the groin—take that you letching smecker—and leapt over him, rolling head over heels and, leaping upright she bolted down the hall. She was thinner and smaller, there was no way the gap would accommodate her gaolers. Captain Snow and the other guard held the doors, trying to force them open again while their colleague, doubled over in pain, blocked their path.

Deirdre was running on adrenalin but she was already out of breath and dizzy; the big black blobs that heralded an imminent loss of consciousness began to appear in the corners of her vision. As she rounded the corner at the end of the corridor she knew she must hide, fast.

Her eyes scanned a second long passageway. This one had doors along each side and one at the end. No stairs. No obvious exit. No chance of fooling her pursuers into running past. She cast about her. She must be quick. The rush wouldn't last long. There was light shining under some of the doors. Presumably the rooms behind them were occupied. Best to avoid those then—the last thing she wanted was to surprise any more Grongles into the chase with three of them after her already. She opened the door to the nearest unlit room. A cupboard. Nothing doing there. She slammed it.

"Doors opening," Deirdre heard the tinny female voice say in the distance. She needed to create some confusion. It was risky, but she had to put her pursuers off the scent. She ran to another darkened room, right at the end of the hall, opened and slammed the door of that one too, and then fled back down the corridor in the direction she had come, to a third darkened door. No light shining underneath. No-one in. Good. She ducked swiftly and quietly inside, closing it silently behind her. She should lock herself in and find another way out but she couldn't find a key or a bolt. Arnold's pants. There must be something to jam it with, surely. A chair?

"If you are looking for the key, I have it here," said a voice.

Aaargh!

Deirdre spun round and stood with her back against the door, arms out sideways, ready to run or fight, but she was under no illusions. The adrenalin coursing through her system was almost gone, leaving her even weaker than before.

The room was lit, very dimly, by the glow of a desk light. It was an office: comfortable, well furnished and in a male and rather austere way, homely. In the right-hand corner there was a desk, and half of the wall opposite it was windows, with a door out onto a balcony. In the left-hand corner of the room, in the half of the wall that wasn't windows, was another door, open, which led into a corridor. She could see there were several more rooms and outside, on the balcony, a doorway leading into one of them. Maybe it wasn't an office, somebody's living quarters perhaps? In the wall facing her was an open fireplace with three sofas in front of it at right angles to one another. There was a rug on the carpet and a coffee table upon which she noticed a plate of food, untouched. She realised she was ravenously hungry.

The occupant of the apartment was sitting at the desk, holding up the key in question. He dropped it casually onto the blotter and stood up slowly. As he walked out into the room, he pressed a button on the wall beside him, switching the main light on. He was very short for a Grongle, six foot, if that, and seemed totally unperturbed by the sudden arrival of a scantily clad female. He wore the same black suede boots as Lord Vernon and Captain Snow but otherwise, his uniform was different to theirs; dark grey with a light stripe down the outside of each trouser leg. He wasn't wearing a jacket, just a loose white shirt, crumpled and half-unbuttoned, with the sleeves rolled up, and his trousers were held up with old-fashioned button braces.

The Resistance operatives in the laundry had told Deirdre that the troops with grey uniforms were almost decent. Perhaps this one had a soft heart she could play on? His face and eyes were hard but not cruel. However, he had an intelligence about him and he was very self-assured—even for a Grongle his air of confidence was striking—and unfortunately, he was clearly a seasoned soldier. He was older but he was lithe and fit and he knew what he was doing. There weren't many people who could equal Deirdre in a fight but she knew, instinctively, that he could. Not that he would need to. He had a laser pistol trained on her and he was smart enough to keep his distance; there would be no disarming him. He'd have plenty of time to shoot before she got near. He looked her up and down but in a different way to the others, there was nothing predatory, no lust, just an air of casual enquiry. He noticed her bruises and the way her eyes were drawn to the food on the table. The two of them stood in silence for a moment and listened to the sound of Captain Snow and his men in the corridor outside. A door banged.

"Clear," shouted a voice. They were searching the rooms one by one. Footsteps stopped outside and the door handle rattled very slightly as if somebody had put their hand on it.

"No, start at that end," said a voice.

The Grongle inside raised his eyebrows in enquiry.

"They are looking for you?"

She said nothing.

"Of course they are. Who are you?"

"I work in the laundry," she mumbled. It was difficult to talk because she was shivering and couldn't stop her teeth from chattering.

"Do you?" He didn't believe her. He reached round, without taking his eyes or his laser pistol off her and picked up his jacket. "Here." He threw it to her. Gratefully, she wrapped it round her shoulders. It was woollen, high quality, soft and warm. "I imagine you'd prefer a towel but I do not think I will trust you alone here while I fetch it."

He waited a moment but she said nothing.

"The usual response is 'thank you'," he said drily.

"Thank you," she said, her tiredness slurring her speech.

"Noted. Do you have a name?"

"Rosa Trampleasure."

He laughed humourlessly.

"I doubt it's that. I meant your real name."

"That is my real name. I have nothing to hide."

"Shall we see?" Without lowering the gun, he took a mobile phone from his pocket, pointed it at her and pressed the screen. She didn't often get to use a mobile as modern as his but she knew he was taking a photograph of her. His phone beeped. "Ah," he said. Deirdre didn't like the way he said that, it was a penny-dropping kind of 'ah' as if he had recognised her for who she really was. Or maybe the phone had face recognition software. He put it back in his pocket and addressed her. "You have been with my master?" His eyes flicked briefly upwards.

She nearly sobbed but managed to keep her composure. This was the enemy. No weakness. No surrender. Instead she nodded.

"Doubtless Captain Snow is going to take you back."

"Not yet."

"Lord Vernon is done with you?" He kept his voice flat, neutral but she could tell he was surprised.

"For now." She couldn't suppress the shudder that ran through her at the thought of another visit, but she was shivering so much from cold and shock that it didn't show, or at least if it did he made no sign that he'd noticed.

"Then I will place you under my protection."

"I don't need your overbearing male protection. I can look after myself."

"If you have been up there with him and you are now down here like this, then, naturally I would assume you can." He was haughty but Deirdre saw a flash of something else in his eyes for a moment, something she couldn't pin down. "However," he continued, "long term, a competency in the art of combat will not save you. And since fate has brought you here, and I can, I suggest you take advantage of my generosity." He nodded at the door. "I believe Captain Snow and his troops will arrive imminently. I would move away from there if I were you. You are clearly tired. You may sit here." He gestured to one of the sofas.

"What if I don't want to?"

"I suggest you do. Your escape will have inconvenienced Captain Snow and in such situations he is not known for his diplomacy."

She wondered if she could reach the balcony doors. Maybe, if she rolled and dived behind the sofa—she'd have to be quick though. He anticipated her thoughts at once.

"I wouldn't try to run. You are too exhausted to get far."

"You don't know that."

"I think I do. Try if you like. I don't usually miss, especially such an easy shot."

He was right, of course. She glared at him.

"I see I will have to incentivise you. This is set to stun." He moved the laser pistol slightly. "If I am forced to use it you will come to no harm but I can assure you, from personal experience, that it is exceedingly painful. I am a Grongle and you are human. My resistance is superior to yours and you are smaller than I am. I believe, for you, it would be excruciating."

Deirdre said nothing.

"Clear!" shouted the voice in the hall. Another door banged.

"So …?"

Slowly, cautiously Deirdre moved to the spot he indicated. Meanwhile he backed round the sofas the other way, maintaining his safe distance, always watching her, never turning his back, never lowering the laser pistol. When he reached the door he opened it revealing a surprised Captain Snow.

"Sir, I am sorry to disturb you."

"Captain. You are looking for this?" he gestured to Deirdre with the laser.

'This?' How dare he?

"Sir."

Deirdre noted that her host ranked higher than Captain.

"I am to return her to the cells until Lord Vernon wants her again." Not exactly what Lord Vernon had ordered, Deirdre noticed.

"No, Captain. I will deal with this."

"Sir, I am under a direct command from Lord Vernon. This female is under his protection."

"My exact point."

"Sir, I do not understand—"

"Captain Snow, this female is a lieutenant in the Resistance, one of Denarghi's most trusted." Well, there was confirmation that he, or the database on his phone, had recognised her. But what was he doing? Deirdre watched, in horror, as this blundering idiot explained to the Captain, in detail, exactly who she was. "As a member of the Grongolian army I assume you are aware how the Resistance chain of command works?"

"Sir."

"How many other lieutenants do you think there are? Let alone ones who are prepared to work with us? Enlighten me, Captain?"

There was a long silence.

"As I thought. Ms Arbuthnot," he pronounced her name and the Ms correctly, "is highly important both to their organisation and to the covert operations which I am undertaking on behalf of Lord Vernon. I cannot achieve his will unless she is returned to her original position in the laundry and allowed to operate there without interference. So, you will return to him, please, and appraise him of this fact. I assure you, he will understand."

"Permission to speak, sir."

"Captain."

"He has guessed she is Resistance, sir, but he is very taken with her. I fear he will not understand."

"Then you will give him this direct message from me; that she is to play a central role in the matters of state he discussed with me earlier this evening and that she is under the protection of my forces on his behalf. When you tell him that, I think you will find he does understand. Completely."

There was a long, long silence.

"My forces, Captain. My regiment, my troops—not yours. Now, unless there is anything else, I am sure you have much to attend to."

"Sir," said the Captain. He was angry but he was also outranked and outmanoeuvred. He clicked his heels and saluted.

"Thank you," said Deirdre's new—whether she wanted or not—protector, closing the door on him.

"How dare you! You … idiot!" she said, leaping up. She stopped. The sudden movement was more painful and difficult than she expected and her voice still sounded slurred.

"I wouldn't do that," he warned her as she grimaced and caught her breath.

"You told them my name."

"I assumed you would not mind."

"You lying—" She took a shaky step forward. He levelled the laser pistol at her and flicked off the safety catch.

"Lieutenant Arbuthnot, I would rather not have to use this but if you force me I swear I shall."

She stopped. She was breathing heavily, her bruised and aching joints beginning to stiffen up.

"You think I'd work with you …?" she asked incredulously.

"I don't believe you have a choice," said the Grongle coolly. He gestured with the pistol to the food on the table, cold chicken, dressed green salad, potato salad. "I should imagine you would like something to eat. The kitchens were kind enough to send this up but I have no appetite tonight. Please, go ahead. I will be back directly."

Deirdre was angry but she was also hungry.

"Where are you going?" she asked him warily.

"To get you some dry clothes and a towel. I am reliably informed females in …" he paused and for the first time he seemed unsure of himself, "your situation are usually grateful for a wash."

A small kindness, but it was unexpected and it caught Deirdre off guard. She fought back the tears, lowering her head so he wouldn't see.

"You're the Grongle, you'd be the expert," she said bitterly.

"No. I would not—as an officer of your rank should realise. Know your enemy; the most basic rule of military strategy, but it appears, one you have neglected."

"I know your kind."

"I doubt that, but be assured, I know yours." He tucked the laser pistol into the back of his trousers and she wondered if she could knock him out and make a run for it. No. Not the way she was now. He stopped and half turned when he noticed her watching him. "You are working with me now; you and I, together, because my colleagues know who you are. You can refuse, of course, but without my protection you know what's going to happen. I'll wager you prefer the laundry to the tender mercies of Captain Snow and Lord Vernon."

"You hateful, arrogant, snot-coloured bastard," she spat. He spun round to face her. For a brief moment she thought he was going to draw the laser pistol and shoot her. Instead, with unexpected irony, he made a low bow.

"I do my best. General Moteurs, at your service." He raised his eyebrows. "Your pique is understandable," he said with a touch too much complacency for her liking. "I doubt a lieutenant in the Resistance appreciates being beaten."

Pique! Beaten! He'd be laughing on the other side of his stuck-up green face just as soon as … the world began to spin and Deirdre put her hand out and steadied herself. He stood on the other side of the room watching her intently. "Lieutenant, eat something." His professional soldier demeanour slipped a little and for a moment his voice was almost gentle. "I will prepare the bathroom …" a euphemism for, 'I will nail closed the window and remove anything that can be used as a weapon'. He made another bow. "You would like me to run the bath?"

"No. I'm not a child. I'll do that myself," she snapped.

"As you wish, then I will bring you a glass of water."

What a lecturing, pompous Grongolian git. He was truly insufferable. Even so, the minute he left the room, Deirdre took his advice. Grabbing his plate of supper, she sat down, to yet more protesting from her aching body, which had only just got used to standing up, and began to eat.

Chapter 73

It was morning and as the sun's first rays stole over the roof of the club, Ruth woke up warm and content under The Pan of Hamgee's cloak, with its owner. She snuggled closer and he put a sleepy arm round her.

"Hello, Chosen One."

"Hmmph …" Ruth closed her eyes and lay there, nestled against him, luxuriating in the sense of warmth and safety. She felt the reassuring weight of his arm around her shoulders and hugged him tightly. She was almost afraid to open her eyes again in case everything turned out to be a dream or a figment of her imagination and he disappeared. As she thought about the previous night, she smiled. It was difficult not to. The Pan had kissed her, quite a lot. Then they'd moved on to other things and they'd done quite a lot of those too, until they had decided they really should stop and try to sleep, at which point they had talked until dawn. So. Quite a lot of talking as well. Ruth was insanely happy and it seemed that so was he. The two of them revelled in every minute together, drinking in as much of each other's company as they could, trying to squeeze the lifetime they could never hope for into one short but idyllic night. Ruth wondered if this was it or whether they would be lucky enough to enjoy another one.

"Would you like a cup of coffee? I think I'm going to need a bit of a kick-start this morning," he said.

She laughed.

"I did warn you. If you'd spent a little less time having your wicked way with me you might have had a bit more sleep."

"You could always have said 'no'—I didn't hear you complaining."

She grabbed one of the cushions and hit him over the head with it.

"Right then, Ms Cochrane. No coffee for you."

She giggled and cuddled up against him.

"None for you either, then. You'll have to stay here."

"I might not want to."

"I'll make you." She gave him a look her mother would certainly not have approved of. The Pan, on the other hand, clearly approved quite a lot.

"You will, will you?" he said.

"Yes, and I don't think it'll be very difficult."

"No, that's probably true."

"You know, the way I feel this morning, I don't think your Pediment's going to be worming his way into my affections for a while. I don't see how he can. We can't just switch this off."

"I think you mean the Architrave and technically he's the Candidate at the moment and …" he stopped and frowned a little. "Switch what off?"

"All these … feelings."

He laughed. "What feelings are those?" He was being deliberately obtuse; teasing her. She propped herself up on one elbow, facing him.

"You know exactly what I'm talking about, Mister Pan. Ours. The ones between us. I'm supposed to love him but I don't see how I can. I'm too busy liking you, you plank."

"You're developing a worrying tendency to blaspheme, Ms Cochrane."

"It's not blasphemy, it's logic." Some of her hair fell over her face and he hooked it gently behind her ear. The electricity was still there and when his hand brushed her cheek it made her shiver. He raised an eyebrow.

"You know, it looks a little more than 'like' from where I am."

"Don't make me mention the L word, Defreville. Not this early on. Apart from the fact it's anathema and will doom our relationship before we begin, don't do it to my dignity."

"Alright, since I have little dignity to speak of, I'll go first shall I? I love you Ruth Cochrane. I love you a fair bit. In fact right now, I can believe that I may even love you till I die. Don't get excited, though, because with my current life expectancy that's hardly a long-term commitment."

She giggled.

"If your heart's attention span matches that of its owner, I give us a couple of weeks at best."

"So little faith … Three weeks at least. If we're lucky and we really work at it we might manage four. What do you think?"

"I think you're a gumby and I see no point in telling you I love you when you quite plainly know."

He ran his hand through her hair, to the back of her neck, leaned forward and kissed her. It made her stomach fizz and her eyes roll, but luckily not enough to stop her from kissing him back. Well … it would be churlish not to.

"And I like the way you do that, Ms Cochrane," he said when they finally came up for air.

"I like it too …" Damn. That wasn't right. "No, I mean …" She looked into his eyes. It made her feel a bit wobbly and it was difficult to concentrate. What was she trying to say? "I meant that I like the way you …"

"The way I …?"

"Oh for heaven's sake! This is no time to try and have a conversation."

"You started it. Anyway, what about the coffee?"

"It can wait. Don't argue, Mister Pan. Stop talking and kiss me again."

He did as she asked and she surrendered happily to his advances. The Candidate would have to pick someone else now. She and The Pan had made some decisions of their own. She couldn't possibly be chosen. Not any more. She had voted with her feet, and her hands and quite a few other parts that were probably better not mentioned; and it was far too late to fall in love with anyone else.

Chapter 74

Ruth and The Pan were late, they had lost track of time. Sir Robin had said nine thirty and it very much wasn't. Mentally, The Pan kicked himself for thinking with his trousers when he should have been using his brain. They ran hand in hand down the hall and stopped outside the study. From within came the sound of low voices.

"Ready?" asked The Pan.

She nodded. She seemed nervous.

"You alright?"

"Yes."

No. Not entirely, The Pan thought.

"Right then," he said. He knocked and without waiting for an answer he opened the door. All conversation in the room died the moment they entered. Well, The Pan supposed, it would. They'd missed breakfast, or at least breakfast with the others, they'd grabbed some things from the kitchen up near the roof garden, and now here they were, together, having been conspicuously absent, also together.

Sir Robin stood up and came over to greet them.

"Ruth, my dear girl …" As he shook her hand vigorously he winked at The Pan. "My boy." Sir Robin took his hand and clapped him on the back. "I see you took my advice."

"Sort of …" he said. "Sir Robin, everyone. I'm sorry we're late." Ruth moved closer, as if for protection. He could feel her body heat. Subtly, he put out his hand, found hers and took it. She held on tightly. "We were," he hesitated, "chatting and forgot the time."

"Gladys, Ada, I am so sorry we missed breakfast, we'd never have done that on purpose," said Ruth. She smiled at the old ladies and The Pan watched as they melted. "I have so many questions and we were blathering on and I lost track of the time and poor Defreville … you know he would never miss one of your meals." There was a pause while The Pan's adopted family absorbed the idea that he had a name and what it was. Ada gave him a look and almost imperceptibly nodded at the Chosen One. The Pan raised his eyebrows, just a tiny bit.

"Blathering? Is that what you youngsters calls sex these days?" said Gladys blowing this discreet exchange clean out of the water.

Ruth shifted uncomfortably and glanced up at him.

"No," he said.

"Whatever it is you has been doing I hopes 'Defreville' was polite," said Gladys.

Arnold!

Ruth looked up at him again with a mischievous smile. Unbidden, The Pan's mind began to recall the previous night and some of the morning's activities. No, no, no. That wouldn't do. He needed to concentrate.

"Look at you, young man!" said Ada. "Standing there smiling like the cat that's got the cream. If we didn't know what you'd been up to we do now." In spite of the old ladies' nosiness The Pan laughed.

"Alright, alright, you've had your fun. Shall we move on now?" he said.

"Yes and hello everyone," said Ruth.

The Pan looked helplessly round the familiar row of faces for aid. Big Merv gave a very leery smile. Lucy hadn't said anything, which surprised him, and while she was definitely giving him a 'look' it wasn't as stern or scary as it might have been. Then he noticed that Big Merv's arm was round her shoulders. His eyes met Big Merv's and Big Merv squeezed Lucy's shoulders and winked. Lucy actually smiled. By The Prophet! Perhaps there was something in the water.

"Mornin' sweets. Mornin' Defreville," said Big Merv chuckling as he said 'Defreville'. Arnold. Less than five minutes since Ruth had used his real name and people were already taking the rip about it. Never mind.

"Yeh, yeh, it's my name," he let go of Ruth's hand and put his arm around her waist before turning to Sir Robin. "Maybe we should sit down?"

"Yes, I suggest you do. Now then, since our last member is not due to arrive until ten, I was going to demonstrate how this," he held up the gold snuff box, "is the real McCoy." He put it on the coffee table and The Pan noticed that the Importance Detector was already there. "Seeing as you're here," the tiniest pause, "Defreville, would you like to ...?"

"If you like but first, you said, 'our last member'." The Pan looked around the room. "You mean to say we're not all here?"

"Speak for yourself," said Trev. "I'm all 'ere, mate."

"We are one short," said Sir Robin when they had settled down. The Pan was worried. Everyone seemed in very good spirits, which was fine but not if they expected Sir Robin to offer them a solution because he was beginning to have graver and graver doubts about that. Unless there was some kind of magic science which Sir Robin was yet to impart, The Pan could see no way out of the situation, not without facing down and defeating Lord Vernon—which was impossible—or being captured. It worried him. He wondered if he should have brought Ruth there at all, whether the two of them should have run, except that running didn't seem to be working.

"Shouldn't we wait until the last person arrives?"

"No, he already knows how the box works and since he has little time to spare, I believe we should make the most of it. You'll meet him in a moment. First, the box."

"What? Now?"

"I see no better time. Come on."

The Pan and Ruth, who were still standing, made their way to three dining chairs with curled arms and upholstered seats which had been lined up along one side of the coffee table. They chose the two closest to each other and sat. Like the other furniture, the chairs were surprisingly comfortable. As he pulled the Importance Detector towards him to alter the settings, The Pan thought he heard a noise and stopped to listen. It sounded like a group of people in the distance, arguing. He wondered if it was coming from the street outside or whether it was in his head, like the chicken noises he kept hearing. He glanced up at the picture behind the desk and shuddered. No-one else seemed to have noticed. He concentrated on blanking it out for a moment and the noise faded away. Sir Robin asked Gladys and Ada's Trev to close the curtains and then turned out the lights. The Pan concentrated on the Importance Detector and was surprised at how easily he remembered the movements. The box glowed green and everyone was duly appreciative.

"Marvellous, my boy. Splendid."

The Pan hesitated. As he had completed the hand movements to change the settings on the Importance Detector, he'd remembered the ring which had been worn by forty generations of Architraves. He took it out of his pocket. "I don't think I should keep this. If you want it hidden, I'm not the best man for the job." He put it on the table, next to the box. Sir Robin seemed touched, but at the same time, a little vexed, as if The Pan had done the wrong thing.

"My boy, that is commendably honest of you—" he began but he was distracted by a sharp rap at the door. "Ah here is our last member now." He strode over to the door and flung it open one-handed, while with the other hand, he switched on the lights.

Chapter 75

Sir Robin spoke to the newcomer.

"Good morning, General."

General? That didn't sound good. The Pan was instantly on his guard, and judging by the reactions of some of the others he wasn't the only one. Sir Robin was still talking.

"Bang on time as usual, I see. Capital, capital. Do come and meet the rest of my team."

Sir Robin ushered the visitor into the room and everyone got a good look at him for the first time.

"This is General Moteurs," said Sir Robin. Silence fell. "The General here is one of the lynchpins of this organisation. His input has been vital to our plans. We could never have got this far without him."

The Pan was the first to move. He stood up quickly and so did Ruth.

"Please sit down. I assure you, there is nothing to fear," said Sir Robin.

"Good morning," said General Moteurs. He made a slight bow to Gladys and Ada and The Pan wondered if he knew them. He spoke with a clipped, upper-class accent; standard, privileged officer type, then. He was green, like all Grongles and decorated extensively judging by the medals on his uniform, though that didn't mean much, the Grongles hadn't fought anything like a proper war against armed opposition for years. His face was hard but the red eyes lacked some of the usual cruelty and they held a trace of something else which The Pan couldn't identify; restlessness, maybe even pain. It was well hidden, whatever it was. Even for a Grongle the contrast between the red, the whites of his eyes and the green of his skin was startling. He was middle-aged by the look of him, but lean and fit and imposing. The Pan swallowed. Very imposing. Arnold's armpits. Like all his fellow officers he positively oozed condescension—and a supreme arrogance. He wasn't as tall as other Grongles, a mere six foot, if that—smaller than Big Merv—but he had more than enough presence to make up for it. He gave off an aura of absolute authority which commanded respect. Clearly he was not only high-ranking but formidable. Most likely he ran a very tight ship.

The Pan stood where he was, with Ruth beside him, and the General eyed them disdainfully. The Pan put his arm round her waist to reassure her, or was it to reassure himself?

"Ohmygod," she said. Slowly she moved closer against him until she could whisper in his ear. "He's a Grongle."

"Yep," The Pan said.

"And he's huge," she whispered.

"Actually, for a Grongle, I think he might be a bit of a short-arse," The Pan whispered back.

"I am also here and not deaf," said the General tartly.

"I apologise," said The Pan who had never been polite to a Grongle and wasn't absolutely sure how to start. He turned to Sir Robin. "What—?" he began.

"The General here is on our side," Sir Robin interrupted him smoothly. "He is our point of liaison with the Underground in Grongolia."

"There's an Underground in Grongolia?" asked Ruth.

"The Underground *is* Grongolian," said the General coldly. "You ill-disciplined rabble are the K'Barthan cell."

"Thank you for that vote of confidence. I'm sure we're all pleased to see you, too," said The Pan.

"You should not be here like this—" began the General.

"But he is. Sit down, Ford." Sir Robin's voice held an authority The Pan hadn't heard before. The General hesitated. "You too, my boy—and Ruth, if you please." The Pan and Ruth did as they were told and for all his Big Man aura so did General Moteurs. In the last free seat, next to The Pan. He sat slightly sideways so he was facing everyone, but most notably The Pan whom he proceeded to fix with a gimlet glare. The Pan returned it for a moment and then pretended it wasn't unsettling him and concentrated on the others. Across the table he could see Big Merv fidgeting. He was angry and staring at General Moteurs the way the General was staring at The Pan, but General Moteurs was too busy glowering at The Pan to notice. Sir Robin began to speak so The Pan tried to forget about it and listen.

"The General is telling the truth, the Underground does have its origins in Grongolia. However, since we were already established when they approached us, I would be more inclined to call us an organisation of like-minded individuals working alongside them."

"Depends who's in charge, donnit?" said Big Merv.

"Exactly, and in this instance, General Moteurs reports to me." Very firm, as much a message to General Moteurs as to the rest of them The Pan suspected. "Now, since we are all here, it is time to discuss our plans for the next few days."

"The next few days? What about afterwards?" said The Pan.

"Oh I don't think it will take much longer than that. We will be dead or in charge by then," said Sir Robin breezily. The General stopped glaring at The Pan long enough to address Sir Robin.

"What about the boy, the Candidate?" he said.

Good question, thought The Pan, as the General glanced dismissively at him for a moment.

"As you can see, he is not with us," said Sir Robin.

"That is evident. I merely ask if we should consider moving without his entire presence."

"We have no choice," said Sir Robin. "He will not let us down but if we wait much longer it will be too late, for him, for us and for you. We must act."

"'S right," said Gladys. "We is ready, isn't we Ada?"

"Indeed we are."

General Moteurs addressed another query to Sir Robin.

"You still trust the Candidate?" he said. "Even now you know who he is?"

"Oh yes. Don't be fooled by appearances. We are ready."

"I find that difficult to believe." He hesitated. "You insist?"

"I do."

The Pan, who had been watching Sir Robin throughout this exchange, risked another glance at General Moteurs. He was projecting an air of strong disapproval; more than strong. Extreme. The Pan had the impression that, like every other Grongle he had met, this one hadn't taken to him. However there was something about General Moteurs which he couldn't place.

"Do I know you?" he asked.

"I doubt it. I do not habitually socialise with those who are classed as vermin," said General Moteurs.

"That must make life tricky living in K'Barth," said The Pan.

"Not necessarily."

"Oh, do tell Defreville where you are based," trilled Ada.

"The Palace." The General, caught off guard, answered her politely and The Pan suddenly realised what a good information gatherer Ada must be. Gladys, too, he suspected. Ada turned to him.

"Isn't that interesting? Such a lovely historic building. Oh, but General, I never asked you when we last met. What do you do?"

"I have a roving remit." General Moteurs was beginning to sound more cautious. "I am in charge of technological advances, mainly."

"Fascinating. You must see such interesting things."

"Alas no, it is mostly equipment used for information gathering; listening devices, computer hacks." The Pan caught an exchange between Ruth and Lucy as Lucy mouthed the word 'espionage' and Ruth nodded. Meanwhile, General Moteurs continued. "I have recently been working on detection systems—"

"The portal detection system?" asked Ruth. General Moteurs gave her an appraising glance which made The Pan proud of her.

"Among other things," said the General.

"Lord Vernon mentioned it. He made a phone call while I was hiding and—" she put her hand over her mouth and gasped. "He was talking to you. You're the General," she stood up and backed away towards the door pointing at him. "You're Lord Vernon's right-hand man." The Pan jumped up too and went to her.

"Wait, Ruth. Are you sure?" he said.

"Of course I am." She was frightened. He put a comforting arm round her and she held onto him tightly. For a moment he revelled in the novel sensation of being needed. It felt good, if a little dishonest. He looked General Moteurs in the eye, which took some doing.

"Well, General, it sounds as if you work quite closely with Lord Vernon." He couldn't begin to ape Ada's conversational tone.

"I would remind you both that I am a Grongle, not a human, but to answer you, the Chosen One is correct. I work closely with Lord Vernon."

"How closely?"

"I report to him and no-one else. I have the same security clearance as him. I am empowered with the same authority as him to commandeer any item or individual I require to carry out my duties in his service. I am his eyes and ears; anonymous, discreet, able to achieve that which, through his notoriety, he cannot. And I advise and guide him."

Arnold.

"And you expect us to believe you're on our side?"

"You have my word. That is usually enough."

"Yeh, to another Grongle maybe, but it ain't to us," muttered Trev.

"'S right pal." Big Merv stood up. "See, I ain't met a Grongle who kept his word to me."

"My friend has a point," said The Pan.

"Yeh," said Merv, his voice had acquired a sinister edge. "An' I've got another one. We ain't never met you, and fair enough, for a Grongle you seem a polite enough bloke. But my mate over there …" another short pause before he could say the word, "'Defreville'. He's smart. I trust him and if he says he's seen you before he ain't lying. So now you got me wondering. There you are, Sir Robin's mate who just happens to be a Grongle. An' thinking about that, I don't reckon Sir Robin knows many Grongles so *that* gets me wondering if you ain't worked at the Bank of Grongolia sometime."

General Moteurs said nothing.

"Yeh. Thought so. I 'spect you get my drift, but just in case, I'm gonna spell it out. We done the leakiest job of all time at the Bank of Grongolia to get that box," he pointed at the gold snuff box on the table, "for your mate there." Big Merv jabbed a finger at Sir Robin. "Ain't that a coincidence?"

"There was nothing wrong with my information. It was not my fault Lord Vernon brought you down."

The Pan winced as he remembered. "Yes, but what my friend Mister Merv is implying is that only a handful of people knew that robbery was going to take place," said The Pan. "Us four, Sir Robin and—"

"You," said Big Merv.

"And you think I betrayed you?"

"Yeh, I think so."

"On the contrary, your colleagues Frank and Harry betrayed you."

"And you think I'm gonna believe that do you, sunshine, with you being Lord Vernon's number one man?"

"I reiterate, I am a Grongle, not a man, and I assist Lord Vernon with security, science, advice, special operations … not police work. I assure you, your colleagues sold you out."

"Handy for you, that they ain't here to ask, innit? I'm wonderin' if their story'd be the same as yours."

"Easy Merv," said The Pan and Big Merv turned on him.

"Stay out of this, son," he growled. His antennae were sticking straight up as if statically charged. Yep, he was. He turned back to General Moteurs.

"Denarghi and his mates killed Frank and Harry and you gotta royal cheek bad-mouthing them like that. I don't like to hear a bloke speak ill of the dead. I reckon I oughta knock your block off."

The air crackled with tension as slowly, without taking his eyes off Big Merv, General Moteurs stood up.

"If you like you can come over here and try."

"I might just do that, pal."

"Then face the facts first," General Moteurs took a step away from his chair, towards Big Merv and stopped. "Your colleagues betrayed you. They are not dead. They changed sides. They are alive and well and working for Denarghi and if required I can prove that to you."

"No way. They wouldn't—"

"I assure you. They did."

"You think I'm gonna believe that?" said Big Merv quietly.

"It would be the clever option."

"I guess I ain't too clever then."

"I had noticed."

"Yeh. I betcha. Then if what you're saying's true you ain't gonna mind proving it, are you, General Snot Face."

Snot face? Oh no no, that was the most insulting thing you could call a Grongle. There'd be no going back now, Big Merv and General Moteurs were going to have a fight unless someone calmed things down. The Pan realised, with a sinking heart, that 'someone' was going to be him. He didn't usually step into situations like this. Usually he ran the other way.

"Merv—" he began.

"Shut it, Defreville," said Big Merv turning his attention back to General Moteurs. "You heard me, pal." There was silence while Big Merv's felt-tip green eyes glared into General Moteurs'. "C'mon then. You gonna show me the money, smart man?"

"I am not a man."

"No, you're right there, sunshine. You ain't half a man."

General Moteurs let Big Merv's insult ride and turned to The Pan.

"You have a portal, you know what to do."

The Pan took the gold thimble from his pocket, pictured Frank and Harry in his mind's eye and looked into it. He expected the grey blur he saw when he looked for his family but instead there they were. It was definitely Frank and Harry, sitting together, eating toast by the looks of things. He glanced up at Big Merv and then at General Moteurs who was exuding an aura now that was, unmistakably, smugness. The Pan was surprised at how angry that made him. He handed the thimble to Big Merv who peered into it.

"That pukka?" Big Merv handed it back. He had taken it badly. He was pallid and shaken but the fight had not gone out of him.

"Yeh. It seems General Moteurs is right," said The Pan.

"Yes, I am. Your friends' disloyalty did you a favour. You would not have evaded us." The Pan wasn't going to let the General have the last word.

"Nothing had stopped us before then, I doubt it would have been any different," he said. So cocky and so absolutely the opposite to how he'd felt when it had happened.

"Without your snurd? We would have had you in minutes."

The Pan thought back to the lengthy trek through the woods and the way the officer who met them had shouted so much that she had risked getting them all killed.

"The Resistance made it worse. Trust me, we'd have been better off without them."

"You are very arrogant for a nothing, Hamgeean. Do not expect to escape again. Not from my troops." Something about the General's tone, his absolute self-confidence, his inability to acknowledge his failings or show any respect for his adversaries annoyed The Pan far more than being called a 'nothing'.

"Is that a challenge?" he said.

"No. It is a warning."

"Yeh. I bet. Watch me, General. Watch," he said.

"Yeh. Remember this next time you're eating our dust, mate," said Big Merv.

"I wouldn't be so sure of yourselves, especially you," he added, glaring at The Pan. "Let me explain something to you, boy. This is a complex operation and it hinges on Lord Vernon trusting me. Your meddling forced me to make concessions which he did not appreciate. It undermined his faith in me and put us all in danger. Neither I, nor my superiors in the Grongolian Underground are pleased or impressed."

"Well, there's something we have in common. I'm not too impressed either," said The Pan. By The Prophet! Why was he arguing? Where would that get him, or Ruth? Nowhere.

"That's enough." Ruth stepped away from him. "Excuse me for butting in while you three do macho battle like this but, before your ballooning egos push the rest of us out into the hall, I have a question for General Moteurs. Were those your men at the Festival Hall?"

"They are not 'men'."

"Oh no of course not. They're Grongles, aren't they?" The General inclined his head. Ruth took a few paces forwards and glared up at him defiantly. "I'm sure that makes them vastly superior to us." The Pan smirked and put his hand over his mouth to try and hide it. "Is that why they tried to kill me?"

"They didn't shoot to kill."

"But you admit they shot at me."

"Yes, they shot *at* you. No-one under my command would miss at such close range. If they had intended to kill you, I assure you they would have done so. Their orders were to ensure you stayed where you were.”

“Oh I’m so sorry, they shot *at* me. And the difference is? Explain please.”

“The difference is that you are here.”

“No, I’m here because of him.” She pointed at The Pan who smiled and bowed. The General paused to glare at him with undisguised contempt.

“Your presence here has nothing to do with this … child,” he said.

“I think it does. All you had to do was talk to me but oh no. You and your people have chased me, hounded me and made me completely miserable. I’ve lived in fear for three months.”

General Moteurs directed another hostile glare at The Pan.

“I see you have ensured the Chosen One shares the same view of my species as the rest of you.”

“I think you did that on your own, General Moteurs. She’s right. Instead of sending people to follow her perhaps you could have tried talking to her. Oh no, but wait, Lord Vernon did the home visit, didn’t he?” The Grongle’s face was an impassive mask, too impassive. Well, well, well. “You didn’t know, did you?” said The Pan.

General Moteurs glanced down at the floor for a moment.

“I confess not. Even so, we are not all barbarians.”

“Maybe, but give Ruth some credit. Anyone who met Lord Vernon first might disagree.”

“Only in so far as, meeting you, I might assume every Hamgeean to be a shiftless, meddling wastrel and a yellow one, at that.”

The Pan laughed mirthlessly.

“You have me down pat then. But that wasn’t what I meant. I think we all know what I’m talking about.”

“Yes, that you would judge a nation and a species on the merits of one individual.”

“No, that you’re happy enough to sit back and let Lord Vernon and others like him take charge.”

“If I were, I would not be here,” said the General evenly.

“Unless Lord Vernon sent you.”

“Which he did and yet, what I say is still true.”

There was silence. The General eyed The Pan who made a point of looking away. He wasn’t going to be drawn into a game of staredown. He would pretend to be big enough not to care about losing.

“Well, you have all made your feelings clear,” said Sir Robin, finally intervening. “General Moteurs has given much, at great personal cost, to become one of us. If I ask you to make him welcome I expect more than this. I trust him implicitly and if any of you cannot, I suggest you leave us." The silence lengthened. The Pan realised the others were looking to him for a decision. He glanced at Sir Robin. Was this a test? Both Sir Robin and General Moteurs were angry, genuinely so and yet there was something behind the General's anger. The Pan had never mixed socially with Grongles, he had no clue how they behaved but he began to have a feeling that this one's actions might be more about making judgements than enemies. Was this how Grongles sized one another up?

"Fair enough. General, I admit I have been prejudiced and I apologise. You're the first Grongle I've met who hasn't tried to kill me, even if you're acting a little as if you'd like to, and frankly, I'm a bit thrown." The General inclined his head. The Pan risked a glance at Sir Robin. He looked grave, but at the same time The Pan had the impression he was pleased. The Pan took Ruth's hand as he passed her and they went back to their chairs, where Ruth sat down. As he was about to follow suit, The Pan noticed Big Merv was still standing.

"Merv, leave it …" he said, putting his hands out, palms down, he motioned towards the ground in a 'calm down' gesture. "Please?" There was a moment of silence while Big Merv and the Grongolian General eyed each other warily. The Pan was a long way out of his comfort zone. The General was right, he was yellow and on his normal form, if a fight looked like breaking out, he'd have been halfway down the corridor by now, but he didn't want to look bad in front of Ruth. She loved him, and for just a little while, he would pretend to be someone worth loving. "Merv, mate. Please … You heard Sir Robin. This isn't going to get us anywhere."

"Merv?" said Lucy quietly. She put her hand up and pulled at his sleeve. Slowly, without taking his eyes off the General, Big Merv sat down. With relief, The Pan sat, too. Ruth leaned over and whispered in his ear.

"Wow. I thought they were going to have a punch-up," she whispered.

"So did I."

"Well done." A beat. "That was quite brave for a coward."

"Not really. I can't stand the sight of blood."

The Pan looked up at General Moteurs; the only one on his feet now, standing alone, he'd moved in front of the fireplace. He seemed a little surprised as if something had punctured his Grongolian arrogance and his eyes showed the tiniest, subtlest hint of … was that …? Yes, amazing, a smile.

"Alright General, if you have something to say we're listening," said The Pan.

Chapter 76

General Moteurs spoke.

"I cannot lie. I am everything you believe of my species and worse. I have done enough to ensure I will burn for eternity. I have dishonoured my family and my ancestors and as the last living member of my line I must make amends while I can or they will be punished in the afterlife, forever. Lord Vernon trusts me. He knows I am here, he knows we plan to overthrow him. He is wily and skilled at reading others. I cannot deceive him or lie to him, but I can manipulate him for our purposes."

That worked two ways, thought The Pan.

"He has sent me here to win your trust. That is why I cannot openly intervene in your favour, any of you. Not yet. Not until it is time to implement our plan."

"We have a plan?"

"Course we has got a plan," said Gladys.

General Moteurs bowed. "The lady is correct," he said. "I am informed that what we have is a plan."

It didn't sound as if he was impressed with it though.

"Great. So what is it?" asked The Pan.

"I will leave the outline to Sir Robin."

"Thank you, Ford," said Sir Robin. "Now, as we all know, Lord Vernon is a rapacious despot intent on world domination."

"And the rest," said Trev.

"Yeh," agreed Big Merv.

"Exactly. He must be stopped."

"He's just about invincible," said The Pan. "How do we stop him?"

"Oh, we don't. The Candidate will do that."

"Whoa, whoa, whoa! How can you be sure? He doesn't even know who he is!"

"True but we have the Chosen One and he is utterly in love with her. It really won't take much more than that. In the meantime, I'm afraid I am going to have to ask you all to bear with a few days' inconvenience and then, I assure you, all will be well."

The Pan and Ruth exchanged glances and she mouthed the word, 'what?' The Pan shrugged.

"Yeh right. Very funny. So what's your real plan?" said The Pan.

"My boy, if you could stop asking questions and listen, I will tell you. Lord Vernon is, as you say, almost invincible. We have no army and there is no time to raise one. I confess it is my fault, I believed the Candidate would appreciate who he was and come to me. As it is, I have been forced to seek him out and even now, he does not begin to understand his calling nor the immense power he commands. It is most vexing and I do believe he would come to his senses given time but, alas, that is a commodity we do not have. I am going to have to force his hand.

"Ford, the date …?"

General Moteurs looked up suddenly. He had been leaning casually against the mantlepiece studying his fingers, except that, to The Pan, he seemed far from relaxed.

"Am I right in thinking that, in the matter of selecting the most auspicious date upon which to be installed as Architrave, Lord Vernon is deferring to my judgement?"

Everyone looked at General Moteurs.

"That is so, Sir Robin," he said.

"More fool him. Do confirm the date for me, there's a good chap."

"Next Saturday, Sir Robin."

"A week today. That is the best date for us, of course, but it is also the last possible point at which the Candidate can oppose Lord Vernon. If he does not wise up and act by then, Lord Vernon's false candidature will succeed and he will be installed as Architrave. The installation is going to be shown on TV. It is rather last minute but I believe our best moment to stop Lord Vernon is at the actual ceremony, when the priest officiating asks if anyone has any objections. It does give the Candidate a nice large audience as well. Everyone who is anyone will be watching."

"Yeh right. The whole nation gets to see him die. I'm sure that will pep up our morale no end," said The Pan.

"But what if they watch him win? How can I put this simply? We all agree that we are too weak to defeat Lord Vernon in an out-and-out fight, yes?"

"Fair point," said The Pan.

Nobody else spoke.

"Exactly. So we have to find another way. To defeat an enemy like Lord Vernon we must use his confidence against him. We play dead, as it were, and wait until he comes close enough to the body to deliver a single, decisive blow. Then we strike. He must be convinced we have nothing left, for only then can we take him by surprise. We have put up an excellent show of resistance and now the time has come to give him almost everything. We will start fighting in earnest next Saturday, at his installation, when he believes he has already won.”

“But if we wait until he thinks he has won, won’t that be when he actually *has*?” demanded The Pan.

“No. If the Candidate reveals himself when all seems lost Lord Vernon will be off guard. He will also be at his highest point, with furthest to fall.”

“I don’t see that working,” said The Pan.

“Then you underestimate the Candidate and the power of tradition.”

“Or am I just being realistic?”

“No, no, my boy. You will understand before long.”

The Pan glanced over at Gladys and Ada who nodded enthusiastically.

“Are you two buying this?” he asked.

“Yer,” said Gladys.

“What’s not to buy?” asked Sir Robin.

“Quite a lot,” said The Pan. “Trev?” Gladys and Ada’s Trev looked uncomfortable and shrugged.

“I has to stand by Mum and Aunt Ada.”

Well yes, fair enough, The Pan could understand that.

“Are you being realistic, my boy, or letting your fear do the talking?”

“I always let my fear do the talking. In this case, I’d say it’s making a lot of sense.”

“My boy, I understand your concerns but you will have to trust me.”

“I don’t trust anyone.”

“Then may I suggest that now is an excellent time to start.”

“Is it? I’m beginning to think Ruth and I shouldn’t be here. That ‘few days’ inconvenience’ you mentioned. It sounds to me as if you are suggesting we give ourselves up to Lord Vernon,” said The Pan. There was a long silence.

“Sir Robin, please tell us Defreville has got that wrong,” said Ruth.

“I’m afraid I cannot, my dear, because that is exactly what I am suggesting,” said Sir Robin gravely.

“Are you crazy?” said Lucy, and everyone started talking at once.

“If you would hear me out …” said Sir Robin and he proceeded to carry on with what he was saying, loudly. As he spoke over them the rumbles of dissent died away again. “It will take courage from all of us but we must let Lord Vernon have his moment of glory or he will not relax his guard. And it is vital that he does so and leaves the General here to get on with the security arrangements in such a way that the Candidate can easily walk in and defeat him.”

“Alright, I admit there is a warped logic to what you’re saying and I was almost with you until we got to the bit where the Candidate walks in, wipes the floor with Lord Vernon and takes power," said The Pan. "Are you expecting him to do that alone?"

"Why, of course. There will be no-one else. Lord Vernon will have the rest of us."

"Hang on a mo. What if the Candidate's a normal bloke?" asked Big Merv.

"That's what I was thinking because if he is, he's not exactly going to defeat Lord Vernon in mortal combat is he?" said The Pan.

"I would not expect him to. He's a very bright boy and he values life. He will not fight. He has wit and intelligence and he will use those."

"Against Lord Vernon," said The Pan flatly.

"Indeed."

"Quite the wunderkind, isn't he?" said Lucy dourly.

"So it would seem," agreed The Pan acidly. "Do we have a choice? Only, I'm not sure I'm up for that, and what about Ruth and Lucy? You can't expect them to take part in this, they're from another reality. This has nothing to do with them."

"On the contrary, as the Chosen One, Ruth is essential for Lord Vernon's strategy to become Architrave. By mere association Lucy will also be on his wish list; for one reason or another, all of us are."

"Then that's all the more reason for us to leave, now, so I can give her and the rest of us a head start."

"I wouldn't do that if I were you," said General Moteurs ominously and without actually moving he somehow contrived to look bigger and more menacing, and to be between everyone else and the door.

The Pan stood up. "Get out of the way, General. Please."

"I do not take orders from you."

The Pan turned to Sir Robin. "Call off your Rottweiler. This is wrong and it's not the K'Barthan way. You have to give us the choice." He glanced round at the others, looking for support and to his surprise, General Moteurs, yes, the same one who was blocking the route to the door, spoke before anyone else.

"Sir Robin, the boy is right."

"I'm twenty-one years old. That's a man by anyone's standards, General," said The Pan wearily. General Moteurs inclined his head and corrected himself.

"The man," he said with heavy irony, "is talking sense. You are basing this on a wish and a prayer. There is a difference between a man of faith making a principled decision and blind foolishness. You are leaning towards the latter."

"We have already discussed this, Ford." Suddenly Sir Robin seemed every bit as authoritative and imposing as the General.

"And …?" said The Pan

"If you agree, I will be using myself, and all of you, excepting the General here, as bait." The Pan took a breath to speak but Sir Robin spoke over him. "And I don't like it either. Nevertheless, I am the High Priest of all K'Barth. I am the last surviving guardian of the Nimmist way and the final living interpreter of the will of The Prophet. When I am gone the knowledge I have," he tapped the side of his head, "will be lost for ever. I am fighting for the preservation of a nation, a way of life and even of some species. How long will the Swamp Things survive if Lord Vernon has total power? Can any of us be so arrogant as to put our lives above that?"

"Are you going to be so arrogant that you don't even give us a choice?" asked The Pan.

"No," said Sir Robin. "You do have a choice. There is the door, run if you must. But deep down, I believe all of you know I am right. I suggest those of us who are in agreement should give the others a few moments to discuss this." He stood up slowly and Gladys, Ada and Their Trev got up too. Together with General Moteurs, they left the room.

There was a long silence. The Pan put his head in his hands. He had found the woman of his dreams and after just a few perfect hours, this.

"What d'you reckon?" asked Big Merv.

"Ruth's the one Lord Vernon wants." The Pan took her hand. "What do you want to do?"

"I don't really have a choice, do I?"

"Well, no, you do," said Lucy. "Defreville is right. Neither you nor I are K'Barthan."

"That makes no difference. The decisions here are being made by other people and I have no access to them and no say." She sounded emotional. "The only thing I have any control over is the way I decide to react. So I can run, which isn't much fun." She stopped and smiled sadly at The Pan. "Not even with you, Defreville. Or I can join in with Sir Robin's plan and be bait with the rest of you. Either way my life here is gone and I'll never see anyone I love—apart from you lot—again. If I run, Lord Vernon will hunt me down eventually and unless he catches me before next week, I know for sure, that I'm dooming a whole world to a regime run by him. It's a different version of my world, I know, but it *is* my world and that's a horrible thought. So, if I do what Sir Robin wants and get captured I will give the Candidate a chance, and if I do that, there is also a remote probability that, in seven days' time, I'll get my life back."

"Or not. You can run, we can all run and I will keep us ahead of Lord

Vernon," said The Pan although he wasn't sure he believed what he was saying. He doubted he could keep all four of them from the Grongles indefinitely but Arnold's armpits, he would try.

Ruth shook her head.

"No, we can't. We can't live the rest of our lives like yesterday."

"It's not always like that."

"I think it will be. I know he was a bit arrogant about it but I think that's what General Moteurs was trying to tell you with all that 'you'll never escape from me' stuff."

The Pan ran his hands through his hair. She was probably right.

"Are you sure you're going to do this?" he asked her.

"Yes. I can't turn my back when a whole planet needs me. Anyway, it will be my reality before long. When Lord Vernon's finished with K'Barth I bet I know what he'll do next."

A very valid argument. Arnold's toe jam! There was only one thing for it, then. Despite the fact that every one of his instincts, the instincts he knew and trusted, was advocating flight, The Pan was going to stay with the Chosen One, because if he couldn't grow old with her, then the rest of his days, all seven of them, would have to do.

"Alright. I'm in. I've run long enough," he said. "Merv? Lucy? What about you two?"

"Someone's gotta keep you in line, you little twerp," said Big Merv. "Count me in."

"Do you think it will be over in a week?" asked Lucy.

"Nah sweets," said Big Merv.

"I think we'll be executed in a week," said The Pan. "Well, except for—"

"Please don't mention that," said Ruth.

"Sir Robin might be right," said Lucy, with a lot more hope than conviction.

"Yeh. Pigs might fly an' all."

"You do have a choice, Lucy. Seriously, even if Merv decides to stay, you, of all of us, don't have to," said The Pan.

"I've booked a week off. What else am I going to do with it?"

"I know it's naff but … group hug?" suggested Ruth. Everyone stood up, put their arms round each other and held on tight for a minute or two.

"I'm sorry I couldn't make it right," said The Pan. They all held each other tighter and The Pan was afraid he would cry. What a plank. Blinking back the tears he buried his face in Ruth's hair and inhaled deeply for a moment.

"It doesn't matter, I know you did your best," said Ruth.

"But it wasn't good enough."

"It nearly were. You done good, son. You got a lot to be proud of," said Big Merv gently.

"It was closer than anyone else would have got. I think we all did OK. It just hasn't worked out," said Ruth.

"I'll go and get Sir Robin," said The Pan. He noticed the box on the table, picked it up and flipped open the lid. Ruth pounced on a distraction.

"How do you do that?" she asked.

"Easy," said The Pan, closing it, flipping it open and closing it a couple of times. "Here." He handed it to her. She tried to do what he had done flicking it with her thumb but it was stuck.

"It doesn't seem to like me. Here, you try," she handed it to Lucy who couldn't open it either.

"If I hadn't seen you do that, I'd think it didn't have a lid," Lucy told The Pan and she held the box out to Big Merv. "Are you going to have a go?" she asked him.

"Nah, it ain't gonna happen for me. I ain't seen no-one open that box apart from this wazzock." He nodded at The Pan. Lucy handed it back to him and he opened it to demonstrate.

"Thinking about it, maybe there is a secret. I opened it in front of Sir Robin and he seemed surprised I was able to." He paused for thought. "Mmm. If it's really that tricky I see no point in making life easy for Lord Vernon, and Sir Robin asked me to hide this." He scooped the ring off the coffee table and put it inside. Then he took the gold thimble, put that in too, and closed the lid. He wondered if he could make it disappear and imagined the box with nothing in it. When he opened it again, the ring and thimble had gone.

"I think it works like the thimble," he said as he showed them.

"Can you get them back though?" asked Ruth.

Good question. The Pan closed the lid, concentrated for a moment and opened it again. There they were. "It would seem so." He held it out to show them.

"Defreville, you're very devious, for a man," said Lucy, as he closed the box again.

"Channelling my inner girl."

"Whadda you mean 'inner'? You are a big girl," said Big Merv.

"Just this once, we'll let you off, Mister Pan," said Lucy.

"Thank you. Wait here you lot, I'll go and tell Sir Robin we're on," said The Pan. He kissed Ruth on the cheek—he couldn't help it—and left the room.

Chapter 77

As The Pan opened the door of the study he heard voices. General Moteurs and Sir Robin, arguing by the sound of it. Shutting the door silently he edged forwards along the hall wall. The door to the dining room was open and yes, they were inside.

"I have grave concerns, Sir Robin," General Moteurs was saying.

"Over what, General?"

"Over the boy's obdurate refusal to acknowledge his calling."

"He will realise soon enough."

"No, Sir Robin. He will not. That boy has no idea who he is."

"Then his ignorance will only keep him safer."

"I think not, and these others will suffer on his account."

"No, General, he will know before Saturday."

"And when he does it will fill him with dread. He will need coaxing, counselling and support. I can give you twenty-four hours to prepare him. My master can wait another day."

"I doubt that, Ford."

"Then you must tell him, now, or Lord Vernon will take him to pieces and us with him."

"I cannot possibly."

"I appreciate it would be a departure from tradition but he must know, fast."

"No. The prophecies are very clear on this, he must realise for himself."

"Forget the prophecies. Sir Robin, this is about defeating a being of great power and intelligence. Your Prophet cannot have foreseen everything. You must act."

"Not now."

"Then when? Once you are in my custody you will not have access to him."

"If I have to, I will find a way. You and I both know that if we disclose his calling now he will run and he is not an easy man to catch."

"Then give him to me. I will tell him and then I will see to it that he cannot run."

Sir Robin chuckled.

"So sure of yourself, Ford. I do believe I see a dash of that famous

Grongolian arrogance in you. My dear fellow, if he has the smallest head start do you honestly think your troops can get hold of him? Nobody else can. I'd say he really is the best escape man in K'Barth and at the moment he's very, very twitchy."

The Pan was irritated, more than irritated. The best escape man in K'Barth was standing right there. It wasn't some custard-coloured git hiding under a sofa. It took all his self-control not to step out of his hiding place and explain.

"I would never hope to catch him if he began to run. But I believe I might be able to break it to him gently. Gently enough for him to heed my words, think on them and stay." There was a pause, while Sir Robin mulled this over.

"Perhaps as a last resort, General, but not now."

"Sir Robin, how can I make you understand? This is our only chance. If we do not tell him now then we are lost." There was urgency in the General's voice, not to mention desperation.

"Oh no, no. There is still time. You forget. He has released the Architraves. I expect they will tell him."

"And if he believes he is delusional instead? He will descend into madness."

"I doubt that will happen in a week. He is a remarkably bright lad."

"'Bright' is not enough. He is young, he lacks confidence and you underestimate his humility."

"What you underestimate is his intelligence, General."

"I would like to think not, but without knowledge his brains alone cannot save him. He has not been guided like his predecessors, he is poorly educated and he has no ready reason to believe. The presence of the others will merely frighten and confuse him."

"I sincerely hope it won't. He cannot survive indefinitely now he has freed them. There is no turning back. He must be installed or he will suffer most horribly."

"And you will stand by and let him or let Lord Vernon take him?"

"If it is the will of the Prophet."

"And if it is not? You said yourself that the prophecies are difficult to interpret and the correct course of action fragile and difficult to maintain."

"They are, but I have absolute faith in him. He will find a way to control the others."

"And defeat Lord Vernon …?" Sir Robin was silent. "As I thought. You fear he will fail."

"It depends what I wish to achieve. He will realise who he is and he will secure the succession. I am absolutely certain of that. The line will not be broken."

"But in saving it, he will be," said General Moteurs bitterly. Sir Robin took a long time to answer and when he did his voice was gentle, sad.

"I very much hope not."

"The honourable course of action would be to tell him and allow him to choose."

"Alas, I do not have that luxury. This is politics, General, and honour is seldom involved. He is the Candidate. He is who he is and he has no choice. It's him and us, or his people." Sir Robin heaved a sigh. "Ford, in times like these we must do our best and hope it is enough. If anyone can defeat Lord Vernon it is that young man and I have done everything in my power to ensure he can do it."

"You think so, do you? Then, I warn you, Sir Robin. I will be watching him. If your Prophet wants your nation to survive I fear he may need a little help from me. There will come a point where the lad must know or die and when that moment comes I will not stand idle. If you do not tell him I will."

"You are a good soul, General, but you are letting your humanity get the better of you." The Pan could hear the fondness in Sir Robin's voice.

"I am a Grongle, I am proud to say I have no humanity," said General Moteurs drily.

"And now you are splitting hairs."

"No. Our philosophy is of honesty, honour, fair play and high principles. We are not perfect, there are good and bad among my species but we are not the monsters that you K'Barthans think. Our current regime is not us. I would like to think I have the same sense of right and wrong as any member of my species, but I didn't expect it to be greater than yours." The Pan smiled wryly. It was clear that Sir Robin annoyed a lot of people.

"As I have already said, this is about more than us, more than the boy. This is about the survival of the succession, a philosophy, a way of life; and several species—possibly every species, General, other than yours."

"And that is all the more reason for you to assure our success. Speak to the boy, Sir Robin."

"With any luck, I just have. Now, General, I believe it is time for you to contact your master."

General Moteurs took out a mobile phone.

"You know what I am about to do. If this laughable scheme you call a plan fails, I cannot save you or them."

"I understand that, Ford, and so do they."

"Then … must I do this, Sir Robin?"

The old man reached up and patted General Moteurs' shoulder.

"Trust me, my good fellow. Trust me and believe. I assure you, one way or another, all will be well."

The Pan trod heavily along the hall and knocked loudly on the half-open dining room door before entering.

"Hello," he said. Their reaction was interesting. A moment of silent understanding seemed to pass between them and then Sir Robin turned to The Pan.

"Well?" he said.

"General, Sir Robin. You have your bait," said The Pan bitterly. "She's too good for the Candidate, too good for any of us. I suppose there might have been some point in it if he'd been less of a weasel."

"We have a saying in Grongolia, 'it takes one to know one'," said General Moteurs.

"Yeh. That's about the size of it. But even I'm not that bad."

"The Candidate is no coward. He is simply humble and uneducated," said Sir Robin. He sounded angry.

"Yeh, yeh. I'm sure he's a top man and my heart bleeds for him," The Pan turned and made to walk away and stopped. Could he resist it? No. He turned round to face them. "Oh and while I'm here. You've been badly misinformed," he jabbed a pointing finger at them to accentuate what he was saying. "The Candidate is *not* the best escape man in K'Barth. I am."

Sir Robin laughed, which was intensely irritating.

"Touché," murmured General Moteurs and Sir Robin shot him a warning look before addressing The Pan.

"A little cocky, aren't we, my boy?"

The Pan looked him in the eye without bothering to hide the full force of his anger and frustration; with the Candidate, with Sir Robin and his own miserable lot in life.

"What do you think?" he said. "Nobody can outrun the Interceptor; no-one, except me. So, until someone else can, I'd say that makes me the best, wouldn't you?"

"More tellingly it proves that you have neither the wit to understand what you have heard nor the wisdom to hide the fact you were listening. You are in no position to be precious about words you had no business hearing, especially when—"

"That is enough, General," said Sir Robin. General Moteurs clearly wanted to say more but bit his lip. Sir Robin continued. "My boy, as the General has reminded you, eavesdroppers seldom hear good of themselves." He held the door open. "Please return to the Architrave's study." The Pan hesitated. "Now, if you please." Their eyes met, Sir Robin's fierce, intense and, yes, a little bit frightening. "Ford, call your master," he said without breaking eye contact with The Pan. Sir Robin took him by the arm and ushered him back to join the others. Gladys, Ada and Their Trev arrived and, after a minute or two, General Moteurs. There was still no sign of Humbert and The Pan thought about how animals always hide before earthquakes. Yeh, the parrot probably knew something he didn't.

Chapter 78

Sir Robin waited for everyone to settle.

"I gather we are decided, yes?" he said addressing his question to The Pan.

"Yeh," he said sullenly.

"And would you confirm your decision to us all?"

"Yes. Gladys, Ada, Trev. We couldn't let you lot be bait on your own."

"Splendid!" Sir Robin clapped his hands. "There, Ford! Wait and see. All will be well." He looked down at the coffee table and noticed the box, sitting alone by the Importance Detector.

"And now, I must ask you to give the box to my esteemed colleague here." Sir Robin gestured to General Moteurs who looked as downcast as Sir Robin did chipper. The Pan picked up the box, walked over to him and dropped it into his outstretched hand.

"The service lift, that's where I saw you; at the Palace, the day before yesterday. I opened the door and it was you. It took me a while to realise because you looked bigger." The General was clearly pained at another reference to his size. Or lack of.

"Did I?" he said and The Pan couldn't help noticing that he looked pretty big now … and intimidating. Very intimidating.

"Yes," said The Pan only it was more of a squeak.

"I was attempting to save your life. If you had come with me, I could have removed you from the Palace before you encountered Lord Vernon."

The Pan still had to take his courage in both hands to look into the red eyes and he could not read them. He decided that, for the sake of continued good relations with Sir Robin, he would take General Moteurs' words at face value.

"I'm sorry I was too quick for you," he said. General Moteurs was unimpressed and gave him a contemptuous look. Mmm well, The Pan supposed that was a bit cocky. "Thank you for making the effort, though," he added to mollify him and then undid his good work almost instantly by adding, "I'm sure Lord Vernon will like the box. If he can open it."

"Doubtless he will," said General Moteurs. He was angry, sulky even but generally, or with Sir Robin, perhaps, rather than specifically with The Pan.

"I'm afraid he will have to have your thimble, too, my boy," said Sir Robin.

"I put it in ..." The Pan turned to General Moteurs who did not even try to open the box but handed it straight to him. He took the thimble out, closed it and handed both back to the General.

"As you may have noticed, there is a knack to opening that," said Sir Robin.

"Yeh," said Big Merv. "Looks like Defreville's the only geezer what can."

"Ask yourself why that might be, Hamgeean," said General Moteurs quietly.

"Ford," warned Sir Robin and the General glowered at him. Sir Robin continued. "Defreville is, in his own way, as much one of the chosen as Ruth. Lord Vernon will expect the box to be difficult to open. It has a secret locking mechanism known only to a few of us."

"But—" began The Pan and Sir Robin eyed him meaningfully. 'Shut up' that look said, so The Pan corrected himself. "Um, right," he said.

"Ford, if I may have that?"

General Moteurs crossed the room and handed the box to Sir Robin who held it up.

"Thank you." Something about the handover didn't ring true. If The Pan hadn't known better, he'd have thought Sir Robin had never taken the box from the General, that the one he held aloft was a replica he'd had concealed in his hand. It was difficult to check but the way General Moteurs put his hands in his pockets afterwards also aroused The Pan's suspicions. He hadn't done that before and it looked unnatural. As if he was unused to it. The Pan gave Sir Robin what he hoped was a searching look and was surprised when he returned it with a wink and a smile. Had he just seen a switch, and if so, why?

Not everyone can resist Truth Serum, said a voice. A voice The Pan had never heard before. Oh no. Please not in his head. Arnold's smelly sandals, this was an inconvenient time to go nuts. Oh well, at least the voice was talking sense. If the box was fake there was no way Sir Robin could say. Perhaps the voice was Sir Robin? Maybe he had a secret talent for ventriloquism. No. That was downright stupid. Anyway, if it had been Sir Robin or any of the others, then The Pan would have recognised it, ventriloquism and voice-throwing or not.

"Are you alright, my boy?" Sir Robin asked.

"I'm ..." he stopped. Should he mention the voices in his head? No. "I'm facing death by Lord Vernon," said The Pan.

"Yes. But future generations will thank you. Now then, I need a volunteer, not you," he told The Pan. "Ruth. Would you like to open the box?"

"OK." She went over to Sir Robin and took the box from his hand.

"Capital. Now, since you have not enjoyed a K'Barthan education, we will need Defreville's help with the next part. My boy, can you help Ruth to find the scene, on the front of the box, where Holy Arnold is laying down the Universal Law?"

"Of course." He went over to Ruth, gave her what he hoped was a look of reassurance and pointed to the scene on the box. "Here."

"Thank you. It should say 'be decent to one another' in tiny letters." Sir Robin took an eyeglass out of his pocket and handed it to Ruth. "You may need this, oh and this," he handed her a pin. "Now, you need to press the 'd' of 'decent'."

Ruth put the eyeglass to her eye and did as Sir Robin asked. The box pinged open. No sign of the ring.

"That's quite complicated," said The Pan dubiously.

"Yes," said Ruth. "So how come it only works for him?"

Excellent question.

"It's designed in such a way as to respond to a particular, rare thumb shape."

What? The Pan almost laughed.

"The majority of the Architraves have had that thumb shape and, by complete coincidence, Defreville is lucky enough to have it too. That is why he can open the box and we cannot."

The Pan had no idea how it worked but if he could put things in it and use his imagination to make them disappear and reappear, there had to be more to it than that. Sure there would be a logical, scientific explanation but it would have to be something quantum mechanical not just … this parlour game, this sleight of hand. It wasn't the real box. General Moteurs had that. Ruth, on the other hand, looked thoughtful.

Arnold's armpits! She believed Sir Robin. That was amazing. Then again, The Pan supposed that to her, the Looking, the Architrave and the Chosen One must come over as total nonsense, so why would this be any different? Maybe that's how the Grongles saw K'Barthan tradition, too. Was that why they thought they were so much better, because they couldn't take it seriously? The thimble would look like magic to Ruth even though The Pan had explained it was science. So she'd be reasoning that with science like the thimble and The Pan's snurd, anything was possible, even this level of complication in a simple mechanism. The fact it didn't add up was blindingly obvious to anyone who would stop to think but, The Pan realised, no-one would. Not even somebody smart like her.

He turned and gave General Moteurs a look. One which, he hoped, said, "I know where the real box is." The General raised his eyebrows and moved his head a tiny fraction; a nod. And this time there was no mistaking it. Despite the poker face and the disapproving demeanour, the red eyes were smiling. Weird.

"Now, I think your first instinct was correct, so would you put the thimble back in the box, my boy?" Unwillingly The Pan put his thimble inside. "Thank you," said Sir Robin but his eyes were saying something else, questioning, hoping. The Pan raised his eyebrows a fraction, wondering if Sir Robin would realise he understood, praying that he had.

"General." Sir Robin was pale. "Are we out of time?"

General Moteurs nodded and Sir Robin took the box from Ruth, closed it and placed it next to the Importance Detector on the table. For a moment The Pan thought of conducting the test to see if it was real but then the door was flung open, the window blew in, the curtains were torn down. Someone fired a smoke grenade and as impenetrable white clouds billowed into the room The Pan just had time to see the General move swiftly forward and scoop up both items. Then visibility deteriorated and he could see nothing.

"Don't anyone move," shouted a voice, a Grongolian voice but one which did not have the clipped upper-class delivery of the General's. It was also filtered with a breathy tinniness that came from speaking through breathing apparatus.

Unseen hands bundled The Pan and Ruth to the floor.

"You cannot do this! You have no right," shouted Sir Robin.

"Shut up or die, old man," said the tinny voice.

"Captain Snow," said General Moteurs calmly, "punctual as usual." The Pan noticed he had something over his mouth, some sort of pocket gas mask or oxygen mask.

"Yes, sir," said Captain Snow smoothly. Then he shouted, "Lie on the floor, vermin. All of you! And put your hands on your heads."

The Pan's eyes stung and he put his cloak over his mouth and buried his face in the carpet to try and filter the air. The dust made him cough, and beside him Ruth was also coughing. He reached out and put his arm round her shoulders. A few feet away a large shape rose up and threw a punch before there was a crunch, like the butt of a gun hitting a head and it crumpled to the floor.

"Merv!" shouted The Pan. His lungs burned and he descended into another fit of coughing. Dull shapes in the smoky air bundled them up and dragged them roughly into the hall where there was less smoke. Members of the

Underground were being rounded up and herded up the stairs to the roof. No. Not them. That wasn't fair. Unless … there were only a few of them, had some of them gone? Had they been given the chance to volunteer? Maybe. At the end of the hall a tall figure appeared, framed in the doorway. The guards, and there were a lot of them, hauled the last remaining members of the Underground to their feet. Big Merv swayed unsteadily, blood running down his forehead. As the figure approached, the guards snapped to attention.

"Lord Vernon," said Sir Robin.

Chapter 79

Lord Vernon laughed and strolled down the hall emanating an aura of unbearable smugness.

"Sir Robin Get. It seems justice has caught up with you at last."

"I'd hardly call it justice," muttered The Pan.

"SILENCE!" roared Captain Snow with a lot more enthusiasm and volume than The Pan deemed necessary.

"This is an outrage," said Sir Robin. "We are unarmed and have put up no resistance. What is more, you are on Free K'Barthan soil."

"Yes, and now the legitimate K'Barthan government is in control."

"Your government is not legitimate."

Lord Vernon walked slowly over to Sir Robin and looked down at him.

"On the contrary, Sir Robin. I think you will find it is." He turned to face General Moteurs.

"Do you have the items, General?"

"Yes, sir. They are both here." He took the gold snuff box from his pocket.

"And the portal?"

"Yes but … I am afraid it is in the box, sir."

Lord Vernon wrenched at the lid.

"There are two, sir. That one is a fake …" he put his hand in his pocket and removed the second box. "This one is the real one."

"I would never have believed this of you, Ford," said Sir Robin.

"Then you were a fool, old man," sneered Lord Vernon. "It seems you are lost. What a pity. I have the Chosen One, the box, the ring, the portals and …" He stopped and turned round slowly, "The Pan of Hamgee. At last," he said softly. "You have caused me a great deal of inconvenience, Hamgeean."

"Good," said The Pan, his mouth running off without his brain as usual.

Lord Vernon laughed.

"Oh, you think so, do you? You will change your mind when I am done with you."

"Leave him alone." Ruth stepped into the space between them. No, no, noooo what was she doing?

"No, Ruth. Don't do this," said The Pan.

"You should take the Hamgeean's advice," snarled Lord Vernon. "It would be unfortunate if I were forced to harm you."

"If I'm your magic Chosen One, I doubt you'd dare."

"Oh, but I would," said Lord Vernon and before she had time to react he grabbed her by the arm and pulled her close to him. "Shall we see what other things I dare to do?" He put his arm around her waist, holding her tight. Ugh! Was he going to kiss her? Arnold no! The Pan's brain let go of the controls.

"Get your hands off her," he said. He was surprised at the authority in his voice. So was everyone else, it seemed, especially Lord Vernon who let go of Ruth, pushing her roughly away from him, and turned back to face The Pan.

"Or what …?" Ah yes, good point. The Pan hadn't thought ahead that far.

"Or she's not going to like it," he said desperately. Arnold, how rubbish could it get?

"What she likes or dislikes does not concern me." Lord Vernon smoothed his gloved hands and clicked his knuckles. "But I know I'm going to like this …" Without taking his eyes off The Pan, he waved a hand in the direction of the others. "Guards, hold them.

"You have stood in my way at every turn, Hamgeean. So now, let me show you and your friends what happens to people who inconvenience me." He glanced over at the others.

"Watch and learn," he said coolly and he walked towards The Pan, who waited, tensely, for the right moment to duck. The Pan dodged a one-two aimed at his jaw but as he ducked to avoid a third punch aimed at his face Lord Vernon's other fist made contact with his stomach at high speed. He felt his eyes bulge and the breath leave his body. Arnold's pants, he'd forgotten the first basic rule of not getting beaten up; watch both fists, and the legs and, in some of the less salubrious places in K'Barth, the head. It was too late now. The Pan rolled into a ball and tried to get his breath back but Lord Vernon hauled him to his feet, clamping one hand round his neck. "Impressive, Hamgeean, but not fast enough. You are not in your snurd now," he whispered as he squeezed harder.

The Pan tried to stay calm and think but it was impossible when the simple business of breathing was such a major issue. What little air he had was running out with alarming speed. Struggling and kicking, he tried to prise Lord Vernon's hand away from his neck but his efforts merely wasted more precious oxygen and accelerated the effects of being throttled. He didn't want to die like this but he was weakening and he could see no way of escape.

Still he fought, writhing, kicking out, fighting to release his neck from the vice-like grip. Deliberately, easily, Lord Vernon plucked his clutching hands away, crushing the fingers painfully to make each of The Pan's efforts to free himself harder than the last. The Pan's legs gave out and he sank to his knees. It was pointless struggling, so he stopped. Lord Vernon smiled, bent down and whispered in his ear.

"You are not dying well, Hamgeean, and your friends are watching. How does it feel?"

Bad. The Lord Protector's slate grey eyes glared into The Pan's with an expression of unwavering hatred. Oh, to reply with something witty and sarcastic but there was no air left to speak. Out of the corner of his eye The Pan could see Big Merv struggling with two of the guards. The world went into slow motion, the shouts of his friends, and the Grongles restraining them, echoed as if coming from far off. The Pan tried to appear calm, courageous. The last thing he would ever see was Lord Vernon's face. That was grim but if he looked away or closed his eyes he would be acknowledging his defeat. He wanted to die, if not defiant, then, with some vestige of pride. Lord Vernon's expression changed and The Pan felt the pressure on his windpipe lessen by the tiniest amount as General Moteurs put his hand on Lord Vernon's arm.

"Before you snap his neck, Your Gracious Exaltedness, a word?" said the General, calmly. Arnold, he was brave. Maybe he had earned all those medals.

"If you must," said Lord Vernon. Wow. Lord Vernon was listening. General Moteurs must command some serious respect to achieve that. The General spoke softly so only Lord Vernon and by incident, The Pan could hear.

"I would urge you not to kill the Hamgeean. Not yet." The Pan glanced up and for the briefest millisecond General Moteurs' eyes met his with a look of warning. The pressure on The Pan's neck was still close to intolerable but it had stopped increasing.

"I am interested to hear why not, General," said Lord Vernon.

"Because if you do, I believe the girl may refuse to cooperate."

"What if I were to kill her friends one by one, starting with this one, until she does?" said Lord Vernon, glaring down at The Pan.

"I think that would be unwise, sir. She is very stubborn."

Yes, she was. The Pan looked into the cold grey eyes and almost smiled. In a battle of wills, the Chosen One would be a match for anyone, even Lord Vernon.

"I doubt I will have trouble persuading her."

"Perhaps not, sir. However, since speed is of the essence, I believe the swiftest, most potent method of persuasion available to you is, as it were, in your hands."

Lord Vernon grimaced and raised his eyes to heaven.

"Again. The Hamgeean."

"In this instance, yes, sir."

"In every instance it would seem," said Lord Vernon petulantly. There was a moment of silence while he thought, or resigned himself, it was difficult for The Pan's oxygen-starved brain to work out which. "I concede you have a point, General. I see that, once again, I must forego my personal indulgences for the benefit of the world at large." He leaned down towards The Pan so their faces were almost touching and again, The Pan looked up into those inhuman, dark, grey eyes, so striking in a Grongolian face. "It seems the General is right. You have the devil's own luck, Hamgeean, but let me assure you it will not hold. His intervention merely allows us a little more time to enjoy each other's company. Oh, I will kill you, but you are not broken. Not yet. And I will break you first." Lord Vernon released his grip and watched, impassively as The Pan sank, coughing, to the floor. "General, please take these verminous scum back to K'Barth and put them in prison where they belong."

"Yes, sir."

"Thank you." He kicked The Pan's prostrate form venomously out of his way with one foot. "Now, I have things to do." He held up his keys and pressed the Interceptor's homing button. Then he strode down the hall, wrenched open the door to the roof garden and slammed it behind him. The sound of his footsteps receded on the stairs.

The Pan rolled over and managed to kneel upright. He looked up at General Moteurs, whom he had distrusted and insulted and who had returned the compliment by saving his life. He was embarrassed and grateful and he wanted to say thank you but when he tried to talk he could only croak.

"I would advise against any unnecessary speech for an hour or two," General Moteurs told him as he helped him to his feet. "Doubtless such unaccustomed peace will come as a relief to your friends, as well as to me." His delivery was deadly serious but that had sounded like a joke. The Pan looked into the inscrutable red eyes searching for the truth. But he found no answer. General Moteurs bowed, clicked his heels and turned to the matter in hand. "Captain Snow," he nodded at the guards, "troops, you heard our orders. Take these vermin back to the Palace. Oh, and Captain, tempting as it may be, I would remind you that these are Lord Vernon's toys and he wants them pristine. While he can—and will—throw them out of the pram, we may not.

Precious cargo, so be gentle, if you please. And now, I will leave this to you." He turned and left by the same route as Lord Vernon, up the stairs to the roof, where an awaiting troop carrier, fitted with a prototype Grongolian portal would carry him back to K'Barth.

The Pan was quite close to Ruth. He wondered dourly why fate had to wait until he was about to die before handing him a real reason to live. They were standing facing each other, separated by no more than three feet of space. But The Pan knew that, surrounded by Grongles, that brief expanse of carpet might as well have been a river of fire. She was already an ocean away. She smiled wanly.

"Thank you," he croaked. It hurt to talk and his voice sounded like a shovel being pushed into sand.

"Don't, you'll make it worse."

"I think this is as bad as it gets," he whispered. His voice was not cooperating. There was so much he wanted to say and he tried to tell her with his eyes. He knew she was frightened and he wanted to hold her and make everything right. Mentally, he kicked himself. Why hadn't he insisted that they run? Now they were at the mercy of the Grongles. The Candidate, their supposed saviour, was still nowhere to be seen and he didn't look like showing up any time soon. Ruth was crying, not sobbing, and The Pan couldn't bear her silent tears. He took a step towards her. She reached for his outstretched hand, but as their fingertips touched Captain Snow took her roughly by the arm.

"I don't think so, vermin," he said and hauled Ruth away, flinging her at the feet of two of his troops. "No!" croaked The Pan, struggling to reach her, but other guards grabbed his arms and wrestled him to the ground. Captain Snow ignored him completely.

"Chain her to that one." He waved a dismissive hand at Lucy. "It's a shame you females belong to Lord Vernon or we could have had some fun with you, right lads?" he sneered. The rest of the troops laughed. "Course, it's not all bad. We'll get what's left of you when he's finished."

Again The Pan tried to reach Ruth, if only to get close enough to Captain Snow to headbutt him but his hands were wrenched behind his back and handcuffed. The Grongles dragged him painfully down the hall to where Big Merv stood, swaying blearily, and chained the two of them together. Ahead, the others were also shackled together in pairs, Gladys to Ada and Sir Robin to Trev. Then the guards hobbled them all, tying their ankles together so they could only shuffle, and dragged them to the bottom of the stairs. The Captain spoke.

"I've been ordered to deliver you back to HQ. Why the smeck I have to lug you all back there I don't know. If I could save myself the bother and despatch you all here, like the non-beings you are, I would. So I warn you, if anyone steps out of line, then orders or no orders, I'll do this job my way."

"You have nothing to fear from us," said Sir Robin. Captain Snow walked over to Sir Robin and grabbed him by the scruff of the neck.

"That's right, old man," he growled, "but if you've got any sense, you'll be very afraid of me. I'll look forward to executing you tomorrow morning—unless Lord Vernon does it himself."

Sir Robin looked calmly up at him. He showed no sign of fear and The Pan admired his courage.

"Oh, we won't be dying just yet, Captain, you can be confident of that."

"I wouldn't be so sure if I were you." He pushed Sir Robin away and turned to his troops. "Let's move," he shouted and slowly The Pan and his friends shuffled forwards through the smoke.

When they reached the stairs, Captain Snow's troops half dragged, half threw their hobbled prisoners up the steps. Once out on the roof, The Pan got to his feet and helped Big Merv to his. He was clearly still woozy after the blow to his head, his antennae drooping dejectedly. Two prison transports stood waiting. One was huge, the other much smaller but both were in aviator mode, wings extended, ready to fly. The ramp at the back of the small one was down, the driver standing ready, but the back of the large one was just closing. Through the diminishing gaps at its sides, The Pan could make out the forms of other prisoners, tightly jammed in, before the door clanged shut. He guessed they were the K'Barthans he'd seen being herded away earlier. As the big snurd taxied for take-off, smashing the fruit trees and gouging tyre tracks across the remaining undamaged lawn, Captain Snow pushed The Pan and his friends towards the smaller one.

"Get in."

The Pan paused a moment to watch the larger prison transport flying upwards until it was engulfed by clouds.

"I said 'get in'." Captain Snow shoved him hard and slowly, with Captain Snow harrying them all the way, The Pan and his friends shuffled up the ramp.

The End

Other Books by M T McGuire

One Man: No Plan, K'Barthan Series: Part 3
The Pan of Hamgee needs answers, although he's not even sure he knows the questions.

He has a chance to go straight but it's been so long that he's almost forgotten how. Despite a death warrant over his head he is released, given a state-sponsored business, and a year's amnesty for all misdemeanours while he adjusts. On the down side, Ruth has left him for his nemesis, Lord Vernon.

The Pan doesn't have a year, either. In only five days Lord Vernon will gain total power and destroy K'Barth. Unless The Pan can stop him. Because even though the Candidate, the person prophesied to save K'Barth, has finally appeared it's still going to be down to The Pan to make things right. But he has no clue where to start or whether he even can.

The future hangs by a thread and the only person who can fix it is The Pan: a man without a plan.

Looking For Trouble, K'Barthan Series: Part 4
The Pan of Hamgee doesn't believe in miracles but if he's going to save K'Barth it looks as if he might need one.

He's not quite as alone as he thought. The punters from The Parrot and Screwdriver are right behind him and he has rescued three of his friends from the Grongolian Security Forces, who are now of course, three of the nation's most wanted, which doesn't make life easy. He even has something of a plan for once. It involves making peace with the Resistance, trying to resurrect the Underground movement, and toppling Lord Vernon.

Now, The Pan just needs to keep his head down and maintain a low profile. He must be brave and clever and stay in control. That's going to be a first. But the hardest part will be staying alive long enough to put his plan into action.

K'Barthan Extras, Hamgeean Misfit

Remember how The Pan had been working for Big Merv for a year, before torching his flats in The Planes? Well, the K'Barthan Extras Series of four stories (so far) describes his adventures during that time. There will be more K'Barthan Extras, coming soon, both about The Pan and other characters:

When trouble comes knocking, be out.
Outlawed and alone, The Pan of Hamgee's only real ambition is to live a normal life, unnoticed by the authorities. With this aim in mind, he travels to the city in the hope of getting lost in the crowds.

Surviving hand to mouth, he meets a selection of colourful characters in his quest for quiet anonymity. But when his very existence is treason trouble is never far away. Especially when the only paid work he can find is delivering messages for Big Merv, one of the scariest gangsters around.

Escape From B-Movie Hell
If you asked Andi Turbot whether she had anything in common with Flash Gordon she'd say no, emphatically. Saving the world is for dynamic, go-ahead, leaders of men and while it would be nice to see a woman getting involved for a change, she believes she could be the least well-equipped being in her galaxy for the job.

Then her best friend, Eric, reveals that he is an extraterrestrial. He's not just any ET either. He's Gamalian: seven-foot, lobster-shaped and covered in Marmite-scented goo. Just when Andi's getting used to that he tells her about the Apocalypse and really ruins her day.

The human race will perish unless Eric's Gamalian superiors step in. Abducted and trapped on an alien ship, Andi must convince the Gamalians her world is worth saving. Or escape from their clutches and save it herself.

Author News

Never miss a new release again! Sign up for M T Mail. Just visit www.hamgee.co.uk/freebook

You will receive a handful of introductory emails, then you can choose to hear about everything or just new releases. You can also keep up to date with all things M T McGuire by joining her K'Barthan Jolly Japery Facebook Group.

To join, go here: https://bit.ly/JollyJapes

Alternatively, you can follow M T McGuire on these social media:

Website: https://www.hamgee.co.uk
Blog: https://www.mtmcguire.co.uk
Facebook: https://www.facebook.com/HamgeeUniversityPress
Instagram: @mtmcguire
Goodreads: https://www.goodreads.com/author/show/8382246

www.ingramcontent.com/pod-product-compliance
Lightning Source LLC
Chambersburg PA
CBHW050959210726
48287CB00004B/1296